BRING UP THE BODIES

HarperCollins Publishers Ltd

HILARY MANTEL

BRING UP THE BODIES

Bring Up the Bodies
Copyright © Tertius Enterprises 2012.
All rights reserved.

Published by HarperCollins Publishers Ltd

First Canadian edition

Hilary Mantel has asserted her right to be identified as the author of this work.

No part of this book may be used or reproduced in any manner whatsoever
without the prior written permission of the publisher, except in the case
of brief quotations embodied in reviews.

HarperCollins books may be purchased for educational, business,
or sales promotional use through our Special Markets Department.

HarperCollins Publishers Ltd
2 Bloor Street East, 20th Floor
Toronto, Ontario, Canada
M4W 1A8

www.harpercollins.ca

Library and Archives Canada Cataloguing in Publication
information is available upon request

ISBN 978-1-55468-779-4 (paperback)
ISBN 978-1-44341-436-4 (library hardcover)

Printed and bound in the United States
RRD 9 8 7 6 5 4 3

Once again to Mary Robertson:
after my right harty commendacions,
and with spede.

CONTENTS

CAST OF CHARACTERS

The Cromwell household

Thomas Cromwell, a blacksmith's son: now Secretary to the king, Master of the Rolls, Chancellor of Cambridge University, and deputy to the king as head of the church in England.

Gregory Cromwell, his son.

Richard Cromwell, his nephew.

Rafe Sadler, his chief clerk, brought up by Cromwell as his son.

Helen, Rafe's beautiful wife.

Thomas Avery, the household accountant.

Thurston, his master cook.

Christophe, a servant.

Dick Purser, keeper of the watchdogs.

Anthony, a jester.

The dead

Thomas Wolsey, cardinal, papal legate, Lord Chancellor: dismissed from office, arrested and died, 1530.

John Fisher, Bishop of Rochester: executed 1535.

Thomas More, Lord Chancellor after Wolsey: executed 1535.

Elizabeth, Anne and Grace Cromwell, Thomas Cromwell's wife
and daughters, died 1527–28; also Katherine Williams and
Elizabeth Wellyfed, his sisters.

The king's family
Henry VIII.
Anne Boleyn, his second wife.
Elizabeth, Anne's infant daughter, heir to the throne.
Henry Fitzroy, Duke of Richmond, the king's illegitimate son.

The king's other family
Katherine of Aragon, Henry's first wife, divorced and under
house arrest at Kimbolton.
Mary, Henry's daughter by Katherine and the alternative heir to
the throne: also under house arrest.
Maria de Salinas, a former lady-in-waiting to Katherine of
Aragon.
Sir Edmund Bedingfield, Katherine's keeper.
Grace, his wife.

The Howard and Boleyn families
Thomas Howard, Duke of Norfolk, uncle to the queen:
ferocious senior peer and an enemy of Cromwell.
Henry Howard, Earl of Surrey, his young son.
Thomas Boleyn, Earl of Wiltshire, the queen's father:
'Monseigneur'.
George Boleyn, Lord Rochford, the queen's brother.
Jane, Lady Rochford, George's wife.
Mary Shelton, the queen's cousin.
And offstage: Mary Boleyn, the queen's sister, now married and
living in the country, but formerly the king's mistress.

The Seymour family of Wolf Hall

Old Sir John, notorious for having had an affair with his daughter-in-law.

Lady Margery, his wife.

Edward Seymour, his eldest son.

Thomas Seymour, a younger son.

Jane Seymour, his daughter, lady-in-waiting to both Henry's queens.

Bess Seymour, her sister, married to Sir Anthony Oughtred, Governor of Jersey: then widowed.

The courtiers

Charles Brandon, Duke of Suffolk: widower of Henry VIII's sister Mary: a peer of limited intellect.

Thomas Wyatt, a gentleman of unlimited intellect: Cromwell's friend: widely suspected of being a lover of Anne Boleyn.

Harry Percy, Earl of Northumberland: a sick and indebted young nobleman, once betrothed to Anne Boleyn.

Francis Bryan, 'the Vicar of Hell', related to both the Boleyns and the Seymours.

Nicholas Carew, Master of the Horse: an enemy of the Boleyns.

William Fitzwilliam, Master Treasurer, also an enemy of the Boleyns.

Henry Norris, known as 'Gentle Norris', chief of the king's privy chamber.

Francis Weston, a reckless and extravagant young gentleman.

William Brereton, a hard-nosed and quarrelsome older gentleman.

Mark Smeaton, a suspiciously well-dressed musician.

Elizabeth, Lady Worcester, a lady-in-waiting to Anne Boleyn.

Hans Holbein, a painter.

The clerics

Thomas Cranmer, Archbishop of Canterbury: Cromwell's
friend.
Stephen Gardiner, Bishop of Winchester: Cromwell's enemy.
Richard Sampson, legal adviser to the king in his matrimonial
affairs.

The officers of state

Thomas Wriothesley, known as Call-Me-Risley, Clerk of the
Signet.
Richard Riche, Solicitor General.
Thomas Audley, Lord Chancellor.

The ambassadors

Eustache Chapuys, ambassador of Emperor Charles V.
Jean de Dinteville, a French envoy.

The reformers

Humphrey Monmouth, wealthy merchant, friend of Cromwell
and evangelical sympathiser: patron of William Tyndale, the
Bible translator, now in prison in the Low Countries.
Robert Packington: a merchant of similar sympathies.
Stephen Vaughan, a merchant at Antwerp, friend and agent of
Cromwell.

The 'old families' with claims to the throne

Margaret Pole, niece of King Edward IV, supporter of
Katherine of Aragon and the Princess Mary.
Henry, Lord Montague, her son.
Henry Courtenay, Marquis of Exeter.
Gertrude, his ambitious wife.

At the Tower of London
Sir William Kingston, the constable.
Lady Kingston, his wife.
Edmund Walsingham, his deputy.
Lady Shelton, aunt of Anne Boleyn.
A French executioner.

The Tudors (simplified)

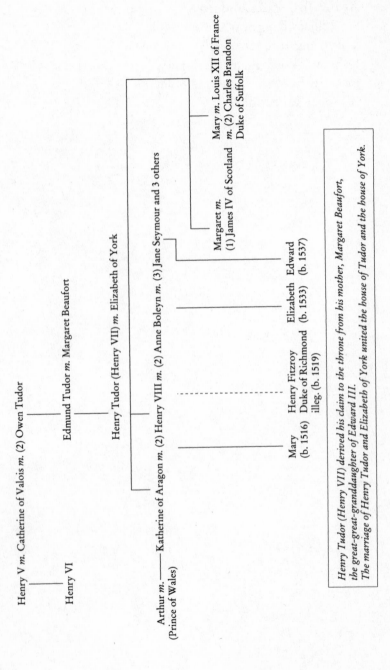

Henry V *m.* Catherine of Valois *m.* (2) Owen Tudor

Henry VI

Edmund Tudor *m.* Margaret Beaufort

Henry Tudor (Henry VII) *m.* Elizabeth of York

Arthur *m.* ——— Katherine of Aragon *m.* (2) Henry VIII *m.* (2) Anne Boleyn *m.* (3) Jane Seymour and 3 others
(Prince of Wales)

Mary   Henry Fitzroy   Elizabeth   Edward
(b. 1516)   Duke of Richmond   (b. 1533)   (b. 1537)
              illeg. (b. 1519)

Margaret *m.*
(1) James IV of Scotland

Mary *m.* Louis XII of France
m. (2) Charles Brandon
Duke of Suffolk

Henry Tudor (Henry VII) derived his claim to the throne from his mother, Margaret Beaufort, the great-great-granddaughter of Edward III.
The marriage of Henry Tudor and Elizabeth of York united the house of Tudor and the house of York.

Henry VIII's rivals from the House of York (simplified)

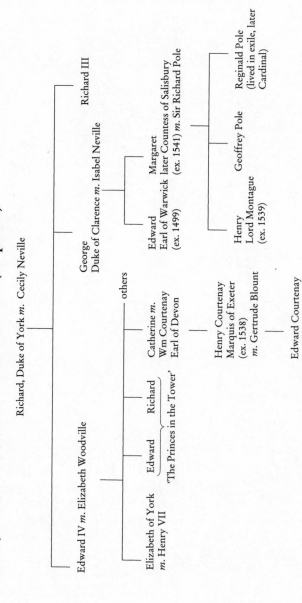

'Am I not a man like other men? Am I not? Am I not?'
HENRY VIII to Eustache Chapuys, Imperial ambassador

PART ONE

I

Falcons
Wiltshire, September 1535

His children are falling from the sky. He watches from horseback, acres of England stretching behind him; they drop, gilt-
winged, each with a blood-filled gaze. Grace Cromwell hovers in
thin air. She is silent when she takes her prey, silent as she glides
to his fist. But the sounds she makes then, the rustle of feathers
and the creak, the sigh and riffle of pinion, the small cluck-cluck
from her throat, these are sounds of recognition, intimate, daugh-
terly, almost disapproving. Her breast is gore-streaked and flesh
clings to her claws.

Later, Henry will say, 'Your girls flew well today.' The hawk
Anne Cromwell bounces on the glove of Rafe Sadler, who rides
by the king in easy conversation. They are tired; the sun is declining, and they ride back to Wolf Hall with the reins slack on the
necks of their mounts. Tomorrow his wife and two sisters will go
out. These dead women, their bones long sunk in London clay,
are now transmigrated. Weightless, they glide on the upper
currents of the air. They pity no one. They answer to no one.
Their lives are simple. When they look down they see nothing
but their prey, and the borrowed plumes of the hunters: they see
a flittering, flinching universe, a universe filled with their dinner.

All summer has been like this, a riot of dismemberment, fur
and feather flying; the beating off and the whipping in of hounds,

3

the coddling of tired horses, the nursing, by the gentlemen, of contusions, sprains and blisters. And for a few days at least, the sun has shone on Henry. Sometime before noon, clouds scudded in from the west and rain fell in big scented drops; but the sun re-emerged with a scorching heat, and now the sky is so clear you can see into Heaven and spy on what the saints are doing.

As they dismount, handing their horses to the grooms and waiting on the king, his mind is already moving to paperwork: to dispatches from Whitehall, galloped down by the post routes that are laid wherever the court shifts. At supper with the Seymours, he will defer to any stories his hosts wish to tell: to anything the king may venture, tousled and happy and amiable as he seems tonight. When the king has gone to bed, his working night will begin.

Though the day is over, Henry seems disinclined to go indoors. He stands looking about him, inhaling horse sweat, a broad, brick-red streak of sunburn across his forehead. Early in the day he lost his hat, so by custom all the hunting party were obliged to take off theirs. The king refused all offers of substitutes. As dusk steals over the woods and fields, servants will be out looking for the stir of the black plume against darkening grass, or the glint of his hunter's badge, a gold St Hubert with sapphire eyes.

Already you can feel the autumn. You know there will not be many more days like these; so let us stand, the horseboys of Wolf Hall swarming around us, Wiltshire and the western counties stretching into a haze of blue; let us stand, the king's hand on his shoulder, Henry's face earnest as he talks his way back through the landscape of the day, the green copses and rushing streams, the alders by the water's edge, the early haze that lifted by nine; the brief shower, the small wind that died and settled; the stillness, the afternoon heat.

'Sir, how are you not burned?' Rafe Sadler demands. A redhead like the king, he has turned a mottled, freckled pink, and even his eyes look sore. He, Thomas Cromwell, shrugs; he hangs an arm around Rafe's shoulders as they drift indoors. He went through the whole of Italy – the battlefield as well as the shaded arena of the counting house – without losing his London pallor. His ruffian childhood, the days on the river, the days in the fields: they left him as white as God made him. 'Cromwell has the skin of a lily,' the king pronounces. 'The only particular in which he resembles that or any other blossom.' Teasing him, they amble towards supper.

The king had left Whitehall the week of Thomas More's death, a miserable dripping week in July, the hoof prints of the royal entourage sinking deep into the mud as they tacked their way across to Windsor. Since then the progress has taken in a swathe of the western counties; the Cromwell aides, having finished up the king's business at the London end, met up with the royal train in mid-August. The king and his companions sleep sound in new houses of rosy brick, in old houses whose fortifications have crumbled away or been pulled down, and in fantasy castles like toys, castles never capable of fortification, with walls a cannon-ball would punch in as if they were paper. England has enjoyed fifty years of peace. This is the Tudors' covenant; peace is what they offer. Every household strives to put forward its best show for the king, and we've seen some panic-stricken plastering these last weeks, some speedy stonework, as his hosts hurry to display the Tudor rose beside their own devices. They search out and obliterate any trace of Katherine, the queen that was, smashing with hammers the pomegranates of Aragon, their splitting segments and their squashed and flying seeds. Instead – if there is no time for carving – the falcon of Anne Boleyn is crudely painted up on hatchments.

Hans has joined them on the progress, and made a drawing of Anne the queen, but it did not please her; how do you please her, these days? He has drawn Rafe Sadler, with his neat little beard and his set mouth, his fashionable hat a feathered disc balanced precariously on his cropped head. 'Made my nose very flat, Master Holbein,' Rafe says, and Hans says, 'And how, Master Sadler, is it in my power to fix your nose?'

'He broke it as a child,' he says, 'running at the ring. I picked him up myself from under the horse's feet, and a sorry bundle he was, crying for his mother.' He squeezes the boy's shoulder. 'Now, Rafe, take heart. I think you look very handsome. Remember what Hans did to me.'

Thomas Cromwell is now about fifty years old. He has a labourer's body, stocky, useful, running to fat. He has black hair, greying now, and because of his pale impermeable skin, which seems designed to resist rain as well as sun, people sneer that his father was an Irishman, though really he was a brewer and a blacksmith at Putney, a shearsman too, a man with a finger in every pie, a scrapper and brawler, a drunk and a bully, a man often hauled before the justices for punching someone, for cheating someone. How the son of such a man has achieved his present eminence is a question all Europe asks. Some say he came up with the Boleyns, the queen's family. Some say it was wholly through the late Cardinal Wolsey, his patron; Cromwell was in his confidence and made money for him and knew his secrets. Others say he haunts the company of sorcerers. He was out of the realm from boyhood, a hired soldier, a wool trader, a banker. No one knows where he has been and who he has met, and he is in no hurry to tell them. He never spares himself in the king's service, he knows his worth and merits and makes sure of his reward: offices, perquisites and title deeds, manor houses and farms. He has a way of getting his way, he has a method; he will charm a man or bribe him, coax him or threaten him, he will explain to a man where his true interests lie, and he will introduce that same man to aspects of himself he didn't know existed. Every day Master Secretary deals with grandees who, if they could, would destroy him with one vindictive swipe, as if he were a fly. Knowing this, he is distinguished by his courtesy, his calmness and his indefatigable attention to England's business. He is not in the habit of explaining himself. He is not in the habit of discussing his successes. But whenever good fortune has called on him, he has been there, planted on the threshold, ready to fling open the door to her timid scratch on the wood.

At home in his city house at Austin Friars, his portrait broods on the wall; he is wrapped in wool and fur, his hand clenched around a document as if he were throttling it. Hans had pushed a table back to trap him and said, 'Thomas, you mustn't laugh'; and they had proceeded on that basis, Hans humming as he worked and he staring ferociously into the middle distance. When he saw the portrait finished he had said, 'Christ, I look like a murderer'; and his son Gregory said, didn't you know? Copies are being made for his friends, and for his admirers among the evangelicals in Germany. He will not part with the original – not now I've got used to it, he says – and so he comes into his hall to find versions of himself in various stages of becoming: a tentative outline, partly inked in. Where to begin with Cromwell? Some start with his sharp little eyes, some start with his hat. Some evade the issue and paint his seal and scissors, others pick out the turquoise ring given him by the cardinal. Wherever they begin, the final impact is the same: if he had a grievance against you, you wouldn't like to meet him at the dark of the moon. His father Walter used to say, 'My boy Thomas, give him a dirty look and he'll gouge your eye out. Trip him, and he'll cut off your leg. But if you don't cut across him, he's a very gentleman. And he'll stand anybody a drink.'

Hans has drawn the king, benign in summer silks, seated after supper with his hosts, the casements open to late birdsong, the first tapers coming in with the candied fruits. At each stage of his progress Henry stops in the principal house, with Anne the queen; his entourage beds down with the local gentlefolk. It is usual for the king's hosts, once at least in the visit, to entertain these peripheral hosts by way of thanks, which places a strain on the housekeeping arrangements. He has counted the provision carts rolling in; he has seen kitchens thrown into turmoil, and he himself has been down in the grey-green hour before dawn, when the brick ovens are swabbed out ready for the first batch of loaves, as carcasses are spitted, pots set on trivets, poultry plucked and jointed. His uncle was a cook to an archbishop, and as a child he hung about the Lambeth Palace kitchens; he knows this business inside out, and nothing about the king's comfort must be left to chance.

These days are perfect. The clear untroubled light picks out each berry shimmering in a hedge. Each leaf of a tree, the sun behind it, hangs like a golden pear. Riding westward in high summer, we have dipped into sylvan chases and crested the downs, emerging into that high country where, even across two counties, you can sense the shifting presence of the sea. In this part of England our forefathers the giants left their earthworks, their barrows and standing stones. We still have, every Englishman and woman, some drops of giant blood in our veins. In those ancient times, in a land undespoiled by sheep or plough, they hunted the wild boar and the elk. The forest stretched ahead for days. Sometimes antique weapons are unearthed: axes that, wielded with double fist, could cut down horse and rider. Think of the great limbs of those dead men, stirring under the soil. War was their nature, and war is always keen to come again. It's not just the past you think of, as you ride these fields. It's what's latent in the soil, what's breeding; it's the days to come, the wars unfought, the injuries and deaths that, like seeds, the soil of England is keeping warm. You would think, to look at Henry laughing, to look at Henry praying, to look at him leading his men through the forest path, that he sits as secure on his throne as he does on his horse. Looks can deceive. By night, he lies awake; he stares at the carved roof beams; he numbers his days. He says, 'Cromwell, Cromwell, what shall I do?' Cromwell, save me from the Emperor. Cromwell, save me from the Pope. Then he calls in his Archbishop of Canterbury, Thomas Cranmer, and demands to know, 'Is my soul damned?'

Back in London, the Emperor's ambassador, Eustache Chapuys, waits daily for news that the people of England have risen against their cruel and ungodly king. It is news that he dearly wishes to hear, and he would spend labour and hard cash to make it come true. His master, the Emperor Charles, is lord of the Low Countries as well as Spain and her lands beyond the seas; Charles is rich and, from time to time, he is angry that Henry Tudor has dared to set aside his aunt, Katherine, to marry a woman whom the people on the streets call a goggle-eyed whore. Chapuys is exhorting his master in urgent dispatches to invade England, to join with the realm's rebels, pretenders and malcontents, and to conquer this unholy island where the king by an act of Parliament has settled his own divorce and declared himself God. The Pope does not take it kindly, that he is laughed at in England and called mere 'Bishop of Rome', that his revenues are cut off and chan-nelled into Henry's coffers. A bull of excommunication, drawn up but not yet promulgated, hovers over Henry, making him an outcast among the Christian kings of Europe: who are invited, indeed, encouraged, to step across the Narrow Sea or the Scots border, and help themselves to anything that's his. Perhaps the Emperor will come. Perhaps the King of France will come. Perhaps they will come together. It would be pleasant to say we are ready for them, but the reality is otherwise. In the case of an armed incursion we may have to dig up the giants' bones to knock them around the head with, as we are short of ordnance, short of powder, short of steel. This is not Thomas Cromwell's fault; as Chapuys says, grimacing, Henry's kingdom would be in better order if Cromwell had been put in charge five years ago.

If you would defend England, and he would – for he would take the field himself, his sword in his hand – you must know what England is. In the August heat, he has stood bare-headed by the carved tombs of ancestors, men armoured *cap à pie* in plate and chain links, their gauntleted hands joined and perched stiffly on their surcoats, their mailed feet resting on stone lions, griffins, greyhounds: stone men, steel men, their soft wives encased beside them like snails in their shells. We think time cannot touch the dead, but it touches their monuments, leaving them snub-nosed and stub-fingered from the accidents and attrition of time. A tiny dismembered foot (as of a kneeling cherub) emerges from a swathe of drapery; the tip of a severed thumb lies on a carved cushion. 'We must get our forefathers mended next year,' the lords of the western counties say: but their shields and support-ers, their achievements and bearings, are kept always paint-fresh, and in talk they embellish the deeds of their ancestors, who they were and what they held: the arms my forefather bore at Agincourt, the cup my forefather was given by John of Gaunt his own hand. If in the late wars of York and Lancaster, their fathers and grandfathers picked the wrong side, they keep quiet about it. A generation on, lapses must be forgiven, reputations remade; otherwise England cannot go forward, she will keep spiralling backwards into the dirty past.

He has no ancestors, of course: not the kind you'd boast about. There was once a noble family called Cromwell, and when he came up in the king's service the heralds had urged him for the sake of appearances to adopt their coat of arms; but I am none of theirs, he had said politely, and I do not want their achievements. He had run away from his father's fists when he was no older than fifteen; crossed the Channel, taken service in the French king's army. He had been fighting since he could walk; and if you're going to fight, why not be paid for it? There are more lucrative trades than soldiering, and he found them. So he decided not to hurry home.

And now, when his titled hosts want advice on the placement of a fountain, or a group of the Three Graces dancing, the king tells them, Cromwell here is your man; Cromwell, he has seen how they do things in Italy, and what will do for them will do for

10

Wiltshire. Sometimes the king departs a place with just his riding household, the queen left behind with her ladies and musicians, as Henry and his favoured few hunt hard across the country. And that is how they come to Wolf Hall, where old Sir John Seymour is waiting to welcome them, in the midst of his flourishing family.

'I don't know, Cromwell,' old Sir John says. He takes his arm, genial. 'All these falcons named for dead women ... don't they dishearten you?'

'I'm never disheartened, Sir John. The world is too good to me.'

'You should marry again, and have another family. Perhaps you will find a bride while you are with us. In the forest of Savernake there are many fresh young women.'

I still have Gregory, he says, looking back over his shoulder for his son; he is always somehow anxious about Gregory. 'Ah,' Seymour says, 'boys are very well, but a man needs daughters too, daughters are a consolation. Look at Jane. Such a good girl.'

He looks at Jane Seymour, as her father directs him. He knows her well from the court, as she was lady-in-waiting to Katherine, the former queen, and to Anne, the queen that is now; she is a plain young woman with a silvery pallor, a habit of silence, and a trick of looking at men as if they represent an unpleasant surprise. She is wearing pearls, and white brocade embroidered with stiff little sprigs of carnations. He recognises considerable expenditure; leave the pearls aside, you couldn't turn her out like that for much under thirty pounds. No wonder she moves with gingerly concern, like a child who's been told not to spill something on herself.

The king says, 'Jane, now we see you at home with your people, are you less shy?' He takes her mouse-paw in his vast hand. 'At court we never get a word from her.'

Jane is looking up at him, blushing from her neck to her hairline. 'Did you ever see such a blush?' Henry asks. 'Never unless with a little maid of twelve.'

'I cannot claim to be twelve,' Jane says.

At supper the king sits next to Lady Margery, his hostess. She was a beauty in her day, and by the king's exquisite attention you would think she was one still; she has had ten children, and six of them are living, and three are in this room. Edward Seymour, the heir, has a long head, a serious expression, a clean fierce profile: a handsome man. He is well-read if not scholarly, applies himself wisely to any office he is given; he has been to war, and while he is waiting to fight again he acquits himself well in the hunting field and tilt yard. The cardinal, in his day, marked him out as better than the usual run of Seymours; and he himself, Thomas Cromwell, has sounded him out and found him in every respect the king's man. Tom Seymour, Edward's younger brother, is noisy and boisterous and more of interest to women; when he comes into the room, virgins giggle, and young matrons dip their heads and examine him from under their lashes.

Old Sir John is a man of notorious family feeling. Two, three years back, the gossip at court was all of how he had tupped his son's wife, not once in the heat of passion but repeatedly since she was a bride. The queen and her confidantes had spread the story about the court. 'We've worked it out at 120 times,' Anne had sniggered. 'Well, Thomas Cromwell has, and he's quick with figures. We suppose they abstained on a Sunday for shame's sake, and eased off in Lent.' The traitor wife gave birth to two boys, and when her conduct came to light Edward said he would not have them for his heirs, as he could not be sure if they were his sons or his half-brothers. The adulteress was locked up in a convent, and soon obliged him by dying; now he has a new wife, who cultivates a forbidding manner and keeps a bodkin in her pocket in case her father-in-law gets too close.

But it is forgiven, it is forgiven. The flesh is frail. This royal visit seals the old fellow's pardon. John Seymour has 1,300 acres including his deer park, most of the rest under sheep and worth two shilling per acre per year, bringing him in a clear twenty-five per cent on what the same acreage would make under the plough. The sheep are little black-faced animals interbred with Welsh mountain stock, gristly mutton but good enough wool. When at their arrival, the king (he is in bucolic vein) says, 'Cromwell, what would that beast weigh?' he says, without picking it up, 'Thirty pounds, sir.' Francis Weston, a young courtier, says with a sneer, 'Master Cromwell used to be a shearsman. He wouldn't be wrong.'

The king says, 'We would be a poor country without our wool trade. That Master Cromwell knows the business is not to his discredit.'

But Francis Weston smirks behind his hand.

Tomorrow Jane Seymour is to hunt with the king. 'I thought it was gentlemen only,' he hears Weston whisper. 'The queen would be angry if she knew.' He murmurs, make sure she doesn't know then, there's a good boy.

'At Wolf Hall we are all great hunters,' Sir John boasts, 'my daughters too, you think Jane is timid but put her in the saddle and I assure you, sirs, she is the goddess Diana. I never troubled my girls in the schoolroom, you know. Sir James here taught them all they needed.'

The priest at the foot of the table nods, beaming: an old fool with a white poll, a bleared eye. He, Cromwell, turns to him: 'And was it you taught them to dance, Sir James? All praise to you. I have seen Jane's sister Elizabeth at court, partnered with the king.'

'Ah, they had a master for that,' old Seymour chuckles. 'Master for dancing, master for music, that's enough for them. They don't want foreign tongues. They're not going anywhere.'

'I think otherwise, sir,' he says. 'I had my daughters taught equal with my son.'

Sometimes he likes to talk about them, Anne and Grace: gone seven years now. Tom Seymour laughs. 'What, you had them in the tilt yard with Gregory and young Master Sadler?'

He smiles. 'Except for that.'

Edward Seymour says, 'It is not uncommon for the daughters of a city household to learn their letters and a little beyond. You might have wanted them in the counting house. One hears of it. It would help them get good husbands, a merchant family would be glad of their training.'

'Imagine Master Cromwell's daughters,' Weston says. 'I dare not. I doubt a counting house could contain them. They would be a shrewd hand with a poleaxe, you would think. One look at them and a man's legs would go from under him. And I do not mean he would be stricken with love.'

Gregory stirs himself. He is such a dreamer you hardly think he has been following the conversation, but his tone is rippling with hurt. 'You insult my sisters and their memory, sir, and you never knew them. My sister Grace ...'

He sees Jane Seymour put out her little hand and touch Gregory's wrist: to save him, she will risk drawing the company's attention. 'I have lately,' she says, 'got some skill of the French tongue.'

'Have you, Jane?' Tom Seymour is smiling.

Jane dips her head. 'Mary Shelton is teaching me.'

'Mary Shelton is a kindly young woman,' the king says; and out of the corner of his eye, he sees Weston elbow his neighbour; they say Shelton has been kind to the king in bed.

'So you see,' Jane says to her brothers, 'we ladies, we do not spend all our time in idle calumny and scandal. Though God he knows, we have gossip enough to occupy a whole town of women.'

'Have you?' he says.

'We talk about who is in love with the queen. Who writes her verses.' She drops her eyes. 'I mean to say, who is in love with us all. This gentleman or that. We know all our suitors and we make inventory head to toe, they would blush if they knew. We say their acreage and how much they have a year, and then we decide

14

if we will let them write us a sonnet. If we do not think they will keep us in fine style, we scorn their rhymes. It is cruel, I can tell you.'

He says, a little uneasy, it is no harm to write verses to ladies, even married ones, at court it is usual. Weston says, thank you for that kind word, Master Cromwell, we thought you might try and make us stop.

Tom Seymour leans forward, laughing. 'And who are your suitors, Jane?'

'If you want to know that, you must put on a gown, and take up your needlework, and come and join us.'

'Like Achilles among the women,' the king says. 'You must shave your fine beard, Seymour, and go and find out their lewd little secrets.' He is laughing, but he is not happy. 'Unless we find someone more maidenly for the task. Gregory, you are a pretty fellow, but I fear your great hands will give you away.'

'The blacksmith's grandson,' Weston says.

'That child Mark,' the king says. 'The musician, you know him? There is a smooth girlish countenance.'

'Oh,' Jane says, 'Mark's with us anyway. He's always loitering. We barely count him a man. If you want to know our secrets, ask Mark.'

The conversation canters off in some other direction; he thinks, I have never known Jane have anything to say for herself; he thinks, Weston is goading me, he knows that in Henry's presence I will not give him a check; he imagines what form the check may take, when he delivers it. Rafe Sadler looks at him out of the tail of his eye.

'So,' the king says to him, 'how will tomorrow be better than today?' To the supper table he explains, 'Master Cromwell cannot sleep unless he is amending something.'

'I will reform the conduct of Your Majesty's hat. And those clouds, before noon –'

'We wanted the shower. The rain cooled us.'

'God send Your Majesty no worse a drenching,' says Edward Seymour.

Henry rubs his stripe of sunburn. 'The cardinal, he reckoned he could change the weather. A good enough morning, he would say, but by ten it will be brighter. And it was.'

Henry does this sometimes; drops Wolsey's name into conversation, as if it were not he, but some other monarch, who had hounded the cardinal to death.

'Some men have a weather eye,' Tom Seymour says. 'That's all it is, sir. It's not special to cardinals.'

Henry nods, smiling. 'That's true, Tom. I should never have stood in awe of him, should I?'

'He was too proud, for a subject,' old Sir John says.

The king looks down the table at him, Thomas Cromwell. He loved the cardinal. Everyone here knows it. His expression is as carefully blank as a freshly painted wall.

After supper, old Sir John tells the story of Edgar the Peaceable. He was the ruler in these parts, many hundreds of years ago, before kings had numbers: when all maids were fair maids and all knights were gallant and life was simple and violent and usually brief. Edgar had in mind a bride for himself, and sent one of his earls to appraise her. The earl, who was both false and cunning, sent back word that her beauty had been much exaggerated by poets and painters; seen in real life, he said, she had a limp and a squint. His aim was to have the tender damsel for himself, and so he seduced and married her. Upon discovering the earl's treachery Edgar ambushed him, in a grove not far from here, and rammed a javelin into him, killing him with one blow.

'What a false knave he was, that earl!' says the king. 'He was paid out.'

'Call him rather a churl than an earl,' Tom Seymour says.

His brother sighs, as if distancing himself from the remark.

16

'And what did the lady say?' he asks; he, Cromwell. 'When she found the earl skewered?'

'The damsel married Edgar,' Sir John says. 'They married in the greenwood, and lived happily ever after.'

'I suppose she had no choice,' Lady Margery sighs. 'Women have to adapt themselves.'

'And the country folk say,' Sir John adds, 'that the false earl walks the woods still, groaning, and trying to pull the lance out of his belly.'

'Just imagine,' Jane Seymour says. 'Any night there is a moon, one might look out of the window and see him, tugging away and complaining all the while. Fortunately I do not believe in ghosts.'

'More fool you, sister,' Tom Seymour says. 'They'll creep up on you, my lass.'

'Still,' Henry says. He mimes a javelin throw: though in the restrained way one must, at a supper table. 'One clean blow. He must have had a good throwing arm, King Edgar.'

He says – he, Cromwell: 'I should like to know if this tale is written down, and if so, by whom, and was he on oath.'

The king says, 'Cromwell would have had the earl before a judge and jury.'

'Bless Your Majesty,' Sir John chuckles, 'I don't think they had them in those days.'

'Cromwell would have found one out.' Young Weston leans forward to make his point. 'He would dig out a jury, he would grub one from a mushroom patch. Then it would be all up with the earl, they would try him and march him out and hack off his head. They say that at Thomas More's trial, Master Secretary here followed the jury to their deliberations, and when they were seated he closed the door behind him and he laid down the law. "Let me put you out of doubt," he said to the jurymen. "Your task is to find Sir Thomas guilty, and you will have no dinner till you have done it." Then out he went and shut the door again and stood outside it with a hatchet in his hand, in case they broke out

17

in search of a boiled pudding; and being Londoners, they care about their bellies above all things, and as soon as they felt them rumbling they cried, "Guilty! He is as guilty as guilty can be!"'

Eyes focus on him, Cromwell. Rafe Sadler, by his side, is tense with displeasure. 'It is a pretty tale,' Rafe tells Weston, 'but I ask you in turn, where is it written down? I think you will find my master is always correct in his dealings with a court of law.'

'You weren't there,' Francis Weston says. 'I heard it from one of those same jurymen. They cried, "Away with him, take out the traitor and bring us in a leg of mutton." And Thomas More was led to his death.'

'You sound as if you regret it,' Rafe says.

'Not I.' Weston holds up his hands. 'Anne the queen says, let More's death be a warning to all such traitors. Be their credit never so great, their treason never so veiled, Thomas Cromwell will find them out.'

There is a murmur of assent; for a moment, he thinks the company will turn to him and applaud. Then Lady Margery touches a finger to her lips, and nods towards the king. Seated at the head of the table, he has begun to incline to the right; his closed eyelids flutter, and his breathing is easeful and deep.

The company exchange smiles. 'Drunk with fresh air,' Tom Seymour whispers.

It makes a change from drunk with drink; the king, these days, calls for the wine jug more often than he did in his lean and sporting youth. He, Cromwell, watches as Henry tilts in his chair. First forward, as if to rest his forehead on the table. Then he starts and jerks backwards. A line of drool trickles down his beard.

This would be the moment for Harry Norris, the chief among the privy chamber gentlemen; Harry with his noiseless tread and his soft unjudging hand, murmuring his sovereign back to wakefulness. But Norris has gone across country, carrying the king's love letter to Anne. So what to do? Henry does not look like a tired child, as five years ago he might have done. He looks like any man in mid-life, lapsed into torpor after too heavy a meal; he looks bloated and puffy, and a vein is burst here and there, and even by candlelight you can see that his faded hair is greying. He, Cromwell, nods to young Weston. 'Francis, your gentlemanly touch is required.'

Weston pretends not to hear him. His eyes are on the king and his face wears an unguarded expression of distaste. Tom Seymour whispers, 'I think we should make a noise. To wake him naturally.'

'What sort of noise?' his brother Edward mouths.

Tom mimes holding his ribs.

Edward's eyebrows shoot up. 'You laugh if you dare. He'll think you're laughing at his drooling.'

The king begins to snore. He lurches to the left. He tilts dangerously over the arm of his chair.

Weston says, 'You do it, Cromwell. No man so great with him as you are.'

He shakes his head, smiling.

'God save His Majesty,' says Sir John, piously. 'He's not as young as he was.'

Jane rises. A stiff rustle from the carnation sprigs. She leans over the king's chair and taps the back of his hand: briskly, as if she were testing a cheese. Henry jumps and his eyes flick open. 'I wasn't asleep,' he says. 'Really. I was just resting my eyes.'

When the king has gone upstairs, Edward Seymour says, 'Master Secretary, time for my revenge.'

Leaning back, glass in hand: 'What I have done to you?'

'A game of chess. Calais. I know you remember.'

Late autumn, the year 1532: the night the king first went to bed with the queen that is now. Before she lay down for him Anne made him swear an oath on the Bible, that he would marry her as soon as they were back on English soil; but the storms trapped them in port, and the king made good use of the time, trying to get a son on her.

'You checkmated me, Master Cromwell,' Edward says. 'But only because you distracted me.'

'How did I?'

'You asked me about my sister Jane. Her age, and so on.'

'You thought I was interested in her.'

'And are you?' Edward smiles, to take the edge off the crude question. 'She is not spoken for yet, you know.'

'Set up the pieces,' he says. 'Would you like the board aligned as it was when you lost your train of thought?'

Edward looks at him, carefully expressionless. Incredible things are related of Cromwell's memory. He smiles to himself. He could set up the board, with only a little guesswork; he knows the type of game a man like Seymour plays. 'We should begin afresh,' he suggests. 'The world moves on. You are happy with Italian rules? I don't like these contests that drag out for a week.'

Their opening moves see some boldness on Edward's part. But then, a white pawn poised between his fingertips, Seymour leans back in his chair, frowning, and takes it into his head to talk about St Augustine; and from St Augustine moves to Martin Luther. 'It is a teaching that brings terror to the heart,' he says. 'That God would make us only to damn us. That his poor creatures, except some few of them, are born only for a struggle in this world and then eternal fire. Sometimes I fear it is true. But I find I hope it is not.'

'Fat Martin has modified his position. Or so I hear. And to our comfort.'

'What, more of us are saved? Or our good works are not entirely useless in God's sight?'

'I should not speak for him. You should read Philip Melanchthon. I will send you his new book. I hope he will visit us in England. We are talking to his people.'

Edward presses the pawn's little round head to his lips. He looks as if he might tap his teeth with it. 'Will the king allow that?'

'He would not let in Brother Martin himself. He does not like his name mentioned. But Philip is an easier man, and it would be good for us, it would be very good for us, if we were to come into some helpful alliance with the German princes who favour the gospel. It would give the Emperor a fright, if we had friends and allies in his own domains.'

'And that is all it means to you?' Edward's knight is skipping over the squares. 'Diplomacy?'

'I cherish diplomacy. It's cheap.'

'Yet they say you love the gospel yourself.'

'It is no secret.' He frowns. 'Do you really mean to do that, Edward? I see my way to your queen. And I should not like to take advantage of you again, and have you say I spoiled your game with small talk about the state of your soul.'

A skewed smile. 'And how is your queen these days?'

'Anne? She is at outs with me. I feel my head wobble on my shoulders when she stares at me hard. She has heard that once or twice I spoke favourably of Katherine, the queen that was.'

'And did you?'

'Only to admire her spirit. Which, anyone must admit, is steadfast in adversity. And again, the queen thinks I am too favourable to the Princess Mary – I mean to say, to Lady Mary, as we should call her now. The king loves his elder daughter still, he says he cannot help it – and it grieves Anne, because she wants the Princess Elizabeth to be the only daughter he knows. She thinks we are too soft towards Mary and that we should tax her to admit her mother was never married lawfully to the king, and that she is a bastard.'

Edward twiddles the white pawn in his fingers, looks at it dubiously, sets it down on its square. 'But is that not the state of affairs? I thought you had made her acknowledge it already.'

'We solve the question by not raising it. She knows she is put out of the succession, and I do not think I should force her beyond a point. As the Emperor is Katherine's nephew and Lady

21

Mary's cousin, I try not to provoke him. Charles holds us in the palm of his hand, do you see? But Anne does not understand the need to placate people. She thinks if she speaks sweetly to Henry, that is enough to do.'

'Whereas you must speak sweetly to Europe.' Edward laughs. His laugh has a rusty sound. His eyes say, you are being very frank, Master Cromwell: why?

'Besides,' his fingers hover over the black knight, 'I am grown too great for the queen's liking, since the king made me his deputy in church affairs. She hates Henry to listen to anyone but herself and her brother George and Monseigneur her father, and even her father gets the rough side of her tongue, and gets called lily-liver and timewaster.'

'How does he take that?' Edward looks down at the board. 'Oh.'

'Now take a careful look,' he urges. 'Do you want to play it out?'

'I resign. I think.' A sigh. 'Yes. I resign.'

He, Cromwell, sweeps the pieces aside, stifling a yawn. 'And I never mentioned your sister Jane, did I? So what's your excuse now?'

When he goes upstairs he sees Rafe and Gregory jumping around near the great window. They are capering and scuffling, eyes on something invisible at their feet. At first he thinks they are playing football without a ball. But then they leap up like dancers and back-heel the thing, and he sees that it is long and thin, a fallen man. They lean down to tweak and jab, to apply torsion. 'Ease off,' Gregory says, 'don't snap his neck yet, I need to see him suffer.'

Rafe looks up, and affects to wipe his brow. Gregory rests hands on knees, getting his breath back, then nudges the victim with his foot. 'This is Francis Weston. You think he is helping put the king to bed, but in fact we have him here in ghostly form. We stood around a corner and waited for him with a magic net.'

'We are punishing him,' Rafe leans down. 'Ho, sir, are you sorry now?' He spits on his palms. 'What next with him, Gregory?'

'Haul him up and out the window with him.'

'Careful,' he says. 'The king favours Weston.'

'Then he'll favour him when he's got a flat head,' Rafe says. They scuffle and push each other out of the way, trying to be the first to stamp Francis flat. Rafe opens a window and both stoop for leverage, hoisting the phantom across the sill. Gregory helps it over, unsnagging its jacket where it catches, and with one shove drops it head first on the cobbles. They peer out after it. 'He bounces,' Rafe observes, and then they dust off their hands, smiling at him. 'Give you good night, sir,' Rafe says.

Later, Gregory sits at the foot of the bed in his shirt, his hair tousled, his shoes kicked off, one bare foot idly scuffing the matting: 'So am I to be married? Am I to be married to Jane Seymour?'

'Early in the summer you thought I was going to marry you to an old dowager with a deer park.' People tease Gregory: Rafe Sadler, Thomas Wriothesley, the other young men of his house; his cousin, Richard Cromwell.

'Yes, but why were you talking to her brother this last hour? First it was chess then it was talk, talk, talk. They say you liked Jane yourself.'

'When?'

'Last year. You liked her last year.'

'If I did I've forgot.'

'George Boleyn's wife told me. Lady Rochford. She said, you may get a young stepmother from Wolf Hall, what will you think of that? So if you like Jane yourself,' Gregory frowns, 'she had better not be married to me.'

'Do you think I'd steal your bride? Like old Sir John?'

Once his head is on the pillow, he says, 'Hush, Gregory.' He closes his eyes. Gregory is a good boy, though all the Latin he has

23

learned, all the sonorous periods of the great authors, have rolled through his head and out again, like stones. Still, you think of Thomas More's boy: offspring of a scholar all Europe admired, and poor young John can barely stumble through his Pater Noster. Gregory is a fine archer, a fine horseman, a shining star in the tilt yard, and his manners cannot be faulted. He speaks reverently to his superiors, not scuffling his feet or standing on one leg, and he is mild and polite with those below him. He knows how to bow to foreign diplomats in the manner of their own countries, sits at table without fidgeting or feeding spaniels, can neatly carve and joint any fowl if requested to serve his elders. He doesn't slouch around with his jacket off one shoulder, or look in windows to admire himself, or stare around in church, or interrupt old men, or finish their stories for them. If anyone sneezes, he says, 'Christ help you!'

Christ help you, sir or madam.

Gregory raises his head. 'Thomas More,' he says. 'The jury. Is that truly what happened?'

He had recognised young Weston's story: in a broad sense, even if he didn't assent to the detail. He closes his eyes. 'I didn't have a hatchet,' he says.

He is tired: he speaks to God; he says: God guide me. Sometimes when he is on the verge of sleep the cardinal's large scarlet presence flits across his inner eye. He wishes the dead man would prophesy. But his old patron speaks only of domestic matters, office matters. Where did I put that letter from the Duke of Norfolk? he will ask the cardinal; and next day, early, it will come to his hand.

He speaks inwardly: not to Wolsey, but to George Boleyn's wife. 'I have no wish to marry. I have no time. I was happy with my wife but Liz is dead and that part of my life is dead with her. Who in the name of God gave you, Lady Rochford, a licence to speculate about my intentions? Madam, I have no time for wooing. I am fifty. At my age, one would be the loser on a long-term contract. If I want a woman, best to rent one by the hour.'

Yet he tries not to say 'at my age': not in his waking life. On a good day he thinks he has twenty years left. He often thinks he will see Henry out, though strictly it is not allowed to have that kind of thought; there is a law against speculating about the term of the king's life, though Henry has been a life-long student of inventive ways to die. There have been several hunting accidents. When he was still a minor the council forbade him to joust, but he did it anyway, face hidden by his helmet and his armour without device, proving himself again and again the strongest man on the field. In battle against the French he has taken the honours, and his nature, as he often mentions, is warlike; no doubt he would be known as Henry the Valiant, except Thomas Cromwell says he can't afford a war. Cost is not the whole consideration: what becomes of England if Henry dies? He was twenty years married to Katherine, this autumn it will be three with Anne, nothing to show but a daughter with each and a churchyard's worth of dead babies, some half-formed and christened in blood, some born alive but dead within hours, within days, within weeks at most. All the turmoil, the scandal, to make the second marriage, and still. Still Henry has no son to follow him. He has a bastard, Harry Duke of Richmond, a fine boy of sixteen: but what use to him is a bastard? What use is Anne's child, the infant Elizabeth? Some special mechanism may have to be created so Harry Richmond can reign, if anything but good should come to his father. He, Thomas Cromwell, stands very well with the young duke; but this dynasty, still new as kingship goes, is not secure enough to survive such a course. The Plantagenets were kings once and they think they will kings be again; they think the Tudors are an interlude. The old families of England are restless and ready to press their claim, especially since Henry broke with Rome; they bow the knee, but they are plotting. He can almost hear them, hidden among the trees.

You may find a bride in the forest, old Seymour had said. When he closes his eyes she slides behind them, veiled in cobwebs and splashed with dew. Her feet are bare, entwined in roots, her feather hair flies into the branches; her finger, beckoning, is a curled leaf. She points to him, as sleep overtakes him. His inner voice mocks him now: you thought you were going to get a holiday at Wolf Hall. You thought there would be nothing to do here except the usual business, war and peace, famine, traitorous connivance; a failing harvest, a stubborn populace; plague ravaging London, and the king losing his shirt at cards. You were prepared for that.

At the edge of his inner vision, behind his closed eyes, he senses something in the act of becoming. It will arrive with morning light; something shifting and breathing, its form disguised in a copse or grove.

Before he sleeps he thinks of the king's hat on a midnight tree, roosting like a bird from paradise.

Next day, so as not to tire the ladies, they cut short the day's sport, and return early to Wolf Hall.

For him, it is a chance to put off his riding clothes and get among the dispatches. He has hopes that the king will sit for an hour and listen to what he needs to tell him. But Henry says, 'Lady Jane, will you walk in the garden with me?'

She is at once on her feet; but frowning, as if trying to make sense of it. Her lips move, she all but repeats his words: Walk … Jane? … In the garden?

Oh yes, of course, honoured. Her hand, a petal, hovers above his sleeve; then it descends, and flesh grazes embroidery.

There are three gardens at Wolf Hall, and they call them the great paled garden, the old lady's garden and the young lady's garden. When he asks who they were, no one remembers; the old lady and the young lady are dust long ago, no difference between them now. He remembers his dream: the bride made of root fibre, the bride made of mould.

He reads. He writes. Something tugs at his attention. He gets up and glances from the window at the walks below. The panes are small and there is a wobble in the glass, so he has to crane his neck to get a proper view. He thinks, I could send my glaziers down, help the Seymours get a clearer idea of the world. He has a team of Hollanders who work for him at his various properties. They worked for the cardinal before him.

Henry and Jane are walking below. Henry is a massive figure and Jane is like a little jointed puppet, her head not up to the king's shoulders. A broad man, a high man, Henry dominates any room; he would do it even if God had not given him the gift of kingship.

Now Jane is behind a bush. Henry is nodding at her; he is speaking at her; he is impressing something on her, and he, Cromwell, watches, scratching his chin: is the king's head becoming bigger? Is that possible, in mid-life?

Hans will have noticed, he thinks, I'll ask him when I get back to London. Most likely I am under a mistake; probably it's just the glass.

Clouds are coming up. A heavy raindrop hits the pane; he blinks; the drop spreads, widens, trickles against the glazing bars. Jane bobs out into his sightline. Henry has her hand clamped firmly on his arm, trapping it with his other hand. He can see the king's mouth, still moving.

He resumes his seat. He reads that the builders working on the fortifications in Calais have downed tools and are demanding sixpence a day. That his new green velvet coat is coming down to Wiltshire by the next courier. That a Medici cardinal has been poisoned by his own brother. He yawns. He reads that hoarders on the Isle of Thanet are deliberately driving up the price of grain. Personally, he would hang hoarders, but the chief of them might be some little lordling who is promoting famine for fat profit, and so you have to tread carefully. Two years ago, at Southwark, seven Londoners were crushed to death in fighting for a dole of bread. It is a shame to England that the king's subjects should starve. He takes up his pen and makes a note.

Very soon – this is not a big house, you can hear everything – he hears a door below, and the king's voice, and a soft hum of solicitation around him ... wet feet, Majesty? He hears Henry's heavy tread approaching, but it seems Jane has melted away without a sound. No doubt her mother and her sisters have swept her aside, to hear all the king said to her.

As Henry comes in behind him, he pushes back his chair to rise. Henry waves a hand: carry on. 'Majesty, the Muscovites have taken three hundred miles of Polish territory. They say fifty thousand men are dead.'

'Oh,' Henry says.

'I hope they spare the libraries. The scholars. There are very fine scholars in Poland.'

'Mm? I hope so too.'

He returns to his dispatches. Plague in town and city ... the king is always very fearful of infection ... Letters from foreign rulers, wishing to know if it is true that Henry is planning to cut off the heads of all his bishops. Certainly not, he notes, we have excellent bishops now, all of them conformable to the king's wishes, all of them recognising him as head of the church in England; besides, what an uncivil question! How dare they imply that the King of England should account for himself to any foreign power? How dare they impugn his sovereign judgement? Bishop Fisher, it is true, is dead, and Thomas More, but Henry's treatment of them, before they drove him to an extremity, was mild to a fault; if they had not evinced a traitorous stubbornness, they would be alive now, alive like you and me.

He has written a lot of these letters, since July. He doesn't sound wholly convincing, even to himself; he finds himself repeating the same points, rather than advancing the argument into new territory. He needs new phrases ... Henry stumps about behind him. 'Majesty, the Imperial ambassador Chapuys asks may he ride up-country to visit your daughter, Lady Mary?'

'No,' Henry says.

He writes to Chapuys, *Wait, just wait, till I am back in London, when all will be arranged ...*

No word from the king: just breathing, pacing, a creak from a cupboard where he rests and leans on it.

'Majesty, I hear the Lord Mayor of London scarcely leaves his house, he is so afflicted by migraine.'

'Mm?' Henry says.

'They are bleeding him. Is that what Your Majesty would advise?'

A pause. Henry focuses on him, with some effort. 'Bleeding him, I'm sorry, for what?'

This is strange. Much as he hates news of plague, Henry always enjoys hearing of other people's minor ailments. Admit to a sniffle or a colic, and he will make up a herbal potion with his own hands, and stand over you while you swallow it.

He puts down his pen. Turns to look his monarch in the face. It is clear that Henry's mind is back in the garden. The king is wearing an expression he has seen before, though on beast, rather than man. He looks stunned, like a veal calf knocked on the head by the butcher.

It is to be their last night at Wolf Hall. He comes down very early, his arms full of papers. Someone is up before him. Stock-still in the great hall, a pale presence in the milky light, Jane Seymour is dressed in her stiff finery. She does not turn her head to acknowledge him, but she sees him from the tail of her eye.

If he had any feeling for her, he cannot find traces of it now. The months run away from you like a flurry of autumn leaves bowling and skittering towards the winter; the summer has gone, Thomas More's daughter has got his head back off London Bridge and is keeping it, God knows, in a dish or bowl, and saying her prayers to it. He is not the same man he was last year, and he doesn't acknowledge that man's feelings; he is starting afresh, always new thoughts, new feelings. Jane, he begins to say, you'll be able to get out of your best gown, will you be glad to see us on the road …?

Jane is facing front, like a sentry. The clouds have blown away overnight. We may have one more fine day. The early sun touches the fields, rosy. Night vapours disperse. The forms of trees swim into particularity. The house is waking up. Unstalled horses tread and whinny. A back door slams. Footsteps creak above them. Jane hardly seems to breathe. No rise and fall discernible, of that flat bosom. He feels he should walk backwards, withdraw, fade back into the night, and leave her here in the moment she occupies: looking out into England.

II

Crows

London and Kimbolton, Autumn 1535

Stephen Gardiner! Coming in as he's going out, striding towards the king's chamber, a folio under one arm, the other flailing the air. Gardiner, Bishop of Winchester: blowing up like a thunderstorm, when for once we have a fine day.

When Stephen comes into a room, the furnishings shrink from him. Chairs scuttle backwards. Joint-stools flatten themselves like pissing bitches. The woollen Bible figures in the king's tapestries lift their hands to cover their ears.

At court you might expect him. Anticipate him. But here? While we are still hunting through the countryside and (notionally) taking our ease? 'This is a pleasure, my lord bishop,' he says. 'It does my heart good to see you looking so well. The court will progress to Winchester shortly, and I did not think to enjoy your company before that.'

'I have stolen a march on you, Cromwell.'

'Are we at war?'

The bishop's face says, you know we are. 'It was you who had me banished.'

'I? Never think it, Stephen. I have missed you every day. Besides, not banished. Rusticated.'

Gardiner licks his lips. 'You will see how I have spent my time in the country.'

31

When Gardiner lost the post of Mr Secretary – and lost it to him, Cromwell – it had been impressed on the bishop that a spell in his own diocese of Winchester might be advisable, for he had too often cut across the king and his second wife. As he had put it, 'My lord of Winchester, a considered statement on the king's supremacy might be welcome, just so that there can be no mistake about your loyalty. A firm declaration that he is head of the English church and, rightfully considered, always has been. An assertion, firmly stated, that the Pope is a foreign prince with no jurisdiction here. A written sermon, perhaps, or an open letter. To clear up any ambiguities in your opinions. To give a lead to other churchmen, and to disabuse ambassador Chapuys of the notion that you have been bought by the Emperor. You should make a statement to the whole of Christendom. In fact, why don't you go back to your diocese and write a book?'

Now here is Gardiner, patting a manuscript as if it were the cheek of a plump baby: 'The king will be pleased to read this. I have called it, *Of True Obedience*.'

'You had better let me see it before it goes to the printer.'

'The king himself will expound it to you. It shows why oaths to the papacy are of none effect, yet our oath to the king, as head of the church, is good. It emphasises most strongly that a king's authority is divine, and descends to him directly from God.'

'And not from a pope.'

'In no wise from a pope; it descends from God without intermediary, and it does not flow upwards from his subjects, as you once stated to him.'

'Did I? Flow upwards? There seems a difficulty there.'

'You brought the king a book to that effect, the book of Marsiglio of Padua, his forty-two articles. The king says you belaboured him with them till his head ached.'

'I should have made the matter shorter,' he says, smiling. 'In practice, Stephen, upwards, downwards – it hardly matters.

"Where the word of a king is, there is power, and who may say to him, what doest thou?"'

'Henry is not a tyrant,' Gardiner says stiffly. 'I rebut any notion that his regime is not lawfully grounded. If I were king, I would wish my authority to be legitimate wholly, to be respected universally and, if questioned, stoutly defended. Would not you?'

'If I were king ...'

He was going to say, if I were king I'd defenestrate you. Gardiner says, 'Why are you looking out of the window?'

He smiles absently. 'I wonder what Thomas More would say to your book?'

'Oh, he would much mislike it, but for his opinion I do not give a fig,' the bishop says heartily, 'since his brain was eaten out by kites, and his skull made a relic his daughter worships on her knees. Why did you let her take the head off London Bridge?'

'You know me, Stephen. The fluid of benevolence flows through my veins and sometimes overspills. But look, if you are so proud of your book, perhaps you should spend more time writing in the country?'

Gardiner scowls. 'You should write a book yourself. That would be something to see. You with your dog Latin and your little bit of Greek.'

'I would write it in English,' he says. 'A good language for all sorts of matters. Go in, Stephen, don't keep the king waiting. You will find him in a good humour. Harry Norris is with him today. Francis Weston.'

'Oh, that chattering coxcomb,' Stephen says. He makes a cuffing motion. 'Thank you for the intelligence.'

Does the phantom-self of Weston feel the slap? A gust of laughter sweeps out from Henry's rooms.

The fine weather did not much outlast their stay at Wolf Hall. They had hardly left the Savernake forest when they were enveloped in wet mist. In England it's been raining, more or less, for a decade, and the harvest will be poor again. The price of wheat is forecast to rise to twenty shillings a quarter. So what will the labourer do this winter, the man who earns five or six pence a day? The profiteers have moved in already, not just on the Isle of Thanet, but through the shires. His men are on their tail.

It used to surprise the cardinal, that one Englishman would starve another and take the profit. But he would say, 'I have seen an English mercenary cut the throat of his comrade, and pull his blanket from under him while he's still twitching, and go through his pack and pocket a holy medal along with his money.'

'Ah, but he was a hired killer,' the cardinal would say. 'Such men have no soul to lose. But most Englishmen fear God.'

'The Italians think not. They say the road between England and Hell is worn bare from treading feet, and runs downhill all the way.'

Daily he ponders the mystery of his countrymen. He has seen killers, yes; but he has seen a hungry soldier give away a loaf to a woman, a woman who is nothing to him, and turn away with a shrug. It is better not to try people, not to force them to desperation. Make them prosper; out of superfluity, they will be generous. Full bellies breed gentle manners. The pinch of famine makes monsters.

When, some days after his meeting with Stephen Gardiner, the travelling court had reached Winchester, new bishops had been consecrated in the cathedral. 'My bishops', Anne called them: gospellers, reformers, men who see Anne as an opportunity. Who would have thought Hugh Latimer would be a bishop? You would rather have predicted he would be burned, shrivelled at Smithfield with the gospel in his mouth. But then, who would have thought that Thomas Cromwell would be anything at all? When Wolsey fell, you might have thought that as Wolsey's servant he was ruined. When his wife and daughters died, you might have thought his loss would kill him. But Henry has turned to him; Henry has sworn him in; Henry has put his time at his disposal and said, come, Master Cromwell, take my arm: through courtyards and throne rooms, his path in life is now made smooth and clear. As a young man he was always shouldering his way through crowds, pushing to the front to see the spectacle. But now crowds scatter as he walks through Westminster or the precincts of any of the king's palaces. Since he was sworn councillor, trestles and packing cases and loose dogs are swept from his path. Women still their whispering and tug down their sleeves and settle their rings on their fingers, since he was named Master of the Rolls. Kitchen debris and clerks' clutter and the footstools of the lowly are kicked into corners and out of sight, now that he is Master Secretary to the king. And no one except Stephen Gardiner corrects his Greek; not now he is Chancellor of Cambridge University.

Henry's summer, on the whole, has been a success: through Berkshire, Wiltshire and Somerset he has shown himself to the people on the roads, and (when the rain isn't bucketing down) they've stood by the roads and cheered. Why would they not? You cannot see Henry and not be amazed. Each time you see him you are struck afresh by him, as if it were the first time: a massive man, bull-necked, his hair receding, face fleshing out; blue eyes, and a small mouth that is almost coy. His height is six feet three inches, and every inch bespeaks power. His carriage, his person, are magnificent; his rages are terrifying, his vows and curses, his molten tears. But there are moments when his great body will stretch and ease itself, his brow clear; he will plump himself down next to you on a bench and talk to you like your brother. Like a brother might, if you had one. Or a father even, a father of an ideal sort: how are you? Not working too hard? Have you had your dinner? What did you dream last night?

The danger of a progress like this is that a king who sits at ordinary tables, on an ordinary chair, can be taken as an ordinary man. But Henry is not ordinary. What if his hair is receding and his belly advancing? The Emperor Charles, when he looks in the glass, would give a province to see the Tudor's visage instead of his own crooked countenance, his hook nose almost touching his chin. King Francis, a beanpole, would pawn his dauphin to have shoulders like the King of England. Any qualities they have, Henry reflects them back, double the size. If they are learned, he is twice learned. If merciful, he is the exemplar of mercy. If they are gallant, he is the pattern of knight errantry, from the biggest book of knights you can think of.

All the same: in village alehouses up and down England, they are blaming the king and Anne Boleyn for the weather: the concubine, the great whore. If the king would take back his lawful wife Katherine, the rain would stop. And indeed, who can doubt that everything would be different and better, if only England were ruled by village idiots and their drunken friends?

They move back towards London slowly, so that by the time the king arrives the city will be free from suspicion of plague. In cold chantry chapels under the gaze of wall-eyed virgins, the king prays alone. He doesn't like him to pray alone. He wants to know what he's praying for; his old master, Cardinal Wolsey, would have known.

His relations with the queen, as the summer draws to its official end, are chary, uncertain, and fraught with distrust. Anne Boleyn is now thirty-four years old, an elegant woman, with a refinement that makes mere prettiness seem redundant. Once sinuous, she has become angular. She retains her dark glitter, now rubbed a little, flaking in places. Her prominent dark eyes she uses to good effect, and in this fashion: she glances at a man's face, then her regard flits away, as if unconcerned, indifferent. There is a pause: as it might be, a breath. Then slowly, as if compelled, she turns her gaze back to him. Her eyes rest on his face. She examines this man. She examines him as if he is the only man in the world. She looks as if she is seeing him for the first time, and considering all sorts of uses for him, all sorts of possibilities which he has not even thought of himself. To her victim the moment seems to last an age, during which shivers run up his spine. Though in fact the trick is quick, cheap, effective and repeatable, it seems to the poor fellow that he is now distinguished among all men. He smirks. He preens himself. He grows a little taller. He grows a little more foolish.

He has seen Anne work her trick on lord and commoner, on the king himself. You watch as the man's mouth gapes a little and he becomes her creature. Almost always it works; it has never worked on him. He is not indifferent to women, God knows, just indifferent to Anne Boleyn. It galls her; he should have pretended. He has made her queen, she has made him minister; but they are uneasy now, each of them vigilant, watching each other for some slip that will betray real feeling, and so give advantage to the one or the other: as if only dissimulation will make them safe. But Anne is not good at hiding her feelings; she is the king's quicksilver darling, slipping and sliding from anger to laughter. There have been times this summer when she would smile secretly at him behind the king's back, or grimace to warn him that Henry was out of temper. At other times she would ignore him, turn her shoulder, her black eyes sweeping the room and resting elsewhere.

To understand this – if it bears understanding – we must go back to last spring, when Thomas More was still alive. Anne had called him in to talk of diplomacy: her object was a marriage contract, a French prince for her infant daughter Elizabeth. But the French proved skittish in negotiation. The truth is, even now they do not fully concede that Anne is queen, they are not convinced that her daughter is legitimate. Anne knows what lies behind their reluctance, and somehow it is his fault: his, Thomas Cromwell's. She had accused him openly of sabotaging her. He did not like the French and did not want the alliance, she claimed. Did he not shirk a chance to cross the sea for face-to-face talks? The French were all ready to negotiate, she says. 'And you were expected, Master Secretary. And you said you were ill, and my lord brother had to go.'

'And failed,' he had sighed. 'Very sadly.'

'I know you,' Anne said. 'You are never ill, are you, unless you wish to be? And besides, I perceive how things stand with you. You think that when you are in the city and not at the court you are not under our eye. But I know you are too friendly with the Emperor's man. I am aware Chapuys is your neighbour. But is that a reason why your servants should be always in and out of each other's houses?'

Anne was wearing, that day, rose pink and dove grey. The colours should have had a fresh maidenly charm; but all he could think of were stretched innards, umbles and tripes, grey-pink intestines looped out of a living body; he had a second batch of recalcitrant friars to be dispatched to Tyburn, to be slit up and gralloched by the hangman. They were traitors and deserved the death, but it is a death exceeding most in cruelty. The pearls around her long neck looked to him like little beads of fat, and as she argued she would reach up and tug them; he kept his eyes on her fingertips, nails flashing like tiny knives.

Still, as he says to Chapuys, while I am in Henry's favour, I doubt the queen can do me any harm. She has her spites, she has her little rages; she is volatile and Henry knows it. It was what fascinated the king, to find someone so different from those soft, kind blondes who drift through men's lives and leave not a mark behind. But now when Anne appears he sometimes looks harassed. You can see his gaze growing distant when she begins one of her rants, and if he were not such a gentleman he would pull his hat down over his ears.

No, he tells the ambassador, it's not Anne who bothers me; it's the men she collects about her. Her family: her father the Earl of Wiltshire, who likes to be known as 'Monseigneur', and her brother George, Lord Rochford, whom Henry has appointed to his privy chamber rota. George is one of the newer staff, because Henry likes to stick with men he is used to, who were his friends when he was young; from time to time the cardinal would sweep them out, but they would seep back like dirty water. Once they were young men of esprit, young men of élan. A quarter of a century has passed and they are grey or balding, flabby or paunchy, gone in the fetlock or missing some fingers, but still as arrogant as satraps and with the mental refinement of a gatepost. And now there is a new litter of pups, Weston and George Rochford and their ilk, whom Henry has taken up because he thinks they keep him young. These men – the old ones and the new – are with the king from his uprising to his downlying, and all his private hours in between. They are with him in his stool chamber, and when he cleans his teeth and spits into a silver basin; they swab him with towels and lace him into his doublet and hose; they know his person, each mole or freckle, each bristle in his beard, and they map the islands of his sweat when he comes from the tennis court and rips off his shirt. They know more than they should, as much as his laundress and his doctor, and they talk of what they know; they know when he visits the queen to try to bounce a son into her, or when, on a Friday (the day no Christian copulates) he dreams of a phantom woman and stains his sheets. They sell their knowledge at a high price: they want favours done, they want their own derelictions ignored, they think they are special and they want you to be aware of it. Ever since he, Cromwell, came up in Henry's service, he has been mollifying these men, flattering them, cajoling them, seeking always an easy way of working, a compromise; but sometimes, when for an hour they block him from access to his king, they can't keep the grins from their faces. I have probably, he thinks, gone as far as I can to accommodate them. Now they must accommodate me, or be removed.

The mornings are chilly now, and fat-bellied clouds bob after the royal party as they dawdle through Hampshire, the roads turning within days from dust to mud. Henry is reluctant to hurry back to business; I wish it were always August, he says. They are en route to Farnham, a small hunting party, when a report is galloped along the road: cases of plague have appeared in the town. Henry, brave on the battlefield, pales almost before their eyes and wrenches around his horse's head: where to? Anywhere will do, anywhere but Farnham.

He leans forward in the saddle, removing his hat as he speaks to the king. 'We can go before our time to Basing House, let me send a fast man to warn William Paulet. Then, so as not to burden him, to Elvetham for a day? Edward Seymour is at home, and I can hunt out supplies if he is unprovided.'

He drops back, letting Henry ride ahead. He says to Rafe, 'Send to Wolf Hall. Fetch Mistress Jane.'

'What, here?'

'She can ride. Tell old Seymour to put her on a good horse. I shall want her at Elvetham for Wednesday evening, any later will be too late.'

Rafe reins in, poised to turn. 'But. Sir. The Seymours will ask why Jane and why the hurry. And why we are going to Elvetham, when there are other houses nearby, the Westons at Sutton Place ...'

Drown or hang the Westons, he thinks. The Westons are no part of this plan. He smiles. 'Say they should do it because they love me.'

He sees Rafe thinking, so my master is going to ask for Jane Seymour after all. For himself or for Gregory?

He, Cromwell, had seen at Wolf Hall what Rafe could not see: silent Jane in his bed, pale and speechless Jane, that is what Henry dreams of now. You cannot account for a man's fantasies, and Henry is no lecher, he has not taken many mistresses. No harm if he, Cromwell, helps ease the king's way towards her. The king does not mistreat his bedfellows. He is not a man who hates a woman once he has had her. He will write her verses, and with prompting he will give her an income, he will advance her folk; there are many families who have decided, since Anne Boleyn came up in the world, that to bask in the sunshine of Henry's regard is an Englishwoman's highest vocation. If they play this carefully, Edward Seymour will rise within the court, and give him an ally where allies are scarce. At this stage, Edward needs advice. Because he, Cromwell, has better business sense than the Seymours. He will not let Jane sell herself cheap.

But what will Anne the queen do, if Henry takes as mistress a young woman she has laughed at since ever Jane waited upon her: whom she calls pasty-face and milksop? How will Anne counter meekness, and silence? Raging will hardly help her. She will have to ask herself what Jane can give the king, that at present he lacks. She will have to think it through. And it is always a pleasure to see Anne thinking.

When the two parties met after Wolf Hall – king's party and queen's party – Anne had been charming to him, laying her hand on his arm and chattering away in French about nothing very much. As if she had never mentioned, a few weeks before, that she would like to cut off his head; as if she was only making conversation. It is well to keep behind her in the hunting field. She is keen and quick but not too accurate. This summer she put a crossbow bolt in a straying cow. And Henry had to pay off the owner.

But look, never mind all this. Queens come and go. So recent history has shown us. Let us think about how to pay for England, her king's great charges, the cost of charity and the cost of justice, the cost of keeping her enemies beyond her shores.

From last year he has been sure of his answer: monks, that parasite class of men, are going to provide. Get out to the abbeys and convents through the realm, he had told his visitors, his inspectors: put to them the questions I will give you, eighty-six questions in all. Listen more than you speak, and when you have listened, ask to see the accounts. Talk to the monks and nuns about their lives and Rule. I am not interested where they think their own salvation lies, whether through Christ's precious blood only or through their own works and merits in part: well, yes, I am interested, but the chief matter is to know what assets they have. To know their rents and holdings, and whether, in the event it please the king as head of the church to take back what he owns, by what mechanism it is best to do it.

Don't expect a warm welcome, he says. They will rush to liquidate their assets ahead of your arrival. Take note of what relics they have or objects of local veneration, and how they exploit them, how much revenue they bring in by the year, for all that money is made off the back of superstitious pilgrims who would do better to stay at home and earn an honest living. Press them on their loyalty, what they think of Katherine, what they think of the Lady Mary, and how they regard the Pope; because if the mother houses of their orders are outside these shores, have they not a higher loyalty, as they might term it, to some foreign power? Put this to them and show them that they are at a disadvantage; it is not enough to assert their fidelity to the king, they must be ready to show it, and they can do that by making your work easy.

His men know better than to try to cheat him, but just to make sure he sends them out in pairs, one to watch the other. The abbeys' bursars will offer bribes, to understate their assets.

Thomas More, in his room in the Tower, had said to him, 'Where will you strike next, Cromwell? You are going to pull all England down.'

He had said, I pray to God, grant me life only as long as I use my power to build and not destroy. Among the ignorant it is said that the king is destroying the church. In fact he is renewing it. It will be a better country, believe me, once it is purged of liars and hypocrites. 'But you, unless you mend your manners towards Henry, will not be alive to see it.'

Nor was he. He doesn't regret what happened; his only regret is that More wouldn't see sense. He was offered an oath upholding Henry's supremacy in the church; this oath is a test of loyalty.

Not many things in life are simple, but this is simple. If you will not swear it, you indict yourself, by implication: traitor, rebel. More would not swear; then what could he do but die? What could he do but splash to the scaffold, on a day in July when the torrents never stopped, except for a brief hour in the evening and that too late for Thomas More; he died with his hose wet, splashed to the knees, and his feet paddling like a duck's. He doesn't exactly miss the man. It's just that sometimes, he forgets he's dead. It's as if they're deep in conversation, and suddenly the conversation stops, he says something and no answer comes back. As if they'd been walking along and More had dropped into a hole in the road, a pit as deep as a man, slopping with rainwater.

You do, in fact, hear of such accidents. Men have died, the track giving way under their feet. England needs better roads, and bridges that don't collapse. He is preparing a bill for Parliament to give employment to men without work, to get them waged and out mending the roads, making the harbours, building walls against the Emperor or any other opportunist. We could pay them, he calculated, if we levied an income tax on the rich; we could provide shelter, doctors if they needed them, their subsistence; we would all have the fruits of their work, and their employment would keep them from becoming bawds or pickpockets or highway robbers, all of which men will do if they see no other way to eat. What if their fathers before them were bawds, pickpockets or highway robbers? That signifies nothing. Look at him. Is he Walter Cromwell? In a generation everything can change.

As for the monks, he believes, like Martin Luther, that the monastic life is not necessary, not useful, not commanded of Christ. There's nothing imperishable about monasteries. They're not part of God's natural order. They rise and decay, like any other institutions, and sometimes their buildings fall down, or they are ruined by lax stewardship. Over the years any number of them have vanished or relocated or become swallowed into some other monastery. The number of monks is diminishing naturally, because these days the good Christian man lives out in the world. Take Battle Abbey. Two hundred monks at the height of its fortunes, and now – what? – forty at most. Forty fat fellows sitting on a fortune. The same up and down the kingdom. Resources that could be freed, that could be put to better use. Why should money lie in coffers, when it could be put into circulation among the king's subjects?

His commissioners go out and send him back scandals; they send him monkish manuscripts, tales of ghosts and curses, meant to keep simple people in dread. The monks have relics that make it rain or make it stop, that inhibit the growth of weeds and cure diseases of cattle. They charge for the use of them, they do not give them free to their neighbours: old bones and chips of wood, bent nails from the crucifixion of Christ. He tells the king and queen what his men have found in Wiltshire at Maiden Bradley. 'The monks have part of God's coat, and some broken meats from the Last Supper. They have twigs that blossom on Christmas Day.'

'That last is possible,' Henry says reverently. 'Think of the Glastonbury thorn.'

'The prior has six children, and keeps his sons in his household as waiting men. He says in his defence he never meddled with married women, only with virgins. And then when he was tired of them or they were with child, he found them a husband. He claims he has a licence given under papal seal, allowing him to keep a whore.'

Anne giggles: 'And could he produce it?'

Henry is shocked. 'Away with him. Such men are a disgrace to their calling.'

But these tonsured fools are commonly worse than other men; does Henry not know that? There are some good monks, but after a few years of exposure to the monastic ideal, they tend to run away. They flee the cloisters and become actors in the world. In times past our forefathers with their billhooks and scythes

44

attacked the monks and their servants with the fury they would bring against an occupying army. They broke down their walls and threatened to burn them out, and what they wanted were the monks' rent-rolls, the items of their servitude, and when they could get them they tore them and put them on bonfires, and they said, what we want is a little liberty: a little liberty, and to be treated like Englishmen, after the centuries we have been treated as beasts.

Darker reports come in. He, Cromwell, says to his visitors, just tell them this, and tell them loud: to each monk, one bed: to each bed, one monk. Is that so hard for them? The world-weary tell him, these sins are sure to happen, if you shut up men without recourse to women they will prey on the younger and weaker novices, they are men and it is only a man's nature. But aren't they supposed to rise above nature? What's the point of all the prayer and fasting, if it leaves them insufficient when the devil comes to tempt them?

The king concedes the waste, the mismanagement; it may be necessary, he says, to reform and regroup some of the smaller houses, for the cardinal himself did so when he was alive. But surely, the great houses, we can trust them to renew themselves?

Possibly, he says. He knows the king is devout and afraid of change. He wants the church reformed, he wants it pristine; he also wants money. But as a native of the sign Cancer, he proceeds crab-wise to his objective: a side-shuffle, a weaving motion. He, Cromwell, watches Henry, as his eyes pass over the figures he has been given. It's not a fortune, not for a king: not a king's ransom. By and by, Henry may want to think of the larger houses, the fatter priors basted in self-regard. Let us for now make a beginning. He says, I've sat at too many abbots' tables where the abbot nibbles raisins and dates, while for the monks it's herring again. He thinks, if I had my way I would free them all to lead a different life. They claim they're living the *vita apostolica*; but you didn't find the apostles feeling each other's bollocks. Those who

want to go, let them go. Those monks who are ordained priest
can be given benefices, do useful work in the parishes. Those
under twenty-four, men and women both, can be sent back into
the world. They are too young to bind themselves for life with
vows.

He is thinking ahead: if the king had the monks' land, not just
a little but the whole of it, he would be three times the man he is
now. He need no longer go cap in hand to Parliament, wheedling
for a subsidy. His son Gregory says to him, 'Sir, they say that if
the Abbot of Glastonbury went to bed with the Abbess of
Shaftesbury, their offspring would be the richest landowner in
England.'

'Very likely,' he says, 'though have you seen the Abbess of
Shaftesbury?'

Gregory looks worried. 'Should I have?'

Conversations with his son are like this: they dart off at angles,
end up anywhere. He thinks of the grunts in which he and Walter
communicated when he was a boy. 'You can look at her if you
like. I must visit Shaftesbury soon, I have something to do there.'

The convent at Shaftesbury is where Wolsey placed his daughter. He says, 'Will you make a note for me, Gregory, a memorandum? Go and see Dorothea.'

Gregory longs to ask, who is Dorothea? He sees the questions
chase each other across the boy's face; then at last: 'Is she pretty?'

'I don't know. Her father kept her close.' He laughs.

But he wipes the smile from his face when he reminds Henry:
when monks are traitors, they are the most recalcitrant of that
cursed breed. When you threaten them, 'I will make you suffer,'
they reply that it is for suffering they were born. Some choose to
starve in prison, or go praying to Tyburn and the attentions of the
hangman. He said to them, as he said to Thomas More, this is not
about your God, or my God, or about God at all. This is about,
which will you have: Henry Tudor or Alessandro Farnese? The
King of England at Whitehall, or some fantastically corrupt

foreigner in the Vatican? They had turned their heads away; died speechless, their false hearts carved out of their chests.

When he rides at last into the gates of his city house at Austin Friars, his liveried servants bunch about him, in their long-skirted coats of grey marbled cloth. Gregory is on his right hand, and on his left Humphrey, keeper of his sporting spaniels, with whom he has had easy conversation on this last mile of the journey; behind him his falconers, Hugh and James and Roger, vigilant men alert for any jostling or threat. A crowd has formed outside his gate, expecting largesse. Humphrey and the rest have money to disburse. After supper tonight there will be the usual dole to the poor. Thurston, his chief cook, says they are feeding two hundred Londoners, twice a day.

He sees a man in the press, a little bowed man, scarcely making an effort to keep his feet. This man is weeping. He loses sight of him; he spots him again, his head bobbing, as if his tears were the tide and were carrying him towards the gate. He says, 'Humphrey, find out what ails that fellow.'

But then he forgets. His household are happy to see him, all his folk with shining faces, and a swarm of little dogs about his feet; he lifts them into his arms, writhing bodies and wafting tails, and asks them how they do. The servants cluster round Gregory, admiring him from hat to boots; all servants love him for his pleasant ways. 'The man in charge!' his nephew Richard says, and gives him a bone-crushing hug. Richard is a solid boy with the Cromwell eye, direct and brutal, and the Cromwell voice that can caress or contradict. He is afraid of nothing that walks the earth, and nothing that walks below it; if a demon turned up at Austin Friars, Richard would kick it downstairs on its hairy arse.

His smiling nieces, young married women now, have slackened the laces on their bodices to accommodate swelling bellies. He kisses them both, their bodies soft against his, their breath sweet, warmed by ginger comfits such as women in their condition use. He misses, for a moment … what does he miss? The pliancy of gentle, willing flesh; the absent, inconsequential conversations of early morning. He has to be careful in any dealings with women, discreet. He should not give his ill-wishers the chance to defame him. Even the king is discreet; he doesn't want Europe to call him Harry Whoremaster. Perhaps he'd rather gaze at the unattainable, for now: Mistress Seymour.

At Elvetham Jane was like a flower, head drooping, modest as a drift of green-white hellebore. In her brother's house, the king had praised her to her family's face: 'A tender, modest, shame-faced maid, such as few be in our day.'

Thomas Seymour, keen as always to crash into the conversation and talk over his elder brother: 'For piety and modesty, I dare say Jane has few equals.'

He saw brother Edward hide a smile. Under his interested eye, Jane's family have begun – with a certain incredulity – to sense which way the wind is blowing. Thomas Seymour said, 'I could not brazen it out, even if I were the king I could not face it, inviting a lady like sister Jane to come to my bed. I wouldn't know how to begin. And would you, anyway? Why would you? It would be like kissing a stone. Rolling her about from one side of the mattress to the other, and your parts growing numb from cold.'

'A brother cannot picture his sister in a man's embrace,' Edward Seymour says. 'At least, no brother can who calls himself a Christian. Though they do say at court that George Boleyn –' He breaks off, frowning. 'And of course the king knows how to propose himself. How to offer himself. He knows how to do it, as a gallant gentleman. As you, brother, do not.'

It's hard to put down Tom Seymour. He just grins.

But Henry had not said much, before they rode away from Elvetham; made his hearty farewells, and never a word about the girl. Jane had whispered to him, 'Master Cromwell, why am I here?'

'Ask your brothers.'

'My brothers say, ask Cromwell.'

'So is it an utter mystery to you?'

'Yes. Unless I am to be married at last. Am I to be married to you?'

'I must forgo that prospect. I am too old for you, Jane. I could be your father.'

'Could you?' Jane says wonderingly. 'Well, stranger things have happened at Wolf Hall. I didn't even realise you knew my mother.'

A fleeting smile and she vanishes, leaving him looking after her. We could be married at that, he thinks; it would keep my mind agile, wondering how she might misconstrue me. Does she do it on purpose?

Though I can't have her till Henry's finished with her. And I once swore I would not take on his used women, did I not?

Perhaps, he had thought, I should scribble an aide-memoire for the Seymour boys, so they are clear on what presents Jane should and should not accept. The rule is simple: jewellery yes, money no. And till the deal is done, let her not take off any item of clothing in Henry's presence. Not even, he will advise, her gloves.

Unkind people describe his house as the Tower of Babel. It is said he has servants from every nation under the sun, except Scotland; so Scots keep applying to him, in hope. Gentlemen and even noblemen from here and abroad are pressing him to take their sons into his household, and he accepts all he thinks he can train. On any given day at Austin Friars a group of German scholars will be deploying the many varieties of their tongue, frowning over the letters of evangelists from their own territories. At dinner young Cambridge men exchange snippets of Greek; they are the scholars he has helped, now come to help him. Sometimes a company of Italian merchants come in for supper, and he chats with them in those languages he learned when he worked for the bankers in Florence and Venice. The retainers of his neighbour Chapuys loll about drinking at the expense of the Cromwell buttery, and gossip in Spanish, in Flemish. He himself speaks in French to Chapuys, as it is the ambassador's first language, and employs French of a more demotic sort to his boy Christophe, a squat little ruffian who followed him home from Calais, and who is never far from his side; he doesn't let him far from his side, because around Christophe fights break out.

There is a summer of gossip to catch up on, and accounts to go through, receipts and expenses of his houses and lands. But first he goes out to the kitchen to see his chief cook. It's that early-afternoon lull, dinner cleared, spits cleaned, pewter scoured and stacked, a smell of cinnamon and cloves, and Thurston standing solitary by a floured board, gazing at a ball of dough as if it were the head of the Baptist. As a shadow blocks his light, 'Inky fingers out!' the cook roars. Then, 'Ah. You, sir. Not before time. We had great venison pasties made against your coming, we had to give them out to your friends before they went bad. We'd have sent some up to you, only you move around so fast.'

He holds out his hands for inspection.

'I beg pardon,' Thurston says. 'But you see I have young Thomas Avery down here fresh from the account books, poking around the stores and wanting to weigh things. Then Master Rafe, look Thurston, we have some Danes coming, what can you make for Danes? Then Master Richard crashing in, Luther has sent his messengers, what sort of cakes do Germans like?'

He gives the dough a pinch. 'Is this for Germans?'

'Never mind what it is. If it works, you'll eat it.'

'Did they pick the quinces? It can't be long before we have frost. I can feel it in my bones.'

'Listen to you,' Thurston says. 'You sound like your own grandam.'

'You didn't know her. Or did you?'

Thurston chuckles. 'Parish drunk?'

Probably. What sort of woman could have suckled his father Walter Cromwell, and not turned to drink? Thurston says, as if it's just struck him, 'Mind you, a man has two grandams. Who were your mother's people, sir?'

'They were northerners.'

Thurston grins. 'Come out of a cave. You know young Francis Weston? He that waits on the king? His people are giving out that you're a Hebrew.' He grunts; he's heard that one before. 'Next time you're at court,' Thurston advises, 'take your cock out and put it on the table and see what he says to that.'

'I do that anyway,' he says. 'If the conversation flags.'

'Mind you ...' Thurston hesitates. 'It's true, sir, you are a Hebrew because you lend money at interest.'

Mounting, in Weston's case. 'Anyway,' he says. He gives the dough another nip; it's a bit solid, is it not? 'What's new on the streets?'

'They're saying the old queen's sick.' Thurston waits. But his master has picked up a handful of currants and is eating them. 'She's sick at heart, I should think. They say she's put a curse on Anne Boleyn, so she won't have a boy. Or if she does have a boy, it won't be Henry's. They say Henry has other women and so Anne chases him around his chamber with a pair of shears, shouting she'll geld him. Queen Katherine used to shut her eyes like wives do, but Anne's not the same mettle and she swears he will suffer for it. So that would be a pretty revenge, wouldn't it?' Thurston cackles. 'She cuckolds Henry to pay him back, and puts her own bastard on the throne.'

They have busy, buzzing minds, the Londoners: minds like middens. 'Do they guess at who the father of this bastard will be?'

'Thomas Wyatt?' Thurston offers. 'Because she was known to favour him before she was queen. Or else her old lover Harry Percy –'

'Percy's in his own country, is he not?'

Thurston rolls his eyes. 'Distance don't stop her. If she wants him down from Northumberland she just whistles and whips him down on the wind. Not that she stops at Harry Percy. They say she has all the gentlemen of the king's privy chamber, one after another. She don't like delay so they all stand in a line frigging their members, till she shouts, "Next."'

'And in they troop,' he says. 'One and then another.' He laughs. Eats the final currant from his palm.

'Welcome home,' Thurston says. 'London, where we believe anything.'

'After she was crowned, I remember she called her whole household together, men and maids, and she sermonised them on how they should behave, no gambling except for tokens, no loose language and no flesh on show. It's slid a bit from there, I agree.'

'Sir,' Thurston says, 'you've got flour on your sleeve.'

'Well, I must go upstairs and sit down in council. Don't let supper be late.'

'When is it ever?' Thurston dusts him tenderly. 'When is it ever?'

This is his household council, not the king's; his familiar advisers, the young men, Rafe Sadler and Richard Cromwell, quick and ready with figures, quick to twist an argument, quick to seize a point. And also Gregory. His son.

This season young men carry their effects in soft pale leather bags, in imitation of the agents for the Fugger bank, who travel all over Europe and set the fashion. The bags are heart-shaped and so to him it always looks as if they are going wooing, but they swear they are not. Nephew Richard Cromwell sits down and gives the bags a sardonic glance. Richard is like his uncle, and keeps his effects close to his person. 'Here's Call-Me,' he says. 'Will you look at the feather in his hat?'

Thomas Wriothesley comes in, parting from his murmuring retainers; he is a tall and handsome young man with a head of burnished copper hair. A generation back, his family were called Writh, but they thought an elegant extension would give them consequence; they were heralds by office, so they were well-placed for reinvention, for the reworking of ordinary ancestors into something more knightly. The change does not go by without mockery; Thomas is known at Austin Friars as Call-Me-Risley. He has grown a trim beard recently, has fathered a son, and is accreting dignity each year. He drops his bag on the table and slides into his place. 'And how is Gregory?' he asks.

Gregory's face opens in delight; he admires Call-Me, and he hardly hears the note of condescension. 'Oh, I am well. I have been hunting all summer and now I will be back to William Fitzwilliam's household to join in his train, for he is a gentleman close to the king and my father thinks I can learn from him. Fitz is good to me.'

'Fitz.' Wriothesley snorts with amusement. 'You Cromwells!'

'Well,' Gregory says, 'he calls my father Crumb.'

'I suggest you don't take that up, Wriothesley,' he says amiably. 'Or at least, Crumb me behind my back. Though I've just been out to the kitchens and Crumb is nothing to what they call the queen.'

Richard Cromwell says, 'It's the women who keep the poison pot stirred. They don't like man-stealers. They think Anne should be punished.'

'When we left for the progress she was all elbows,' Gregory says, unexpectedly. 'Elbows and points and spikes. She looks more plush now.'

'So she does.' He is surprised the boy has noticed such a thing. The married men, experienced, watch Anne for signs of fattening as keenly as they watch their own wives. There are glances around the table. 'Well, we shall see. They have not been together the whole summer, but as I judge, enough.'

'It had better be enough,' Wriothesley says. 'The king will grow impatient with her. How many years has he waited, for a woman to do her duty? Anne promised him a son if he would wed her, and you wonder, would he do so much for her, if it were all to do again?'

Richard Riche joins them last, with a muttered apology. No heart-shaped bag for this Richard either, though once he would have been just the kind of young gallant to have five in different colours. What a change a decade brings! Riche was once the worst kind of law student, the kind with a file of pleas in mitigation to set against his sins; the kind who seeks out low taverns where lawyers are called vermin, and so is obliged in honour to start a fight; who arrives back at his lodgings in the Temple in the small hours stinking of cheap wine and with his jacket in shreds; the kind who halloos with a pack of terriers over Lincoln's Inn Fields. But Riche is sobered and subdued now, protégé of the Lord Chancellor Thomas Audley, and constantly to and fro between that dignitary and Thomas Cromwell. The boys call him Sir Purse; Purse is getting fatter, they say. The cares of office have fallen on him, the duties of the father of a growing family; once a golden boy, he looks to be covered by a faint patina of dust. Who would have thought he would be Solicitor General? But then he has a good lawyer's brain, and when you want a good lawyer, he is always at hand.

'Bishop Gardiner's book is not to your purpose,' Riche begins. 'Sir.'

'It is not wholly bad. On the king's powers, we concur.'

'Yes, but,' Riche says.

'I was moved to quote to Gardiner this text: "Where the word of a king is, there is power, and who shall say to him, what doest thou?"'

Riche raises his eyebrows. 'Parliament shall.'

Mr Wriothesley says, 'Trust Master Riche to know what Parliament can do.'

It was on the questions of Parliament's powers, it seems, that Riche tripped Thomas More, tripped and tipped him and perhaps betrayed him into treason. No one knows what was said in that room, in that cell; Riche had come out, pink-faced, hoping and half-suspecting that he had got enough, and gone straight from the Tower of London to him, to Thomas Cromwell. Who had said calmly, yes, this will do; we have him, thank you. Thank you, Purse, you did well.

Now Richard Cromwell leans towards him: 'Tell us, my little friend Purse: in your good opinion, can Parliament put an heir in the queen's belly?'

Riche blushes a little; he is nearly forty now, but because of his complexion he can still blush. 'I never said Parliament can do what God will not. I said it could do more than Thomas More would allow.'

'Martyr More,' he says. 'The word is in Rome that he and Fisher are to be made saints.' Mr Wriothesley laughs. 'I agree it is ridiculous,' he says. He darts a look at his nephew: enough now, say nothing more about the queen, her belly or any other part.

For he has confided to Richard Cromwell something at least of the events at Elvetham, at Edward Seymour's house. When the royal party was so suddenly diverted, Edward had stepped up and entertained them handsomely. But the king could not sleep that night, and sent the boy Weston to call him from his bed. A dancing candle flame, in a room of unfamiliar shape: 'Christ, what time is it?' 'Six o'clock,' Weston said maliciously, 'and you are late.'

In fact it was not four, the sky still dark. The shutter opened to let in air, Henry sat whispering to him, the planets their only witnesses: he had made sure that Weston was out of earshot, refused to speak till the door was shut. Just as well. 'Cromwell,' the king said, 'what if I. What if I were to fear, what if I were to begin to suspect, there is some flaw in my marriage to Anne, some impediment, something displeasing to Almighty God?'

He had felt the years roll away: he was the cardinal, listening to the same conversation: only the queen's name then was Katherine.

'But what impediment?' he had said, a little wearily. 'What could it be, sir?'

'I don't know,' the king had whispered. 'I don't know now but I may know. Was she not pre-contracted to Harry Percy?'

'No, sir. He swore not, on the Bible. Your Majesty heard him swear.'

'Ah, but you had been to see him, had you not, Cromwell, did you not trail him to some low inn and haul him up from his bench and pound his head with your fist?'

'No, sir. I would never so mistreat any peer of the realm, let alone the Earl of Northumberland.'

'Ah well. I am relieved to hear that. I may have got the details wrong. But that day the earl said what he thought I wanted him to say. He said that there was no union with Anne, no promise of marriage, let alone consummation. What if he lied?'

'On oath, sir?'

'But you are very frightening, Crumb. You would make a man forget his manners before God. What if he did lie? What if she made a contract with Percy amounting to a lawful marriage? If that were so, she cannot be married to me.'

He had kept silence, but he saw Henry's mind running; his own was darting like a startled deer. 'And I much suspect,' the king had whispered. 'I much suspect her with Thomas Wyatt.'

'No, sir,' he said, vehement even before he had time to think. Wyatt is his friend; his father, Sir Henry Wyatt, had charged him to make the boy's path smooth; Wyatt is not a boy any more, but never mind.

'You say no.' Henry leaned towards him. 'But did not Wyatt avoid the realm and go to Italy, because she would not favour him and he had no peace of mind while her image was before him?'

'Well, there you have it. You say it yourself, Majesty. She would not favour him. If she had, no doubt he'd have stayed.'

'But I cannot be sure,' Henry insists. 'Suppose she denied him then but favoured him some other time? Women are weak and easily conquered by flattery. Especially when men write verses to them, and there are some who say that Wyatt writes better verses than me, though I am the king.'

He blinks at him: four o'clock, sleepless; you could call it harmless vanity, God love him, if only it were not four o'clock. 'Majesty,' he says, 'put your mind at rest. If Wyatt had made any inroads on that lady's immaculate chastity, I feel sure he could not have resisted boasting about it. In verse, or common prose.'

Henry only grunts. But he looks up: Wyatt's well-dressed shade, silken, slides across the window, blocks the cold starlight. On your way, phantom: his mind brushes it before him; who can understand Wyatt, who absolve him? The king says, 'Well. Perhaps. Even if she did give way to Wyatt, it would be no impediment to my marriage, there can be no question of a contract between them since he himself was married as a boy and so not free to promise anything to Anne. But I tell you, it would be impediment to my trust in her. I would not take it kindly to have any woman lie to me, and say she came a virgin to my bed if she did not.'

Wolsey, where are you? You have heard all this before. Advise me now.

He stands up. He is easing this interview to an end. 'Shall I tell them to bring you something, sir? Something to help you sleep again for an hour or two?'

'I need something to sweeten my dreams. I wish I knew what it was. I have consulted Bishop Gardiner in this matter.'

He had tried to keep the shock off his face. Gone to Gardiner: behind my back?

'And Gardiner said,' Henry's face was the picture of desolation, 'he said there was doubt enough in the case, but that if the marriage were not good, if I were forced to put away Anne, I must return to Katherine. And I cannot do it, Cromwell. I am resolved that even if the whole of Christendom comes against me, I can never touch that stale old woman again.'

'Well,' he had said. He was looking at the floor, at Henry's large white naked feet. 'I think we can do better than that, sir. I do not pretend to follow Gardiner's reasoning, but then the bishop knows more canon law than me. I do not believe, however, you can be constrained or compelled in any matter, as you are master of your own household, and your own country, and of your own church. Perhaps Gardiner meant only to prepare Your Majesty for the obstacles others might raise.'

Or perhaps, he thought, he just meant to make you sweat and give you nightmares. Gardiner's like that. But Henry had sat up: 'I can do as it pleases me,' his monarch said. 'God would not allow my pleasure to be contrary to his design, nor my designs to be impeded by his will.' A shadow of cunning had crossed his face. 'And Gardiner himself said so.'

Henry yawned. It was a signal. 'Crumb, you don't look very dignified, bowing in a nightgown. Will you be ready to ride at seven, or shall we leave you behind and see you at supper?'

If you'll be ready, I'll be ready, he thinks, as he pads back to his bed. Come sunrise, will you forget we ever had this conversation? The court will be astir, the horses tossing their heads and sniffing the wind. By mid-morning we will be reunited with the queen's band; Anne will be chirruping atop her hunter; she will never know, unless her little friend Weston tells her, that last night at Elvetham the king sat gazing at his next mistress: Jane Seymour ignoring his pleading eyes, and placidly working her way through a chicken. Gregory had said, his eyes round: 'Doesn't Mistress Seymour eat a lot?'

And now the summer is over. Wolf Hall, Elvetham, fade into the dusk. His lips are sealed on the king's doubts and fears; it is autumn, he is at Austin Friars; with bowed head he listens to the court news, watches Riche's fingers twisting the silk tag on a document. 'Their households have been provoking each other in the streets,' his nephew Richard says. 'Thumbing of noses, curses, hands on daggers.'

'Sorry, who?' he says.

'Nicholas Carew's people. Scrapping with Lord Rochford's servants.'

'As long as they keep it away from the court,' he says sharply. The penalty for drawing a blade within the precincts of the royal court is amputation of the offending hand. What is the quarrel about, he begins to ask, then changes his question: 'What is their excuse?'

For picture Carew, one of Henry's old friends, one of his privy chamber gentlemen, and devoted to the queen that was. See him, an antique man with his long grave face, his cultivated air of having stepped straight from a book of knight-errantry. No surprise if Sir Nicholas, with his rigid sense of the fitness of things, has found it impossible to bend to George Boleyn's parvenu pretensions. Sir Nicholas is a papist to his steel-capped toes, and is offended to his marrow by George's support of reformed teaching. So an issue of principle lies between them; but what trivial event has sparked the quarrel into life? Did George and his evil company make a racket outside the chamber of Sir Nicholas, while he was at some solemn business like admiring himself in the looking glass? He stifles a smile. 'Rafe, have a word with both gentlemen. Tell them to leash their dogs.' He adds, 'You do right to mention it.' He is interested, always, to hear of divisions between the courtiers and how they arose.

Soon after his sister became queen, George Boleyn had called him in and given him some instruction, about how he should handle his career. The young man was flaunting a bejewelled gold chain, which he, Cromwell, weighed in his mind's eye; in his mind's eye he removed George's jacket, unstitched it, wound the fabric on to the bolt and priced it; once you have been in the cloth trade, you don't lose your eye for texture and drape, and if you are charged with raising revenue, you soon learn to estimate a man's worth.

Young Boleyn had kept him standing, while he occupied the room's single chair. 'Remember, Cromwell,' he began, 'that though you are of the king's council, you are not a gentleman born. You should confine yourself to speech where it is demanded of you, and for the rest, leave it alone. Do not meddle in the affairs of those set above you. His Majesty is pleased to bring you often into his presence, but remember who it was who placed you where he could see you.'

It's interesting, George Boleyn's version of his life. He had always supposed it was Wolsey who trained him up, Wolsey who promoted him, Wolsey who made him the man he is: but George says no, it was the Boleyns. Clearly, he has not been expressing proper gratitude. So he expresses it now, saying yes sir and no sir, and I see you are a man of singular good judgement for your years. Why, your father Monseigneur the Earl of Wiltshire, your uncle Thomas Howard Duke of Norfolk, they could not have instructed me better. 'I shall profit by this, I assure you sir, and from now on conduct myself more humble-wise.'

George was mollified. 'See you do.'

He smiles now, thinking of it; returns to the scribbled agenda. His son Gregory's eyes flit about the table, as he tries to pick up what isn't said: now cousin Richard Cromwell, now Call-Me-Risley, now his father, and the other gentlemen who have come in. Richard Riche frowns over his papers, Call-Me fiddles with his pen. Troubled men both, he thinks, Wriothesley and Riche, and alike in some ways, sidling around the peripheries of their own souls, tapping at the walls: oh, what is that hollow sound? But he has to produce to the king men of talent; and they are agile, they are tenacious, they are unsparing in their efforts for the Crown, and for themselves.

'One last thing,' he says, 'before we break up. My lord the Bishop of Winchester has so pleased the king that, at my urging, the king has sent him again to France as ambassador. It is thought his embassy will not be a short one.'

Slow smiles ripple around the table. He watches Call-Me. He was once a protégé of Stephen Gardiner. But he seems as joyful as the rest. Richard Riche turns pink, rises from the table and wrings his hand.

'Get him on the road,' Rafe says, 'and let him stay away. Gardiner is double in everything.'

'Double?' he says. 'He has a tongue like a three-pronged eel spear. First he is for the Pope, then Henry, then, mark what I say, he will be for the Pope again.'

'Can we trust him abroad?' Riche says.

'We can trust him only to know where his advantage lies. Which is with the king for now. And we can keep an eye on him, put some of our men in his train. Master Wriothesley, you can see to that, I think?'

Only Gregory seems dubious. 'My lord Winchester, an ambassador? Fitzwilliam tells me, an ambassador's first duty is to give no affront.'

He nods. 'And Stephen gives nothing but affront, does he?'

'Is not an ambassador supposed to be a cheerful fellow and affable? So Fitzwilliam tells me. He should be pleasant in any company, conversable and easy, and he should endear himself to his hosts. So he has chances to visit their homes, sit at their boards, become friendly with their wives and their heirs, and corrupt their household to his service.'

Rafe's eyebrows shoot up. 'Is that what Fitz teaches you?' The boys laugh.

'It's true,' he says. 'That is what an ambassador must do. So I hope Chapuys is not corrupting you, Gregory? If I had a wife, he would be sneaking sonnets to her, I know it, and bringing in bones for my dogs. Ah well … Chapuys, he is pleasant company, you see. Not like Stephen Gardiner. But the truth is, Gregory, we need a stout ambassador for the French, a man full of spleen and spite. And Stephen has been among them before, and done himself credit. The French are hypocrites, pretending false friendship and demanding money as the price of it. You see,' he says, setting himself to educate his son. 'Just now the French have a plan to take the duchy of Milan from the Emperor, and they want us to subsidise them. And we must accommodate them, or seem to, for fear they will veer about and join with the Emperor and over-whelm us. So when the day comes that they say, "Deliver over the gold you have promised," we need that kind of ambassador, like Stephen, who will brazen it out and say, "Oh, the gold? Just take it out of what you already owe King Henry." King Francis will be spitting fire, yet in a manner we will have kept our word. You understand? We save our fiercest champions for the French court. Recall that my lord Norfolk was sometime ambassador there.'

Gregory dips his head. 'Any foreigner would fear Norfolk.'

'And any Englishman too. With good reason. Now the duke is like one of those giant cannon the Turks have. The blast is shock-ing but it needs three hours' cooling time before it can fire again. Whereas Bishop Gardiner, he can explode at ten-minute intervals, dawn to dusk.'

'But sir,' Gregory bursts out, 'if we promise them money, and we don't deliver it, what will they do?'

'By then, I hope, we will be firm friends with the Emperor again.' He sighs. 'It is an old game and it seems we must go on playing it, until I think of something better, or the king does. You have heard of the Emperor's recent victory at Tunis?'

'The whole world is talking of it,' Gregory says. 'Every Christian knight wishes he had been there.'

He shrugs. 'Time will tell how glorious it is. Barbarossa will soon find another base for his piracy. But with such a victory behind him, and the Turk quiet for the moment, the Emperor may turn on us and invade our shores.'

'But how do we stop him?' Gregory looks desperate. 'Must we not have Queen Katherine back?

Call-Me laughs. 'Gregory begins to perceive the difficulties of our trade, sir.'

'I liked it better when we talked of the present queen,' Gregory says in a low voice. 'And I got the credit for observing she was fatter.'

Call-Me says kindly, 'I should not laugh. You have the right of it, Gregory. All our labours, our sophistry, all our learning both acquired or pretended; the stratagems of state, the lawyers' decrees, the churchmen's curses, and the grave resolutions of judges, sacred and secular: all and each can be defeated by a woman's body, can they not? God should have made their bellies transparent, and saved us the hope and fear. But perhaps what grows in there has to grow in the dark.'

'They say that Katherine is ailing,' Richard Riche says. 'If she should die within the year, I wonder what world would be then?'

But look: we have sat here too long! Let's be up and out into the gardens of Austin Friars, Master Secretary's pride; he wants the plants he saw flowering abroad, he wants better fruit, so he nags the ambassadors to send him shoots and cuttings in the diplomatic bag. The keen young clerks stand by, ready to break a code, and all that tumbles out is a rootball, still pulsing with life after a journey through the straits of Dover.

He wants tender things to live, young men to thrive. So he has built a tennis court, a gift to Richard and Gregory and all the young men of his house. He is not quite beyond the game himself … if he could play a blind man, he says, or an opponent with one leg. Much of the game is tactics; his foot drags, he has to rely on cunning rather than speed. But he is proud of his building and glad to stand the expense. He has recently consulted with the king's keepers of tennis at Hampton Court, and had the measurements adjusted to those Henry prefers; the king has been to

Austin Friars to dine, so it is not unpossible that one day he may call in for an afternoon on the court.

In Italy, when he was a servant in Frescobaldi's household, the boys would go out in the hot evening and play games in the street. It was tennis of a kind, a *jeu de paume*, no racquets but just the hand; they would jostle and push and scream, bounce the ball off the walls and run it along a tailor's awning, till the master himself would come out and scold: 'If you boys don't respect my awning, I'll shear off your testicles and hang them over the doorway on a ribbon.' They would say sorry, master, sorry, and back off down the street, and play subdued in a back court. But half an hour later they would be back again, and he can still hear it in his dreams, the rattle as the ball's crude seam hit metal and skimmed into the air; he can feel the slap of leather against his palm. In those days, though he was carrying an injury he tried to run the stiffness off: this injury he'd got the other year, when he was at Garigliano with the French army. The *garzoni* would say, look Tommaso, how is it you got the wound in the back of the leg, were you running away? He would say, Mother of God, yes: I was only paid enough for running away, if you want me facing the front you have to pay me extra.

From this massacre the French scattered, and in those days he was French; the King of France paid his wages. He had crawled then limped, he and his comrades dragging their battered bodies as fast as they could from the victorious Spanish, trying to struggle back to ground not bogged with blood; they were wild Welsh bowmen and renegade Switzers, and a few English boys like himself, all of them more or less confused and penniless, gathering their wits in the aftermath of the rout, plotting a course, changing their nation and their names at need, washing up in the cities to the north, looking for the next battle or some safer trade.

At the back gate of a great house, a steward had interrogated him: 'French?'

'English.'

The man had rolled his eyes. 'So what can you do?'

'I can fight.'

'Evidently, not well enough.'

'I can cook.'

'We have no need of barbarous cuisine.'

'I can cast accounts.'

'This is a banking house. We are well supplied.'

'Tell me what you want done. I can do it.' (Already he boasts like an Italian.)

'We want a labourer. What is your name?'

'Hercules,' he says.

Against his better judgement, the man laughs. 'Come in, Ercole.'

Ercole limps in, over the threshold. The man bustles about his own duties. He sits down on a step, nearly weeping with pain. He looks around him. All he has is this floor. This floor is his world. He is hungry, he is thirsty, he is over seven hundred miles from home. But this floor can be improved. 'Jesus, Mary and Joseph!' he shouts. 'Water! Bucket! *Allez, allez!*'

They go. Quick they go. A pail arrives. He improves this floor. He improves this house. He does not improve it without resistance. They start him off in the kitchen, where as a foreigner he is ill-received, and where with the blades and spits and boiling water there is so much possibility for violence. But he is better at fighting than you would think: lacking in height, without skill or craft, but almost impossible to knock over. And what aids him is the fame of his countrymen, feared through Europe as brawlers and looters and rapists and thieves. As he cannot abuse his colleagues in their own language, he uses Putney. He teaches them terrible English oaths – 'By the bleeding nail-holes of Christ' – which they can use to relieve their feelings behind the backs of their masters. When the girl comes in the mornings, the herbs in her basket damp with dew, they step back, appreciate her and ask,

'Well, sweetheart, and how are you today?' When somebody interrupts a tricky task, they say, 'Why don't you fuck off out of here, or I'll boil your head in this pot.'

Before long he understood that fortune had brought him to the door of one of the city's ancient families, who not only dealt in money and silk, wool and wine, but also had great poets in their lineage. Francisco Frescobaldi, the master, came to the kitchen to talk to him. He did not share the general prejudice against Englishmen, rather he thought of them as lucky; although, he said, some of his ancestors had been brought close to ruin by the unpaid debts of kings of England long ago dead. He had little English himself and he said, we can always use your countrymen, there are many letters to write; you can write, I hope? When he, Tommaso or Ercole, had improved in Tuscan so much that he was able to express himself and make jokes, Frescobaldi had promised, one day I will call you to the counting house. I will make trial of you.

That day came. He was tried and he won. From Florence he went to Venice, to Rome: and when he dreams of those cities, as sometimes he does, a residual swagger trails him into his day, a trace of the young Italian he was. He thinks back to his younger self with no indulgence, but no blame either. He has always done what was needed to survive, and if his judgement of what was necessary was sometimes questionable … that is what it is to be young. Nowadays he takes poor scholars into his family. There's always a job for them, some niche where they can scribble away at tracts on good government or translations of the psalms. But he will also take in young men who are rough and wild, as he was rough and wild, because he knows if he is patient with them they will be loyal to him. Even now, he loves Frescobaldi like a father. Custom stales the intimacies of marriage, children grow truculent and rebel, but a good master gives more than he takes and his benevolence guides you through your life. Think of Wolsey. To his inner ear, the cardinal speaks. He says, I saw you, Crumb, when you were at Elvetham: scratching your balls in the dawn and wondering at the violence of the king's whims. If he wants a new wife, fix him one. I didn't, and I am dead.

Thurston's cake must have failed because it doesn't appear that evening at supper, but there is a very good jelly in the shape of a castle. 'Thurston has a licence to crenellate,' Richard Cromwell says, and immediately throws himself into a dispute with an Italian across the table: which is the best shape for a fort, circular or star-shaped?

The castle is made in stripes of red and white, the red a deep crimson and the white perfectly clear, so the walls seem to float. There are edible archers peeping from the battlements, shooting candied arrows. It even makes the Solicitor General smile. 'I wish my little girls could see it.'

'I'll send the moulds to your house. Though perhaps not a fort. A flower garden?' What pleases little girls? He's forgotten.

After supper, if there are no messengers pounding at the door, he will often steal an hour to be among his books. He keeps them at all his properties: at Austin Friars, at the Rolls House at Chancery Lane, at Stepney, at Hackney. There are books these days on all sorts of subjects. Books that advise you how to be a good prince, or a bad one. Poetry books and volumes that tell you how to keep accounts, books of phrases for use abroad, dictionaries, books that tell you how to wipe your sins clean and books that tell you how to preserve fish. His friend Andrew Boorde, the physician, is writing a book on beards; he is against them. He thinks of what Gardiner said: you should write a book yourself, that would be something to see.

If he did, it would be The Book Called Henry: how to read him, how to serve him, how best to preserve him. In his mind he writes the preamble. 'Who shall number the qualities, both public and private, of this most blessed of men? Among priests, he is devout: among soldiers, valiant: among scholars, erudite: among courtiers, most gentle and refined: and all these qualities, King Henry possesses in such a remarkable degree that the like was never seen since the world began.'

Erasmus says that you should praise a ruler even for qualities he does not have. For the flattery gives him to think. And the qualities he presently lacks, he might go to work on them.

He looks up as the door opens. It is his little Welsh boy, backing in: 'Ready for your candles, master?'

'Yes, more than ready.' The light shivers, then settles against dark wood like discs pared from a pearl. 'You see that stool,' he says. 'Sit on it.'

The boy flops down. The demands of the household have had him on the run since early morning. Why is it always little legs that have to save big legs? *Just run upstairs and fetch me* ... It flattered you, when you were young. You thought you were important, indeed essential. He used to hurtle around Putney, on errands for Walter. More fool him. Now it pleases him to say to a boy, take your ease. 'I used to speak a bit of Welsh when I was a boy. I can't now.'

He thinks, that's the bleat of the man of fifty: Welsh, tennis, I used to, I can't now. There are compensations: the head is better stored with information, the heart better proof against chips and fractures. Just now he is undertaking a survey of the queen's Welsh properties. For this and weightier reasons, he keeps a keen eye on the principality. 'Tell me your life,' he asks the child. 'Tell me how you came here.' With the boy's own bit of English, he pieces together his tale: arson, cattle raids, the usual borderlands story, ending in destitution, the making of orphans.

'Can you say the Pater Noster?' he asks.

'Pater Noster,' says the boy. 'Or, Our Father.'

'In Welsh?'

'No, sir. There are no prayers in Welsh.'

'Dear Jesus. I'll get a man on it.'

'Do, sir. Then I can pray for my father and mother.'

'Do you know John ap Rice? He was at supper with us tonight.'

'Married to your niece Johane, sir?'

The boy darts off. Little legs at work again. It's his aim that all the Welsh will speak English, but that can't be yet, and meanwhile they need God on their side. Brigands cover the whole principality, and bribe and threaten their way out of gaol; pirates savage the coasts. Those gentlemen with territory there, like Norris and Brereton of the king's privy chamber, seem resistant to his interest. They put their own dealings before the king's peace. They do not care to have their activities overseen. They do not care for justice: whereas he means to make an equal justice, from Essex to Anglesey, Cornwall to the Scots border.

Rice brings in with him a little velvet box, which he puts down on the desk: 'Present. You have to guess.'

He rattles it. Something like grains. His finger explores fragments, scaly, grey. Rice has been surveying abbeys for him. 'It wouldn't be St Apollonia's teeth?'

'Guess again.'

'Is it teeth from the comb of Mary Magdalene?'

Rice relents. 'St Edmund's nail parings.'

'Ah. Tip them in with the rest. The man must have had five hundred fingers.'

In the year 1257, an elephant died in the Tower menagerie and was buried in a pit near the chapel. But the following year he was dug up and his remains sent to Westminster Abbey. Now, what did they want at Westminster Abbey, with the remains of an elephant? If not to carve a ton of relics out of him, and make his animal bones into the bones of saints?

According to the custodians of holy relics, part of the power of these artefacts is that they are able to multiply. Bone, wood and stone have, like animals, the ability to breed, yet keep their intact nature; the offspring are in no wise inferior to the originals. So the crown of thorns blossoms. The cross of Christ puts out buds; it flourishes, like a living tree. Christ's seamless coat weaves copies of itself. Nails give birth to nails.

John ap Rice says, 'Reason cannot win against these people. You try to open their eyes. But ranged against you are statues of the virgin that weep tears of blood.'

'And they say I play tricks!' He broods. 'John, you must sit down and write. Your compatriots must have prayers.'

'They must have a Bible, sir, in their own tongue.'

'Let me first get the king's assured blessing for the English to have it.' It is his daily, covert crusade: for Henry to sponsor a great Bible, put it in every church. He is very close now and he thinks he can win Henry to it. His ideal would be a single country, single coinage, just one method of weighing and measuring, and above all one language that everybody owns. You don't have to go to Wales to be misunderstood. There are parts of this realm not fifty miles from London, where if you ask them to cook you a herring they give you a blank look instead. Only when you've pointed to the pan and impersonated a fish do they say, ah, now I see what you mean.

But his greatest ambition for England is this: the prince and his commonwealth should be in accord. He doesn't want the kingdom to be run like Walter's house in Putney, with fighting all the time and the sound of banging and shrieking day and night. He wants it to be a household where everybody knows what they have to do, and feels safe doing it. He says to Rice, 'Stephen Gardiner says I should write a book. What do you think? Perhaps I might if one day I retire. Till then, why should I give my secrets away?'

He remembers reading Machiavelli's book, shut up in the dark days after his wife's death: that book which now begins to make such a stir in the world, though it is more talked about than actually read. He had been confined to the house, he, Rafe, the immediate household, so as not to take fever into the city; turning the book over, he had said, you cannot really pluck out lessons from

Italian principalities and apply them to Wales and the northern border. We don't work the same way. The book seemed almost trite to him, nothing in it but abstractions – virtue, terror – and small particular instances of base conduct or flawed calculation. Perhaps he could improve on it, but he has no time; all he can do, when business is so pressing, is to toss phrases to clerks, poised with their pens for his dictation: '*I heartily commend me to you ... your assured friend, your loving friend, your friend Thomas Cromwell.*' No fee attaches to the post of Secretary. The scope of the job is ill-defined and this suits him; whereas the Lord Chancellor has his circumscribed role, Mr Secretary can inquire into any office of state or corner of government. He has letters from throughout the shires, asking him to arbitrate in land disputes or lend his name to some stranger's cause. People he doesn't know send him tittle-tattle about their neighbours, monks send accounts of disloyal words spoken by their superiors, priests sift for him the utterances of their bishops. The affairs of the whole realm are whispered in his ear, and so plural are his offices under the Crown that the great business of England, parchment and roll awaiting stamp and signet, is pushed or pulled across his desk, to himself or from himself. His petitioners send him malmsey and muscatel, geldings, game and gold; gifts and grants and warrants, lucky charms and spells. They want favours and they expect to pay for them. This has been going on since first he came into the king's favour. He is rich.

And naturally, envy follows. His enemies dig out what they can, about his early life. 'So, I went down to Putney,' Gardiner had said. 'Or, to be accurate, I sent a man. They said down there, who'd have thought that Put-an-edge-on-it would have risen so high? We all thought he'd be hanged by now.'

His father would sharpen knives; people would hale him in the street: Tom, can you take this, ask your father can he do aught with it? And he'd scoop it up, whatever blunt instrument: leave it with me, he'll put an edge on it.

'It's a skill,' he told Gardiner. 'Honing a blade.'

'You've killed men. I know it.'

'Not in this jurisdiction.'

'Abroad doesn't count?'

'No court in Europe would convict a man who struck in self-defence.'

'But do you ask yourself why people want to kill you?'

He had laughed. 'Why, Stephen – much in this life is a mystery but that is no mystery at all. I was always first up in the morning. I was always the last man standing. I was always in the money. I always got the girl. Show me a heap, and I'm on top of it.'

'Or a whore,' Stephen murmured.

'You were young once. Have you been to the king with your findings?'

'He should know what kind of man he employs.' But then, Gardiner had broken off; he, Cromwell, approached him smiling. 'Do your worst, Stephen. Put your men on the road. Lay out money. Search Europe. You will not hear of any talent I possess, that England cannot use.' He had eased from within his coat an imaginary knife; he pressed it home, softly, easily, under Gardiner's ribs. 'Stephen, have I not begged you often and often to reconcile with me? And have you not refused?'

Credit to Gardiner, he didn't flinch. Only with a kind of creeping of his flesh, and a pull on his robe, eased himself away from the airy blade. 'The lad you knifed in Putney died,' he said. 'You did well to run, Cromwell. His family had a noose for you. Your father bought them off.'

He is amazed. 'What? Walter? Walter did?'

'He didn't pay much. They had other children.'

'Even so.' He had stood dumbfounded. Walter. Walter paid them off. Walter, who never gave him anything more than a kick.

Gardiner laughed. 'You see. I know things about your life you don't know yourself.'

* * *

It is late now; he will finish up at his desk, then go to his cabinet to read. Before him is an inventory from the abbey at Worcester. His men are thorough; everything is here, from a fireball to warm the hands to a mortar for crushing garlic. And a chasuble of changeable satin, an alb of cloth of gold, the Lamb of God cut out in black silk; an ivory comb, a brass lamp, three leather bottles and a scythe; psalm books, song books, six fox-nets with bells, two wheelbarrows, sundry shovels and spades, some relics of St Ursula and her eleven thousand virgins, together with St Oswald's mitre and a stack of trestle tables.

These are sounds of Austin Friars, in the autumn of 1535: the singing children rehearsing a motet, breaking off, beginning again. The voices of these children, small boys, calling out to each other from staircases, and nearer at hand the scrabbling of dogs' paws on the boards. The chink of gold pieces into a chest. The susurration, tapestry-muffled, of polyglot conversation. The whisper of ink across paper. Beyond the walls the noises of the city: the milling of the crowds at his gate, distant cries from the river. His inner monologue, running on, soft-voiced: it is in public rooms that he thinks of the cardinal, his footsteps echoing in lofty vaulted chambers. It is in private spaces that he thinks of his wife Elizabeth. She is a blur now in his mind, a whisk of skirts around a corner. That last morning of her life, as he left the house he thought he saw her following him, caught a flash of her white cap. He had half turned, saying to her, 'Go back to bed': but no one was there. By the time he came home that night her jaw was bound and there were candles at her head and feet.

It was only a year before his girls died of the same cause. In his house at Stepney he keeps in a locked box their necklaces of pearl and coral, Anne's copy books with her Latin exercises. And in the store room where they keep their play costumes for Christmas, he still has the wings made of peacock feathers that Grace wore in a parish play. After the play she walked upstairs, still in her wings; frost glittered at the window. I am going to say my prayers, she said: walking away from him, furled in her feathers, fading into dusk.

And now night falls on Austin Friars. Snap of bolts, click of key in lock, rattle of strong chain across wicket, and the great bar fallen across the main gate. The boy Dick Purser lets out the watchdogs. They pounce and race, they snap at the moonlight, they flop under the fruit trees, heads on paws and ears twitching. When the house is quiet – when all his houses are quiet – then dead people walk about on the stairs.

Anne the queen sends for him to her own chamber; it is after supper. Only a step for him, as at every major palace rooms are reserved for him now, near the king's. Just a staircase: and there, with the light of a sconce lapping at its gold trim, is the stiff new doublet of Mark Smeaton. Mark himself is lurking inside it.

What brings Mark here? He is without musical instruments as an excuse, and he is got up as gorgeously as any of the young lords who wait on Anne. Is there justice? he wonders. Mark does naught and gets more bonny each time I see him, and I do every-thing and get more grey and paunchy by the day.

Since unpleasantness usually ensues between them, it is in his mind to pass by with a nod, but Mark stands up straight and smiles: 'Lord Cromwell, how are you?'

'Ah, no,' he says. 'Still plain master.'

'It is a natural mistake. You seem every inch the lord. And surely, the king will do something for you soon.'

'Perhaps not. He needs me in the House of Commons.'

'Even so,' the boy murmurs, 'it would seem ungracious in him, when others are rewarded for much less service. Tell me, they say you have got music scholars in your house?'

A dozen or so merry little boys, saved from the cloister. They work at their books and practise their instruments, and at table they learn their manners; at supper they entertain his guests. They practise with the bow, and play fetch with the spaniels, and the littlest ones drag their hobby horses over the cobbles, and follow him about, sir, sir, sir, look at me, do you want to see me stand on my hands? 'They keep the household lively,' he says.

'If you should ever want someone to put a polish on their performance, think of me.'

'I will, Mark.' He thinks, I wouldn't trust you around my little boys.

'You will find the queen discontented,' the young man says. 'You know her brother Rochford has lately gone into France on a special embassy, and today he has sent a letter; it seems to be the common talk over there that Katherine has been writing to the Pope, asking him to put into effect that wicked sentence of excommunication he has pronounced against our master. And which would result in untold hurts and perils to our realm.' He nods, yes, yes, yes; he does not need Mark to tell him what excommunication is; can he not make it short? 'The queen is angry,' the boy says, 'for if this is so, Katherine is a plain traitor, and the queen wonders, why do we not act against her?'

'Suppose I tell you the reason, Mark? Would you take it in to her? It seems you could save me an hour or two.'

'If you would entrust me –' the boy begins; then sees his cold smile. He blushes.

'I'd trust you with a motet, Mark. Although.' He looks at him thoughtfully. 'It does seem to me that you must stand high in the queen's favour.'

'Master Secretary, I believe that I do.' Flattened, Mark is already bouncing back. 'It is we lesser men, often, who are most fit for royal confidence.'

'Well then. Baron Smeaton, eh, before long? I shall be the first to congratulate you. Even if I am still toiling on the benches of the Commons.'

* * *

With a whisk of her hand, Anne shoos away the ladies around her, who bob to him and whisper out. Her sister-in-law, George's wife, lingers: Anne says, 'Thank you, Lady Rochford, I shall not need you again tonight.'

Only her fool stays with her: a dwarf woman, peeping at him from behind the queen's chair. Anne's hair is loose beneath a cap of silver tissue shaped like a crescent moon. He makes a mental note of it; the women about him always enquire what Anne is wearing. This is how she receives her husband, the dark tresses displayed only for him, and incidentally for Cromwell, who is a tradesman's son and doesn't matter, any more than the boy Mark does.

She begins, as she often does, as if in the middle of a sentence. 'So I want you to go. Up-country to see her. Very secret. Only take the men you need. Here, you may read my brother Rochford's letter.' She flourishes it at her fingers' ends, then changes her mind, whips it back. 'Or … no,' she says, and decides to sit on it instead. Perhaps, amid the news, it contains dispraise of Thomas Cromwell? 'I am very suspicious of Katherine, very suspicious. It seems they know in France what we only guess at. Your people are not vigilant, perhaps? My lord brother believes the queen is urging the Emperor to invade, as is the ambassador Chapuys, who by the way should be banished this kingdom.'

'Well, you know,' he says. 'We can't go throwing ambassadors out. Because then we don't get to know anything at all.'

Truth is, he is not afraid of Katherine's intrigues: the mood between France and the Empire is at the moment unremittingly hostile, and if open war breaks out, the Emperor will have no troops to spare for invading England. These things swing about in a week, and the Boleyn reading of any situation, he has noticed, is always a little behind the times, and influenced by the fact that they pretend to have special friends at the Valois court. Anne is still in pursuit of a royal marriage for her ginger little daughter. He used to admire her as a person who learned from her mistakes,

76

who would pull back, re-calculate; but she has a streak of stubbornness to equal that of Katherine, the old queen, and it seems in this matter she will never learn. George Boleyn has been over to France again, intriguing for the match, but with no result. What's George Boleyn *for*? That's a question he asks himself. He says, 'Highness, the king could not compromise his honour by any ill-treatment of the queen that was. If it became known, it would be a personal embarrassment to him.'

Anne looks sceptical; she does not grasp the idea of embarrassment. The lights are low; her silver head bobs, glittering and small; the dwarf fusses and chuckles, muttering to herself out of sight; seated on her velvet cushions, Anne dangles her velvet slipper, like a child about to dip a toe in a stream. 'If I were Katherine, I too would intrigue. I would not forgive. I would do as she does.' She gives him a dangerous smile. 'You see, I know her mind. Though she is a Spaniard, I can put myself in her place. You would not see me meek, if Henry cast me off. I too would want war.' She takes a strand of hair between fingers and thumb, runs its length, thoughtful. 'However. The king believes she is ailing. She and her daughter both, they are always mewling, their stomachs are disordered or their teeth falling out, they have agues or rheum, they are up all night puking and down all day moaning, and all their pain is due to Anne Boleyn. So look. Do you, Cremuel, go and see her without warning. Then tell me if she is feigning, or no.'

She maintains, as an affectation, a skittish slur in her speech, the odd French intonation, her inability to say his name. There is a stir at the door: the king is coming in. He makes a reverence. Anne does not rise or curtsey; she says without preliminary, 'I have told him, Henry, to go.'

'I wish you would, Cromwell. And give us your own report. There is no one like you for seeing into the nature of things. When the Emperor wants a stick to beat me with, he says his aunt is dying, of neglect and cold, and shame. Well, she has servants. She has firewood.'

'And as for shame,' Anne says, 'she should die inside, when she thinks of the lies she has told.'

'Majesty,' he says, 'I shall ride at dawn and tomorrow send Rafe Sadler to you, if you permit, with the day's agenda.'

The king groans. 'No escape from your big lists?'

'No, sir, for if I gave you a respite you would forever have me on the road, on some pretext. Till I return, would you just … sit on the situation?'

Anne shifts in her chair, brother George's letter under her. 'I shall do nothing without you,' Henry says. 'Take care, the roads are treacherous. I shall be your beadsman. Good night.'

He looks about the outer chamber, but Mark has vanished, and there is only a knot of matrons and maids: Mary Shelton, Jane Seymour and Elizabeth, the Earl of Worcester's wife. Who's missing? 'Where is Lady Rochford?' he says, smiling. 'Do I see her shape behind the arras?' He indicates Anne's chamber. 'Going to bed, I think. So you girls get her installed and then you will have the rest of the night for your ill behaviour.'

They giggle. Lady Worcester makes creepy motions with her finger. 'Nine of the clock, and here comes Harry Norris, bare beneath his shirt. Run, Mary Shelton. Run rather slowly …'

'Who do you run from, Lady Worcester?'

'Thomas Cromwell, I could not possibly tell you. A married woman like myself?' Teasing, smiling, she creeps her fingers along his upper arm. 'We all know where Harry Norris would like to lie tonight. Shelton is only his bedwarmer for now. He has royal ambitions. He will tell anyone. He is sick with love for the queen.'

'I shall play cards,' Jane Seymour says. 'With myself, so there will be no undue losses. Master, is there any news of the Lady Katherine?'

'I have nothing to tell you. Sorry.'

Lady Worcester's glance follows him. She is a fine woman, careless and rather free-spending, no older than the queen. Her husband is away and he feels she too could run rather slowly, if he gave her the nod. But then, a countess. And he a humble master. And sworn to the road before sunrise.

They ride up-country towards Katherine without banner or display, a tight knot of armed men. It is a clear day and bitter cold. The brown tussocky land shows through layers of hard frost, and herons flap from frozen pools. Clouds stack and shift on the horizon, slate-grey and a mild deceptive rose; leading them from early afternoon is a silvered moon as mean as a clipped coin. Christophe rides beside him, growing more voluble and disgusted the further they travel from urban comfort. '*On dit* the king chose a hard country for Katherine. He hopes the mould will get into her bones and she will die.'

'He has no such thought. Kimbolton is an old house but very sound. She has every comfort. Her household costs the king four thousand pounds a year. It is no mean sum.'

He leaves Christophe to ponder that locution: no mean sum. At last the boy says, 'Spaniards are *merde*, anyway.'

'You watch the track and keep Jenny's feet out of holes. Any spills and I'll have you follow me home on a donkey.'

'*Hi-han*,' Christophe bellows, loud enough to make the men at arms turn in their saddles. 'French donkey,' he explains.

French fuckwit, one says, amiably enough. Riding beneath dark trees at the close of that first day's travel, they sing; it lifts the tired heart, and dispels spirits lurking in the verges; never underestimate the superstition of the average Englishman. As this year closes, the favourite will be variations on the song the king wrote himself, 'Pastime with good company/I love and shall until I die.' The variations are only mildly obscene, or he would feel obliged to check them.

The landlord of their inn is a harassed wisp of a man, who does his futile best to find out whom he is entertaining. His wife is a strong, discontented young woman, with angry blue eyes and a loud voice. He has brought his own travelling cook. 'What, my lord?' she says. 'You think we'd poison you?' He can hear her banging around in the kitchen, laying down what shall and shan't be done with her skillets.

She comes to his chamber late and asks, do you want anything? He says no, but she comes back: what, really, nothing? You might lower your voice, he says. This far from London, the king's deputy in church affairs can perhaps relax his caution? 'Stay, then,' he tells her. Noisy she may be, but safer than Lady Worcester.

He wakes before dawn, so suddenly that he doesn't know where he is. He can hear a woman's voice from below, and for a moment he thinks he is back at the sign of the Pegasus, with his sister Kat crashing about, and that it is the morning of his flight from his father: that all his life is before him. But cautiously, in the dark chamber without a candle, he moves each limb: no bruises; he is not cut; he remembers where he is and what he is, and moves into the warmth the woman's body has left, and dozes, an arm thrown across the bolster.

Soon he hears his landlady singing on the stairs. Twelve virgins went out on a May morning, it seems. And none of them came back. She has scooped up the money he left her. On her face, as she greets him, no sign of the night's transaction; but she comes out and speaks to him, her voice low, as they prepare to ride. Christophe, with a lordly air, pays the reckoning to their host. The day is milder and their progress swift and without event. Certain images will be all that remain from his ride into middle England. The holly berries burning in their bushes. The startled flight of a woodcock, flushed from almost beneath their hooves. The feeling of venturing into a watery place, where soil and marsh are the same colour and nothing is solid under your feet.

* * *

Kimbolton is a busy market town, but at twilight the streets are empty. They have made no great speed, but it is futile to wear out horses on a task that is important, but not urgent; Katherine will live or die at her own pace. Besides, it is good for him to get out to the country. Squeezed in London's alleys, edging horse or mule under her jetties and gables, the mean canvas of her sky pierced by broken roofs, one forgets what England is: how broad the fields, how wide the sky, how squalid and ignorant the populace. They pass a wayside cross that shows recent signs of excavation at its base. One of the men at arms says, 'They think the monks are burying their treasure. Hiding it from our master here.'

'So they are,' he says. 'But not under crosses. They're not that foolish.'

In the main street they draw rein at the church. 'What for?' says Christophe.

'I need a blessing,' he says.

'You need to make your confession, sir,' one of the men says.

Smiles are exchanged. It is harmless, no one thinks the worse of him: only that their own beds were cold. He has noticed this: that men who have not met him dislike him, but when they have met him, only some of them do. We could have put up at a monastery, one of his guard had complained; but no girls in a monastery, I suppose. He had turned in the saddle: 'You really think that?' Knowing laughter from the men.

In the church's frigid interior, his escort flap their arms across their bodies; they stamp their feet and cry 'Brr,' like bad actors. 'I'll whistle for a priest,' Christophe says.

'You will do no such thing.' But he grins; can imagine his young self saying it, and doing it too.

But there is no need to whistle. Some suspicious janitor is edging in with a light. No doubt a messenger is stumbling towards the great house with news: watch out, make ready, lords are here. It is decorous for Katherine to have some warning, he feels, but not too much. 'Imagine it,' Christophe says, 'we might burst in on her when she is plucking her whiskers. Which women of that age do.'

To Christophe, the former queen is a broken jade, a crone. He thinks, Katherine would be my age, or thereabouts. But life is harsher to women, particularly women who, like Katherine, have been blessed with many children and seen them die.

Silently the priest arrives at his elbow, a timid fellow who wants to show the church's treasures. 'Now you must be …' He runs through a list in his head. 'William Lord?'

'Ah. No.' This is some other William. A long explanation ensues. He cuts it short. 'As long as your bishop knows who you are.' Behind him is an image of St Edmund, the man with five hundred fingers; the saint's feet are pointed daintily, as if he is dancing. 'Hold up the lights,' he says. 'Is that a mermaid?'

'Yes, my lord.' A shadow of anxiety crosses the priest's face. 'Must she come down? Is she forbidden?'

He smiles. 'I just thought she's a long way from the sea.'

'She's stinking fish.' Christophe yells with laughter.

'Forgive the boy. He's no poet.'

A feeble smile from the priest. On an oak screen St Anne holds a book for the instruction of her little daughter, the Virgin Mary; St Michael the Archangel hacks away with a scimitar at a devil entwining his feet. 'Are you here to see the queen, sir? I mean,' the priest corrects himself, 'the Lady Katherine?'

This priest doesn't know me from Adam, he thinks. I could be any emissary. I could be Charles Brandon, Duke of Suffolk. I could be Thomas Howard, Duke of Norfolk. They have both tried on Katherine their scant persuasive powers and their best bully-boy tricks.

He doesn't give his name, but he leaves an offering. The priest's hand enfolds the coins as if to warm them. 'You will forgive my slip, my lord? Over the lady's title? I swear I meant no harm by it. For an old countryman such as I am, it is hard to keep up with the changes. By the time we have understood one report from London, it is contradicted by the next.'

'It's hard for us all,' he says, shrugging. 'You pray for Queen Anne every Sunday?'

'Of course, my lord.'

'And what do your parishioners say to that?'

The priest looks embarrassed. 'Well, sir, they are simple people. I would not pay heed to what they say. Though they are all very loyal,' he adds hastily. 'Very loyal.'

'No doubt. Will you please me now, and this Sunday in your prayers remember Tom Wolsey?'

The late cardinal? He sees the old fellow revising his ideas. This can't be Thomas Howard or Charles Brandon: for if you speak the name of Wolsey, they can hardly restrain themselves from spitting at your feet.

When they leave the church, the last light is vanishing into the sky, and a stray snowflake drifts along towards the south. They remount; it has been a long day; his clothes feel heavy on his back. He doesn't believe the dead need our prayers, nor can they use them. But anyone who knows the Bible as he does, knows that our God is a capricious God, and there's no harm in hedging your bets. When the woodcock flew up in its flash of reddish brown, his heart had knocked hard. As they rode he was aware of it, each beat a heavy wing-beat; as the bird found the conceal-ment of trees, its tracing of feathers inked out to black.

They arrive in the half-dark: a hallooing from the walls, and an answering shout from Christophe: 'Thomas Cremuel, Secretary to the king and Master of the Rolls.'

'How do we know you?' a sentry bellows. 'Show your colours.'

'Tell him show a light and let me in,' he says, 'or I'll show his backside my boot.'

He has to say these things, when he's up-country; it's expected of him, the king's common adviser.

The drawbridge must come down for them: an antique scrape, a creak and rattling of bolts and chains. At Kimbolton they lock in early: good. 'Remember,' he says to his party, 'do not make the priest's mistake. When you talk to her household she is the Dowager Princess of Wales.'

'What?' Christophe says.

'She is not the king's wife. She never was the king's wife. She is the wife of the king's deceased brother, Arthur, Prince of Wales.'

'Deceased means dead,' Christophe says. 'I know it.'

'She is not a queen, or former queen, as her second so-called marriage was not licit.'

'That is, not permissible,' Christophe says. 'She make the mistake of conjugation with both brothers, Arthur first then Henry.'

'And what are we to think of such a woman?' he says, smiling.

Flare of torches and, taking form out of dimness, Sir Edmund Bedingfield: Katherine's keeper. 'I think you might have warned us, Cromwell!'

'Grace, you didn't want warning of me, did you?' He kisses Lady Bedingfield. 'I didn't bring my supper. But there's a mule cart behind me, it will be here tomorrow. I have venison for your own table, and some almonds for the queen, and a sweet wine that Chapuys says she favours.'

'I am glad of anything that will tempt her appetite.' Grace Bedingfield leads the way into the great hall. In the firelight she stops and turns to him: 'Her doctor suspects she has a growth in her belly. But it may take a long course. When you would think she has suffered enough, poor lady.'

He hands his gloves, his riding coat, to Christophe. 'Will you wait upon her straight away?' Bedingfield asks. 'Though we were not expecting you, she may be. It is hard for us, because the townspeople favour her and word slips in with servants, you cannot prevent it, I believe they stand and signal from beyond the moat. I think she knows most of what goes on, who passes on the road.'

Two ladies, Spanish by their dress and well-advanced in age, press themselves against a plaster wall and look at him with resentment. He bows to them, and one remarks in her own tongue that this is the man who has sold the King of England's soul. The wall behind them is painted, he sees, with the fading figures of a scene from paradise: Adam and Eve, hand in hand, stroll among beasts so new to creation they have not yet learned their names. A small elephant with a rolling eye peeps shyly through the foliage. He has never seen an elephant, but understood them to be higher by far than a warhorse; perhaps it's not had time to grow yet. Branches bowed with fruit hang above its head.

'Well, you know the form,' Bedingfield says. 'She lives in that room and has her ladies – those ones – cook for her over the fire. You knock and go in, and if you call her Lady Katherine she kicks you out, and if you call her Your Highness she lets you stay. So I call her nothing. You, I call her. As if she were a girl that scrubs the steps.'

Katherine is sitting by the fire shrunk into a cape of very good ermines. The king will want that back, he thinks, if she dies. She glances up, and puts out a hand for him to kiss: unwilling, but more because of the chill, he thinks, than because she is reluctant to acknowledge him. She is jaundiced, and there is an invalid fug in the room – the faint animal scent of the furs, a vegetal stench of undrained cooking water, and the sour reek from a bowl with which a girl hurries away: containing, he suspects, the evacuated contents of the dowager's stomach. If she is ill in the night, perhaps she dreams of the gardens of the Alhambra, where she grew up: the marble pavements, the bubbling of crystal water into basins, the drag of a white peacock's tail and the scent of lemons. I could have brought her a lemon in my saddlebag, he thinks.

As if reading his thoughts, she speaks to him in Castilian. 'Master Cromwell, let us abandon this weary pretence that you do not speak my language.'

He nods. 'It has been hard in times past, standing by while your maids talked about me. "Jesu, isn't he ugly, do you think he has a hairy body like Satan?"'

'My maids said that?' Katherine seems amused. She withdraws her hand, out of his sight. 'They are long gone, those lively girls. Only old women remain, and a handful of licensed traitors.'

'Madam, those about you love you.'

'They report on me. All my words. They even listen in to my prayers. Well, master.' She raises her face to the light. 'How do you think I look? What will you say of me when the king asks you? I have not seen myself in a mirror these many months.' She pats her fur cap, pulls its lappets over her ears; laughs. 'The king used to call me an angel. He used to call me a flower. When my first son was born, it was the depths of winter. All England lay under snow. There were no flowers to be had, I thought. But Henry gave me six dozen roses made of the purest white silk. "White as your hand, my love," he said, and kissed my finger-tips.' A twitch beneath the ermine tells him where a bunched fist lies now. 'I keep them in a chest, the roses. They at least do not fade. Over the years I have given them to those who have done me some service.' She pauses; her lips move, a silent invocation: prayers for departed souls. 'Tell me, how is Boleyn's daughter? They say she prays a good deal, to her reformed God.'

'She has indeed a reputation for piety. As she has the approbation of the scholars and bishops.'

'They are using her. As she is using them. If they were true churchmen they would shrink from her in horror, as they would shrink from an infidel. But I expect she is praying for a son. She lost the last child, I am told. Ah well, I know how that is. I pity her from the bottom of my heart.'

'She and the king have hopes of another child soon.'

'What? Particular hope, or general hope?'

He pauses; nothing definite has been said; Gregory could be wrong. 'I thought she confided in you,' Katherine says sharply. She scans his face: is there some rift, some *froideur*? 'They say Henry pursues other women.' Katherine's finger strokes the fur: absently round and round, rubbing at the pelt. 'It is so soon. They have only been married such a little space. I suppose she looks at the women about her, and says to herself, always questioning, is it you, madam? Or you? It has always surprised me that those who are untrustworthy themselves are blind when placing their own trust. La Ana thinks she has friends. But if she does not give the king a son soon, they will turn on her.'

He nods. 'You may be right. Who will turn first?'

'Why should I alert her?' Katherine asks drily. 'They say that when she is crossed she carps like a common scold. I am not surprised. A queen, and she calls herself a queen, must live and suffer under the world's eye. No woman is above her but the Queen of Heaven, so she can look for no companionship in her troubles. If she suffers she suffers alone, and she needs a special grace to bear it. It appears Boleyn's daughter has not received this grace. I ask myself why that could be.'

She breaks off; her lips open and her flesh draws itself together, as if squirming away from her clothes. You are in pain, he starts to say, but she waves him to silence, it's nothing, nothing. 'Gentlemen about the king, who swear now they will lay down their lives for her smile, will soon offer their devotion to another. They used to offer that same devotion to me. It was because I was the king's wife, it was nothing to do with my person. But La Ana takes it as a tribute to her charms. And besides, it is not just the men she should fear. Her sister-in-law, Jane Rochford, now there is a vigilant young woman ... when she served me she often brought secrets to me, love secrets, secrets I would perhaps rather not know, and I doubt her ears and eyes are less sharp nowadays.' Still her fingers work away, now massaging a spot near her breastbone. 'You wonder, how can Katherine, who is banished, know the workings of the court? That is for you to ponder.'

I don't have to ponder long, he thinks. It is Nicholas Carew's wife, a particular friend of yours. And it is Gertrude Courtenay, the Marquis of Exeter's wife; I caught her out in plotting last year, I should have locked her up. Perhaps even little Jane Seymour; though Jane has her own career to serve, since Wolf Hall. 'I know you have your sources,' he says. 'But should you trust them? They act in your name, but not in your best interests. Or those of your daughter.'

'Will you let the princess visit me? If you think she needs counsel to steady her, who better than I?'

'If it stood to me, madam ...'

'What harm can it do the king?'

'Put yourself in his place. I believe your ambassador Chapuys has written to Lady Mary, saying he can get her out of the country.'

'Never! Chapuys can have no such thought. I guarantee it in my own person.'

'The king thinks that perhaps Mary might corrupt her guards, and if permitted to make a journey to see you she might spur away, and take ship for the territories of her cousin the Emperor.'

It almost brings a smile to his lips, to think of the skinny, scared little princess embarking on such a desperate and criminal course of action. Katherine smiles too; a twisted, malicious smile. 'And then what? Does Henry fear my daughter will come riding back, with a foreign husband by her side, and turn him out of his kingdom? You can assure him, she has no such intention. I will answer for her, again, with my own person.'

'Your own person must do a good deal, madam. Guarantee this, answer for that. You have only one death to suffer.'

'I wish it might do Henry good. When my death arrives, in whatever manner, I hope to meet it in such a way as to set him an example when the time comes for his own.'

'I see. Do you think a lot about the king's death?'

'I think about his afterlife.'

'If you want to do his soul good, why do you continually obstruct him? It hardly makes him a better man. Do you never think that, if you had bowed to the king's wishes years ago, if you had entered a convent and allowed him to remarry, he would never have broken with Rome? There would have been no need. Sufficient doubt was cast upon your marriage for you to retire with a good grace. You would have been honoured by all. But now the titles you cling to are empty. Henry was a good son of Rome. You drove him to this extremity. You, not he, split Christendom. And I expect that you know that, and that you think about it in the silence of the night.'

There is a pause, while she turns the great pages of her volume of rage, and puts her finger on just the right word. 'What you say, Cromwell, is … contemptible.'

She's probably right, he thinks. But I will keep tormenting her, revealing her to herself, stripping her of any illusions, and I will do it for her daughter's sake: Mary is the future, the only grown child the king has, England's only prospect if God calls away Henry and the throne is suddenly empty. 'So you won't be giving me one of those silk roses,' he says. 'I thought you might.'

A long look. 'At least, as an enemy, you stand in plain sight. I wish my friends could bear to be as conspicuous. The English are a nation of hypocrites.'

'Ingrates,' he agrees. 'Natural liars. I've found it myself. I would rather the Italians. The Florentines, so modest. The Venetians, transparent in all their dealing. And your own race, the Spaniards. Such an honest people. They used to say of your royal father Ferdinand, that his open heart would undo him.'

'You are amusing yourself,' she says, 'at the expense of a dying woman.'

'You want a great deal of credit for dying. You offer guarantees on the one hand, you want privileges on the other.'

'A state such as mine, it usually buys kindness.'

'I am trying to be kind, but you do not see it. At the last, madam, can you not put your own will aside, and for the sake of your daughter, reconcile with the king? If you leave this world at odds with him, blame will be visited on her. And she is young and has her life to live.'

'He will not blame Mary. I know the king. He is not so mean a man.'

He is silent. She still loves her husband, he thinks: in some kink or crevice of her old leathern heart, she is still hoping for his footstep, his voice. And with his gift to her hand, how can she forget that he once loved her? After all, there must have been weeks of work in the silk roses, he must have ordered them long before he knew the child was a boy. 'We called him the New Year's prince,' Wolsey had said. 'He lived fifty-two days, and I counted every one.' England in winter: the pall of sliding snow, blanketing the fields and palace roofs, smothering tile and gable, slipping silent over window glass; feathering the rutted tracks, weighting the boughs of oak and yew, sealing the fishes under ice and freezing the bird to the branch. He imagines the cradle, curtained in crimson, gilded with the arms of England: the rockers huddled into their clothes: a brazier burning and the air fresh with the New Year scents of cinnamon and juniper. The roses brought to her triumphant bedside – how? In a gilded basket? In a long box like a coffin, a casket inlaid with polished shells? Or tumbled to her coverlet from a silk sheath embroidered with pomegranates? Two happy months pass. The child thrives. It is understood through the world that the Tudors have an heir. And then on the fifty-second day, a silence behind a curtain: a breath, not a breath. The women of the chamber snatch up the prince, crying in shock and fear; hopelessly crossing themselves, they cower by the cradle to pray.

'I will see what can be done,' he says. 'About your daughter. About a visit.' How perilous can it be to bring one little girl across country? 'I do think the king would permit it, if you would advise Lady Mary to be in all respect conformable to his will, and recognise him, as now she does not, as head of the church.'

'In that matter the Princess Mary must consult her own conscience.' She holds up a hand, palm towards him. 'I see you pity me, Cromwell. You should not. I have been prepared for death a long time. I believe that Almighty God will reward my efforts to serve him. And I shall see my little children again, who have gone before me.'

Your heart could break for her, he thinks: if it were not proof against breaking. She wants a martyr's death on the scaffold. Instead she will die in the Fens, alone: choke on her own vomit, like as not. He says, 'What about Lady Mary, is she also ready to die?'

'The Princess Mary has meditated on Christ's passion since she was an infant in the nursery. She will be ready when he calls.'

'You are an unnatural parent,' he says. 'What parent would risk a child's death?'

But he remembers Walter Cromwell. Walter used to jump on me with his big boots: on me, his only son. He gathers himself for one last effort. 'I have instanced to you, madam, a case where your stubbornness in setting yourself against the king and his council served only to bring about a result you most abhor. So you can be wrong, do you see? I ask you to consider that you may be wrong more than once. For the love of God, advise Mary to obey the king.'

'The Princess Mary,' she says, dully. She does not seem to have the breath for any further protest. He watches her for a moment, and prepares to withdraw. But then she looks up. 'I have wondered, master, in what language do you confess? Or do you not confess?'

'God knows our hearts, madam. There is no need for an idle formula, or for an intermediary.' No need for language either, he thinks: God is beyond translation.

* * *

He falls out of the door and almost into the arms of Katherine's keeper: 'Is my chamber ready?'

'But your supper ...'

'Send me up a bowl of broth. I am talked out. All I want is my bed.'

'Anything in it?' Bedingfield looks roguish.

So, his escort has informed on him. 'Just a pillow, Edmund.'

Grace Bedingfield is disappointed he has retired so early. She thought she would get all the court news; she resents being stuck out here with the silent Spaniards, a long winter ahead. He must repeat the king's instructions: utmost vigilance against the outside world. 'I don't mind if Chapuys's letters get through, it will keep her occupied working the cipher. She isn't important to the Emperor now, it's Mary he cares about. But no visitors, except under the king's seal or mine. Although –' He breaks off; he can see the day, next spring and if Katherine is still alive, when the Emperor's army is riding up-country, and it is necessary to snatch her out of their path and hold her hostage; it would be a poor show if Edmund refused to yield her. 'Look.' He shows his turquoise ring. 'You see this? The late cardinal gave it me, and I am known to wear it.'

'Is that it, the magic one?' Grace Bedingfield takes his hand. 'Melts stone walls, makes princesses fall in love with you?'

'This is the one. If any messenger brings you this, let him in.'

When he closes his eyes that night a vault rises above him, the carved roof of Kimbolton's church. A man ringing handbells. A swan, a lamb, a cripple with a stick, two lovers' hearts entwined. And a pomegranate tree. Katherine's emblem. That might have to go. He yawns. Chisel them into apples, that'll fix it. I'm too tired for unnecessary effort. He remembers the woman at the inn and feels guilty. He pulls a pillow towards him: just a pillow, Edmund.

When the innkeeper's wife spoke to him as they were mounting their horses, she had said, 'Send me a present. Send me a present from London, something you can't get here.' It will have to be something she can wear on her back, otherwise it will be vanished away by some light-fingered traveller. He will remember his obligation, but very likely by the time he returns to London he will have forgotten what she looked like. He had seen her by candlelight, and then the candle was out. When he saw her by daylight she could have been a different woman. Perhaps she was.

When he sleeps he dreams of the fruit of the Garden of Eden, outstretched in Eve's plump hand. He wakes momentarily: if the fruit is ripe, when did those boughs blossom? In what possible month, in what possible spring? Schoolmen will have addressed the question. A dozen furrowed generations. Tonsured heads bent. Chilblained fingers fumbling scrolls. It's the sort of silly question monks are made for. I'll ask Cranmer, he thinks: my archbishop. Why doesn't Henry ask Cranmer's advice, if he wants to be rid of Anne? It was Cranmer who divorced him from Katherine; he would never tell him he must go back to her stale bed.

But no, Henry cannot speak of his doubts in that quarter. Cranmer loves Anne, he thinks her the pattern of a Christian woman, the hope of good Bible readers all over Europe.

He sleeps again and dreams of the flowers made before the dawn of the world. They are made of white silk. There is no bush or stem to pluck them from. They lie on the bare uncreated ground.

He looks closely at Anne the queen, the day he brings back his report; she looks sleek, contented, and the benign domestic hum of their voices, as he approaches, tell him that she and Henry are in harmony. They are busy, their heads together. The king has his drawing instruments to hand: his compasses and pencils, his rules, inks and penknives. The table is covered in unscrolling plans, and in artificers' moulds and batons.

He makes them his reverence, and comes to the point: 'She is not well, and I believe it would be a kindness to let her have a visit from ambassador Chapuys.'

Anne shoots out of her chair. 'What, so he can intrigue with her more conveniently?'

'Her doctors suggest, madam, that she will soon be in her grave, and not able to work you any displeasure.'

'She would come out of it, flapping in her shroud, if she saw the chance to thwart me.'

Henry stretches out a hand: 'Sweetheart, Chapuys has never acknowledged you. But when Katherine is gone, and can no longer make trouble for us, I will make sure he bends his knee.'

'Nevertheless, I do not think he should go out of London. He encourages Katherine in her perversity, and she encourages her daughter.' She darts a glance at him. 'Cremuel, you agree, do you not? Mary should be brought to court and made to kneel before her father and swear the oath, and there on her knees she should beg pardon for her treasonous obstinacy, and acknowledge that my daughter, and not she, is heir to England.'

He indicates the plans. 'Not building, sir?'

Henry looks like a child caught with its fingers in the sugar box. He pushes one of the batons towards him. The designs, still novel to the English eye, are those he grew accustomed to in Italy: fluted urns and vases, mantled and winged, and the sightless heads of emperors and gods. These days the native flowers and trees, the winding stems and blossoms, are disdained for wreathed arms, for the laurels of victory, the shaft of the lictor's axe, the shaft of the spear. He sees that Anne's status is not served by simplicity; for more than seven years now, Henry has been adapting his taste to hers. Henry used to enjoy hedge wines, the fruits of the English summer, but now the wines he favours are heavy, perfumed, drowsy; his body is heavy, so sometimes he seems to block out the light. 'Are we building from the foundations?' he enquires. 'Or just a layer of ornamentation? Both cost money.'

'How ungracious you are,' Anne says. 'The king is sending you some oak for your own building at Hackney. And some for Master Sadler, for his new house.'

With a dip of his head he signals his thanks. But the king's mind is up-country, with the woman who still claims to be his wife. 'What use is Katherine's life to her, now?' Henry asks. 'I am sure she is tired of contention. God knows, I am tired of it. She were better to join the saints and holy martyrs.'

'They have waited for her long enough.' Anne laughs: too loudly.

'I picture the lady dying,' the king says. 'She will be making speeches and forgiving me. She is always forgiving me. It is she who needs forgiveness. For her blighted womb. For poisoning my children before they were born.'

He, Cromwell, flits his eyes to Anne. Surely now, if she has anything to tell, is the moment? But she turns away, leans down and scoops her spaniel Purkoy into her lap. She buries her face in his fur, and the little dog, startled from his sleep, whimpers and twists in her hands and watches Master Secretary bow himself out.

Outside waiting for him, George Boleyn's wife: her confiding hand, drawing him aside, her whisper. If someone said to Lady Rochford, 'It's raining,' she would turn it into a conspiracy; as she passed the news on, she would make it sound somehow indecent, unlikely, but sadly true.

'Well?' he says. 'Is she?'

'Ah. Has she said nothing still? Of course, the wise woman says nothing till she feels it quickening.' He regards her: stony-eyed. 'Yes,' she says at last, casting a nervous glance over her shoulder. 'She has been wrong before. But yes.'

'Does the king know?'

'You should tell him, Cromwell. Be the man with good news. Who knows, he might knight you on the spot.'

He is thinking, fetch me Rafe Sadler, fetch me Thomas Wriothesley, send a letter to Edward Seymour, whistle up my nephew Richard, cancel supper with Chapuys, but don't let our dishes go to waste: let's invite Sir Thomas Boleyn.

'I suppose it is to be expected,' Jane Rochford says. 'She was with the king for much of the summer, was she not? A week here, a week there. And when he was not with her, he would write her love letters, and send them by the hand of Harry Norris.'

'My lady, I must leave you, I have business.'

'I'm sure you have. Ah well. And you are usually such a good listener. You always attend to what I say. And I say that this summer he wrote her love letters, and sent them by the hand of Harry Norris.'

He is moving too fast to make much of her last sentence; though, as he will admit later, the detail will affix itself and adhere to certain sentences of his own, not yet formed. Phrases only. Elliptic. Conditional. As everything is conditional now. Anne blossoming as Katherine fails. He pictures them, their faces intent and skirts bunched, two little girls in a muddy track, playing teeter-totter with a plank balanced on a stone.

Thomas Seymour says at once, 'This is Jane's chance, now. He will hesitate no more, he will want a new bedfellow. He will not touch the queen till she gives birth. He cannot. There is too much to lose.'

He thinks, already perhaps the secret king of England has fingers, has a face. But I thought that before, he reminds himself. At her coronation, when Anne carried her belly so proudly; and after all, it was only a girl.

'I still don't see it,' says old Sir John, the adulterer. 'I don't see how he'd want Jane. Now if it were my daughter Bess. The king has danced with her. He liked her very well.'

'Bess is married,' Edward says.

Tom Seymour laughs. 'The more fit for his purpose.'

Edward is irate. 'Don't talk of Bess. Bess would not have him. Bess is not in question.'

'It could turn to good,' Sir John says, tentative. 'For until now Jane's never been any use to us.'

'True,' Edward says. 'Jane is as much use as a blancmange. Now let her earn her keep. The king will need a companion. But we do not push her in his way. Let it be as Cromwell here has advised. Henry has seen her. He has formed his intent. Now she must avoid him. No, she must repel him.'

'Oh, hoity-toity,' old Seymour says. 'If you can afford it.'

'Afford what's chaste, what's seemly?' Edward snaps. 'You never could. Be quiet, you old lecher. The king pretends to forget your crimes, but no one really forgets. You are pointed at: the old goat who stole his son's bride.'

'Yes, hold your peace, Father,' Tom says. 'We're talking to Cromwell.'

'One thing I am afraid of,' he says. 'Your sister loves her old mistress, Katherine. This is well known to the present queen, who spares no opportunity for harshness. If she sees that the king is looking at Jane, I am afraid she will be further persecuted. Anne is not one to sit by while her husband makes a – a companion – of another woman. Even if she thought it a temporary arrangement.'

'Jane will pay no heed,' Edward says. 'What though she gets a pinch or a slap? She will know how to bear herself patiently.'

'She will play him for some great reward,' says old Seymour.

Tom Seymour says, 'He made Anne a marquise before he had her.'

Edward's face is as grim as if he is ordering up an execution. 'You know what he made her. Marquise first. Queen thereafter.'

Parliament is prorogued, but London lawyers, flapping their black gowns like crows, settle to their winter term. The happy news seeps and leaks through the court. Anne lets out her bodices. Bets are laid. Pens scribble. Letters are folded. Seals pressed to wax. Horses are mounted. Ships set sail. The old families of England kneel and ask God why he favours the Tudors. King Francis frowns. Emperor Charles sucks his lip. King Henry dances.

The conversation at Elvetham, that early hour's confabulation: it is as if it had never been. The king's doubts about his marriage, it seems, have vanished.

Though in the desolate winter gardens, he has been seen walking with Jane.

Her family surround her; they call him in. 'What did he say, sister?' Edward Seymour demands. 'Tell me everything, everything he said.'

Jane says, 'He asked me if I would be his good mistress.'

They exchange glances. There is a difference between a mistress and a good mistress: does Jane know that? The first implies concubinage. The second, something less immediate: an exchange of tokens, a chaste and languorous admiration, a prolonged courtship ... though it can't be very prolonged, of course, or Anne will have given birth and Jane will have missed her chance. The women cannot predict when the heir will see the light, and he can get no further with Anne's doctors.

'Look, Jane,' Edward tells her, 'this is no time to be shy. You must give us particulars.'

'He asked me if I would look kindly on him.'

'Kindly on him when?'

'For instance, if he wrote me a poem. Praising my beauty. So I said I would. I would thank him for it. I wouldn't laugh, even behind my hand. And I wouldn't raise any objection to any statements he might make in verse. Even if they were exaggerated. Because in poems it is usual to exaggerate.'

He, Cromwell, congratulates her. 'You have it covered from every angle, Mistress Seymour. You would have made a sharp lawyer.'

'You mean, if I had been born a man?' She frowns. 'But still, it is not likely, Master Secretary. The Seymours are not tradesmen.'

Edward Seymour says, 'Good mistress. Write you verse. Very well. Good so far. But if he attempts anything on your person, you must scream.'

Jane says, 'What if nobody came?'

He puts his hand on Edward's arm. He wants to stop this scene developing any further. 'Listen, Jane. Don't scream. Pray. Pray aloud, I mean. Mental prayer will not do it. Say a prayer with the Holy Virgin in it. Something that will appeal to His Majesty's piety and sense of honour.'

'I understand,' Jane says. 'Do you have a prayer book on your person, Master Secretary? Brothers? No matter. I will go and look for mine. I am sure I can find something that will fit the bill.'

In early December, he receives word from Katherine's doctors that she is eating better, though praying no less. Death has moved, perhaps, from the head of the bed to its foot. Her recent pains have eased and she is lucid; she uses the time to make her bequests. She leaves her daughter Mary a gold collar she brought from Spain, and her furs. She asks for five hundred masses to be said for her soul, and for a pilgrimage to be made to Walsingham.

Details of the dispositions make their way back to Whitehall. 'These furs,' Henry says, 'have you seen them, Cromwell? Are they any good? If they are, I want them sent down to me.'

Teeter-totter.

The women around Anne say, you would not think she was *enceinte*. In October she looked well enough, but now she seems to be losing flesh, rather than gaining. Jane Rochford tells him, 'You would almost think she is ashamed of her condition. And His Majesty is not attentive to her, as formerly he was attentive when her belly was big. Then, he could not do enough for her. He would cater to her whims and wait on her like a maid. I once came in to find her feet in his lap, and he rubbing them like an ostler nursing some splay-hooved mare.'

'Rubbing doesn't help a splayed hoof,' he says, earnest. 'You have to trim it and fit a special shoe.'

Rochford stares at him. 'Have you been talking to Jane Seymour?'

'Why?'

'Never mind,' she says.

He has seen Anne's face as she watches the king, as she watches the king watching Jane. You expect black anger, and the enactment of it: scissored-up sewing, broken glass. Instead, her face is narrow; she holds her jewelled sleeve across her body, where the child is growing. 'I must not disturb myself,' she says. 'It could injure the prince.' She pulls her skirts aside when Jane passes. She huddles into herself, narrow shoulders shrinking; she looks cold as a doorstep orphan.

Teeter-totter.

The rumour in the country is that Master Secretary has brought a woman back from his recent trip to Hertfordshire, or Bedfordshire, and set her up in his house at Stepney, or at Austin Friars, or at King's Place in Hackney, which he is rebuilding for her in lavish style. She is the keeper of an inn, and her husband has been seized and locked up, for a new crime invented by Thomas Cromwell. The poor cuckold is to be charged and hanged at the next assize; though, by some reports, he has already been found dead in his prison, bludgeoned, poisoned, and with his throat cut.

III

Angels

Stepney and Greenwich,
Christmas 1535–New Year 1536

Christmas morning: he comes hurtling out in pursuit of whatever trouble is next. A huge toad blocks his path. 'Is that Matthew?'

From the amphibian mouth, a juvenile chortle. 'Simon. Merry Christmas, sir, how do you?'

He sighs. 'Overworked. Did you send your duties to your mother and father?'

The singing children go home in the summer. At Christmas, they are busy singing. 'Will you be going to see the king, sir?' Simon croaks. 'I bet their plays at court are not so good as ours. We are playing Robin Hood, and King Arthur is in it. I play Merlin's toad. Master Richard Cromwell plays the Pope and has a begging bowl. He cries "Mumpsimus sumpsimus, hocus pocus." We give him stones for alms. He threatens us with Hell.'

He pats Simon's warty skin. The toad clears his path with a ponderous hop.

Since his return from Kimbolton, London has closed around him: late autumn, her fading and melancholy evenings, her early dark. The sedate and ponderous arrangements of the court have enfolded him, entrapped him into desk-bound days prolonged by candlelight into desk-bound nights; sometimes he would give a king's ransom to see the sun. He is buying land in the lusher parts of England, but he has no leisure to visit it; so these farms, these ancient manors in their walled gardens, these watercourses with their little quays, these ponds with their gilded fish rising to the hook; these vineyards, flower gardens, arbours and walks, remain to him flat, each one a paper construct, a set of figures on a page of accounts: not sheep-nibbled margins, nor meadows where kine stand knee-deep in grass, not coppices nor groves where a white doe shivers, a hoof poised; but parchment domains, leases and freeholds delimited by inky clauses, not by ancient hedges or boundary stones. His acres are notional acres, sources of income, sources of dissatisfaction in the small hours, when he wakes up and his mind explores their geography: in these waking nights before sullen or frozen dawns, he thinks not of the freedom his holdings allow, but of the trampling intrusion of others, their easements and rights of way, their fences and vantage points, that allow them to impinge on his boundaries and interfere with his quiet possession of his future. Christ knows, he is no country boy: though where he grew up, in the streets near the quays, Putney Heath was at his back, a place to go missing. He spent long days there, running with his brethren, boys as rough as himself: all of them in flight from their fathers, from their belts and fists, and from the education they were threatened with if they ever stood still. But London pulled him to her urban gut; long before he sailed the Thames in Master Secretary's barge, he knew the currents and the tide, and he knew how much could be picked up, casually, at watermen's trades, by unloading boats and running crates in barrows uphill to the fine houses that lined the Strand, the houses of lords and bishops: the houses of men with whom, daily, he now sits down at the council board.

The winter court perambulates, its accustomed circuit: Greenwich and Eltham, the houses of Henry's childhood; Whitehall and Hampton Court, once the cardinal's houses. It is usual these days for the king, wherever the court resides, to dine alone in his private rooms. Outside the royal apartments, in the outer Watching Chamber or the Guard Chamber – in whatever that outer hall is named, in the palaces in which we find ourselves – there is a top table, where the Lord Chamberlain, head of the king's private household, holds court for the nobility. Uncle Norfolk sits at this table, when he is with us at court; so does Charles Brandon, Duke of Suffolk, and the queen's father, the Earl of Wiltshire. There is a table, somewhat lower in status, but served with due honour, for functionaries like himself, and for the old friends of the king who happen not to be peers. Nicholas Carew sits there, Master of the Horse; and William Fitzwilliam, Master Treasurer, who of course has known Henry since he was a boy. William Paulet, Master Comptroller, presides at the head of this board: and he wonders, until it is explained to him, at their habit of lifting their goblets (and their eyebrows) in a toast to someone not there. Till Paulet explains, half-embarrassed, 'We toast the man who sat here before me. Master Comptroller who was. Sir Henry Guildford, his blessed memory. You knew him, Cromwell, of course.'

Indeed: who did not know Guildford, that practised diplomat, that most studied of courtiers? A man of the king's own age, he had been Henry's right arm since he came to the throne, he an unpractised, well-meaning, optimistic prince of nineteen. Two glowing spirits, earnest in pursuit of glory and a good time, the master and servant had aged together. You would have backed Guildford to survive an earthquake; but he did not survive Anne Boleyn. His partisanship was clear: he loved Queen Katherine and said so. (And if I did not love her, he said, then propriety alone, and my Christian conscience, would compel me to back her case.) The king had excused him out of long friendship; only let us, he had pleaded, leave the matter unmentioned, the disagreement unstated. Do not mention Anne Boleyn. Make it possible for us to stay friends.

But silence had not been enough for Anne. The day I am queen, she had told Guildford, is the day you lose your job.

Madam, said Sir Henry Guildford: the day you become queen, is the day I resign.

And so he did. Henry said: Come on, man! Don't let a woman nag you out of your post! It's just women's jealousy and spite, ignore it.

But I fear for myself, Guildford said. For my family and my name.

Do not abandon me, said the king.

Blame your new wife, Henry Guildford said.

And so he quit the court. And went home to the country. 'And died,' says William Fitzwilliam, 'within a few short months. They say, of a broken heart.'

A sigh runs around the table. That's the way it takes men; life's work over, rural ennui stretching ahead: a procession of days, Sunday to Sunday, all without shape. What is there, without Henry? Without the radiance of his smile? It's like perpetual November, a life in the dark.

'Wherefore we remember him,' Sir Nicholas Carew says. 'Our old friend. And we drink a toast – Paulet here does not mind – to the man who would still be Master Comptroller, if the times were not out of joint.'

He has a gloomy way of making a toast, Sir Nicholas Carew. Levity is unknown to one so dignified. He, Cromwell, had been sitting at table for a week before Sir Nicholas deigned to turn a cold eye upon him, and nudge the mutton his way. But their relations have eased since then; after all, he, Cromwell, is an easy man to get along with. He sees that there is a camaraderie among men such as these, men who have lost out to the Boleyns: a defiant camaraderie, such as exists among those sectaries in Europe who are always expecting the end of the world, but who hope that, after the earth has been consumed by fire, they will be seated in glory: grilled a little, crisp at the edges and blackened in parts, but still, thanks be to God, alive for eternity, and seated at his right hand.

He knew Henry Guildford himself, as Paulet reminds him. It must be five years ago now that he had been entertained by him handsomely, at Leeds Castle down in Kent. It was only because Guildford wanted something, of course: a favour, from my lord cardinal. But still, he had learned from Guildford's table talk, from the way he ordered his household, from his prudence and discreet wit. More lately, he had learned from Guildford's example how Anne Boleyn could break a career; and how far they were from forgiving her, his companions at table. Men like Carew, he knows, tend to blame him, Cromwell, for Anne's rise in the world; he facilitated it, he broke the old marriage and let in the new. He does not expect them to soften to him, to include him in their companionship; he only wants them not to spit in his dinner. But Carew's stiffness bends a little, as he joins them in talk; sometimes the Master of the Horse swivels towards him his long, indeed somewhat equine head; sometimes he gives him a slow courser's blink and says, 'Well, Master Secretary, and how are you today?'

And as he searches for a reply that Nicholas will understand, William Fitzwilliam will catch his eye, and grin.

During December a landslide, an avalanche of papers has crossed his desk. Often he ends the day smarting and thwarted, because he has sent Henry vital and urgent messages and the gentlemen of the privy chamber have decided it's easier for them if they keep the business back till Henry's in the mood. Despite the good news he has had from the queen, Henry is testy, capricious. At any moment he may demand the oddest item of information, or pose questions with no answer. What's the market price of Berkshire wool? Do you speak Turkish? Why not? Who does speak Turkish? Who was the founder of the monastery at Hexham?

Seven shilling the sack, and rising, Majesty. No. Because I was never in those parts. I will find a man if one can be got. St Wilfred, sir. He closes his eyes. 'I believe the Scots razed it, and it was built up again in the time of the first Henry.'

'Why does Luther think,' the king demands, 'that I should come into conformity with his church? Should he not think of coming into conformity with me?'

About St Lucy's Day, Anne calls him in, taking him from the affairs of Cambridge University. But Lady Rochford is there to check him before he reaches her, put a hand on his arm. 'She is a sorry sight. She cannot stop blubbing. Have you not heard? Her little dog is dead. We could not face telling her. We had to ask the king himself to do it.'

Purkoy? Her favourite? Jane Rochford conducts him in, glances at Anne. Poor lady: her eyes are cried to slits. 'Do you know,' Lady Rochford murmurs, 'when she miscarried her last child, she did not shed a tear?'

The women skirt around Anne, keeping their distance as if she were barbed. He remembers what Gregory said: Anne is all elbows and points. You could not comfort her; even a hand extended, she would regard as a presumption, or a threat. Katherine is right. A queen is alone, whether in the loss of her husband, her spaniel or her child.

She turns her head: 'Cremuel.' She orders her women out: a vehement gesture, a child scaring crows. Unhurried, like bold corvines of some new and silky kind, the ladies gather their trains, flap languidly away; their voices, like voices from the air, trail behind them: their gossip broken off, their knowing cackles of laughter. Lady Rochford is the last to take wing, trailing her feathers, reluctant to yield the ground.

Now there is no one in the room but himself and Anne and her dwarf, humming in the corner, waggling her fingers before her face.

'I am so sorry,' he says, his eyes down. He knows better than to say, you can get another dog.

'They found him –' Anne throws out a hand, 'out there. Down in the courtyard. The window was open above. His neck was broken.'

She does not say, he must have fallen. Because clearly this is not what she thinks. 'Do you remember, you were here, that day my cousin Francis Bryan brought him from Calais? Francis walked in and I had Purkoy off his arm before you could blink. He was a creature who did no one harm. What monster would find it in their heart to pick him up and kill him?'

He wants to soothe her; she seems as torn, as injured, as if the attack had been on her person. 'Probably he crept out on the sill and then his paws slipped. Those little dogs, you expect them to fall on their feet like a cat, but they don't. I had a spaniel jumped out of my son's arms because she saw a mouse, and she snapped her leg. It's easily done.'

'What happened to her?'

He says gently, 'We could not mend her.' He glances up at the fool. She is grinning in her corner, and jerking her fists apart in a snapping motion. Why does Anne keep the thing? She should be sent to a hospital. Anne scrubs at her cheeks; all her fine French manners fallen away, she uses her knuckles, like a little girl. 'What is the news from Kimbolton?' She finds a handkerchief and blows her nose. 'They say Katherine could live six months.'

He does not know what to say. Perhaps she wants him to send a man to Kimbolton to drop Katherine from a height?

'The French ambassador complains he came twice to your house and you would not see him.'

'I was busy,' he shrugs.

'With?'

'I was playing bowls in the garden. Yes, twice. I practise constantly, because if I lose a game I am in a rage all day, and I go looking for papists to kick.'

Once, Anne would have laughed. Not now. 'I myself do not care for this ambassador. He does not give me his respect, as the envoy before did. None the less, you must be careful of him. You must do him all honour, because it is only King Francis who is keeping the Pope from our throats.'

Farnese as wolf. Snarling and dripping bloody drool. He is not sure she is in a mood to be talked to, but he will try. 'It is not for love of us that Francis helps us.'

'I know it is not for love.' She teases out her wet handkerchief, looking for a dry bit. 'Not for love of me, anyway. I am not such a fool.'

'It is only that he does not want the Emperor Charles to over-run us and make himself master of the world. And he does not like the bull of excommunication. He does not think it right that the Bishop of Rome or any priest should set himself up to deprive a king of his own country. But I wish France would see his own interest. It is a pity there is not a skilled man to open to him the advantages of doing as our sovereign lord has done, and taking the headship of his own church.'

'But there are not two Cremuels.' She manages a sour smile.

He waits. Does she know how the French now see her? They no longer believe she can influence Henry. They think she is a spent force. And though the whole of England has taken an oath to uphold her children, no one abroad believes that, if she fails to give Henry a son, the little Elizabeth can reign. As the French ambassador said to him (the last time he let him in): if the choice is between two females, why not prefer the elder? If Mary's blood is Spanish, at least it is royal. And at least she can walk straight and has control of her bowels.

From her corner the creature, the dwarf, comes shuffling towards Anne on her bottom; she pulls at her mistress's skirts. 'Get away, Mary,' Anne says. She laughs at his expression. 'Did you not know I have rebaptised my fool? The king's daughter is almost a dwarf, is she not? Even more squat than her mother. The French would be shocked if they saw her, I think a glimpse of her would scuttle their intentions. Oh, I know, Cremuel, I know what they are trying to do behind my back. They had my brother to and fro for talks, but they never meant to make a marriage with Elizabeth.' Ah, he thinks, she grasps it at last. 'They are trying for a match between the dauphin and the Spanish bastard. All the time they are smiling to my face and are working away behind my back. You knew this and you did not tell me.'

'Madam,' he murmurs, 'I tried.'

'It is as if I did not exist. As if my daughter had never been born. As if Katherine were still queen.' Her voice sharpens. 'I will not endure it.'

So what will you do? In the next breath she tells him. 'I have thought of a way. With Mary.' He waits. 'I might visit her,' she says. 'And not alone. With some gallant young gentlemen.'

'You do not lack for those.'

'Or why should you not visit her, Cremuel? You have some handsome boys in your train. Do you know the wretch has never had a compliment in her life?'

'From her father she has, I believe.'

'When a girl is eighteen, her father no longer counts with her. She craves other company. Believe me, I know, because once I was as foolish as any girl. A maiden of that age, she wants some-one to write her a verse. Someone who turns his eyes to her and sighs when she enters the room. Admit now, this is what we have not tried. To flatter her, seduce her.'

'You want me to compromise her?'

'Between us we can contrive it. Do it yourself even, I care not, someone told me she liked you. And I should like to see Cremuel pretending to be in love.'

'It would be a foolish man who came near Mary. I think the king would kill him.'

'I am not suggesting he bed her. God save me, I would not impose it on any friend of mine. All that is needed is to have her make a fool of herself, and do it in public, so she loses her reputation.'

'No,' he says.

'What?'

'That is not my aim and those are not my methods.'

109

Anne flushes. Anger mottles her throat. She will do anything, he thinks. Anne has no limits. 'You will be sorry,' she says, 'for the way you speak to me. You think you are grown great and that you no longer need me.' Her voice is shaking. 'I know you are talking to the Seymours. You think it is secret but nothing is secret from me. It shocked me when I heard it, I can tell you, I did not think you would put your money on such a bad risk. What has Jane Seymour got but a maidenhead, and what use is a maidenhead, the morning after? Before the event she is the queen of his heart, and after it she is just another drab who could not keep her skirts down. Jane has neither looks nor wit. She will not hold Henry a week. She will be packed off to Wolf Hall and forgotten.'

'Perhaps so,' he says. There is a chance that she is right; he would not discount it. 'Madam, things were once happier between us. You used to listen to my advice. Let me advise you now. Drop your plans and schemes. Lay down the burden of them. Keep yourself in quietness till the child is born. Do not risk its wellbeing by agitating your mind. You have said yourself, strife and contention can mark a child even before it sees the light. Bend your mind to the king's desires. As for Jane, she is pale and inconspicuous, is she not? Pretend you do not see her. Turn your head from sights that are not for you.'

She leans forward in her chair, hands clenched on her knees. 'I will advise you, Cremuel. Make terms with me before my child is born. Even if it is a girl I will have another. Henry will never abandon me. He waited for me long enough. I have made the wait worth his while. And if he turns his back on me he will turn his back on the great and marvellous work done in this realm since I became queen – I mean the work for the gospel. Henry will never return to Rome. He will never bow his knee. Since my coronation there is a new England. It cannot subsist without me.'

Not so, madam, he thinks. If need be, I can separate you from history. He says, 'I hope we are not at odds. I give you homely advice, as friend to friend. You know I am, or I was, the father of a family. I always did counsel my wife to calmness at such a time. If there is anything I can do for you, tell me and I will do it.' He looks up at her. His eyes glitter. 'But do not threaten me, good madam. I find it uncomfortable.'

She snaps, 'Your comfort is not my concern. You must study your advantage, Master Secretary. Those who are made can be unmade.'

He says, 'I entirely agree.'

He bows himself out. He pities her; she is fighting with the women's weapons that are all she has. In the anteroom to her presence chamber, Lady Rochford is alone. 'Still snivelling?' she asks.

'I think she has gathered herself.'

'She is losing her looks, don't you think? Was she too much in the sun this summer? She is beginning to line.'

'I don't look at her, my lady. Well, no more than a subject ought.'

'Oh, you don't?' She is amused. 'Then I'll tell you. She looks every day of her age and more. Faces are not incidental. Our sins are written on them.'

'Jesus! What have I done?'

She laughs. 'Mr Secretary, that is what we all would like to know. But then, perhaps it is not always true. Mary Boleyn down in the country, I hear she blossoms like the month of May. Fair and plump, they say. How is it possible? A jade like Mary, through so many hands you can't find a stable lad who hasn't had her. But put the two side by side, and it is Anne who looks – how would you express it? Well-used.'

Chattering, the other ladies flock into the room. 'Have you left her alone?' says Mary Shelton: as if Anne ought not to be alone. She picks up her skirts and flits back to the inner chamber.

He takes his leave of Lady Rochford. But something is scuffling about his feet, impeding him. It is the dwarf woman, on all fours. She growls in her throat and makes as if to nip him. He just restrains himself from kicking her away.

He goes about his day. He wonders, how can it be for Lady Rochford, to be married to a man who humiliates her, preferring to be with his whores and making no secret of it? He has no means of answering the question, he admits; no point of entry into her feelings at all. He knows he doesn't like her hand on his arm. Misery seems to leak and seep from her pores. She laughs but her eyes never laugh; they flit from face to face, they take in everything.

The day Purkoy came from Calais to the court, he had held Francis Bryan by the sleeve: 'Where can I get one?' Ah, for your mistress, that one-eyed devil had enquired: fishing for gossip. No, he had said, smiling, just for myself.

Soon Calais was in an uproar. Letters flitting across the Narrow Sea. Master Secretary would like a pretty dog. Find him one, find him one quick, before someone else gets the credit. Lady Lisle, the governor's wife, wondered if she should part with her own dog. By one hand and another, a half-dozen spaniels were whisked in. Each was parti-coloured and smiling, with a feathered tail and delicate miniature feet. Not one of them was like Purkoy, with his ears pricked, his habit of interrogation. *Pourquoi?*

Good question.

Advent: first the fast and then the feast. In the store rooms, raisins, almonds, nutmegs, mace, cloves, liquorice, figs and ginger. The King of England's envoys are in Germany, holding talks with the League of Schmalkald, the confederation of Protestant princes. The Emperor is at Naples. Barbarossa is at Constantinople. The servant Anthony is in the great hall at Stepney, perched on a ladder and wearing a robe embroidered with the moon and stars. 'All right, Tom?' he shouts.

The Christmas star sways above his head. He, Cromwell, stands looking up at its silvered edges: sharp as blades.

It was only last month that Anthony joined the household, but it is hard to think of him as a beggar at the gate. When he had rode back from his visit to Katherine, the usual press of Londoners had gathered outside Austin Friars. They might not know him up-country, but they know him here. They come to stare at his servants, at his horses and their tack, at his colours flying; but today he rides in with an anonymous guard, a bunch of tired men coming from nowhere. 'Where've you been, Lord Cromwell?' a man bawls: as if he owes the Londoners an explanation. Sometimes he sees himself, in his mind's eye, dressed in filched cast-offs, a soldier from a broken army: a starving boy, a stranger, a gawper at his own gate.

They are about to pass into the courtyard, when he says, wait; a wan face bobs by his side; a little man has weaselled through the crowd, and catches at his stirrup. He is weeping, and so evidently harmless that no one even raises a hand to him; only he, Cromwell, feels his neck bristle: this is how you are trapped, your attention snared by some staged incident while the killer comes behind with the knife. But the men at arms are a wall at his back, and this bowed wretch is shaking so much that if he whipped out a blade he would peel his own knees. He leans down. 'Do I know you? I saw you here before.'

Tears trickle down the man's face. He has no visible teeth, a state that would upset anyone. 'God bless you, my lord. May he cherish you and increase your wealth.'

'Oh, he does.' He is tired of telling people he is not their lord.

'Give me a place,' the man begs. 'I am in rags, as you see. I will sleep with the dogs if it please you.'

'The dogs might not like it.'

One of his escort closes in: 'Shall I whip him off, sir?'

At this, the man sets up a fresh wailing. 'Oh, hush,' he says, as if to a child. The lament redoubles, the tears spurt as if he had a pump behind his nose. Perhaps he cried his teeth right out of his head? Is that possible?

'I am a masterless man,' the poor creature sobs. 'My dear lord was killed in an explosion.'

'God forgive us, what kind of explosion?' His attention is riveted: are people wasting gunpowder? We may need that if the Emperor comes.

The man is rocking himself, his arms clasped across his chest; his legs seem about to give way. He, Cromwell, reaches down and hauls him up by his sagging jerkin; he doesn't want him rolling on the ground and panicking the horses. 'Stand up. Give your name.'

A choked sob: 'Anthony.'

'What can you do, besides weep?'

'If it please you, I was much valued before ... alas!' He breaks down entirely, wracked and swaying.

'Before the explosion,' he says patiently. 'Now, what was it you did? Water the orchard? Swill out the privies?'

'Alas,' the man wails. 'Neither of those. Nothing so useful.' His chest heaves. 'Sir, I was a jester.'

He lets go of his jerkin, stares at him, and begins to laugh. A disbelieving snigger runs from man to man through the crowd. His escort bow over their saddles, giggling.

The little man seems to bounce from his grip. He regains his balance and looks up at him. His cheeks are quite dry, and a sly smile has replaced the lineaments of despair. 'So,' he says, 'am I coming in?'

Now as Christmas approaches Anthony keeps the household open-mouthed with stories of the horrors that have come to people he knows, round and about the time of the Nativity: assault by innkeepers, stables catching fire, livestock wandering the hills. He does different voices for men and women, can make dogs talk impertinently to their masters, can mimic ambassador Chapuys and anyone else you name. 'Do you impersonate me?' he asks.

'You grudge me the opportunity,' Anthony says. 'A man could wish for a master who rolls his words around his mouth, or is always crossing himself and crying Jesu-Maria, or grinning, or frowning, or a man with a twitch. But you don't hum, or shuffle your feet or twirl your thumbs.'

'My father had a savage temper. I learned as a child to be still. If he noticed me, he hit me.'

'As for what is in there,' Anthony looks him in the eye, taps his forehead, 'as for what's in there, who knows? I may as well impersonate a shutter. A plank has more expression. A water butt.'

'I'll give you a good character, if you want a new master.'

'I'll get you in the end. When I learn to imitate a gatepost. A standing stone. A statue. There are statues who move their eyes. In the north country.'

'I have some of them in custody. In the strong rooms.'

'Can I have the key? I want to see if they are still moving their eyes, in the dark without their keepers.'

'Are you a papist, Anthony?'

'I may be. I like miracles. I have been a pilgrim in my time. But the fist of Cromwell is more proximate than the hand of God.'

On Christmas Eve Anthony sings 'Pastime With Good Company', in the person of the king and wearing a dish for a crown. He expands before your eyes, his meagre limbs fleshing out. The king has a silly voice, too high for a big man. It's something we pretend not to notice. But now he laughs at Anthony, his hand covering his mouth. When has Anthony seen the king? He seems to know his every gesture. I wouldn't be surprised, he thinks, if Anthony has been bustling about the court these many years, drawing a *per diem* and nobody asking what he's for or how he got on to the payroll. If he can imitate a king, he can easily imitate a busy useful fellow with places to be and business to see to.

Christmas Day comes. The bells peal at Dunstan's church. Snowflakes drift on the wind. Spaniels wear ribbons. It is Master Wriothesley who is first to arrive; he was a great actor when he was at Cambridge, and these last years he has been in charge of the plays in their household. 'Give me just a small role,' he had begged him. 'I could be a tree? Then I need not learn anything. Trees have an impromptu wit.'

'In the Indies,' Gregory says, 'trees can ambulate. They lift themselves up by their roots and if the wind blows they can move to a more sheltered spot.'

'Who told you that?'

'I'm afraid it was me,' says Call-Me-Risley. 'But he was so pleased to hear of it, I'm sure it was none harm.'

Wriothesley's pretty wife is dressed as Maid Marion, her hair loose and falling to her waist. Wriothesley is simpering in skirts, to which his toddling daughter clings. 'I've come as a virgin,' he says. 'They're so rare these days that they send unicorns out looking for them.'

'Go and change,' he says. 'I don't like it.' He lifts Master Wriothesley's veil. 'You're not very convincing, with that beard.'

Call-Me drops a curtsey. 'But I must have a disguise, sir.'

'We have a worm costume left,' Anthony says. 'Or you could be a giant striped rose.'

'St Uncumber was a virgin and grew a beard,' Gregory volunteers. 'The beard was to repulse her suitors and so guard her chastity. Women pray to her if they wish to be rid of their husbands.'

Call-Me goes to change. Worm or flower? 'You could be the worm in the bud,' Anthony suggests.

Rafe and his nephew Richard have come in; he sees them exchange a glance. He lifts Wriothesley's child in his arms, asks after her baby brother and admires her cap. 'Mistress, I have forgot your name.'

'I am called Elizabeth,' the child says.

Richard Cromwell says, 'Aren't you all, these days?'

I will win Call-Me, he thinks. I will win him away from Stephen Gardiner completely, and he will see where his true interest lies, and be loyal only to me and to his king.

When Richard Riche comes in with his wife he admires her new sleeves of russet satin. 'Robert Packington charged me six shillings,' she says, her tone outraged. 'And fourpence to line them.'

'Has Riche paid him?' He is laughing. 'You don't want to pay Packington. It only encourages him.'

When Packington himself arrives, it's with a grave face; it's clear he has something to say, and it's not just 'How do you?' His friend Humphrey Monmouth is by his side, a stalwart of the Drapers' Guild. 'William Tyndale is still in prison, and likely to be killed as I hear.' Packington hesitates, but clearly he must speak. 'I think of him in durance, as we enjoy our feast. What will you do for him, Thomas Cromwell?'

Packington is a gospel man, a reformer, one of his oldest friends. As a friend, he lays his difficulties before him: he himself cannot negotiate with the authorities in the Low Countries, he needs Henry's permission. And Henry will not grant it, as Tyndale would never give him a good opinion in the matter of his divorce. Like Martin Luther, Tyndale believes Henry's marriage to Katherine is valid, and no consideration of policy will sway him. You would think he would bend, to suit the King of England, to make a friend of him; but Tyndale is an obdurate man, plain and stubborn as a boulder.

'So must our brother burn? This is what you are telling me? A merry Christmas to you, Master Secretary.' He turns away. 'They say money follows you these days like a spaniel his master.'

He puts a hand on his arm: 'Rob –' Then pulls back, says heartily, 'They're not wrong.'

He knows what his friend thinks. Master Secretary is so powerful that he can move the king's conscience; and if he can, why does he not, unless he is too busy lining his pocket? He wants to ask, give me a day off, in Christ's name.

Monmouth says, 'You have not forgot our brothers whom Thomas More burned? And those he hounded to death? Those broken by months in prison?'

'He didn't break you. You lived to see More come down.'

'But his arm reached out of his grave,' Packington says. 'More had men everywhere, all about Tyndale. It was More's agents who betrayed him. If you cannot move the king, perhaps the queen can?'

'The queen needs help herself. And if you want to help her, tell your wives to curb their poisoned tongues.'

He moves away. Rafe's children – his stepchildren rather – are crying out to him to come and see their disguises. But the conversation, broken off, leaves a sour taste in his mouth that persists throughout the festival. Anthony pursues him with jokes, but he turns his eyes to the child dressed as an angel: it is Rafe's step-daughter, the elder child of his wife Helen. She is wearing the peacock wings he made long ago for Grace.

Long ago? It is not ten years, not nearly ten. The feathers' eyes gleam; the day is dark, but banks of candles pick out threads of gold, the scarlet splash of holly berries bound on the wall, the points of the silver star. That night, as snowflakes float to earth, Gregory asks him, 'Where do the dead live now? Do we have Purgatory or not? They say it still exists, but no one knows where. They say we do no good by praying for the suffering souls. We cannot pray them out, as once we could.'

When his family died, he had done everything as was the custom in those days: offerings, masses. 'I don't know,' he says. 'The king will not allow preaching on Purgatory, it is so contentious. You can talk to Archbishop Cranmer.' A twist of his mouth. 'He'll tell you the latest thinking.'

'I take it very hard if I cannot pray for my mother. Or if they let me pray but say I am wasting my breath because nobody hears me.'

Imagine the silence now, in that place which is no-place, that anteroom to God where each hour is ten thousand years long. Once you imagined the souls held in a great net, a web spun by God, held safe till their release into his radiance. But if the net is cut and the web broken, do they spill into freezing space, each year falling further into silence, until there is no trace of them at all?

He takes the child to a looking glass so she can see her wings. Her steps are tentative, she is in awe at herself. Mirrored, the peacock eyes speak to him. Do not forget us. As the year turns, we are here: a whisper, a touch, a feather's breath from you.

Four days later, Eustache Chapuys, the ambassador of Spain and the Holy Roman Empire, arrives in Stepney. He comes in to a warm welcome from the household, who approach him and wish him well in Latin and French. Chapuys is a Savoyard, speaks some Spanish but English hardly at all, though he is beginning to understand more than he speaks.

Back in the city their two households have been fraternising since a gusty autumn night when a fire started at the ambassador's lodging, and his wailing attendants, soot-blackened and carrying all they could salvage, came banging at the gates of Austin Friars. The ambassador lost his furniture and his wardrobe; one could not help laughing at the sight of him, wrapped in a scorched curtain with only a shirt beneath. His entourage spent the night on pallets on the floor of the hall, brother-in-law John Williamson having quit his chamber to allow the unexpected dignitary to occupy it. Next day the ambassador suffered the embarrassment of going into company in borrowed clothes too large for him; it was either that, or take the Cromwell livery, a spectacle from which an ambassador's career could never recover. He had set tailors to work at once. 'I don't know where we will replicate that violent flame-coloured silk you favour. But I'll put the word out in Venice.' Next day, he and Chapuys had walked over the ground together, under the blackened beams. The ambassador gave a low moan as he stirred with a stick the wet black sludge that had been his official papers. 'Do you think,' he had said, glancing up, 'that the Boleyns did this?'

The ambassador has never acknowledged Anne Boleyn, never been presented to her; he must forgo that pleasure, Henry has decreed, till he is ready to kiss her hand and call her queen. His allegiance is to the other queen, the exile at Kimbolton; but Henry says, Cromwell, sometime we will practise to bring Chapuys face to face with the truth. I should like to see what he would do, the king says, if he were put in Anne's path and could not avoid her.

Today the ambassador is wearing a startling hat. More like the sort that George Boleyn sports, than a hat for a grave councillor. 'What do you think, Cremuel?' He tilts it.

'Very becoming. I must get one of those.'

'Allow me to present you ...' Chapuys removes it from his head with a flourish, then reconsiders. 'No, it would not fit your big head. I shall have one made for you.' He takes his arm. '*Mon cher*, your household is a delight as always. But may we talk apart?'

In a private room, the ambassador attacks. 'They say that the king will command priests to marry.'

He is caught off-guard; but he does not mean to be jolted out of his good humour. 'There is some merit in it, for the avoiding of hypocrisy. But I can be clear with you, that will not happen. The king will not hear of it.' He looks closely at Chapuys; has he perhaps heard that Cranmer, Archbishop of Canterbury, has a secret wife? Surely he cannot know. If he did, he would denounce and ruin him. They hate Thomas Cranmer, these so-called Catholics, almost as much as they hate Thomas Cromwell. He indicates the best chair to the ambassador. 'Will you not sit and take a glass of claret?'

But Chapuys will not be diverted. 'I hear you are going to put all the monks and nuns out on the road.'

'From whom did you hear that?'

'From the mouths of the king's own subjects.'

'Listen to me, Monsieur. As my commissioners go about, I hear little from the monks but petitions to be let go. And nuns too, they cannot endure their bondage, they come to my men weeping and asking for their liberty. I have it in hand to pension the monks, or find them useful posts. If they are scholars they can be given stipends. If they are ordained priests, the parishes will use them. And the money the monks are sitting on, I should like to see some of that go to the parish priests. I do not know how it may be in your country, but some benefices only bring a man four or five shillings a year. Who will take on a cure of souls, for a sum that won't pay for his firewood? And when I have got the clergy an income they can live on, I mean to make each priest mentor to a poor scholar, so he helps him through the university. The next generation of priests will be learned, and they will instruct in their turn. Tell your master this. Tell him I mean good religion to increase, not wither.'

But Chapuys turns away. He is plucking nervously at his sleeve and his words fall over each other. 'I do not tell my master lies. I tell him what I see. I see a restless population, Cremuel, I see discontent, I see misery; I see famine, before the spring. You are buying corn from Flanders. Be thankful to the Emperor that he allows his territories to feed yours. That trade could be stopped, you know.'

'What would he gain by starving my countrymen?'

'He would gain this, that they would see how evilly they are governed, and how opprobrious are the king's proceedings. What are your envoys doing with the German princes? Talk, talk, talk, month after month. I know they hope to conclude some treaty with the Lutherans and import their practices here.'

'The king will not have the form of the Mass varied. He is clear on it.'

'Yet,' Chapuys stabs a finger in the air, 'the heretic Melanchthon has dedicated a book to him! You cannot hide a book, can you? No, deny it as you will, Henry will end by abolishing half the sacraments and making common cause with these heretics, on purpose to upset my master, who is their emperor and overlord.

Henry begins by mocking the Pope, and he will end up embracing the devil.'

'You appear to know him better than I do. Henry, I mean. Not the devil.'

He is amazed by the turn the conversation has taken. It is only ten days since he enjoyed a genial supper with the ambassador, and Chapuys assured him that the Emperor's only thought was for the realm's tranquillity. There was no talk of blockades then, no talk of starving England. 'Eustache,' he says, 'what has happened?'

Chapuys sits down abruptly, slumps forward with his elbows on his knees. His hat sinks lower, till he removes it altogether, and puts it on the table; not without a glance of regret. 'Thomas, I have heard from Kimbolton. They say the queen cannot keep her food down, she cannot even take water. In six nights she has not slept two hours together.' Chapuys grinds his fists into his eyes. 'I fear she cannot live more than a day or two. I do not want her to die alone, without anyone who loves her. I fear the king will not let me go. Will you let me go?'

The man's grief touches him; it comes from the heart, it is beyond his remit as envoy. 'We'll go to Greenwich and ask him,' he says. 'This very day. We'll go now. Put your hat back on.'

On the barge he says, 'That's a thaw wind.' Chapuys seems not to appreciate it. He huddles into himself, wrapped in layers of lambskin.

'The king intended to joust today,' he says.

Chapuys sniffs, 'In the snow?'

'He can have the field cleared.'

'No doubt by toiling monks.'

He has to laugh, at the ambassador's tenacity. 'We must hope the sport went forward, then Henry will be in a good humour. He has just come from the little princess at Eltham. You must ask after her health. And you must make her a New Year's gift, have you thought of it?'

The ambassador glowers at him. All he would give Elizabeth is a knock on the head.

'I am glad we are not iced up. Sometimes we cannot use the river for weeks. Have you seen it when it's frozen over?' No reply. 'Katherine is strong, you know. If there is no more snow and the king permits, you can ride tomorrow. She has been ill before and she has regained her ground. You will find her sitting up in bed and asking why you've come.'

'Why are you chattering?' Chapuys says gloomily. 'It is not like you.'

Why indeed? If Katherine dies it will be a great thing for England. Charles may be her fond nephew but he will not keep up a quarrel for a dead woman. The threat of war will vanish. It will be a new era. Only he hopes she does not suffer. There would be no point in that.

They tie up at the king's landing stage. Chapuys says, 'Your winters are so long. I wish I was still a young man in Italy.'

The snow is banked up on the quay, the fields are still blanketed. The ambassador received his education in Turin. You don't get this sort of wind there, shrieking around the towers like a soul in torment. 'You forget the swamps and the bad air, don't you?' he says. 'I'm like you, I only remember the sunshine.' He puts a hand under the ambassador's elbow to steer him on to dry land. Chapuys himself keeps a firm hold on his hat. Its tassels are damp and drooping, and the ambassador himself looks as if he might cry.

Harry Norris is the gentleman who greets them. 'Ah, "gentle Norris",' Chapuys whispers. 'One could do worse.'

Norris is, as always, the pattern of courtesy. 'We ran a few courses,' he says, in answer to enquiry. 'His Majesty had the best of it. You will find him cheerful. Now we are getting dressed for the masque.'

He never sees Norris but he remembers Wolsey stumbling from his own home before the king's men, fleeing to a cold empty house at Esher: the cardinal kneeling in the mud and gibbering his thanks, because the king by way of Norris had sent him a token of good-will. Wolsey was kneeling to thank God, but it looked as if he were kneeling to Norris. It doesn't matter how Norris oils around him now; he can never wipe that scene from his mind's eye.

Inside the palace, a roaring heat, stampeding feet; musicians toting their instruments, upper servants bawling brutish orders at lower. When the king comes out to greet them, it is with the French ambassador at his side. Chapuys is taken aback. An effusive greeting is *de rigueur*; kiss-kiss. How smoothly, easily, Chapuys has slipped back into his persona; with what a courteous flourish he makes his reverence to His Majesty. Such a practised diplomat can even cajole his stiff knee joints; not for the first time, Chapuys reminds him of a dancing master. The remarkable hat he holds by his side.

'Merry Christmas, ambassador,' the king says. He adds hopefully, 'The French have already made me great gifts.'

'And the Emperor's gifts will be with Your Majesty at New Year,' Chapuys boasts. 'You will find them even more magnificent.'

The French ambassador eyes him. 'Merry Christmas, Cremuel. Not bowling today?'

'Today I am at your disposal, Monsieur.'

'I take my leave,' the Frenchman says. He looks sardonic; the king has already linked his arm with Chapuys's. 'Majesty, may I assure you in parting that my master King François has knit his heart to yours?' His glance sweeps over Chapuys. 'With the friendship of France, you may be assured you will reign unmolested, and need no longer fear Rome.'

'Unmolested?' he says: he, Cromwell. 'Well, ambassador, that's gracious of you.'

124

The Frenchman skims by him with a curt nod. Chapuys stiffens as French brocade grazes his own person; snatches his hat away, as if to save it from contamination. 'Shall I hold that for you?' Norris whispers.

But Chapuys has fastened his attention on the king. 'Katherine the queen ...' he begins.

'The Dowager Princess of Wales,' Henry says sternly. 'Yes, I hear the old woman is off her food again. Is that what you're here about?'

Harry Norris whispers, 'I have to dress up as a Moor. Will you excuse me, Mr Secretary?'

'Gladly, in this case,' he says. Norris melts away. For the next ten minutes he has to stand and hear the king lying fluently. The French, he says, have made him great promises, all of which he believes. The Duke of Milan is dead, both Charles and Francis claim the duchy, and unless they can resolve it there will be war. Of course, he is always a friend to the Emperor, but the French have promised him towns, they have promised him castles, a seaport even, so in duty to the commonweal he must think seriously about a formal alliance. However, he knows the Emperor has it in his power to make offers as good, if not better ...

'I will not dissemble with you,' Henry tells Chapuys. 'As an Englishman, I am always straight in my dealings. An Englishman never lies nor deceives, even for his own profit.'

'It seems,' Chapuys snaps, 'that you are too good to live. If you cannot mind your country's interests, I must mind them for you. They will not give you territory, whatever they say. May I remind you what poor friends the French have been to you these last months while you have not been able to feed your people? If it were not for the shipments of grain my master permits, your subjects would be corpses piled from here to the Scots border.'

Some exaggeration there. Lucky that Henry is in holiday humour. He likes feasts, pastimes, an hour in the lists, a masque in prospect; he likes even more the idea that his former wife is lying in the fens gasping her last. 'Come, Chapuys,' he says. 'We will have private conference in my chamber.' He draws the ambassador with him and, over his head, winks.

But Chapuys stops dead. The king must stop too. 'Majesty, we can speak of this hereafter. My mission now brooks no delay. I beg for permission to ride where the ... where Katherine is. And I implore you to allow her daughter to see her. It may be for the last time.'

'Oh, I could not be moving the Lady Mary around without my council's advice. And I see no hope of convening them today. The roads, you know. As for you, how do you propose to travel? Have you wings?' The king chuckles. He reasserts his grip and bears the ambassador away. A door closes. He, Cromwell, stands glaring at it. What further lies will be told behind it? Chapuys will have to bargain his mother's bones away to match these great offers Henry claims he has from the French.

He thinks, what would the cardinal do? Wolsey used to say, 'Never let me hear you claim, "You don't know what goes on behind closed doors." Find out.'

So. He is going to think of some reason to follow them in there. But here is Norris blocking his path. In his Moorish drapery, his face blacked, he is playful, smiling, but still vigilant. Prime Christmas game: let's fuck about with Cromwell. He is about to spin away Norris by his silken shoulder, when a small dragon comes waggling along. 'Who is in that dragon?' he asks.

Norris snorts. 'Francis Weston.' He pushes back his woolly wig to reveal his noble forehead. 'Said dragon is going to waggle waggle to the queen's apartments to beg for sweetmeats.'

He grins. 'You sound bitter, Harry Norris.'

Why would he not? He's served his time at the queen's door. On her threshold.

Norris says, 'She will play with him and pat his little rump. She's fond of puppy dogs.'

'Did you find out who killed Purkoy?'

'Don't say that,' the Moor beseeches. 'It was an accident.'

At his elbow, causing him to turn, is William Brereton. 'Where's that thrice-blasted dragon?' he enquires. 'I'm supposed to get after it.'

Brereton is dressed as an antique huntsman, wearing the skin of one of his victims. 'Is that real leopard skin, William? Where did you catch it, up in Chester?' He feels it critically. Brereton seems to be naked beneath it. 'Is that proper?' he asks.

Brereton snarls, 'It's the season of licence. If you were forced to impersonate an antique hunter, would you wear a jerkin?'

'As long as the queen is not treated to the sight of your *attributi*.'

The Moor giggles. 'He wouldn't be showing her anything she hasn't seen.'

He raises an eyebrow. 'Has she?'

Norris blushes easily, for a Moor. 'You know what I meant. Not William's. The king's.'

He holds up a hand. 'Please take note, I am not the one who introduced this topic. By the way, the dragon went in that direction.'

He remembers last year, Brereton swaggering through Whitehall, whistling like a stable boy; breaking off to say to him, 'I hear the king, when he does not like the papers you bring in to him, knocks you well about the pate.'

You'll be knocked, he had said to himself. Something in this man makes him feel he is a boy again, a sullen belligerent little ruffian fighting on the riverbank at Putney. He has heard it before, this rumour put about to demean him. Anyone who knows Henry knows it is impossible. He is the first gentleman of Europe, his courtesy unflawed. If he wants someone stricken, he employs a subject to do it; he would not sully his own hand. It is true they sometimes disagree. But if Henry were to touch him, he would walk away. There are princes in Europe who want him. They make him offers; he could have castles.

Now he watches Brereton, as he heads towards the queen's suite, bow slung over his furry shoulder. He turns to speak to Norris, but his voice is drowned out by a metallic clatter, a clash as of guardsmen: shouts of 'Make way for my lord the Duke of Suffolk.'

The duke's upper body is still armed; perhaps he has been out there in the yard, jousting by himself. His large face is flushed, his beard – more impressive year on year – spreads over his breastplate. The valiant Moor steps forward to say, 'His Majesty is in conference with –' but Brandon knocks him aside, as if he were on a crusade.

He, Cromwell, follows on the duke's heels. If he had a net, he would drop it over him. Brandon bangs once on the king's door with his fist, then throws it open before him. 'Leave what you're doing, Majesty. You want to hear this, by God. You're quit of the old lady. She is on her deathbed. You will soon be a widower. Then you can get rid of the other one, and marry into France, by God, and lay your hands on Normandy as dowry ...' He notices Chapuys. 'Oh. Ambassador. Well, you can take yourself off. No use you staying for scraps. Go home and make your own Christmas, we don't want you here.'

Henry has turned white. 'Think what you are saying.' He approaches Brandon as if he might knock him down; which, if he had a poleaxe, he could. 'My wife is carrying a child. I am lawfully married.'

'Oh.' Charles blows out his cheeks. 'Yes, as far as that goes. But I thought you said –'

He, Cromwell, hurls himself towards the duke. Where in the name of Satan's sister did Charles get this notion? Marry into France? It must be the king's plan, as Brandon has none of his own. It looks as if Henry is carrying on two foreign policies: one he knows about and one he doesn't. He takes a grip on Brandon. He is a head shorter. He doesn't think he can move half a ton of idiot, still padded and partly armed. But it seems he can, he can move him fast, fast, and try to get him out of earshot of the ambassador, whose face is astonished. Only when he has propelled Brandon across the presence chamber does he stop and demand, 'Suffolk, where do you get this from?'

'Ah, we noble lords know more than you do. The king makes plain to us his real intentions. You think you know all his secrets, but you are mistaken, Cromwell.'

'You heard what he said. Anne is carrying his child. You are mad if you think he will turn her out now.'

'He's mad if he thinks it's his.'

'What?' He pulls back from Brandon as if the breastplate were hot. 'If you know anything against the queen's honour, you are bound as a subject to speak plainly.'

Brandon wrenches his arm away. 'I spoke plain before and look where it got me. I told him about her and Wyatt, and he kicked me out of the court and back to the east country.'

'Drag Wyatt into this, and I'll kick you to China.'

The duke's face is congested with rage. How has it come to this? Only weeks ago, Brandon was asking him to be godfather to the son he has with his new little wife. But now the duke snarls, 'Get back to your abacus, Cromwell. You are only for fetching in money, when it comes to the affairs of nations you cannot deal, you are a common man of no status, and the king himself says so, you are not fit to talk to princes.'

Brandon's hand in his chest, shoving him back: once again, the duke is making for the king's person. It is Chapuys, frozen in dignity and sorrow, who imposes some order, stepping between the king and the heaving, boiling mass of the duke. 'I take my leave, Majesty. As always I find you a most gracious prince. If I am in time, as I trust I shall be, my master will be consoled to have news of his aunt's final hours from the hand of his own envoy.'

'I can do no less,' Henry says, sobered. 'God speed.'

'I ride at first light,' Chapuys tells him; rapidly, they walk away, through the morris men and the bobbing hobby horses, through a merman and his shoal, skirting round a castle that rumbles towards them, painted masonry on oiled wheels.

Outside on the quay Chapuys turns to him. Within his mind, oiled wheels must be revolving; what he has heard about the woman he calls the concubine, he will already be coding into dispatches. They cannot pretend between them that he did not hear; when Brandon bawls, trees fall in Germany. It would not be surprising if the ambassador were cawing in triumph: not at the thought of a French marriage, to be sure, but at the thought of Anne's eclipse.

But Chapuys keeps his countenance; he is very pale, very earnest. 'Cremuel,' he says, 'I note the duke's comments. About your person. About your position.' He clears his throat. 'For what it is worth, I am myself a man of humble origins. Though not perhaps so low ...'

He knows Chapuys's history. His people are petty lawyers, two generations away from the soil.

'And again for what it is worth, I believe you are fit to deal. I would back you in any assemblage this side of Heaven. You are an eloquent and learned man. If I wanted an advocate to argue for my life, I would give you the brief.'

'You dazzle me, Eustache.'

'Go back to Henry. Move him that the princess might see her mother. A dying woman, what policy can it hurt, what interest ...' One angry, dry sob breaks out of the poor man's throat. In a moment he recovers himself. He removes his hat, stares at it, as if he cannot think where he got it. 'I do not think I should wear this hat,' he says. 'It is more a Christmas hat, would you say? Still, I am loath to lose it, it is quite unique.'

'Give it to me. I will have it sent to your house and you can wear it on your return.' When you are out of mourning, he thinks. 'Look ... I will not raise your hopes about Mary.'

'You being an Englishman, who never lies or deceives.' Chapuys gives a bark of laughter. 'Jesu-Maria!'

130

'The king will not permit any meeting that could strengthen Mary's spirit of disobedience.'

'Even if her mother is on her deathbed?'

'Especially then. We do not wants oaths, deathbed promises. You see that?'

He speaks to his bargemaster: I shall stay here and see how it goes with the dragon, whether he eats the hunter or what. Convey the ambassador up to London, he must prepare for a journey. 'But how will you get back yourself?' Chapuys says.

'Crawl, if Brandon has his way.' He puts his hand on the little man's shoulder. Says softly, 'This clears the way, you know? For an alliance with your master. Which will be very good for England and her trade, and is what you and I both want. Katherine has come between us.'

'And what about the French marriage?'

'There will be no French marriage. It is a fairy tale. Go. It will be dark in an hour. I hope you rest tonight.'

Already, twilight steals across the Thames; there are crepuscular deeps in the lapping waves, and a blue dusk creeps along the banks. He says to one of the boatmen, do you think the roads north will be open? God help me, sir, the man says: I only know the river, and anyway I've never stirred north of Enfield.

When he arrives back in Stepney torchlight spills out of the house, and the singing children, in a state of high excitement, are carolling in the garden; dogs are barking, black shapes bobbing against the snow, and a dozen mounds, ghostly white, tower over the frozen hedges. One, taller than the rest, wears a mitre; it has a stub of blue-tinged carrot for its nose, and a smaller stub for its cock. Gregory pitches towards him, a swirl of excitement: 'Look, sir, we have made the Pope out of snow.'

'First we made the Pope.' The glowing face beside him belongs to Dick Purser, the boy who keeps the watchdogs. 'We made the

Pope, sir, and then he looked harmless by himself and so we made a set of cardinals. Do you like them?'

His kitchen boys swarm about him, frosted and dripping. The whole household has turned out, or at least everyone under thirty. They have lit a bonfire – well away from the snowmen – and appear to be dancing around it, led by his boy Christophe.

Gregory gets his breath. 'We only did it for the better setting forth of the king's supremacy. I do not think it is wrong, because we can blow a trumpet then kick them flat, and cousin Richard said we may, and he himself moulded the Pope's head, and Master Wriothesley who was here looking for you thrust in the Pope's little member and laughed at it.'

'Such children you are!' he says. 'I like them very much. We will have the fanfare tomorrow when there's more light, shall we?'

'And can we fire a cannon?'

'Where would I get a cannon?'

'Speak to the king, sir.' Gregory is laughing; he knows the cannon is a step too far.

Dick Purser's sharp eye has fallen on the ambassador's hat. 'Might we borrow that? We have done ill with the Pope's tiara, because we did not know how it should look.'

He spins the hat in his hand. 'You're right, this is more the sort of thing Farnese wears. But no. This hat is a sacred charge. I have to answer to the Emperor for it. Now, let me go,' he says, laughing, 'I must write letters, we look for great changes soon.'

'Stephen Vaughan is here,' Gregory says.

'Is he? Ah. Good. I have a use for him.'

He tramps towards the house, firelight licking his heels. 'Pity Master Vaughan,' Gregory says. 'I think he came for his supper.'

'Stephen!' A hasty embrace. 'No time,' he says. 'Katherine is dying.'

'What?' his friend says. 'I heard nothing of this in Antwerp.'

132

Vaughan is always in transit. He is about to be in transit again. He is Cromwell's servant, he is the king's servant, he is the king's eyes and ears across the Narrow Sea; nothing passes with the Flemish merchants or the guilds at Calais that Stephen does not know and report. 'I am bound to say, Master Secretary, you keep a disorderly household. One might as well eat supper in a field.'

'You are in a field,' he says. 'More or less. Or you soon will be. You must get on the road.'

'But I am just off the ship!'

This is how Stephen manifests his friendship: constant complaints, carping and grumbles. He turns and issues orders: feed Vaughan, water Vaughan, bed down Vaughan, have a good horse ready to go at dawn. 'Don't fret, you can sleep the night. Then you must escort Chapuys up to Kimbolton. You speak the languages, Stephen! Nothing must pass in French or Spanish or Latin, but I know every word.'

'Ah. I see.' Stephen draws his person together.

'Because I think that if Katherine dies, Mary will be desperate to take ship for the Emperor's domains. He is her cousin, after all, and though she should not trust him, she cannot be convinced of that. And we can hardly chain her to the wall.'

'Keep her up-country. Keep her where there is no port in two days' ride.'

'If Chapuys saw an exit for her, she would fly on the wind and set to sea in a sieve.'

'Thomas.' Vaughan, a grave man, lays a hand upon him. 'What is all this agitation? It is not like you. You are afraid of being bested by a little girl?'

He would like to tell Vaughan what has passed, but how to convey the texture of it: the smoothness of Henry's lies, the solid weight of Brandon when he shoved him, dragged him, man-handled him away from the king; the raw wetness of the wind on his face, the taste of blood in his mouth. It will always be like this, he thinks. It will go on being like this. Advent, Lent, Whitsuntide. 'Look,' he sighs, 'I must go and write to Stephen Gardiner in France. If this is the end of Katherine, I must make sure he knows it from me.'

'No more grovelling to Frenchmen for our salvation,' Stephen says. Is that a grin? It is a wolfish one. Stephen is a merchant, and he values the Low Countries trade. When relations with the Emperor founder, England runs out of money. When the Emperor is on our side, we grow rich. 'We can patch all the quarrels,' Stephen says. 'Katherine was the cause of all. Her nephew will be as relieved as we are. He never wanted to invade us. And now he has enough to do with Milan. Let him scrap with the French if he must. Our king will be free. A free hand to do as he likes.'

That is what worries me, he thinks. This free hand. He makes his apologies to Stephen. Vaughan stops him. 'Thomas. You will wreck yourself with this pace you keep up. Do you ever consider, that half your years be spent?'

'Half? Stephen, I am fifty.'

'I forget.' A little laugh. 'Fifty already? I don't know you have changed much since ever I knew you.'

'That is an illusion,' he says. 'But I promise to take a rest, when you do.'

In his cabinet it is warm. He closes the shutters, insulating himself from the white glare without. He sits down to write to Gardiner, commending him. The king is very pleased with his embassy to France. He is sending funds.

He puts down his pen. Whatever possessed Charles Brandon? He knows there has been gossip that Anne's child is not Henry's. There has even been gossip that she is not with child at all, only pretending; and it is true she seems very uncertain when it will be born. But he had thought these rumours were blowing from France into England; and what would they know at the French court? He has dismissed it as empty malice. It is what Anne attracts; that is her misfortune, or one of them.

Under his hand there is a letter from Calais, from Lord Lisle. He feels exhausted at the thought of it. Lisle is telling him all about his Christmas Day, from his first waking in the frosty dawn. At some point in the festivities, Lord Lisle received an insult: the Mayor of Calais kept him waiting. So he, in his turn, kept the Mayor waiting … and now both parties are writing to him: which is more important, Master Secretary, governor or mayor? Say it is me, say it is me!

Arthur Lord Lisle is the pleasantest man in the world; except, clearly, when the mayor cuts across him. But he is in debt to the king and has not paid a penny in seven years. He should perhaps do something about that; the treasurer of the king's chamber has sent him a note about it. And on that subject … Harry Norris, by virtue of his position in the king's immediate household, by some custom the origin and use of which he has never fathomed, is in charge of the secret funds which the king has stashed in his principal houses, for use in some exigency; it is not clear what would free up these funds, or where they come from, or how much coin is stored, or who has access if Norris were to … if Norris were to be off duty when the need arose. Or if Norris were to meet with some accident. Once again he lays down his quill. He starts to imagine accidents. He puts his head in his hands, fingertips over tired eyes. He sees Norris flying from his horse. Sees Norris tumbled in the mud. Says to himself, 'Get back to your abacus, Cromwell.'

His New Year gifts have started to come in already. A supporter in Ireland has sent him a roll of white Irish blankets and a flask of aqua vitae. He would like to swaddle himself in the blankets, drain the flask, roll over on the floor and sleep.

Ireland is quiet this Christmas, in greater peace than she has seen for forty years. Mainly he has brought this about by hanging people. Not many: just the right ones. It's an art, a necessary art; the Irish chiefs have been begging the Emperor to use the country as a landing stage, for his invasion of England.

He takes a breath. Lisle, mayor, insults, Lisle. Calais, Dublin, secret funds. He wants Chapuys to get to Kimbolton in time. But he doesn't want Katherine to rally. You should not desire, he knows, the death of any human creature. Death is your prince, you are not his patron; when you think he is engaged elsewhere, he will batter down your door, walk in and wipe his boots on you.

He sifts his papers. More chronicles of monks who sit in the alehouse all night and come reeling to the cloister at dawn; more priors found under hedges with prostitutes; more prayers, more pleas; tales of neglectful clergy who won't christen children or bury the dead. He sweeps them away. Enough. A stranger writes to him – an old man judging by his hand – to say that the conversion of the Mohammedans is imminent. But what sort of church can we offer them? Unless there is sweeping change soon, the letter says, the heathens will be in more darkness than before. And you are Vicar General, Master Cromwell, you are the king's vicegerent: what are you going to do about it?

He wonders, does the Turk work his people as hard as Henry works me? If I had been born an infidel I could have been a pirate. I could have sailed the Middle Sea.

As he turns up the next paper he almost laughs; some hand has laid before him a fat land grant, from the king to Charles Brandon. It is pastureland and woodland, furze and heath, and the manors sprinkled through it: Harry Percy, the Earl of Northumberland, has made over this land to the Crown in part payment of his massive debts. Harry Percy, he thinks: I told him I would bring him down for his part in destroying Wolsey. And by God, I have not broken sweat; with his manner of life he has destroyed himself. It only remains to take his earldom away, as I swore I would.

The door opens, discreetly; it is Rafe Sadler. He looks up, surprised. 'You should be with your household.'

'I heard you had been at court, sir. I thought there might be letters to write.'

'Go through these, but not tonight.' He bundles over the papers for the grants. 'Brandon may not get many such presents this New Year.' He tells Rafe what has passed: Suffolk's outburst, Chapuys's amazed face. He does not tell him what Suffolk said, about how he was not fit to deal in the affairs of his betters; he shakes his head and says, 'Charles Brandon, I was looking at him today ... you know how he used to be cried up as a handsome fellow? The king's own sister fell in love with him. But now, that big slab face of his ... he has no more grace than a dripping pan.'

Rafe pulls up a low stool and sits thinking, forearms laid on the desk, his head pillowed on them. They are used to each other's silent company. He inches a candle closer and frowns at some more papers, makes marginal marks. The king's face rises before him: not Henry as he was today, but Henry as he was at Wolf Hall, coming from the garden, his expression dazed, drops of rain on his jacket: and the pale circle of Jane Seymour's face by his side.

After a time he glances at Rafe: 'Are you all right down there, little man?'

Rafe says, 'This house always smells of apples.'

It is true; Great Place is set among orchards, and the summer seems to linger in the garrets where the fruit is stored. At Austin Friars the gardens are raw, saplings bound to stakes. But this is an old house; it was a cottage once, but it was built up for his own use by Sir Henry Colet, father of the learned Dean of St Paul's. When Sir Henry died Lady Christian lived out her days here, and then by Sir Henry's will the house devolved to the Mercers' Guild. He holds it on a fifty-year sub-lease, which should see him out, and Gregory in. Gregory's children can grow up wrapped in the aroma of baking, of honey and sliced apples, raisins and cloves. He says, 'Rafe. I must get Gregory married.'

'I'll make a memorandum,' Rafe says, and laughs.

A year ago, Rafe could not laugh. Thomas, his first child, had lived only a day or two after he was baptised. Rafe took it like a

Christian man, but it sobered him, and he was a sober young man already. Helen had children by her first husband, but had never lost one; she took it badly. Yet this year, after a long and harsh labour that frightened her, she has another son in the cradle, and they have called him Thomas too. May it bring him better fortune than his brother; reluctant as he was to come out and face the world, he seems strong, and Rafe has relaxed into fatherhood.

'Sir,' Rafe says. 'I have been wanting to ask. Is that your new hat?'

'No,' he says gravely. 'It is the hat of the ambassador of Spain and the Empire. Would you like to try it on?'

A commotion at the door. It is Christophe. He cannot enter in the ordinary way; he treats doors as his foe. His face is still black from the bonfire. 'A woman is here for you, sir. Very urgent. She will not be sent away.'

'What manner of woman?'

'Quite old. But not so old you would kick her downstairs. Not on a cold night like this.'

'Oh, for shame,' he says. 'Wash your face, Christophe.' He turns to Rafe. 'An unknown woman. Am I inky?'

'You'll do.'

In his great hall, waiting for him by the light of sconces, a lady who lifts her veil and speaks to him in Castilian: Maria, Lady Willoughby, once Maria de Salinas. He is aghast: how is this possible, he asks, she has come alone from her house in London, at night, in the snow?

She cuts him short. 'I come to you in desperation. I cannot get to the king. There is no time to lose. I must have a pass. You must give me a paper. Or when I arrive at Kimbolton they will not let me in.'

But he switches her to English; in any dealings with Katherine's friends, he wants witnesses. 'My lady, you cannot travel in this weather.'

'Here.' She fumbles for a letter. 'Read this, it is from the queen's physician, his own hand. My mistress is in pain and afraid and alone.'

He takes the paper. Some twenty-five years ago, when Katherine's entourage had first arrived in England, Thomas More had described them as hunchbacked pygmies, refugees from Hell. He cannot comment; he was still out of England himself, and far from the court, but it sounds like one of More's poetic exaggerations. This lady came a little later; she was Katherine's favourite; only her marriage to an Englishman had parted them. She was beautiful then, and now, a widow, she is beautiful still; she knows it and will use it, even when she is shrinking with misery and blue with cold. She swirls out of her cloak, and gives it to Rafe Sadler, as if he stood there for that purpose. She crosses the room and takes his hands. 'Mother of God, Thomas Cromwell, let me go. You will not refuse me this.'

He glances at Rafe. The boy is as immune to Spanish passion as he might be to a wet dog buffeting the door. 'You must understand, Lady Willoughby,' Rafe says coolly, 'that this is a family matter, not even a council matter. You may beseech Master Secretary all you like, but it is for the king to say who visits the dowager.'

'Look, my lady,' he says. 'The weather is filthy. Even if it thaws tonight, it will be worse up-country. I cannot guarantee your safety, even if I give you an escort. You might fall from your horse.'

'I will walk there!' she says. 'How will you stop me, Master Secretary? Keep me in chains? Will you have your black-faced peasant tie me up and lock me in a closet till the queen is dead?'

'You are ridiculous, madam,' Rafe says. He seems to feel some need to step in and protect him, Cromwell, from women's wiles. 'It is as Master Secretary says. You cannot ride in this weather. You are no longer young.'

Under her breath she utters a prayer, or curse. 'Thank you for your gallant reminder, Master Sadler, without your advice I might have thought myself sixteen. Ah, do you see, I am an Englishwoman now! I know how to say the opposite of what I mean.' A shadow of calculation crosses her face. 'The cardinal would have let me go.'

'Then what a pity he is not here to tell us about it.' But he takes the cloak from Rafe, places it around her shoulders. 'Go, then. I see you are determined. Chapuys is riding up there with a pass, so perhaps …'

'I am sworn to be on the road at dawn. God turn his back on me, if I am not. I shall outpace Chapuys, he is not impelled as I am.'

'Even if you get there … it is a harsh country and the roads barely worth the name. You might reach the castle itself and have a fall. Even under the walls.'

'What?' she says. 'Oh, I see.'

'Bedingfield has his orders. But he could not leave a lady in a snowdrift.'

She kisses him. 'Thomas Cromwell. God and the Emperor will requite you.'

He nods. 'I trust in God.'

She sweeps out. They can hear her voice raised in enquiry: 'What are these strange mounds of snow?'

'I hope they do not tell her,' he says to Rafe. 'She is a papist.'

'One never kisses me like that,' Christophe complains.

'Perhaps if you washed your face,' he says. He looks keenly at Rafe. 'You would not have let her go.'

'I would not,' Rafe says stiffly. 'The ruse would not have occurred to me. And even if it had … no, I would not, I would have been afraid to cross the king.'

'That's why you will thrive and live to be old.' He shrugs. 'She will ride. Chapuys will ride. And Stephen Vaughan will watch them both. Are you coming tomorrow morning? Bring Helen and her daughters. Not the baby, it's too cold. We are going to have a fanfare, Gregory says, and then trample the papal court into the ground.'

'She loved the wings,' Rafe says. 'Our little girl. She wants to know if she can wear them every year.'

'I don't see why not. Till Gregory has a daughter big enough.'

They embrace. 'Try to sleep, sir.'

He knows Brandon's words will go round in his head when that head touches the pillow. 'When it comes to the affairs of nations you cannot deal, you are not fit to talk to princes.' Useless to swear vengeance on Duke Dripping Pan. He will undo himself, and perhaps for good this time, shouting around Greenwich that Henry is a cuckold. Surely even an old favourite cannot get away with that?

Besides, Brandon's right. A duke can represent his master at the court of a foreign king. Or a cardinal; even if he is low-born like Wolsey, his office in the church dignifies him. A bishop like Gardiner; he may be of dubious provenance, but by his office he is Stephen Winchester, incumbent of England's richest see. But Cremuel remains a nobody. The king gives him titles that no one abroad understands, and jobs that no one at home can do. He multiplies offices, duties pile on him: plain Master Cromwell goes out at morning, plain Master Cromwell comes in at night. Henry had offered him the Lord Chancellor's post; no, don't disturb Lord Audley, he had said. Audley does a good job; Audley, in fact, does as he's told. Perhaps, though, he should have agreed? He sighs, at the thought of wearing the chain. You cannot, surely, be both Lord Chancellor and Master Secretary? And he will not give up that post. It doesn't matter if it gives him a lesser status. It doesn't matter if the French don't comprehend. Let them judge by results. Brandon can make a racket, unreproved, near the royal person; he can slap the king on the back and call him Harry; he can chuckle with him over ancient jests and tilt-yard escapades. But chivalry's day is over. One day soon moss will grow in the tilt yard. The days of the moneylender have arrived, and the days of the swaggering privateer; banker sits down with banker, and kings are their waiting boys.

Last thing, he opens the shutter to say good night to the Pope. He hears a drip from a drainage spout above, he hears the deep groan as snow slides across the tiles above him, and falls in a clean sheet of white that for a second obliterates his view. His eyes follow it; with a little puff like white smoke, the fallen snow joins the trodden slush on the ground. He was right about the wind on the river. He draws the shutter closed. The thaw has begun. The great spoiler of souls, with his conclave, is left dripping in the dark.

At New Year he visits Rafe in his new house at Hackney, three storeys of brick and glass by St Augustine's church. On his first visit at summer's end, he had noted everything in place for Rafe's happy life: pots of basil on the kitchen sills, garden plots seeded and the bees in their hives, the doves in their cote and the frames in place for the roses that will climb them; the pale oak-panelled walls gleaming in expectation of paint.

Now the house is settled, bedded in, scenes from the gospels glowing on the wall: Christ as fisher of men, a startled steward tasting the good wine at Cana. In an upper room reached by the steep steps from the parlour, Helen reads Tyndale's gospel as her maids sew: '... by grace are ye saved.' St Paul may not suffer a woman to teach, but it is not exactly teaching. Helen has put off the poverty of her early life. The husband who beat her is dead, or gone so far away that we count him dead. She can become Sadler's wife, a rising man in Henry's service; she can become a serene hostess, a learned woman. But she cannot lose her history. One day the king will say, 'Sadler, why do you not bring your wife to court, is she very ugly?'

He will interrupt: 'No sir; very beautiful.' But Rafe will add, 'Helen is lowly born and does not know court manners.'

'Why did you wed her?' Henry will demand. And then his face will soften: Ah, I see, for love.

Now Helen takes his hands and wishes him a continuance of good fortune. 'I pray to God every day for you, for you were the origin of my happiness when you took me into your house. I pray him send you health and good luck and the king's listening ear.'

He kisses her and holds her close as if she were his daughter. His godson is howling in the next room.

On Twelfth Night the last marzipan moon is eaten up. The star is taken down, Anthony supervising. Its wicked points are fitted into their sleeves, and it is carried carefully to its store room. The peacock wings sigh into their linen shroud, and are hung on their peg behind the door.

Reports come from Vaughan that the old queen is better. Chapuys thinks so well of her that he is on the road back to London. He found her wasted, so weak that she could not sit up. But now she is eating again, taking comfort in the company of her friend Maria de Salinas; her gaolers were forced to admit this lady, after she suffered an accident under the very walls.

But later he, Cromwell, will hear of how on the evening of 6 January – just about the time, he thinks, that we were seeing our Christmas into store – Katherine grew restless. She felt herself failing, and during the night she told her chaplain that she would like to take communion: asking anxiously, what hour is it now? It is not yet four o'clock, he told her, but in case of urgency, the canonical hour can be advanced. Katherine waits it out, lips moving, a holy medal folded in her palm.

She will die that day, she says. She has studied death, many times anticipated it, and she is not shy at its approach. She dictates her wishes about her burial arrangements, which she does not expect to be observed. She asks for her household to be paid off, her debts to be settled.

At ten in the morning a priest anoints her, touching the holy oil to her eyelids and lips, her hands and feet. These lids will now seal and not reopen, she will neither look nor see. These lips have finished their prayers. These hands will sign no more papers. These feet have finished their journey. By noon her breathing is stertorous, she is labouring to her end. At two o'clock, light cast into her chamber by the fields of snow, she resigns from life. As she draws her last breath, the sombre forms of her keepers close in. They are reluctant to disturb the aged chaplain, and the old women shuffling from her bedside. Before they have washed her, Bedingfield has put his fastest rider on the road.

8 January: the news arrives at court. It filters out from the king's rooms then runs riot up staircases to the rooms where the queen's maids are dressing, and through the cubby holes where kitchen boys huddle to doze, and along lanes and passages through the breweries and the cold rooms for keeping fish, and up again through the gardens to the galleries and bounces up to the carpeted chambers where Anne Boleyn sinks to her knees and says, 'At last God, not before time!' The musicians tune up for the celebrations.

Anne the queen wears yellow, as she did when she first appeared at court, dancing in a masque: the year, 1521. Everyone remembers it, or they say they do: Boleyn's second daughter with her bold dark eyes, her speed, her grace. The fashion for yellow had started among the wealthy in Basle; for a few months, if a draper could get hold of it, he could make a killing. And then suddenly it was everywhere, in sleeves and hose and even hairbands for those who couldn't afford more than a sliver. By the time of Anne's debut it had slid down the scale abroad; in the domains of the Emperor, you'd see a woman in a brothel hoisting her fat dugs and tight-lacing her yellow bodice.

Does Anne know this? Today her gown is worth five times the one she wore when her father was her only banker. It is sewn over with pearls, so that she moves in a blur of primrose light. He says to Lady Rochford, do we call it a new colour, or an old colour come back? Will you be wearing it, my lady?

She says, I don't think it suits any complexion, myself. And Anne should stick to black.

On this happy occasion, Henry wants to show off the princess. You would think such a small child – she is now almost two and a half – would be looking about her for her nurse, but Elizabeth chuckles as she is passed hand-to-hand by the gentlemen, scuffing up their beards and batting at their hats. Her father bounces her in his arms. 'She looks forward to seeing her little brother, don't you, dumpling?'

There is a stir from the courtiers; all Europe knows Anne's condition, but it is the first time it has been mentioned in public. 'And I share her impatience,' the king says. 'It's been long enough to wait.'

Elizabeth's face is losing its baby roundness. Hail Princess Ferret Face. The older courtiers say they can see the king's father in her, and his brother, Prince Arthur. She has her mother's eyes though, busy and full in their orbits. He thinks Anne's eyes beautiful, though best when they gleam with interest, as a cat's do when she sees the whisk of some small creature's tail.

The king seizes back his darling and coos to her. 'Up to the sky!' he says, and tosses her up, then swoops her down and plants a kiss on her head.

Lady Rochford says, 'Henry has a tender heart, does he not? Of course, he is pleased with any child. I have seen him kiss a stranger's baby in much the same way.'

At the first sign of fractiousness the child is taken away, wrapped tight in furs. Anne's eyes follow her. Henry says, as if remembering his manners, 'We must accept that the country will mourn for the dowager.'

Anne says, 'They didn't know her. How can they mourn? What was she to them? A foreigner.'

'I suppose it is proper,' the king says, reluctant. 'As she was once given the title of queen.'

'Mistakenly,' Anne says. She is relentless.

The musicians strike up. The king tows Mary Shelton into the dance. Mary is laughing. She has been missing this last half hour, and now she's pink-cheeked, her eyes brilliant; no mistaking what she's been doing. He thinks, if old Bishop Fisher could see this kick-up, he would think the Antichrist has arrived. He is surprised to find himself, even for a moment, viewing the world through Bishop Fisher's eyes.

On London Bridge after his execution, Fisher's head remained in such a state of preservation that the Londoners began to talk of a miracle. Eventually he had the bridge keeper pull it down and drop it in a weighted sack into the Thames.

At Kimbolton, Katherine's body has been turned over to the embalmers. He imagines a rustle in the dark, a sigh, as the nation arranges itself to pray. 'She sent me a letter,' Henry says. He slides it from among the folds of his yellow jacket. 'I don't want it. Here, Cromwell, take it away.'

As he folds it he glances at it: *'And lastly I make this vow, that mine eyes desire you above all things.'*

After the dancing, Anne calls him in. She is sombre, dry, attentive: all business. 'I wish to make my thoughts known to Lady Mary the king's daughter.' He notes the respectful address. It isn't 'the Princess Mary'. But it isn't 'the Spanish bastard' either. 'Now that her mother is gone and cannot influence her,' Anne says, 'we may hope she will be less stiff in maintaining her errors. I have no need to conciliate her, God knows. But I think if I could put an end to the ill-feeling between the king and Mary, he would thank me for it.'

'He would be beholden to you, madam. And it would be an act of charity.'

'I wish to be a mother to her.' Anne flushes; it does sound unlikely. 'I do not expect her to call me "my lady mother", but I expect her to call me Your Highness. If she will conform herself to her father I shall be pleased to have her at court. She will have an honoured place, and not much below mine. I shall not expect a deep reverence from her, but the ordinary form of courtesy which royal persons use among themselves, within their families, the younger to the elder. Assure her, I shall not make her carry my train. She will not have to sit at table with her sister the Princess Elizabeth, so no question of her lower rank will arise. I think this is a fair offer.' He waits. 'If she will render me the respect which is my due, I shall not walk before her on ordinary occasions, but we will walk hand in hand.'

For one so tender about her dignities as Anne the queen, it is an unparalleled set of concessions. But he imagines Mary's face when it is put to her. He is glad he will not be there to see it in person.

He makes a respectful good night, but Anne calls him back. She says, in a low voice: 'Cremuel, this is my offer, I will go no further. I am resolved to make it and then I cannot be blamed. But I do not think she will take it, and then we will both be sorry, for we are condemned to fight till the breath goes out of our bodies. She is my death, and I am hers. So tell her, I shall make sure she does not live to laugh at me after I am gone.'

He goes to Chapuys's house to pay his condolences. The ambassador is wrapped in black. A draught is cutting through his rooms that seems to blow straight from the river, and his mood is one of self-reproach. 'How I wish I had not left her! But she seemed better. She sat up that morning and they dressed her hair. I had seen her eat some bread, a mouthful or two, I thought that was an advance. I rode away in hope, and within hours she was failing.'

'You must not blame yourself. Your master will know you did all you could. After all, you are sent here to watch the king, you cannot be too long from London in the winter.'

He thinks, I have been there since Katherine's trials began: a hundred scholars, a thousand lawyers, ten thousand hours of argument. Almost since the first word was spoken against her marriage, for the cardinal kept me informed; late at night with a glass of wine, he would talk about the king's great matter and how he saw it would work out.

Badly, he said.

'Oh, this fire,' Chapuys says. 'Do you call this a fire? Do you call this a climate?' Smoke from the wood eddies past them. 'Smoke and smells and no heat!'

'Get a stove. I've got stoves.'

'Oh, yes,' the ambassador moans, 'but then the servants stuff them with rubbish and they blow up. Or the chimneys fall apart and you have to send across the sea for a man to fix them. I know all about stoves.' He rubs his blue hands. 'I told her chaplain, you know. When she is on her deathbed, I said, ask her whether Prince Arthur left her a virgin or not. All the world must believe a declaration made by a dying woman. But he is an old man. In his grief and trouble he forgot. So now we will never be sure.'

That is a large admission, he thinks: that the truth may be other than what Katherine told us all these years. 'But do you know,' Chapuys says, 'before I left her, she said a troubling thing to me. She said, "It might be all my fault. That I stood out against the king, when I could have made an honourable withdrawal and let him marry again." I said to her, madam – because I was amazed – madam, what are you thinking, you have right on your side, the great weight of opinion, both lay and clerical – "Ah but," she said to me, "to the lawyers there was doubt in the case. And if I erred, then I drove the king, who does not brook opposition, to act according to his worse nature, and therefore I partly share in the guilt of his sin." I said to her, good madam, only the harshest authority would say so; let the king bear his own sins, let him answer for them. But she shook her head.' Chapuys shakes his, distressed, perplexed. 'All those deaths, the good Bishop Fisher, Thomas More, the sainted monks of the Charterhouse … "I am going out of life," she said, "dragging their corpses."'

He is silent. Chapuys crosses the room to his desk and opens a little inlaid box. 'Do you know what this is?'

He picks up the silk flower, carefully in case it falls to dust in his fingers. 'Yes. Her present from Henry. Her present when the New Year's prince was born.'

'It shows the king in a good light. I would not have believed him so tender. I am sure I would not have thought to do it.'

'You are a sad old bachelor, Eustache.'

'And you a sad old widower. What did you give your wife, when your lovely Gregory was born?'

'Oh, I suppose … a gold dish. A gold chalice. Something to set up on her shelf.' He hands back the silk flower. 'A city wife wants a present she can weigh.'

'Katherine gave me this rose as we parted,' Chapuys says. 'She said, it is all I have to bequeath. She told me, choose a flower from the coffer and go. I kissed her hand and took to the road.' He sighs. He drops the flower on his desk and slides his hands into his sleeves. 'They tell me the concubine is consulting diviners to tell the sex of her child, although she did that before and they all told her it was a boy. Well, the queen's death has altered the position of the concubine. But not perhaps in the way she would like.'

He lets that pass. He waits. Chapuys says, 'I am informed that Henry paraded his little bastard about the court when he heard the news.'

Elizabeth is a forward child, he tells the ambassador. But then you must remember that, when he was hardly a year older than his daughter is now, the young Henry rode through London, perched on the saddle of a warhorse, six feet from the ground and gripping the pommel with fat infant fists. You should not discount her, he tells Chapuys, just because she is young. The Tudors are warriors from their cradle.

'Ah, well, yes,' Chapuys flicks a speck of ash from his sleeve. 'Assuming she is a Tudor. Which some people do doubt. And the

149

hair proves nothing, Cremuel. Considering I could go out on the street and catch half a dozen redheads without a net.'

'So,' he says, laughing, 'you consider Anne's child could have been fathered by any passer-by?'

The ambassador hesitates. He does not like to admit he has been listening to French rumours. 'Anyway,' he sniffs, 'even if she is Henry's child, she is still a bastard.'

'I must leave you.' He stands up. 'Oh. I should have brought back your Christmas hat.'

'You may have custody of it.' Chapuys huddles into himself. 'I shall be in mourning for some time. But do not wear it, Thomas. You will stretch it out of shape.'

Call-Me-Risley comes straight from the king, with news of the funeral arrangements.

'I said to him, Majesty, you will bring the body to St Paul's? He said, she can be laid to rest in Peterborough, Peterborough is an ancient and honourable place and it will cost less. I was astonished. I persisted, I said to him, these things are done by precedent. Your Majesty's sister Mary, the Duke of Suffolk's wife, was taken to Paul's to lie in state. And do you not call Katherine your sister? And he said, ah but, my sister Mary was a royal lady, once married to the King of France.' Wriothesley frowns. 'And Katherine is not royal, he claims, though both her parents were sovereigns. The king said, she will have all she is entitled to as Dowager Princess of Wales. He said, where is the cloth of estate that was put over the hearse when Arthur died? It must be somewhere in the Wardrobe. It can be re-used.'

'That makes sense,' he says. 'The Prince of Wales's feathers. There wouldn't be time to weave a new one. Unless we keep her lingering above ground for it.'

'It appears that she asked for five hundred masses for her soul,' Wriothesley says. 'But I was not about to tell Henry that, because from day to day one never knows what he believes. Anyway, the trumpets blew. And he marched off to Mass. And the queen with him. And she was smiling. And he had a new gold chain.'

Wriothesley's tone suggests he is curious: just that. It passes no judgement on Henry.

'Well,' he says, 'if you're dead, Peterborough is as good a place as any.'

Richard Riche is up in Kimbolton taking an inventory, and has started a spat with Henry about Katherine's effects; not that Riche loved the old queen, but he loves the law. Henry wants her plate and her furs, but Riche says, Majesty, if you were never married to her, she was a *feme sole* not a *feme covert*, if you were not her husband you have no right to lay hands on her property.

He has been laughing over it. 'Henry will get the furs,' he says. 'Riche will find the king a way around it, believe me. You know what she should have done? Bundled them up and given them to Chapuys. There's a man who feels the chill.'

A message comes, for Anne the queen from the Lady Mary, in reply to her kind offer to be a mother to her. Mary says she has lost the best mother in the world and has no need for a substitute. As for fellowship with her father's concubine, she would not degrade herself. She would not hold hands with someone who has shaken paws with the devil.

He says, 'Perhaps the timing was awry. Perhaps she had heard of the dancing. And the yellow dress.'

Mary says she will obey her father, so far as her honour and her conscience allow. But that is all she will do. She will not make any statement or take any oath that requires her to recognise that her mother was not married to her father, or to accept a child of Anne Boleyn as heir of England.

Anne says, 'How does she dare? Why does she even think she can negotiate? If my child is a boy, I know what will happen to her. She had better make her peace with her father now, not come crying to him for mercy when it is too late.'

'It's good advice,' he says. 'I doubt she will take it.'

'Then I can do no more.'

'I honestly think you cannot.'

And he does not see what more he can do for Anne Boleyn. She is crowned, she is proclaimed, her name is written in the statutes, in the rolls: but if the people do not accept her as queen …

Katherine's funeral is planned for 29 January. The early bills are coming in, for the mourning attire and candles. The king continues elated. He is ordering up court entertainments. There is to be a tournament in the third week of the month and Gregory is down as a contestant. Already the boy is in a sweat of preparation. He keeps calling in his armourer, sending him off and calling him back again; changing his mind about his horse. 'Father, I hope I am not drawn against the king,' he says. 'Not that I fear him. But it will be hard work, trying to remember it is him, and also trying to forget it is him, trying your best to get a touch but please God no more than a touch. Suppose I should have the bad luck to unhorse him? Can you imagine if he came down, and to a novice like me?'

'I wouldn't worry,' he says. 'Henry was jousting before you could walk.'

'That's the whole difficulty, sir. He is not as quick as he was. So the gentlemen say. Norris says, he's lost his apprehension. Norris says you can't do it if you're not scared, and Henry is convinced he is the best, so he fears no opponent. And you should fear, Norris says. It keeps you sharp.'

'Next time,' he says, 'get drawn on the king's team at the start. That avoids the problem.'

'How would one do that?'

Oh, dear God. How would one do anything, Gregory? 'I'll have a word,' he says patiently.

'No, don't.' Gregory is upset. 'How would that stand with my honour? If you were there arranging matters? This is something

152

I must do for myself. I know you know everything, father. But you were never in the lists.'

He nods. As you please. His son clanks away. His tender son.

As the New Year begins, Jane Seymour continues her duties about the queen, unreadable expressions drifting across her face as if she were moving within a cloud. Mary Shelton tells him: 'The queen says that if Jane gives way to Henry he will be tired of her after a day, and if she does not give way he will be tired of her anyway. Then Jane will be sent back to Wolf Hall, and her family will lock her in a convent because she is no further use to them. And Jane says nothing.' Shelton laughs, but kindly enough. 'Jane does not feel it would be very different. As she is now in a portable convent, and bound by her own vows. She says, "Master Secretary thinks I would be very sinful to let the king hold my hand, though he begs me, 'Jane, give me your little paw.' And as Master Secretary is second only to the king in church affairs, and a very godly man, I take notice of what he says."'

One day Henry seizes Jane as she is passing and sits her on his knee. It is a sportive gesture, boyish, impetuous, no harm in it; so he says later, excusing himself sheepishly. Jane does not smile or speak. She sits calmly till she is released, as if the king were any joint-stool.

Christophe comes to him, whispering: 'Sir, they are saying on the streets that Katherine was murdered. They are saying that the king locked her in a room and starved her to death. They are saying that he sent her almonds, and she ate, and was poisoned. They are saying that you sent two murderers with knives, and that they cut out her heart, and that when it was inspected, your name was branded there in big black letters.'

'What? On her heart? "Thomas Cromwell"?'

Christophe hesitates. '*Alors* ... Perhaps just your initials.'

PART TWO

I

The Black Book
London, January–April 1536

When he hears the shout of 'Fire!' he turns over and swims back into his dream. He supposes the conflagration is a dream; it's the sort he has.

Then he wakes to Christophe bellowing in his ear. 'Get up! The queen is on fire.'

He is out of bed. The cold slices into him. Christophe yells, 'Quick, quick! She is totally incinderated.'

Moments later, when he arrives on the queen's floor, he finds the smell of singed cloth heavy in the air, and Anne surrounded by gibbering women, but unhurt, in a chair, wrapped in black silk, with a chalice of warmed wine in her hands. The cup jiggles, spills a little; Henry is tearful, hugging her, and his heir who is inside her. 'If only I had been with you, sweetheart. If only I had spent the night. I could have put you out of danger in an instant.'

On and on he goes. Thank the Lord God who watches over us. Thank the God who protects England. If only I. With a blanket, a quilt, stifling them. I, in an instant, beating out the flames.

Anne takes a gulp of her wine. 'It is over. I am not harmed. Please, my lord husband. Peace. Let me drink this.'

He sees, in a flash, how Henry irritates her; his solicitude, his doting, his clinging. And in the depth of a January night she can't disguise the irritation. She looks grey, her sleep broken. She turns to him, Cromwell, and speaks in French. 'There is a prophecy that a queen of England will be burned. I did not think it meant in her own bed. It was an unattended candle. Or so one assumes.'

'By whom unattended?'

Anne shudders. She looks away.

'We had better take order,' he says to the king, 'that water be kept to hand, and one woman be appointed on every rota to check that all lights are extinguished about the queen. I cannot think why it is not the custom.'

All these things are written down in the Black Book, which comes from King Edward's time. It orders the household: orders everything, in fact, except the king's privy chamber, whose workings are not transparent.

'If only I had been with her,' says Henry. 'But, you see, our hopes being what they are ...'

The King of England cannot afford carnal relations with the woman carrying his child. The risk of miscarriage is too great. And for company he looks elsewhere too. Tonight you can see how Anne's body stiffens as she pulls away from her husband's hands, but in daylight hours, their position is reversed. He has watched Anne as she tries to draw the king into conversation. His abruptness, all too often. His turned shoulder. As if to deny his need of her. And yet his eyes follow her ...

He is irritated; these are women's things. And the fact that the queen's body, wrapped only in a damask nightgown, seems too narrow for that of a woman who will give birth in spring; that is a woman's thing too. The king says, 'The fire did not come very near her. It is the corner of the arras that is burned up. It is Absalom hanging in the tree. It is a very good piece and I would like you to ...'

'I'll get someone over from Brussels,' he says.

The fire has not touched King David's son. He hangs from the branches, strung up by his long hair: his eyes are wild and his mouth opens in a scream.

It is hours yet till daylight. The rooms of the palace seem hushed, as if they are waiting for an explanation. Guards patrol through the dark hours; where were they? Should not some woman have been with the queen, sleeping on a pallet at the foot of her bed? He says to Lady Rochford, 'I know the queen has enemies, but how were they allowed to come so near her?'

Jane Rochford is on her high horse; she thinks he is attempting to blame her. 'Look, Master Secretary. Shall I be plain with you?'

'I wish you would.'

'First, this is a household matter. It is not within your remit. Second, she was in no danger. Third, I do not know who lit the candle. Four, if I did I would not tell you.'

He waits.

'Five: no one else will tell you either.'

He waits.

'If, as it may happen, some person visits the queen after the lights are out, then it is an event over which we should draw a veil.'

'Some person.' He digests this. 'Some person for the purposes of arson, or for purposes of something else?'

'For the usual purposes of bedchambers,' she says. 'Not that I say there is such a person. I would not have any knowledge of it. The queen knows how to keep her secrets.'

'Jane,' he says, 'if the time comes when you wish to disburden your conscience, do not go to a priest, come to me. The priest will give you a penance, but I will give you a reward.'

What is the nature of the border between truth and lies? It is permeable and blurred because it is planted thick with rumour, confabulation, misunderstandings and twisted tales. Truth can break the gates down, truth can howl in the street; unless truth is pleasing, personable and easy to like, she is condemned to stay whimpering at the back door.

Tidying up after Katherine's death, he had been moved to explore some legends of her early life. Account books form a narrative as engaging as any tale of sea monsters or cannibals. Katherine had always said that, between the death of Arthur and her marriage to the young Prince Henry, she had been miserably neglected, wretchedly poor: eaten yesterday's fish, and so on. One had blamed the old king for it, but when you look at the books, you see he was generous enough. Katherine's household were cheating her. Her plate and jewels were leaking on to the market; in that she must have been complicit? She was lavish, he sees, and generous; regal, in other words, with no idea of living within her means.

You wonder what else you have always believed, believed without foundation. His father Walter had laid out money for him, or so Gardiner said: compensation, for the stab wound he inflicted, the injured family paid off. What if, he thinks, Walter didn't hate me? What if he was just exasperated with me, and showed it by kicking me around the brewery yard? What if I deserved it? Because I was always crowing, 'Item, I have a better head for drink than you; Item, I have a better head for everything. Item, I am prince of Putney and can wallop anybody from Wimbledon, let them come from Mortlake and I will mince them. Item, I am already one inch taller than you, look at the door where I have put a notch, go on, go on, father, go and stand against the wall.'

He writes:

Anthony's teeth.
Question: What happened to them?

Anthony's testimony, in answer to me, Thomas Cromwell: They were knocked out by his brutal father.

160

To Richard Cromwell: He was in a fortress besieged by the Pope. Abroad somewhere. Some year. Some Pope. The fortress was undermined and a charge planted. As he was standing in an unlucky spot, his teeth were blown clear out of his head.

To Thomas Wriothesley: When he was a sailor off Iceland his captain traded them for provisions with a man who could carve chessmen out of teeth. Did not understand the nature of the bargain until men in furs came to knock them out.

To Richard Riche: He lost them in a dispute with a man who impugned the powers of Parliament.

To Christophe: Somebody put a spell on him and they all fell out. Christophe says, 'I was told as a child about diabolists in England. There is a witch in every street. Practically.'

To Thurston: He had an enemy was a cook. And this enemy painted a batch of stone to look like hazelnuts, and invited him to a handful.

To Gregory: They were sucked out of his head by a great worm that crawled out of the ground and ate his wife. This was in Yorkshire, last year.

He draws a line under his conclusions. Says, 'Gregory, what should I do about the great worm?'

'Send a commission against it, sir,' the boy says. 'It must be put down. Bishop Rowland Lee would go up against it. Or Fitz.'

He gives his son a long look. 'You do know it's Arthur Cobbler's tales?'

Gregory gives him a long look back. 'Yes, I do know.' He sounds regretful. 'But it makes people so happy when I believe them. Mr Wriothesley, especially. Though now he has grown so grave. He used to amuse himself by holding my head under a water spout. But now he turns his eyes up to Heaven and says "the King's Majesty". Though he used to call him, His High Horridness. And imitate how he walks.' Gregory plants his fists on his hips and stamps across the room.

He raises a hand to cover his smile.

The day of the tournament comes. He is at Greenwich but excuses himself from the spectators' stand. The king had been at him that morning, as they sat side by side in his closet at early Mass: 'How much does the lordship of Ripon bring in? To the Archbishop of York?'

'A little over two hundred and sixty pounds, sir.'

'And what does Southwell bring in?'

'Scant one hundred and fifty pounds, sir.'

'Do you say so? I thought that it would be more.'

Henry is taking the closest interest in the finances of the bishops. Some people say, and he would not demur, that we should put the bishops on a fixed stipend and take the profits of their sees for the treasury. He has worked out that the money raised could pay for a standing army.

But this is not the time to put it to Henry. The king falls to his knees and prays to whatever saint guards knights in the lists. 'Majesty,' he says, 'if you run against my son Gregory, will you forbear to unhorse him? If you can help it?'

But the king says, 'I would not mind if little Gregory unhorsed me. Though it is unlikely, I would take it in good part. And we cannot help what we do, really. Once you are thundering down at a man, you cannot check.' He stops himself and says kindly, 'It is quite a rare event, you know, to bring your opponent down. It is not the sole aim of the contest. If you are concerned about what showing he will make, you need not be. He is very able. He would not be a combatant otherwise. One cannot break a lance on a timid opponent, he must run at full pace against you. Besides, no one ever does badly. It is not allowed. You know how the heralds put it. As it might be, "Gregory Cromwell has jousted well, Henry Norris has jousted very well, but our Sovereign Lord the king has jousted best of all."'

'And have you, sir?' He smiles to take any sting from the words.

'I know you councillors think I should take to the spectators' bench. And I will, I promise, it has not escaped me that a man of my age is past his best. But you see, Crumb, it is hard to give up what you have worked at since you were a boy. There were some Italian visitors once, they were cheering us on, Brandon and myself, and they thought that Achilles and Hector had come back to life. So they said.'

But which is which? One dragged through the dust by the other …

The king says, 'You turn your boy out beautifully, and your nephew Richard too. No nobleman could do more. They are a credit to your house.'

Gregory has done well. Gregory has done very well. Gregory has done best of all. 'I don't want him to be Achilles,' he says, 'I only want him not to be flattened.'

There is a correspondence between the score sheet and the human body, in that the paper has divisions marked off, for the head and the torso. A touch on the breastplate is recorded, but not fractured ribs. A touch on the helm is recorded, but not a cracked skull. You can pick up the score sheets afterwards and read back a record of the day, but the marks on paper do not tell you about the pain of a broken ankle or the efforts of a suffocating man not to vomit inside his helmet. As the combatants will always tell you, you really needed to see it, you had to be there.

Gregory was disappointed when his father had excused himself from watching. He pleaded a prior engagement with his papers. The Vatican is offering Henry three months to return to obedience, or the bull of excommunication against him will be printed and distributed through Europe, and every Christian hand will be against him. The Emperor's fleet is set for Algiers, with forty thousand armed men. The abbot of Fountains has been systematically robbing his own treasury, and entertains six whores, though presumably he needs a rest between. And the parliamentary session opens in a fortnight.

He had met an old knight once, in Venice, one of those men who had made a career of riding to tournaments all over Europe. The man had described his life to him, crossing frontiers with his band of esquires and his string of horses, always on the move from one prize to the next, till age and the accumulation of injuries put him out of the game. On his own now, he tried to pick up a living teaching young lords, enduring mockery and time-wasting; in my day, he had said, the young were taught manners, but now I find myself fettling horses and polishing breastplates for some little tosspot I wouldn't have let clean my boots in the old days; for look at me now, reduced to drinking with, what are you, an Englishman?

The knight was a Portuguese, but he spoke dog-Latin and a kind of German, interspersed with technicalities which are much the same in all languages. In the old days each tournament was a testing-ground. There was no display of idle luxury. Women, instead of simpering at you from gilded pavilions, were kept for afterwards. In those days the scoring was complex and the judges had no mercy on any infringement of the rules, so you could shatter all your lances but lose on points, you could flatten your opposer and come out not with a bag of gold but with a fine or a blot on your record. A breach of rules would trail you through Europe, so some infringements committed, let's say, in Lisbon, would catch up with you in Ferrara; a man's reputation would go before him, and in the end, he said, given a bad season, a run of ill-luck, reputation's all you've got; so don't you push your luck, he said, when fortune's star is shining, because the next minute, it isn't. Come to that, don't pay out good money for horoscopes. If things are going to go badly for you, is that what you need to know as you saddle up?

One drink in, the old knight talked as if everybody had followed his trade. You should set your squires, he said, at each end of the barrier, to make your horse swerve wide if he tries to cut the corner, or else you may catch your foot, easy done if there's no end-guard, bloody painful: have you ever done that? Some fools collect their boys in the middle, where the atteint will occur; but what's the use? Indeed, he agreed, what use at all: and wondered at that delicate word, *atteint*, for the brutal shock of contact. These spring-loaded shields, the old man said, have you seen them, they jump apart when they're hit? Babies' tricks. The old-time judges didn't need a device like that to tell them when a man had got a touch – no, they used their eyes, they had eyes in those days. Look, he said: there are three ways to fail. Horse can fail. Boys can fail. Nerve can fail.

You have to get your helmet on tightly so that you have a good line of sight. You keep your body square-on, and when you are about to strike, then and only then turn your head so that you have a full view of your opposer, and watch the iron tip of your lance straight on to your target. Some people veer away in the second before the clash. It is natural, but forget what is natural. Practise till you break your instinct. Given a chance you will always swerve. Your body wants to preserve itself and your instinct will try to avoid crashing your armoured warhorse and your armoured self into another man and horse coming at full gallop the other way. Some men don't swerve, but instead they close their eyes at the moment of impact. These men are of two kinds: the ones who know they do it and can't help it, and the ones who don't know they do it. Get your boys to watch you when you practise. Be neither of these kinds of men.

So how shall I improve, he said to the old knight, how shall I succeed? These were his instructions: you must sit easily in your saddle, as if you were riding out to take the air. Hold your reins loosely, but have your horse collected. In the *combat à plaisance*, with its fluttering flags, its garlands, its rebated swords and lances tipped with buffering coronals, ride as if you were out to kill. In the *combat à l'outrance*, kill as if it were a sport. Now look, the knight said, and slapped the table, here's what I've seen, more times than I care to count: your man braces himself for the atteint, and at that final moment, the urgency of desire undoes him: he tightens his muscles, he pulls in his lance-arm against his body, the tip tilts up, and he's off the mark; if you avoid one fault, avoid that. Carry your lance a little loose, so when you tense your frame and draw in your arm your point comes exactly on the target. But remember this above all: defeat your instinct. Your love of glory must conquer your will to survive; or why fight at all? Why not be a smith, a brewer, a wool merchant? Why are you in the contest, if not to win, and if not to win, then to die?

The next day he saw the knight again. He, Tommaso, was coming back from drinking with his friend Karl Heinz, and when they spotted the old man he was lying with his head on *terra firma*, his feet in the water; in Venice at dusk, it can so easily be the other way around. They pulled him on to the bank and turned him over. I know this man, he said. His friend said, who owns him? Nobody owns him, but he curses in German, therefore let us take him to the German House, for I myself am staying not at the Tuscan House but with a man who runs a foundry. Karl Heinz said, you are dealing in arms? and he said, no, altar cloths. Karl Heinz said, you are as likely to shit rubies as learn an Englishman's secrets.

As they were talking they were hauling the old man upright, and Karl Heinz said, they have cut his purse, look. A wonder they did not kill him. In a boat they took him to the Fondaco where the German merchants stay, and which was just then rebuilding after the fire. You can bed him down in the warehouse among the crates, he said. Find something to cover him, and give him food and drink when he wakes. He will live. He is an old man but tough. Here is money.

A whimsical Englishman, Karl Heinz said. He said, I myself have benefited from strangers who were angels in disguise.

There is a guard on the water gate, not set by the merchants but by the state, as the Venetians wish to know all that goes on within the houses of the nations. So more coins are passed, to the guard. They pull the old man out of the boat; he is half-awake now, flailing his arms and speaking something, perhaps Portuguese. They are dragging him in, under the portico, when Karl Heinz says, 'Thomas, have you seen our paintings? Here,' he says, 'you, guard, give us the benefit of holding up your torch, or must we pay you for that too?'

Light flares against the wall. Out of the brick blossoms a flow of silk, red silk or pooled blood. He sees a white curve, a slender moon, a sickle cut; as the light washes over the wall, he sees a woman's face, the curve of her cheek edged with gold. She is a goddess. 'Hold up the torch,' he says. On her blown and tangled hair there is a gilded crown. Behind her are the planets and stars. 'Who did you hire for this?' he asks.

Karl Heinz says, 'Giorgione is painting it for us, his friend Tiziano is painting the Rialto front, the Senate is paying their fees. But by God, they will milk it from us in commissions. Do you like her?'

The light touches her white flesh. It falters away from her, patching her with dark. The watchman lowers his torch and says, what, you think I am standing here all night for your pleasure in the gnawing cold? Which is an exaggeration, to get more money, but it is true that mist creeps over the bridges and walkways, and a chill wind has got up from the sea.

Parting from Karl Heinz, the moon herself a stone in the waters of the canal, he sees an expensive whore out late, her servants supporting her elbows, teetering over the cobbles on her high chopines. Her laughter rings on the air, and the fringed end of her yellow scarf snakes away from her white throat and into the mist. He watches her; she does not notice him. Then she is gone. Somewhere a door opens for her and somewhere a door is closed. Like the woman on the wall, she melts and is lost in the dark. The square is empty again; and he himself only a black shape against the brickwork, a fragment cut out of the night. If I ever need to vanish, he says, this is where I shall do it.

But that was long ago and in another country. Now Rafe Sadler is here with a message: he must return suddenly to Greenwich, to this raw morning, the rain just holding off. Where is Karl Heinz today? Dead probably. Since the night he saw the goddess growing on the wall, he has intended to commission one himself, though other purposes – making money and drafting legislation – have taken up his time.

'Rafe?'

Rafe stands in the doorway and does not speak. He looks up at the young man's face. His hand lets go his quill and ink splashes the paper. He stands up at once, wrapping his furred robe about him as if it will buffer him from what is to come. He says, 'Gregory?' and Rafe shakes his head.

Gregory is intact. He did not run a course.

The tournament is interrupted.

It is the king, Rafe says. It is Henry, he is dead.

Ah, he says.

He dries the ink with dust from the box of bone. Blood everywhere, no doubt, he says.

He keeps at hand a gift he was given once, a Turkish dagger made of iron, the sheath engraved with a pattern of sunflowers. Until now he had always thought of it as an ornament, a curio. He tucks it away amongst his garments.

* * *

He will recall, later, how difficult it was to get through the doorway, to turn his steps to the tilting ground. He feels weak, the
backwash of the weakness that had made him drop the pen when
he thought that Gregory was hurt. He says to himself, it is not
Gregory; but his body is dazed, slow to catch up with the news,
as if he himself had received a killing blow. Whether, now, to go
forward to try to seize command, or to seize this moment,
perhaps the last moment, to quit the scene: to make good an
escape, before the ports are blocked, and to go where? Perhaps to
Germany? Is there any principality, state, in which he would be
safe from the reach of Emperor or Pope, or the new ruler of
England, whoever that may be?

He has never backed off; or once, perhaps, from Walter when he
was seven years old: but Walter came on. Since then: forward,
forward, *en avant!* So his hesitation is not long, but afterwards he
will have no recollection of how he arrived in a lofty and gilded
tent, embroidered with the arms and devices of England, and
standing over the corpse of King Henry VIII. Rafe says, the
contests had not begun, he was running at the ring, the point of his
lance scooped the eye of the circle. Then the horse stumbled under
him, man and rider down, horse rolling with a scream and Henry
beneath it. Now Gentle Norris is on his knees by the bier, praying,
tears cascading down his cheeks. There is a blur of light on plate
armour, helms hiding faces, iron jaws, frog mouths, the slits of
visors. Someone says, the beast went down as if its leg were broke,
no one was near the king, no one to blame. He seems to hear the
appalling noise of it, the horse's roar of terror as it pitches, the
screams from the spectators, the grating clatter of steel and hooves
on steel as one huge animal entangles with another, warhorse and
king collapsing together, metal driven into flesh, hoof into bone.

'Fetch a mirror,' he says, 'to hold to his lips. Fetch a feather to
see if it stirs.'

The king has been manhandled out of his armour, but is still
laced in his tournament jacket of wadded black, as if in mourning

for himself. There is no evident blood, so he asks, where was he hurt? Someone says, he knocked his head; but that is all the sense he can glean from the wailing and babbling that fills the tent. Feathers, mirrors, they intimate it has been done; tongues clamour like bell tongues, their eyes are like pebbles in their heads, one shocked and vacant face turns to another, oaths are uttered and prayers, and they move slowly, slowly; no one wants to carry the corpse inside, it is too much to take on oneself, it will be seen, it will be reported. It is a mistake to think that when the king dies his councillors shout, 'Long live the king.' Often the fact of the death is hidden for days. As this must be hidden ... Henry is waxen, and he sees the shocking tenderness of human flesh evicted from steel. He is lying on his back, all his magnificent height stretched on a piece of ocean-blue cloth. His limbs are straight. He looks uninjured. He touches his face. It is still warm. Fate has not spoiled him or mangled. He is intact, a present for the gods. They are taking him back as he was sent.

He opens his mouth and shouts. What do they mean, leaving the king lying here, untouched by Christian hand, as if he were already excommunicate? If this were any other fallen man they would be enticing his senses with rose petals and myrrh. They would be pulling his hair and tweaking his ears, burning a paper under his nose, wrenching open his jaw to trickle in holy water, blowing a horn next to his head. All this should be done and – he looks up and sees Thomas Howard, the Duke of Norfolk, running at him like a demon. Uncle Norfolk: uncle to the queen, premier nobleman of England. 'By God, Cromwell!' he snarls. And his import is clear. By God, I've got you now; by God, your presumptuous guts will be drawn: by God, before the day is over your head will be spiked.

Perhaps. But in the next seconds he, Cromwell, seems to body out and fill all the space around the fallen man. He sees himself, as if he were watching from the canvas above: his girth expands, even his height. So that he occupies more ground. So that he takes up more space, breathes more air, is planted and solid when Norfolk careers into him, twitching, trembling. So he is a fortress on a rock, serene, and Thomas Howard just bounces back from his walls, wincing, flinching, and blethering God knows what about God knows who. 'MY LORD NORFOLK!' he roars at him. 'My lord Norfolk, where is the queen?'

Norfolk is panting hard. 'On the floor. I told her. I myself. My place to do it. My place, am her uncle. Fallen in a fit. Fell down. Dwarf trying to pull her up. Kicked it away. Oh God Almighty!'

Now who governs, for Anne's unborn child? When Henry purposed to go to France, he said he would leave Anne as regent, but that was more than a year ago, and besides he never did go, and so we don't know if he would have done it; Anne had said to him, Cremuel, if I am regent, watch yourself, I will have your obedience or I will have your head. Anne as regent would have made short work of Katherine, of Mary: Katherine is passed beyond her reach, but Mary there for the killing. Uncle Norfolk, lurched down by the corpse for a quick prayer, has stumbled up again: 'No, no, no,' he is saying. 'No woman with a big belly. Such cannot rule. Anne cannot rule. Me, me, me.'

Gregory is pushing through the crowd. He has had the sense to fetch Fitzwilliam, Master Treasurer. 'The Princess Mary,' he says to Fitz. 'How to get her. I must have her. Or the realm is done for.'

Fitzwilliam is one of Henry's old friends, a man of his own age: too capable by nature, thank God, to panic and gibber. 'Her keepers are Boleyns,' Fitz says. 'I don't know if they'll yield her.'

Yes, and what a fool I was, he thinks, not to get among them and suborn them and advance-bribe them for an occasion such as this; I said I would send my ring for Katherine's deliverance, but for the princess I made no such arrangement. Let Mary remain in the hands of the Boleyns, and she is dead. Let her fall into the hands of the papists, they will set her up as queen, and I am dead. There will be civil war.

171

Courtiers are now pouring into the tent, all inventing how Henry died, all exclaiming, denying, lamenting; the noise rises, and he grips Fitz's arm: 'If this news gets up-country before we do, we will never see Mary alive.' Her guardians will not hang her up from the staircase, they will not stab her, but they will make sure she meets with an accident, a broken neck on the road. Then if Anne's unborn child is a girl, Elizabeth is queen, as we have no other.

Fitzwilliam says, 'Wait now, let me think. Where is Richmond?' The king's bastard, sixteen years old. He is a commodity, he is to be reckoned with, he is to be secured. Richmond is Norfolk's son-in-law. Norfolk must know where he is, Norfolk is best placed to lay hands on him, bargain with him, lock him up or turn him loose: but he, Cromwell, does not fear a bastard boy, and besides, the young man favours him, in all their dealings he has buttered him like a parsnip.

Norfolk is now buzzing from side to side, a maddened wasp, and as if he were a wasp the onlookers shrink from him, eddying away, then swaying back. The duke buzzes into him; he, Cromwell, bats the duke away. He stares down at Henry. He thinks he has seen, but it might be fantasy, a twitch of an eyelid. It is enough. He stands over Henry, like a figure on a tomb: a broad, mute, ugly guardian. He waits: then he sees that flicker again, he thinks he does. His heart lurches. He puts his hand on the king's chest, slapping it down, like a merchant closing a deal. Says calmly, 'The king is breathing.'

There is an unholy roar. It is something between a moan and a cheer and a wail of panic, a shout to God, a riposte to the devil.

Beneath the jacket, within the horsehair padding, a fibrillation, a quiver of life: his hand heavy and flat on the regal breast, he feels he is raising Lazarus. It is as if his palm, magnetised, is drawing life back into his prince. The king's respiration, though shallow, seems steady. He, Cromwell, has seen the future; he has seen England without Henry; he prays aloud, 'Long live the king.'

'Fetch the surgeons,' he says. 'Fetch Butts. Fetch any man with skill. If he dies again, they will not be blamed. My word on that. Get me Richard Cromwell my nephew. Fetch a stool for my lord Norfolk, he has had a shock.' He is tempted to add, throw a bucket of water on Gentle Norris: whose prayers, he has time to notice, are of a marked papist character.

The tent is now so crowded that it seems to have been picked up by its moorings, to be carried on men's heads. He takes a last look at Henry before his still form disappears under the ministrations of doctors and priests. He hears a long, retching gasp; but one has heard the same from corpses.

'Breathe,' Norfolk shouts. 'Let the king breathe!' And as if in obedience, the fallen man takes a deep, sucking, scraping breath. And then he swears. And then he tries to sit up.

And it is over.

But not entirely: not until he has studied the Boleyn expressions around. They look numb, bemused. Their faces are pinched in the bitter cold. Their great hour has passed, before they realised it has arrived. How have they all got here so fast? Where have they come from? he asks Fitz. Only then he realises that the light is fading. What felt like ten minutes has been two hours: two hours since Rafe stood in the doorway, and he dropped his pen on the page.

He says to Fitzwilliam, 'Of course, it never happened. Or if it did, it was an incident of no importance.'

For Chapuys and the other ambassadors, he will stick by his original version: the king fell, hit his head, and was unconscious for ten minutes. No, at no time did we think he was dead. After ten minutes he sat up. And now he is perfectly well.

The way I tell it, he says to Fitzwilliam, you would think that the blow on the head had improved him. That he actually set out to get it. That every monarch needs a blow on the head, from time to time.

Fitzwilliam is amused. 'A man's thoughts at such a time hardly bear scrutiny. I recall thinking, should we not send for the Lord Chancellor? But I don't know what I thought he was to do.'

'My thought,' he confesses, 'was, somebody get the Archbishop of Canterbury. I think I believed a king couldn't die without his supervision. Imagine trying to bustle Cranmer across the Thames. He would make you join him in a gospel reading first.'

What does the Black Book say? Nothing to the purpose. No one has made a plan for a king struck down between one moment and the next, one second mounted tall and riding full tilt, next second mashed into the ground. No one dares. No one dares think about it. Where protocol fails, it is war to the knife. He remembers Fitzwilliam beside him; Gregory in the crowd; Rafe by his side, and then Richard his nephew. Was it Richard who helped lever the king upright as he tried to sit, while the doctors cried, 'No, no, lie him down!' Henry had clasped his hands to his chest, as if to squeeze his own heart. He had struggled to rise, he had made inarticulate noises, that sounded like words but were not, as if the Holy Ghost had descended upon him and he was speaking in tongues. He had thought, panic darting through him, what if he never makes sense again? What does the Black Book say if a king is rendered simple? Outside he remembers the roaring of Henry's fallen horse, struggling to rise; but surely that cannot be what he heard, surely they had slaughtered it?

Then Henry himself was roaring. That night, the king rips the bandage from his head. The bruising, the swelling, is God's verdict on the day. He is determined to show himself to his court, to counter any rumours that he is mauled or dead. Anne approaches him, supported by her father, 'Monseigneur'. The earl is really supporting her, not pretending to. She looks white and frail; now her pregnancy shows. 'My lord,' she says, 'I pray, the whole of England prays, that you will never joust again.'

Henry beckons her to approach. Beckons her till her face is close to his own. His voice low and vehement: 'Why not geld me while you are at it? That would suit you, would it not, madam?'

Faces open in shock. The Boleyns have the sense to draw Anne backwards, backwards and away, Mistress Shelton and Jane Rochford flapping and tut-tutting, the whole Howard, Boleyn clan closing around her. Jane Seymour, alone of the ladies, does not move. She stands and looks at Henry and the king's eyes fly straight to her, a space opens around her and for a moment she stands in the vacancy, like a dancer left behind when the line moves on.

Later he is with Henry in his bedchamber, the king collapsed in a velvet chair. Henry says, when I was a boy, I was walking with my father in a gallery at Richmond, one night in summer about eleven of the clock, he had my arm in his and we were deep in talk or he was: and suddenly there was a great crashing and a splintering, the whole building gave a deep groan, and the floor fell away at our feet. I will remember it all my life, standing on the brink, and the world vanished from beneath us. But for a moment I did not know what I heard, whether it was the timbers splintering or our bones. Both of us by God's grace still stood on solid ground, and yet I had seen myself plummeting, down and down through the floor below till I hit the earth and smelled it, damp like the grave. Well ... when I fell today, that was how it was. I heard voices. Very distant. I could not make out the words. I felt myself borne through the air. I did not see God. Or angels.

'I hope you were not disappointed when you woke. Only to see Thomas Cromwell.'

'You were never more welcome,' Henry says. 'Your own mother on the day you were born was no gladder to see you than I was today.'

The grooms of the chamber are here, going soft-footed about their usual duties, sprinkling the king's sheets with holy water.

'Steady,' Henry says crossly. 'Do you want me to take a chill? A drowning is not more efficacious than a drop.' He turns and says, low-voiced, 'Crumb, you know this never happened?'

He nods. What records are already made, he is in the process of expunging. Afterwards it will be known that on such a date, the king's horse stumbled. But God's hand plucked him from the ground and set him back laughing on his throne. Another item of note, for The Book Called Henry: knock him down and he bounces.

But the queen has a point. You've seen these jousters from the old king's time, limping about the court, the wincing and addle-pated survivors of the lists; men who've taken a blow on the head once too often, men who walk crooked, bent like a dog-leg brick. And all your skill counts for nothing when your day of reckoning comes. Horse can fail. Boys can fail. Nerve can fail.

That night he says to Richard Cromwell, 'It was a bad moment for me. How many men can say, as I must, "I am a man whose only friend is the King of England"? I have everything, you would think. And yet take Henry away and I have nothing.'

Richard sees the helpless truth of it. Says, 'Yes.' What else can he say?

Later he voices the same thought, in a cautious and modified form, to Fitzwilliam. Fitzwilliam looks at him: thoughtful, not without sympathy. 'I don't know, Crumb. You are not without support, you know.'

'Forgive me,' he says sceptically, 'but in what way does this support manifest?'

'I mean that you would have support, should you need it against the Boleyns.'

'Why should I? The queen and I are perfect friends.'

'That's not what you tell Chapuys.'

He inclines his head. Interesting, the people who talk to Chapuys; interesting too, what the ambassador chooses to pass on, from one party to another.

'Did you hear them?' Fitz says. His tone is disgusted. 'Outside the tent, when we thought the king was dead? Shouting "Boleyn, Boleyn!" Calling out their own name. Like cuckoos.'

He waits. Of course he heard them; what is the real question here? Fitz is close to the king. He was brought up at court with Henry since they were small boys, though his family is good gentry, not noble. He has been to war. Has had a crossbow bolt in him. Has been abroad on embassies, knows France, knows Calais, the English enclave there and its politics. He is of that select company, the Garter knights. He writes a good letter, to the point, neither abrupt nor circumlocutory, nor larded with flattery, nor cursory in expressions of regard. The cardinal liked him, and he is affable to Thomas Cromwell when they dine daily in the guard chamber. He is always affable: and now more so? 'What would have happened, Crumb, if the king had not come back to life? I shall never forget Howard pitching in, "Me, me, me!"'

'It is not a spectacle we will erase from our minds. As for …' he hesitates, 'well, if the worst had been, the king's body dies but the body politic continues. It might be possible to convene a ruling council, made up from the law officers, and from those chief councillors that are now …'

'… amongst whom, yourself …'

'Myself, granted.' Myself in several capacities, he thinks: who more trusted, who closer, and not just Master Secretary but a law officer, Master of the Rolls? 'If Parliament were willing, we might bring together a body who would have ruled as regent till the queen was delivered, and perhaps with her permission during a minority …'

'But you know Anne would give no such permission,' Fitz says.

'No, she would have all to rule herself. Though she would have to fight Uncle Norfolk. Between the two of them I do not know who I would back. The lady, I think.'

'God help the realm,' Fitzwilliam says, 'and all the men in it. Of the two, I would sooner have Thomas Howard. At least if it came to it, one could challenge him to come outside and fight. Let the lady be regent and the Boleyns would walk on our backs. We would be their living carpet. She would have "AB" sewn into our skins.' He rubs his chin. 'But so she will anyway. If she gives Harry a son.'

He is aware that Fitz is watching him. 'On the topic of sons,' he says, 'have I thanked you in proper form? Let me know if there is anything I can do for you. Gregory has thrived under your guidance.'

'The pleasure is mine. Send him back to me soon.'

I will, he thinks, and with the lease on a little abbey or two, when my new laws are passed. His desk is piled high with business for the new session of Parliament. Before many years are out he would like Gregory to have a seat beside him in the Commons. He must see all aspects of how the realm is governed. A term in Parliament is an exercise in frustration, it is a lesson in patience: whichever way you like to look at it. They commune of war, peace, strife, contention, debate, murmur, grudges, riches, poverty, truth, falsehood, justice, equity, oppression, treason, murder and the edification and continuance of the common-wealth; then do as their predecessors have done – that is, as well as they might – and leave off where they began.

After the king's accident, everything is the same, yet nothing is the same. He is still on the wrong side of the Boleyns, of Mary's supporters, the Duke of Norfolk, the Duke of Suffolk, and the absent Bishop of Winchester; not to mention the King of France, the Emperor, and the Bishop of Rome, otherwise known as the Pope. But the contest – every contest – is sharper now.

On the day of Katherine's funeral, he finds himself downcast. How close we hug our enemies! They are our familiars, our other selves. When she was sitting on a silk cushion at the Alhambra, a seven-year-old working her first embroidery, he was scrubbing roots in the kitchen at Lambeth Palace, under the eye of his uncle John, the cook.

So often in council he has taken Katherine's part, as if he were one of her appointed lawyers. 'You make this argument, my lords,' he has said, 'but the dowager princess will allege ...' And 'Katherine will refute you, thus.' Not because he favours her cause but because it saves time; as her opponent, he enters into her concerns, he judges her stratagems, he reaches every point before she does. It has long been a puzzle to Charles Brandon: 'Whose side is this fellow on?' he would demand.

But even now Katherine's cause is not considered settled, in Rome. Once the Vatican lawyers have started a case, they don't stop just because one of the parties is dead. Possibly, when all of us are dead, from some Vatican oubliette a skeleton secretary will rattle along, to consult his fellow skeletons on a point of canon law. They will chatter their teeth at each other; their absent eyes will turn down in the sockets, to see that their parchments have turned to dust motes in the light. Who took Katherine's virginity, her first husband or her second? For all eternity we will never know.

He says to Rafe, 'Who can understand the lives of women?'

'Or their deaths,' Rafe says.

He glances up. 'Not you! You don't think she was poisoned, do you?'

'It is rumoured,' Rafe says gravely, 'that the poison was introduced to her in some strong Welsh beer. A brew which, it seems, she had taken a delight in, these last few months.'

He catches Rafe's eye, and snorts with suppressed laughter. The dowager princess, swigging strong Welsh beer. 'From a leather tankard,' Rafe says. 'And think of her slapping it down on the table. And roaring "Fill it up."'

He hears running feet approaching. What now? A bang at the door, and his little Welsh boy appears, out of breath. 'Master, you are to go at once to the king. Fitzwilliam's people have come for you. I think somebody is dead.'

'What, somebody else?' he says. He picks up his sheaf of papers, throws them into a chest, turns the key on them and gives it to Rafe. From now on he leaves no secret unattended, no fresh ink exposed to the air. 'Who have I to raise this time?'

You know what it's like when a cart overturns in the street? Everybody you meet has witnessed it. They saw a man's leg sliced clean off. They saw a woman gasp her last. They saw the goods looted, thieves stealing from the back-end while the carter was crushed at the front. They heard a man roar out his last confession, while another whispered his last will and testament. And if all the people who say they were there had really been there, then the dregs of London would have drained to the one spot, the gaols emptied of thieves, the beds empty of whores, and all the lawyers standing on the shoulders of the butchers to get a better look.

Later that day, 29 January, he will be on his way to Greenwich, shocked, apprehensive, at the news Fitzwilliam's men had brought. People will tell him, 'I was there, I was there when Anne broke off her talk, I was there when she put down her book, her sewing, her lute, I was there when she broke off her merriment at the thought of Katherine lowered into the ground. I saw her face change. I saw her ladies close about her. I saw them sweep her to her chamber and bolt the door, and I saw the trail of blood left on the ground as she walked.'

We need not believe that. Not the trail of blood. They saw it in their minds perhaps. He will ask, what time did the queen's pains begin? But no one seemed able to tell him, despite their close knowledge of the incident. They have concentrated on the blood trail and left out the facts. It will take all day for the bad news to leak from the queen's bedside. Sometimes women do bleed but the child clings on and grows. Not this time. Katherine is too fresh in her tomb to lie quiet. She has reached out and shaken Anne's child free, so it is brought untimely into the world and no bigger than a rat.

At evening, outside the queen's suite, the dwarf sits on the flags, rocking and moaning. She is pretending to be in labour, someone says: unnecessarily. 'Can you not remove her?' he asks the women.

Jane Rochford says, 'It was a boy, Mr Secretary. She had carried it under four months, as we judge.'

Early October, then. We were still on progress. 'You will have a note of the itinerary,' Lady Rochford murmurs. 'Where was she then?'

'Does it matter?'

'I should think you would like to know. Oh, I know that plans were changed, sometimes on the instant. That sometimes she was with the king, sometimes not, that sometimes Norris was with her, and sometimes others of the gentlemen. But you are right, Master Secretary. It is of no moment. The doctors can be sure of very little. We cannot say when it was conceived. Who was here and who was there.'

'Perhaps we should leave it like that,' he says.

'So. Now that she has lost another chance, poor lady ... what world will be?'

The dwarf scrambles to her feet. Watching him, holding his gaze, she pulls her skirts up. He is not quick enough to look away. She has shaved herself or someone has shaved her, and her parts are bald, like the parts of an old woman or a little child.

Later, before the king, holding Mary Shelton's hand, Jane Rochford is unsure of everything. 'The child had the appearance of a male,' she says, 'and of about fifteen weeks' gestation.'

'What do you mean, the appearance of?' the king demands. 'Could you not tell? Oh, get away, woman, you have never given birth, what do you know? It should have been matrons at her bedside, what did you want there? Could not you Boleyns give way to someone more useful, must you be there in a crowd whenever disaster strikes?'

Lady Rochford's voice shakes, but she sticks to her point. 'Your Majesty may interview the doctors.'

'I have.'

'I only repeat their words.'

Mary Shelton bursts into tears. Henry looks at her and says humbly, 'Mistress Shelton, forgive me. Sweetheart, I did not mean to make you cry.'

Henry is in pain. His leg has been bound up by the surgeons, the leg he injured in the joust over ten years ago; it is prone to ulcerate, and it seems that the recent fall has opened a channel into his flesh. All his bravado has melted away; it is like the days when he dreamed of his brother Arthur, the days he was run ragged by the dead. It is the second child she has lost, he says that night, in private: though who knows, there could have been others, the women keep these things to themselves till their bellies show, we do not know how many of my heirs have bled away. What does God want of me now? What must I do to please him? I see he will not give me male children.

He, Cromwell, stands back while Thomas Cranmer, pale and smooth, takes charge of the king's bereavement. We much misconstrue our creator, the archbishop says, if we blame him for every accident of fallen nature.

I thought he regarded every sparrow that falls, the king says, truculent as a child. Then why does he not regard England?

Cranmer will have some reason. He hardly listens. He thinks of the women about Anne: wise as serpents, mild as doves. Already a certain line is being spun, about the day's events; it is spun in the queen's chamber. Anne Boleyn is not to blame for this misfortune. It is her uncle Thomas Howard, the Duke of Norfolk, who is at fault. When the king took his tumble, it was Norfolk who burst in on the queen, shouting that Henry was dead, and giving her such a shock that the unborn heart stopped.

And further: it is Henry's fault. It is because of the way he has been behaving, mooning over old Seymour's daughter, dropping letters in her place in chapel and sending her sweetmeats from his table. When the queen saw he loved another, she was struck to the quick. The sorrow she has taken has made her viscera revolt and reject the tender child.

Just be clear, Henry says coldly, when he stands at the foot of the lady's bed and hears this reading of events. Just be clear on this, madam. If any woman is to blame, it is the one I am looking at. I will speak to you when you are better. And now fare you well, because I am going to Whitehall to prepare for the Parliament, and you had better stay in bed till you are restored. Which I myself, I doubt I will ever be.

Then Anne shouts after him – or so Lady Rochford says – 'Stay, stay my lord, I will soon give you another child, and all the quicker now Katherine is dead …'

'I do not see how that will speed the business.' Henry limps away. Then in his own rooms the privy chamber gentlemen move carefully about him, as if he were made of glass, making their preparations for departure. Henry is repenting now of his hasty pronouncement, because if the queen stays behind all the women must stay behind, and he will not be able to feast his eyes on his little bun-face, Jane. Further reasoning follows him, conveyed by Anne in a note perhaps: this lost foetus, conceived when Katherine was alive, is inferior to the conception that will follow, at some unknown date, but soon. For even if the child had lived and grown up, there would have been some who still doubted his claim; whereas now Henry is a widower, no one in Christendom can dispute that his marriage to Anne is licit, and any son they beget is heir to England.

'Well, what do you make of that chain of reasoning?' Henry demands. Leg stout with bandages, he heaves himself into a chair in his private rooms. 'No, do not confer, I want an answer from each of you, each Thomas alone.' He grimaces, though he means to smile. 'Do you know the confusion you cause among the French? They have made of you one composite counsellor, and in dispatches they call you Dr Chramuel.'

They exchange glances, he and Cranmer: the pork butcher and the angel. But the king does not wait for their advice, joint or several; he talks on, like a man sticking a dagger into himself to prove how much it hurts. 'If a king cannot have a son, if he cannot do that, it matters not what else he can do. The victories, the spoils of victory, the just laws he makes, the famous courts he holds, these are as nothing.'

It is true. To maintain the stability of the realm: this is the compact a king makes with his people. If he cannot have a son of his own, he must find an heir, name him before his country falls into doubt and confusion, faction and conspiracy. And who can Henry name, that will not be laughed at? The king says, 'When I remember what I did for the present queen, how I raised her from a gentleman's daughter … I cannot think now why I did it.' He looks at them as if to say, do you know, Dr Chramuel? 'It seems to me,' he is groping, perplexed, for the right phrases, 'it seems to me I was somehow dishonestly led into this marriage.'

He, Cromwell, eyes the other half of himself, as if through a mirror: Cranmer looks thrown. 'How, dishonestly?' the archbishop asks.

'I feel sure I was not in my clear mind then. Not as I am now.'

'But sir,' Cranmer says. 'Majesty. Saving Your Grace, your mind cannot be clear. You have suffered a great loss.'

Two, in fact, he thinks: today your son was born dead, and your first wife buried. No wonder you tremble.

'It seems to me I was seduced,' Henry says, 'that is to say, I was practised upon, perhaps by charms, perhaps by spells. Women do use such things. And if that were so, then the marriage would be null, would it not?'

Cranmer holds out his hands, like a man trying to send back the tide. He sees his queen vanishing into thin air: his queen who has done so much for true religion. 'Sir, sir ... Majesty ...'

'Oh, peace!' Henry says: as if it were Cranmer who had started it. 'Cromwell, when you were soldiering, did you ever hear of anything that would heal a leg like mine? I have knocked it again now and the surgeons say the foul humours must come out. They fear that the rot has got as far as the bone. But do not tell anybody. I would not like word to spread abroad. Will you send a page to find Thomas Vicary? I think he must bleed me. I need some relief. Give you good night.' He adds, almost under his breath, 'For I suppose even this day must end.'

Dr Chramuel goes out. In an antechamber, one of him turns to the other. 'He will be different tomorrow,' the archbishop says.

'Yes. A man in pain will say anything.'

'We should not heed it.'

'No.'

They are like two men crossing thin ice; leaning into each other, taking tiny, timid steps. As if that will do you any good, when it begins to crack on every side.

Cranmer says uncertainly, 'Grief for the child sways him. Would he wait so long for Anne, to throw her over so quickly? They will soon be perfect friends.'

'Besides,' he says. 'He is not a man to admit he was wrong. He may have his doubts about his marriage. But God help anyone else who raises them.'

'We must calm these doubts,' Cranmer says. 'Between us we must do it.'

'He would like to be the Emperor's friend. Now that Katherine is not there to cause ill-feeling between them. And so we must face the fact that the present queen is ...' He hesitates to say, superfluous; he hesitates to say, an obstacle to peace.

'She is in his way,' Cranmer says bluntly. 'But he will not sacrifice her? Surely he will not. Not to please Emperor Charles or any man. They need not think it. Rome need not think it. He will never revert.'

'No. Have some faith in our good master to maintain the church.'

Cranmer hears the words he has left unspoken: the king does not need Anne, to help him do that.

Although, he says to Cranmer. It is hard to remember the king, before Anne; hard to imagine him without her. She hovers around him. She reads over his shoulder. She gets into his dreams. Even when she's lying next to him it's not close enough for her. 'I tell you what we'll do,' he says. He squeezes Cranmer's arm. 'Let's give a dinner, shall we, and invite the Duke of Norfolk?'

Cranmer shrinks. 'Norfolk? Why would we?'

'For reconciliation,' he says breezily. 'I fear that on the day of the king's accident, I may have, um, slighted his pretensions. In a tent. When he raced in. Well-founded pretensions,' he adds reverently. 'For is he not our senior peer? No, I pity the duke from the bottom of my heart.'

'What did you do, Cromwell?' The archbishop is pale. 'What did you do in that tent? Did you lay violent hands upon him, as I hear you did recently with the Duke of Suffolk?'

'What, Brandon? I was only moving him.'

'When he was not of a mind to be moved.'

'It was for his own good. If I had left him there in the king's presence, Charles would have talked himself into the Tower. He was slandering the queen, you see.' And any slander, any doubt, he thinks, must come from Henry, out of his own mouth, and not from mine, or any other man's. 'Please, please,' he says, 'let us have a dinner. You must give it at Lambeth, Norfolk will not come to me, he will think I plan to put a sleeping draught in the claret and convey him on board ship to be sold into slavery. He will like to come to you. I will supply the venison. We will have jellies in the shape of the duke's major castles. It will be no cost to you. And no trouble to your cooks.'

186

Cranmer laughs. At last, he laughs. It has been a hard-fought campaign, to get him even to smile. 'As you wish, Thomas. We shall have a dinner.'

The archbishop sets his hands on his upper arms, kisses him right and left. The kiss of peace. He does not feel soothed, or assuaged, as he returns to his own rooms through the palace unnaturally quiet: no music from distant rooms, perhaps the murmur of prayer. He tries to imagine the lost child, the manikin, its limbs budding, its face old and wise.

Few men have seen such a thing. Certainly he has not. In Italy, once, he stood holding up a light for a surgeon, while in a sealed room draped in shadows he sliced a dead man apart to see what made him work. It was a fearful night, the stench of bowel and blood clogging the throat, and the artists who had jostled and bribed for a place tried to elbow him away: but he stood firm, for he had guaranteed to do so, he had said he would hold the light. And so he was among the elect of that company, the luminaries, who saw muscle stripped from bone. But he has never seen inside a woman, still less a gravid corpse; no surgeon, even for money, would perform that work for an audience.

He thinks of Katherine, embalmed and entombed. Her spirit cut free, and gone to seek out her first husband: wandering now, calling his name. Will Arthur be shocked to see her, she such a stout old woman, and he still a skinny child?

King Arthur of blessed memory could not have a son. And what happened after Arthur? We don't know. But we know his glory vanished from the world.

He thinks of Anne's chosen motto, painted up with her coat of arms: 'The Most Happy'.

He had said to Jane Rochford, 'How is my lady the queen?'

Rochford had said, 'Sitting up, lamenting.'

He had meant, has she lost much blood?

Katherine was not without sin, but now her sins are taken off her. They are all heaped upon Anne: the shadow who flits after her, the woman draped in night. The old queen dwells in the radiance of God's presence, her dead infants swaddled at her feet, but Anne dwells in this sinful world below, stewed in her childbed sweat, in her soiled sheet. But her hands and feet are cold and her heart is like a stone.

So here's the Duke of Norfolk, expecting to be fed. Dressed in his best, or at least what's good enough for Lambeth Palace, he looks like a piece of rope chewed by a dog, or a piece of gristle left on the side of a trencher. Bright fierce eyes under unruly brows. Hair an iron stubble. His person is meagre, sinewy, and he smells of horses and leather and the armourer's shop, and mysteriously of furnaces or perhaps of cooling ash: dust-dry, pungent. He fears no one alive except Henry Tudor, who could at a whim take his dukedom away, but he fears the dead. They say that at any of his houses at close of day you can hear him slamming the shutters and shooting the bolts, in case the late Cardinal Wolsey is blowing through a window or slithering up a stair. If Wolsey wanted Norfolk he would lie quiet inside a table top, breathing along the grain of the wood; he would ooze through a keyhole, or flop down a chimney with a soft flurry like a soot-stained dove.

When Anne Boleyn came up in the world, and she a niece of his illustrious family, the duke thought his troubles were over. Because he has troubles; the greatest nobleman has his rivals, his ill-wishers, his defamers. But he believed that, with Anne crowned in due time, he would be always at the king's right hand. It hasn't worked out like that, and the duke has become disaffected. The match hasn't brought the Howards the riches and honours he expected. Anne has taken the rewards for herself, and Thomas Cromwell has taken them. The duke thinks Anne should be guided by her male kin, but she won't be guided; in fact she has made it plain that she sees herself, and not the duke, as the head of the family now. Which is unnatural, in the duke's view: a woman cannot be head of anything, subordination and submission is her role. Let her be a queen and a rich woman, still she should know her place, or be taught it. Howard sometimes grumbles in public: not about Henry, but about Anne Boleyn. And he has found it expedient to spend his time in his own country, harassing his duchess, who often writes to Thomas Cromwell with complaints of his treatment of her. As if he, Thomas Cromwell, could turn the duke into one of the world's great lovers, or even into a semblance of a reasonable man.

But then when Anne's latest pregnancy was known, the duke had come to court, flanked by his smirking retainers and soon joined by his peculiar son. Surrey is a young man with a great conceit of himself as handsome, talented and lucky. But his face is lopsided, and he does himself no favours, in having his hair cut like a bowl. Hans Holbein admits he finds him a challenge. Surrey is here tonight at Lambeth, forfeiting an evening in the brothel. His eyes roam about the room; perhaps he thinks Cranmer keeps naked girls behind the arras.

'Well, now,' says the duke, rubbing his hands. 'When are you coming down to see me at Kenninghall, Thomas Cromwell? We have good hunting, by God, we have something to shoot at every season of the year. And we can get you a bedwarmer if you want one, a common woman of the type you like, we have a maidservant just now,' the duke sucks in his breath, 'you should see her titties.' His knotty fingers knead the air.

'Well, if she's yours,' he murmurs. 'I wouldn't like to deprive you.'

The duke shoots a glance at Cranmer. Perhaps one ought not to talk about women? But then, Cranmer's not a proper archbishop, not in Norfolk's view; he's some petty clerk Henry found in the fens one year, who promised to do anything he asked in return for a mitre and two good meals a day.

'By God, you look ill, Cranmer,' the duke says with gloomy relish. 'You look as if you can't keep the flesh on your bones. No more can I. Look at this.' The duke thrusts himself back from the table, elbowing a poor youth who stands ready with the wine jug. He stands up and parts his gown, thrusting out a skinny calf. 'What do you make of that?'

That's horrible, he agrees. It's humiliation, surely, that wears Thomas Howard to the bone? In company his niece interrupts him and talks over him. She laughs at his holy medals and the relics he wears, some of them very sacred. At table she leans towards him, says, Come, uncle, take a crumb from my hand, you are wasting away. 'And I am,' he says. 'I don't know how you do it, Cromwell. Look at you, all fleshed out in your gown, an ogre would eat you roasted.'

'Ah, well,' he says, smiling, 'that's the risk I run.'

'I think you drink some powder that you got in Italy. Keeps you sleek. I suppose you wouldn't part with the secret?'

'Eat up your jelly, my lord,' he says patiently. 'If I do hear of a powder I will get a sample for you. My only secret is that I sleep at night. I am at peace with my maker. And of course,' he adds, leaning back at his ease, 'I have no enemies.'

'What?' says the duke. His eyebrows shoot up into his hair. He serves himself some more of Thurston's jelly crenellations, the scarlet and the pale, the airy stone and the bloody brick. As he swills them around his mouth he opines on several topics. Chiefly Wiltshire, the queen's father. Who should have brought Anne up properly and with more attention to discipline. But no, he was too busy boasting about her in French, boasting about what she would become.

'Well, she did become,' says young Surrey. 'Didn't she, my lord father?'

'I think it's she who's wasting me away,' the duke says. 'She knows all about powders. They say she keeps poisoners in her house. You know what she did to old Bishop Fisher.'

'What did she do?' young Surrey says.

'Do you know nothing, boy? Fisher's cook was paid to put a powder in the broth. It nigh killed him.'

'That would have been no loss,' the boy says. 'He was a traitor.'

'Yes,' Norfolk says, 'but in those days his treason stood still to be proved. This is not Italy, boy. We have courts of law. Well, the old fellow pulled around, but he was never well after. Henry had the cook boiled alive.'

'But he never confessed,' he says: he, Cromwell. 'So we cannot say for sure the Boleyns did it.'

Norfolk snorts. 'They had motive. Mary had better watch herself.'

'I agree,' he says. 'Though I do not think poison is the chief danger to her.'

'What then?' Surrey says.

'Bad advice, my lord.'

'You think she should listen to you, Cromwell?' Young Surrey now lays down his knife and begins to complain. Noblemen, he laments, are not respected as they were in the days when England was great. The present king keeps about himself a collection of men of base degree, and no good will come of it. Cranmer creeps forward in his chair, as if to intervene, but Surrey gives him a glare that says, you're exactly who I mean, archbishop.

He nods to a boy to refill the young man's glass. 'You do not suit your talk to your audience, sir.'

'Why should I?' Surrey says.

'Thomas Wyatt says you are studying to write verse. I am fond of poems, as I passed my youth among the Italians. If you would favour me, I would like to read some.'

'No doubt you would,' Surrey says. 'But I keep them for my friends.'

When he gets home his son comes out to greet him. 'Have you heard what the queen is doing? She has risen from her childbed and things incredible are spoken of her. They say she was seen toasting cobnuts over the fire in her chamber, tossing them about in a latten pan, ready to make poisoned sweetmeats for the Lady Mary.'

'It would be someone else with the latten pan,' he says, smiling. 'A minion. Weston. That boy Mark.'

Gregory sticks stubbornly by his version: 'It was herself. Toasting. And the king came in, and frowned to see her at the occupation, for he didn't know what it meant, and he has suspicions of her, you see. What are you at, he asked, and Anne the queen said, oh my lord, I am but making sweetmeats to reward the poor women who stand at the gate and call out their greetings to me. The king said, is it even so, sweetheart? Then bless you. And so he was utterly misled, you see.'

'And where did this happen, Gregory? You see, she is at Greenwich, and the king at Whitehall.'

'No matter,' Gregory says cheerfully. 'In France witches can fly, latten pan and cobnuts and all. And that is where she learned it. In truth the whole Boleyn affinity are become witches, to witch up a boy for her, for the king fears he can give her none.'

His smile becomes pained. 'Do not spread this about the household.'

Gregory says happily, 'Too late, the household has spread it about me.'

He remembers Jane Rochford saying to him, it must be two years back: 'The queen has boasted she will give Katherine's daughter a breakfast she will not recover from.'

Merry at breakfast, dead by dinner. It was what they used to say about the sweating sickness, that killed his wife and daughters. And unnatural ends, when they occur, are usually swifter than that; they cut down at a stroke.

'I am going to my rooms,' he says. 'I have to draw up a paper. Do not let me be interrupted. Richard may come in if he will.'

'What about me, can I come in? For instance, if the house were on fire, you would like to hear of it?'

'Not from you. Why would I believe you?' He pats his son. Hurries off to his private room and shuts the door.

The meeting with Norfolk has, on the face of it, no pay-off. But. He takes his paper. At the top he writes:

THOMAS BOLEYN

This is the lady's father. He pictures him in his mind. An upright man, still lithe, proud of his looks, who pays great attention to turning himself out, just like his son George: a man to test the ingenuity of London goldsmiths, and to swivel around his fingers jewels which he says have been given him by foreign rulers. These many years he has served Henry as a diplomat, a trade for which he is fitted by his cold emollience. He is not a man wedded to action, Boleyn, but rather a man who stands by, smirking and stroking his beard; he thinks he looks enigmatic, but instead he looks as if he's pleasuring himself.

Still, he knew how to act when the chance presented itself, how to set his family climbing, climbing, to the highest branches of the tree. It's cold up there when the wind blows, the cutting wind of 1536.

As we know, his title of Earl of Wiltshire seems to him insufficient to indicate his special status, so he has invented for himself a French title, *Monseigneur*. And it gives him pleasure, to be so addressed. He lets it be known this title should be universally adopted. From whether the courtiers comply, you can tell a great deal about where they stand.

He writes:

Monseigneur: All the Boleyns. Their women. Their chaplains.
   Their servants.
All the Boleyn toadies in the privy chamber, that is to say,

Henry Norris
Francis Weston
William Brereton, etc.

But plain old 'Wiltshire', delivered in accents brisk:
The Duke of Norfolk.
Sir Nicholas Carew (of the privy chamber) who is cousin to
    Edward Seymour, and married to the sister of:
Sir Francis Bryan, cousin to the Boleyns, but cousin to the
    Seymours also, and friend of:
Mr Treasurer, William Fitzwilliam.

He looks at this list. He adds the names of two grandees:

The Marquis of Exeter, Henry Courtenay.
Henry Pole, Lord Montague.

These are the old families of England; they draw their claims
from ancient lines; they smart, more than any of us, under the
pretensions of the Boleyns.

He rolls up his paper. Norfolk, Carew, Fitz. Francis Bryan. The
Courtenays, the Montagues, and their ilk. And Suffolk, who
hates Anne. It is a set of names. You cannot take too much from
it. These people are not necessarily friends of each other. They are
just, to one degree and another, friends of the old dispensation
and enemies of the Boleyns.

    He closes his eyes. He sits, his breathing calm. In his mind, a
picture appears. A lofty hall. Into which he commands a table.

    The trestles are lugged up by menials.

    The top is fixed in place.

    Liveried officials unroll the cloth, tweaking and smoothing; like
the king's tablecloth, it is blessed, its attendants murmuring a Latin
formula as they stand back to take a view and even up the edges.

So much for the table. Now for somewhere for the guests to sit.

The servants scrape over the floor a weighty chair, the Howard coat of arms carved into its back. That's for the Duke of Norfolk, who lowers his bony bum. 'What have you got,' he asks plaintively, 'to tempt my appetite, Crumb?'

Now bring up another chair, he commands the servants. Set it down at my lord Norfolk's right hand.

This one is for Henry Courtenay, the Marquis of Exeter. Who says, 'Cromwell, my wife insisted on coming!'

'It does my heart good to see you, Lady Gertrude,' he says, bowing. 'Take your seat.' Until this dinner, he has always tried to avoid this rash and interfering woman. But now he puts on his polite face: 'Any friend of the Lady Mary is welcome to dine.'

'The Princess Mary,' Gertrude Courtenay snaps.

'As you will, my lady,' he sighs.

'Now here comes Henry Pole!' Norfolk exclaims. 'Will he steal my dinner?'

'There is food for all,' he says. 'Bring up another chair for Lord Montague. A fitting chair, for a man of royal blood.'

'We call it a throne,' Montague says. 'By the way, my mother is here.'

Lady Margaret Pole, the Countess of Salisbury. Rightful queen of England, according to some. King Henry has taken a wise course with her and all her family. He has honoured them, cherished them, kept them close. Much good it's done him: they still think the Tudors are usurpers, though the countess is fond of Princess Mary, whose childhood governor she was: honouring her more for her royal mother, Katherine, than for her father, whom she regards as the spawn of Welsh cattle-raiders.

Now the countess, in his mind, creaks to her place. She stares around her. 'You have a magnificent hall here, Cromwell,' she says, peeved.

'The rewards of vice,' says her son Montague.

He bows again. He will swallow any insult, at this point.

'Well,' Norfolk says, 'where's my first dish?'

'Patience, my lord,' he says.

He takes his own place, a humble three-legged stool, down at the end of the table. He gazes up at his betters. 'In a moment the platters will come in. But first, shall we say a grace?'

He glances up at the beams. Up there are carved and painted the faces of the dead: More, Fisher, the cardinal, Katherine the queen. Below them, the flower of living England. Let us hope the roof doesn't fall in.

The day after he, Thomas Cromwell, has exercised his imagination in this way, he feels the need to clarify his position, in the real world; and to add to the guest list. His daydream has not got as far as the actual feast, so he does not know what dishes he is going to offer. He must cook up something good, or the magnates will storm out, pulling off the cloth and kicking his servants.

So: he now speaks to the Seymours, privately yet plainly. 'As long as the king holds by the queen that is now, I will hold by her too. But if he rejects her, I must reconsider.'

'So you have no interest of your own in this?' Edward Seymour says sceptically.

'I represent the king's interests. That is what I am for.'

Edward knows he will get no further. 'Still ...' he says. Anne will soon be recovered from her mishap and Henry can have her back in bed, but it is clear that the prospect has not made him lose interest in Jane. The game has changed, and Jane must be repositioned. The challenge puts a glint in Seymour eyes. Now Anne has failed again, it is possible that Henry may wish to remarry. The whole court is talking of it. It is Anne Boleyn's former success that allows them to imagine it.

'You Seymours should not raise your hopes,' he says. 'He falls out with Anne and falls in again, and then he cannot do too much for her. That is how they have always been.'

Tom Seymour says, 'Why would one prefer a tough old hen to a plump little chick? What use is it?'

'Soup,' he says: but not so that Tom can hear.

The Seymours are in mourning, though not for the dowager Katherine. Anthony Oughtred is dead, the governor of Jersey, and Jane's sister Elizabeth is left a widow.

Tom Seymour says, 'If the king takes on Jane as his mistress, or whatever, we should look to make some great match for Bess.'

Edward says, 'Just stick to the matter in hand, brother.'

The brisk young widow comes to court, to help the family in their campaign. He'd thought they called her Lizzie, this young woman, but it seems that was just her husband's name for her, and to her family she's Bess. He is glad, though he doesn't know why. It is unreasonable of him to think other women shouldn't have his wife's name. Bess is no great beauty, and darker than her sister, but she has a confident vivacity that compels the eye. 'Be kind to Jane, Master Secretary,' Bess says. 'She is not proud, as some people think. They wonder why she doesn't speak to them, but it's only because she can't think what to say.'

'But she will speak to me.'

'She will listen.'

'An attractive quality in women.'

'An attractive quality in anyone. Wouldn't you say? Though Jane above all women looks to men to tell her what she should do.'

'Then does she do it?'

'Not necessarily.' She laughs. Her fingertips brush the back of his hand. 'Come. She is ready for you.'

Warmed by the sun of the King of England's desire, which maiden would not glow? Not Jane. She is in deeper black, it seems, than the rest of her family, and she volunteers that she has been praying for the soul of the late Katherine: not that she needs it, for surely, if any woman has gone straight to Heaven …

'Jane,' Edward Seymour says, 'I am warning you now and I want you to listen carefully and heed what I say. When you come into the king's presence, it must be as if no such woman as the late Katherine ever existed. If he hears her name in your mouth, he will cease his favour, upon the instant.'

'Look,' Tom Seymour says. 'Cromwell here wants to know, are you truly and entirely a virgin?'

He could blush for her. 'If you aren't, Mistress Jane,' he says, 'it can be managed. But you must tell us now.'

Her pale, oblivious regard: 'What?'

Tom Seymour: 'Jane, even you must understand the question.'

'Is it correct that no one has ever asked for you in marriage? No contract or understanding?' He feels desperate. 'Did you never like anybody, Jane?'

'I liked William Dormer. But he married Mary Sidney.' She looks up: one flash of those ice-blue eyes. 'I hear they're very miserable.'

'The Dormers didn't think we were good enough,' Tom says. 'But now look.'

He says, 'It is to your credit, Mistress Jane, that you have formed no attachments till your family were ready to marry you. For young women often do, and then it ends badly.' He feels that he should clarify the point. 'Men will tell you that they are so in love with you that it is making them ill. They will say they have stopped eating and sleeping. They say that they fear unless they can have you they will die. Then, the moment you give in, they get up and walk away and lose all interest. The next week they will pass you by as if they don't know you.'

'Did you do this, Master Secretary?' Jane asks.

He hesitates.

'Well?' Tom Seymour says. 'We would like to know.'

'I probably did. When I was young. I am telling you in case your brothers cannot bring themselves to tell you. It is not a pretty thing for a man to have to admit to his sister.'

'So you see,' Edward urges. 'You must not give in to the king.'

Jane says, 'Why would I want to do that?'

'His honeyed words –' Edward begins.

'His what?'

The Emperor's ambassador has been skulking indoors, and won't come out to meet Thomas Cromwell. He would not go up to Peterborough for Katherine's funeral because she was not being buried as a queen, and now he says he has to observe his mourning period. Finally, a meeting is arranged: the ambassador will happen to be coming back from Mass at the church of Austin Friars, while Thomas Cromwell, now in residence at the Rolls House at Chancery Lane, has called by to inspect his building work, extensions to his principal house nearby. 'Ambassador!' he cries: as if he were wildly surprised.

The bricks ready for use today were fired last summer, when the king was still on his progress through the western counties; the clay for them was dug the winter before, and the frost was breaking down the clumps while he, Cromwell, was trying to break down Thomas More. Waiting for Chapuys to appear, he has been haranguing the bricklayers' gaffer about water penetration, which he definitely does not want. Now he takes hold of Chapuys and steers him away from the noise and dust of the sawpit. Eustache is seething with questions; you can feel them, jumping and agitating in the muscles of his arm, buzzing in the weave of his garments. 'This Semer girl ...'

It is a lightless day, still, the air frigid. 'Today would be a good day to fish for pike,' he says.

The ambassador struggles to master his dismay. 'Surely your servants ... if you must have this fish ...'

'Ah, Eustache, I see you do not understand the sport. Have no fear, I will teach you. What could be better for the health than to be out from dawn to dusk, hours and hours on a muddy bank, with the trees dripping above, watching your own breath on the air, alone or with one good companion?'

Various ideas are fighting inside the ambassador's head. On the one hand, hours and hours with Cromwell: during which he might drop his guard, say anything. On the other hand, what good am I to my Imperial master if my knees seize up entirely, and I have to be carried to court in a litter? 'Could we not fish for it in the summer?' he asks, without much hope.

'I could not risk your person. A summer pike would pull you in.' He relents. 'The lady you mean is called Seymour. As in, "Ambassador, I would like to see more of you." Though some old folk pronounce it Semer.'

'I make no progress in this tongue,' the ambassador complains. 'Anyone may say his name any way he likes, different on different days. What I hear is, the family is ancient, and the woman herself not so young.'

'She served the dowager princess, you know. She was fond of Katherine. She lamented, in fact, what had befallen her. She is troubled about the Lady Mary, and they say she has sent her messages to be of good cheer. If the king continues his favour to her, she may be able to do Mary some good.'

'Mm.' The ambassador looks sceptical. 'I have heard this, and also that she is of a very meek and pious character. But I fear there may be a scorpion lurking under the honey. I would like to see Mistress Semer, can you arrange that? Not to meet her. To glimpse her.'

'I am surprised that you take so much interest. I should have thought you would be more interested in which French princess Henry will marry, should he dissolve his present arrangements.'

Now the ambassador is stretched tight on the ladder of terror. Better the devil you know? Better Anne Boleyn, than a new threat, a new treaty, a new alliance between France and England?

'But surely not!' he explodes. 'Cremuel, you told me that this was a fairy tale! You have expressed yourself a friend of my master, you will not countenance a French match?'

'Calmly, ambassador, calmly. I do not claim I can govern Henry. And after all, he may decide to continue with his present marriage, or if not, to live chaste.'

'You are laughing!' the ambassador accuses. 'Cremuel! You are laughing behind your hand.'

And so he is. The builders skirt around them, giving them space, rough London craftsmen with tools stuck in their belts. Penitent, he says, 'Do not get your hopes up. When the king and his woman have one of their reconciliations, it goes hard with anyone who has spoken out against her in the interim.'

'You would maintain her? You would support her?' The ambassador's whole body has stiffened, as if he had really been on that riverbank all day. 'She may be your co-religionist –'

'What?' He opens his eyes wide. 'My co-religionist? Like my master the king, I am a faithful son of the holy Catholic church. Only just now we are not in communion with the Pope.'

'Let me put it another way,' Chapuys says. He squints up at the grey London sky, as if seeking help from above. 'Let us say your ties to her are material, not spiritual. I understand that you have had preferment from her. I am aware of that.'

'Do not mistake me. I owe Anne nothing. I have preferment from the king, from no one else.'

'You have sometimes called her your dear friend. I remember occasions.'

'I have sometimes called you my dear friend. But you're not, are you?'

Chapuys digests the point. 'There is nothing I wish to see more,' he says, 'than peace between our nations. What could better mark an ambassador's success in his post, than a rapprochement after years of trouble? And now we have the opportunity.'

'Now Katherine is gone.'

Chapuys does not argue with that. He just winds his cloak closer about him. 'The king has got no good of the concubine, and will get none now. No power in Europe recognises his marriage. Even the heretics do not recognise it, though she has done her best to make friends of them. What profit can there be to you, in keeping matters as they are: the king unhappy, Parliament fretful, the nobility fractious, the whole country revolted by the woman's pretensions?'

Slow drops of rain have begun to fall: ponderous, icy. Chapuys glances up again irritably, as if God were undermining him at this crucial point. Taking a grip on the ambassador once more, he tows him over the rough ground towards shelter. The builders have put up a canopy, and he turns them out, saying, 'Give us a minute, boys, will you?' Chapuys huddles by the brazier, and grows confidential. 'I hear the king talks of witchcraft,' he whispers. 'He says that he was seduced into the marriage by certain charms and false practices. I see he does not confide in you. But he has spoken to his confessor. If this is so, if he entered into the match in a state of entrancement, then he might find he is not married at all, and free to take a new wife.'

He gazes over the ambassador's shoulder. Look, he says, this is how it will be: in a year these damp and freezing spaces will be inhabited rooms. His hand sketches the line of the jettied upper storeys, the glazed bays.

Inventories for this project: lime and sand, oak timbers and special cements, spades and shovels, baskets and ropes, tackets, pin nails, roof nails, lead pipes; tiles yellow and tiles blue, window locks, latches, bolts and hinges, iron door handles in the shape of roses; gilding, painting, 2 lb. of frankincense to perfume the new rooms; 6d per day per labourer, and the cost of candles for labour by night.

'My friend,' Chapuys says, 'Anne is desperate and dangerous. Strike first, before she strikes you. Remember how she brought down Wolsey.'

His past lies about him like a burnt house. He has been building, building, but it has taken him years to sweep up the mess.

At the Rolls House, he finds his son, who is packing to go away for the next phase of his education. 'Gregory, you know St Uncumber? You say that women pray to her to be rid of useless husbands. Now, is there a saint that men can pray to if they wish to be quit of their wives?'

'I don't think so.' Gregory is shocked. 'The women pray because they have no other means. A man can consult a cleric to find why the marriage is not licit. Or he can chase her away and pay her money to stay in a separate house. As the Duke of Norfolk pays his wife.'

He nods. 'That's very helpful, Gregory.'

Anne Boleyn comes up to Whitehall to celebrate the feast of St Matthias with the king. She has changed, all in a season. She is light, starved, she looks as she did in her days of waiting, those futile years of negotiations before he, Thomas Cromwell, came along and cut the knot. Her flamboyant liveliness has faded to something austere, narrow, almost nun-like. But she does not have a nun's composure. Her fingers play with the jewels at her girdle, tug at her sleeves, touch and retouch the jewels at her throat.

Lady Rochford says, 'She thought that when she was queen, she would take comfort in going over the days of her coronation, hour by hour. But she says she has forgotten them. When she tries to remember, it's as if it happened to someone else, and she wasn't there. She didn't tell me this, of course. She told brother George.'

From the queen's rooms comes a dispatch: a prophetess has told her that she will not bear Henry a son while his daughter Mary is alive.

You have to admire it, he says to his nephew. She is on the offensive. She is like a serpent, you do not know when she will strike.

He has always rated Anne highly as a strategist. He has never believed in her as a passionate, spontaneous woman. Everything she does is calculated, like everything he does. He notes, as he has these many years, the careful deployment of her flashing eyes. He wonders what it would take to make her panic.

The king sings:

> 'My most desire my hand may reach,
> My will is always at my hand;
> Me need not long for to beseech,
> Her that has power me to command.'

So he thinks. He can beseech and beseech, but it has no effect on Jane.

But the nation's business must go forward, and this is how: an act to give Wales members of Parliament, and make English the language of the law courts, and to cut from under them the powers of the lords of the Welsh marches. An act to dissolve the small monasteries, those houses worth under two hundred pounds a year. An act to set up a Court of Augmentations, a new body to deal with the inflow of revenue from these monasteries: Richard Riche to be its chancellor.

In March, Parliament knocks back his new poor law. It was too much for the Commons to digest, that rich men might have some duty to the poor; that if you get fat, as gentlemen of England do, on the wool trade, you have some responsibility to the men turned off the land, the labourers without labour, the sowers without a field. England needs roads, forts, harbours, bridges. Men need work. It's a shame to see them begging their bread, when honest labour could keep the realm secure. Can we not put them together, the hands and the task?

But Parliament cannot see how it is the state's job to create work. Are not these matters in God's hands, and is not poverty and dereliction part of his eternal order? To everything there is a season: a time to starve and a time to thieve. If rain falls for six months solid and rots the grain in the fields, there must be providence in it; for God knows his trade. It is an outrage to the rich and enterprising, to suggest that they should pay an income tax, only to put bread in the mouths of the workshy. And if Secretary Cromwell argues that famine provokes criminality: well, are there not hangmen enough?

The king himself comes to the Commons to argue for the law. He wants to be Henry the Beloved, a father to his people, a shepherd to his flock. But the Commons sit stony-faced on their benches and stare him out. The wreckage of the measure is comprehensive. 'It has ended up as an act for the whipping of beggars,' Richard Riche says. 'It is more against the poor than for them.'

'Perhaps we can bring it in again,' Henry says. 'In a better year. Do not lose heart, Master Secretary.'

So: there will be better years, will there? He will keep trying; sneak it past them when they're off their guard, start off the measure in the Lords and face down the opposition ... there are ways and ways with Parliament, but there are times he wishes he could kick the members back to their own shires, because he could get on faster without them. He says, 'If I were king, I would not take it so quietly. I would make them shake in their shoes.'

Richard Riche is Mr Speaker in this Parliament; he says nervously, 'Don't incense the king, sir. You know what More used to say. "If the lion knew his own strength, it were hard to rule him."'

'Thank you,' he says. 'That consoles me mightily, Sir Purse, a text from the grave from that blood-soaked hypocrite. Has he anything else to say about the situation? Because if so I'm going to get his head back off his daughter and boot it up and down Whitehall till he shuts up for good and all.' He bursts into laughter. 'The Commons. God rot them. Their heads are empty. They never think higher than their pockets.'

Still, if his fellows in Parliament are worried about their incomes, he is buoyant about his own. Though the lesser monastic houses are to be dissolved, they may apply for exemptions, and all these applications come to him, accompanied by a fee or a pension. The king will not keep all his new lands in his own name, but lease them out, so continual application is made to him, for this place or that, for manors, farms, pasture; each applicant offers him a little something, a one-off payment or an annuity, an annuity that will pass to Gregory in time. It's the way business has always been done, favours, sweeteners, a timely transfer of funds to secure attention, or a promise of split proceeds: just now there is so much business, so many transactions, so many offers he can hardly, in civility, decline. No man in England works harder than he does. Say what you like about Thomas Cromwell, he offers good value for what he takes. And he's always ready to lend: William Fitzwilliam, Sir Nicholas Carew, that ageing one-eyed reprobate Francis Bryan.

He gets Sir Francis round and gets him drunk. He, Cromwell, can trust himself; when he was young, he learned to drink with Germans. It's over a year since Francis Bryan quarrelled with George Boleyn: over what, Francis hardly remembers, but the grudge remains, and until his legs go from under him he is able to act out the more florid bits of the row, standing up and waving his arms. Of his cousin Anne he says, 'You like to know where you are with a woman. Is she a harlot, or a lady? Anne wants you to treat her like the Virgin Mary, but she also wants you to put your cash on the table, do the business and get out.'

Sir Francis is intermittently pious, as conspicuous sinners tend to be. Lent is here: 'It is time for you to enter into your yearly frenzy of penitence, is it not?'

Francis pushes up the patch on his blind eye, and rubs the scar tissue; it itches, he explains. 'Of course,' he says, 'Wyatt's had her.'

He, Thomas Cromwell, waits.

But then Francis puts his head down on the table, and begins to snore.

'The Vicar of Hell,' he says thoughtfully. He calls for boys to come in. 'Take Sir Francis home to his own people. But wrap him up warm, we may need his testimony in the days to come.'

He wonders exactly how much you'd have to leave on the table, for Anne. She's cost Henry his honour, his peace of mind. To him, Cromwell, she is just another trader. He admires the way she's laid out her goods. He personally doesn't want to buy; but there are customers enough.

Now Edward Seymour is promoted into the king's privy chamber, a singular mark of favour. And the king says to him, 'I think I should have young Rafe Sadler among my grooms. He is a gentleman born, and a pleasant young man to have near me, and I think it would help you, Cromwell, would it not? Only he is not for ever to be putting papers under my nose.'

Rafe's wife Helen bursts into tears when she hears the news. 'He will be away at court,' she says, 'for weeks at a time.'

He sits with her in the parlour at Brick Place, consoling her as best he can. 'This is the best thing that has ever happened for Rafe, I know,' she says. 'I am a fool to weep over it. But I cannot bear to be parted from him, nor he from me. When he is late I send men to look along the road. I wish we could be under the same roof every night we live.'

'He is a lucky man,' he says. 'And I don't mean just lucky in the king's favour. You are both of you lucky. To love so much.'

Henry used to sing a song, in his Katherine days:

'I hurt no man, I do no wrong,
I love true where I did marry.'

Rafe says, 'You need a steady nerve, to be always with Henry.'

'You have a steady nerve, Rafe.'

He could give him advice. Extracts from The Book Called Henry. As a child, a young man, praised for the sweetness of his nature and his golden looks, Henry grew up believing that all the world was his friend and everybody wanted him to be happy. So any pain, any delay, frustration or stroke of ill-luck seems to him an anomaly, an outrage. Any activity he finds wearying or displeasant, he will try honestly to turn into an amusement, and if he cannot find some thread of pleasure he will avoid it; this to him seems reasonable and natural. He has councillors employed to fry their brains on his behalf, and if he is out of temper it is probably their fault; they shouldn't block him or provoke him. He doesn't want people who say, 'No, but ...' He wants people who say, 'Yes, and ...' He doesn't like men who are pessimistic and sceptical, who turn down their mouths and cost out his brilliant projects with a scribble in the margin of their papers. So do the sums in your head where no one can see them. Do not expect consistency from him. Henry prides himself on understanding his councillors, their secret opinions and desires, but he is resolved that none of his councillors shall understand him. He is suspicious of any plan that doesn't originate with himself, or seem to. You can argue with him but you must be careful how and when. You are better to give way on every possible point until the vital point, and to pose yourself as one in need of guidance and instruction, rather than to maintain a fixed opinion from the start and let him think you believe you know better than he does. Be sinuous in argument and allow him escapes: don't corner him, don't back him against the wall. Remember that his mood depends on other people, so consider who has been with him since you were with him last. Remember he wants more than to be advised of his power, he wants to be told he is right. He is never in error. It is only that other people commit errors on his behalf or deceive him with false information. Henry wants to be told that he is behaving well, in the sight of God and man. 'Cromwell,' he says, 'you know what we should try? Cromwell, would it not reflect well on my honour if I …? Cromwell, would it not confound my enemies if …?' And all these are the ideas you put to him last week. Never mind. You don't want the credit. You just want action.

But there is no need for these lessons. All his life Rafe has been training for this. A scrap of a boy, he is no athlete, he could never exercise himself in tilt or tournament, a stray breeze would whisk him out of the saddle. But he has the heft for this. He knows how to watch. He knows how to listen. He knows how to send a message encrypted, or a message so secret that no message appears to be there; a piece of information so solid that its meaning seems to be stamped out in the earth, yet its form so fragile that it seems to be conveyed by angels. Rafe knows his master; Henry is his master. But Cromwell is his father and his friend.

You can be merry with the king, you can share a joke with him. But as Thomas More used to say, it's like sporting with a tamed lion. You tousle its mane and pull its ears, but all the time you're thinking, those claws, those claws, those claws.

In Henry's new church, Lent is as raw and cold as ever it was under the Pope. Miserable, meatless days fray a man's temper. When Henry talks about Jane, he blinks, tears spring to his eyes. 'Her little hands, Crumb. Her little paws, like a child's. She has no guile in her. And she never speaks. And if she does I have to bend my head to hear what she says. And in the pause I can hear my heart. Her little bits of embroidery, her scraps of silk, her halcyon sleeves she cut out of the cloth some admirer gave her once, some poor boy struck with love for her … and yet she has never succumbed. Her little sleeves, her seed pearl necklace …

she has nothing … she expects nothing …' A tear at last sneaks from Henry's eye, meanders down his cheek and vanishes into the mottled grey and ginger of his beard.

Notice how he speaks of Jane: so humble, so shy. Even Archbishop Cranmer must recognise the portrait, the black reverse portrait of the present queen. All the riches of the New World would not sate her; while Jane is grateful for a smile.

I am going to write Jane a letter, Henry says. I am going to send her a purse, for she will need money for herself now she is removed from the queen's chamber.

Paper and quills are brought to his hand. He sits down and sighs and sets about it. The king's handwriting is square, the hand he learned as a child from his mother. He has never picked up speed; the more effort he puts into it, the more the letters seem to turn back on themselves. He takes pity on him: 'Sir, would you like to dictate it, and I will write for you?'

It would not be the first time he has written a love letter for Henry. Over their sovereign's bent head, Cranmer looks up and meets his eyes: full of accusation.

'Have a look,' Henry says. He doesn't offer it to Cranmer. 'She'll understand, yes, that I want her?'

He reads, trying to put himself in the place of a maiden lady. He looks up. 'It is very delicately expressed, sir. And she is very innocent.'

Henry takes the letter back and writes in a few reinforcing phrases.

It is the end of March. Mistress Seymour, stricken with panic, seeks an interview with Mr Secretary; it is set up by Sir Nicholas Carew, though Sir Nicholas himself is absent, not yet ready to commit himself to talks. Her widowed sister is with her. Bess gives him a searching glance; then drops her bright eyes.

'Here is my difficulty,' Jane says. She looks at him wildly; he thinks, maybe that's all she means to say: here is my difficulty.

She says, 'You can't ... His Grace, His Majesty, you can't for one moment forget who he is, even though he demands you do. The more he says, "Jane I am your humble suitor," the less humble you know he is. And every moment you are thinking, what if he stops talking and I have to say something? I feel as if I'm standing on a pincushion, with the pins pointing up. I keep thinking, I'll get used to it, next time I'll be better, but when he comes in, "Jane, Jane ..." I'm like a scalded cat. Though, have you ever seen a scalded cat, Master Secretary? I have not. But I think, if after this short time I'm so frightened of him –'

'He wants people to be frightened.' With the words arrives the truth of them. But Jane is too intent on her own struggles to hear what he has said.

'– if I'm frightened of him now, what will it be like to see him every day?' She breaks off. 'Oh. I suppose you know. You do see him, Master Secretary, most days. Still. Not the same, I suppose.'

'No, not the same,' he says.

He sees Bess, in sympathy, raise her eyes to her sister. 'But Master Cromwell,' Bess says, 'it cannot always be acts of Parliament and dispatches to ambassadors and revenue and Wales and monks and pirates and traitorous devices and Bibles and oaths and trusts and wards and leases and the price of wool and whether we should pray for the dead. There must sometimes be other topics.'

He is struck by her overview of his situation. It is as if she has understood his life. He is taken by an impulse to clasp her hand and ask her to marry him; even if they did not get on in bed, she seems to have a gift for précis that eludes most of his clerks.

'Well?' Jane says. 'Are there? Other topics?'

He can't think. He squashes his soft hat between his hands. 'Horses,' he says. 'Henry likes to know about trades and crafts, simple things. In my youth I learned to shoe a horse, he likes to know about that, the right shoe for the job, so he can confound his own smiths with secret knowledge. The archbishop, too, he is a man who will ride any horse that comes to his hand, he is a timid man but horses like him, he learned to manage them when he was young. When he is tired of God and men we speak of these matters with the king.'

'And?' Bess says. 'You are together many hours.'

'Dogs, sometimes. Hunting dogs, their breeding and virtues. Fortresses. Building them. Artillery. The range of it. Cannon foundries. Dear God.' He runs his hand through his hair. 'We sometimes say, we will have a day out together, ride down to Kent, to the weald, to see the ironmasters there, study their operations, and propose them new ways of casting cannon. But we never do it. Something is always in our way.'

He feels irredeemably sad. As if he has been plunged into mourning. And at the same time he feels, if someone tossed a feather bed into the room (which is unlikely) he would throw Bess on to it, and have to do with her.

'Well, that's that,' Jane says, her tone resigned. 'I could not found a cannon to save my life. I am sorry to have taken your time, Master Secretary. You had better get back to Wales.'

He knows what she means.

Next day, the king's love letter is brought to Jane, with a heavy purse. It is a scene staged before witnesses. 'I must return this purse,' Jane says. (But she does not say it before she has weighed it, fondled it, in her tiny hand.) 'I must beg the king, if he wishes to make me a present of money, to send it again when I should contract an honourable marriage.'

Given the king's letter, she declares she had better not open it. For well she knows his heart, his gallant and ardent heart. For herself, her only possession is her womanly honour, her maidenhead. So – no, really – she had better not break the seal.

And then, before she returns it to the messenger, she holds it in her two hands: and places, on the seal, a chaste kiss.

'She kissed it!' Tom Seymour cries. 'What genius possessed her? First his seal. Next,' he sniggers, 'his sceptre!'

In a fit of joy, he knocks his brother Edward's hat off. He has been playing this joke for twenty years or more, and Edward has never been amused. But just this once, he fetches up a smile.

When the king gets the letter back from Jane, he listens closely to what his messenger has to tell him, and his face lights up. 'I see I was wrong to send it. Cromwell here has spoken to me of her innocence and her virtue, and with good reason, as it appears. From this point I will do nothing that will offend her honour. In fact, I shall only speak to her in the presence of her kin.'

If Edward Seymour's wife were to come to court, they could make a family party, with whom the king could take supper without any affront to Jane's modesty. Perhaps Edward should have a suite in the palace? Those rooms of mine at Greenwich, he reminds Henry, that communicate directly with yours: what if I were to move out and let the Seymours move in? Henry beams at him.

He has been studying the Seymour brothers intently since the visit to Wolf Hall. He will have to work with them; Henry's women come trailing families, he does not find his brides in the forest hiding under a leaf. Edward is grave, serious, yet he is ready to unfold his thoughts to you. Tom is close, that's what he thinks; close and cunning, brain busily working beneath that show of bonhomie. But it's perhaps not the best brain. Tom Seymour will give me no trouble, he thinks, and Edward I can carry with me. His mind is already moving ahead, to a time when the king indicates his pleasure. Gregory and the Emperor's ambassador, between them, have suggested the way forward. 'If he can annul twenty years with his true wife,' Chapuys has said to him, 'I am sure it is not beyond your wit to find some grounds to free him from his concubine. No one has ever believed the marriage was good in the first place, except those who are employed to say yes to him.'

He wonders, though, about the ambassador's 'no one'. No one in the Emperor's court, perhaps: but all England has sworn to the marriage. It is not a light matter, he tells his nephew Richard, to undo it legally, even if the king commanded it. We shall wait a little, we will not go to anyone, let them come to us.

He asks for a document to be drawn up, showing all grants to the Boleyns since 1524. 'Such a thing would be good to have at my hand, in case the king calls for it.'

He does not mean to take anything away. Rather, enhance their holdings. Load them with honours. Laugh at their jokes.

Though you must be careful what you laugh at. Master Sexton, the king's jester, has jested about Anne and called her a ribald. He thought he had licence, but Henry lumbered across the hall and clouted him, banged his head on the panelling and banished him the court. They say Nicholas Carew gave the man refuge, out of pity.

Anthony is aggrieved about Sexton. One jester does not like to hear of the downfall of another; especially, Anthony says, when his only vice is foresight. Oh, he says, you have been listening to the gossip in the kitchen. But the fool says, 'Henry kicks out the truth and Master Sexton with it. But these days it has a way of creeping under the bolted door and down the chimney. One day he will give in and invite it to stand by the hearth.'

William Fitzwilliam comes to the Rolls House and sits down with him. 'So how does the queen, Crumb? Still perfect friends, though you dine with the Seymours?'

He smiles.

Fitzwilliam jumps up, wrenches the door open to see no one is lurking, then sits down again, and resumes. 'Cast your mind back. This Boleyn courtship, this Boleyn marriage. How did the king look, in the eyes of grown men? Like one who only studies his own pleasures. Like a child, that is to say. To

214

be so impassioned, to be so enslaved by a woman, who after all is made just as other women are – some said it was unmanly.'

'Did they? Well, I am shocked. We cannot have it said of Henry that he is not a man.'

'A man' – and Fitzwilliam stresses the word – 'a man should be governor of his passions. Henry shows much force of will but little wisdom. It harms him. She harms him. The harm will go on.'

It seems he will not name her, Anna Bolena, La Ana, the concubine. So, if she harms the king, would it be the act of a good Englishman to remove her? The possibility lies between them, approached but still unexplored. It is treason, of course, to speak against the present queen and her heirs; a treason from which the king alone is exempt, for he could not violate his own interest. He reminds Fitzwilliam of this: he adds, even if Henry speaks against her, do not be drawn.

'But what do we look for in a queen?' Fitzwilliam asks. 'She should have all the virtues of an ordinary woman, but she must have them to a high degree. She must be more modest, more humble, more discreet and more obedient even than they: so that she sets an example. There are those who ask themselves, is Anne Boleyn any of these things?'

He looks at Master Treasurer: go on.

'I think I can speak frankly to you, Cromwell,' Fitz says: and (after checking at the door once again) he does. 'A queen should be mild and pitiful. She should move the king to mercy – not drive him on to harshness.'

'You have some particular case in mind?'

Fitz was in Wolsey's household as a young man. No one knows what part Anne played in the fall of the cardinal; her hand was hidden in her sleeve. Wolsey knew he could hope for no mercy from her, and he received none. But Fitz seems to brush away the cardinal. He says, 'I hold no brief for Thomas More. He was not the adept in affairs of state that he thought he was. He thought he could sway the king, he thought he could control him, he thought that Henry was still a sweet young prince he could lead by the hand. But Henry is a king and he will be obeyed.'

'Yes, and?'

'And I wish that with More it could have ended another way. A scholar, a man who was Lord Chancellor, to drag him out in the rain and cut off his head ...'

He says, 'You know, sometimes I forget he's gone. There is some piece of news and I think, what will More say to this?'

Fitz glances up. 'You don't talk to him, do you?'

He laughs. 'I don't go to him for advice.' Though I do, of course, consult the cardinal: in the privacy of my short hours of sleep.

Fitz says, 'Thomas More scuttled his chances with Anne when he would not come to see her crowned. She would have seen him dead a year before it happened, if she could have proved treason on him.'

'But More was a clever lawyer. Amongst the other things he was.'

'The Princess Mary – the Lady Mary, I should say – she is no lawyer. A friendless girl.'

'Oh, I would think that her cousin the Emperor counts as her friend. And a very good friend to have, too.'

Fitz looks irritated. 'The Emperor is a great idol, set up in another country. Day by day, she needs a more proximate defender. She needs someone to push forward her interests. Stop this, Crumb – this dancing around the point.'

'Mary just needs to keep breathing,' he says. 'I am not often accused of dancing.'

Fitzwilliam stands up. 'Well now. A word to the wise.'

The feeling is that something is wrong in England and must be set right. It's not the laws that are wrong or the customs. It's something deeper.

Fitzwilliam leaves the room, then he comes back in. Says abruptly, 'If it is old Seymour's daughter next, there will be some jealousy among those who think their own noble house should be preferred – but after all, the Seymours are an ancient family, and he won't have this trouble with her. I mean, men running after her like dogs after a – well … You just look at her, Seymour's little girl, and you know that nobody's ever pulled her skirts up.' This time he does go; but giving him, Cromwell, a sort of mock salute, a flourish in the direction of his hat.

Sir Nicholas Carew comes to see him. The very fibres of his beard are bristling with conspiracy. He half-expects the knight to wink as he sits down.

When it comes to it, Carew is surprisingly brisk. 'We want the concubine ousted. We know you want it too.'

'We?'

Carew looks up at him, from beneath bristling brows; like a man who has shot off his one crossbow bolt, he must now plod over the terrain, seeking friend or foe or just a place to hide for the night. Ponderously, he clarifies. 'My friends in this matter do comprise a good part of the ancient nobility of this nation, those of honourable lineage, and …' He sees Cromwell's face and hurries on. 'I speak of those very near the throne, those in the line of old King Edward. Lord Exeter, the Courtenay family. Also Lord Montague and his brother Geoffrey Pole. Lady Margaret Pole, who as you know was governor to the Princess Mary.'

He casts up his eyes. 'Lady Mary.'

'If you must. We call her the princess.'

He nods. 'We will not let that stop us discussing her.'

'Those I have named,' Carew says, 'are the principal persons on whose behalf I speak, but as you will be aware, the most part of England would rejoice to see the king free of her.'

'I don't think the most part of England knows or cares.' Carew means, of course, the most part of *my* England, the England of ancient blood. Any other country, for Sir Nicholas, does not exist.

He says, 'I suppose Exeter's wife Gertrude is active in this matter.'

'She has been,' Carew leans forward to impart something very secret, 'in communication with Mary.'

'I know,' he sighs.

'You read their letters?'

'I read everybody's letters.' Including yours. 'But look,' he says, 'this smells of intrigue against the king himself, does it not?'

'In no wise. His honour is at the heart of it.'

He nods. Point taken. 'And so? What do you require of me?'

'We require you to join with us. We are content to have Seymour's girl crowned. The young woman is my kin, and she is known to favour true religion. We believe she will bring Henry back to Rome.'

'A cause close to my heart,' he murmurs.

Sir Nicholas leans forward. 'This is our difficulty, Cromwell. You are a Lutheran.'

He touches his jacket: round about his heart. 'No, sir, I am a banker. Luther condemns to Hell those who lend at interest. Is it likely that I should take his part?'

Sir Nicholas laughs heartily. 'I did not know. Where would we be, without Cromwell to lend us money?'

He asks, 'What is to happen to Anne Boleyn?'

'I don't know. Convent?'

So the bargain is struck and sealed: he, Cromwell, is to assist the old families, the true faithful; and afterwards, under the new regime, they will keep his services in consideration: his zeal in this matter may cause them to forget the blasphemies of these last three years, which otherwise would invite condign punishment.

'Just one thing, Cromwell.' Carew stands up. 'Don't keep me waiting next time. It ill becomes a man of your stamp to keep a man of my stamp kicking his heels in an anteroom.'

'Ah, was that the noise?' Though Carew wears the padded satin of the courtier, he always imagines him in show-armour: not the kind you fight in, the kind you buy from Italy to impress your friends. Heel-kicking would be a noisy business, then: clatter, clang. He looks up. 'I meant no slight, Sir Nicholas. From now we will make all speed. Consider me at your right hand, furnished for the fight.'

That's the sort of bombast Carew understands.

Now Fitzwilliam is talking to Carew. Carew is talking to his wife, who is Francis Bryan's sister. His wife is talking, or writing at least, to Mary to let her know that her prospects are improving by the hour, that La Ana may be displaced. At the very least, it's a way of keeping Mary quiet for the while. He doesn't want her to hear the rumours that Anne is launching fresh hostilities. She may panic, and try to escape; they say she has various absurd plans, like drugging the Boleyn women about her and spurring off by night. He has warned Chapuys, though not in so many words of course, that if Mary does escape Henry is likely to hold him responsible, and to have no regard for the protection of his diplomatic status. At the very least, he will be booted around like Sexton the jester. At worst, he may never see his native shores again.

Francis Bryan is keeping the Seymours at Wolf Hall abreast of events at court. Fitzwilliam and Carew are talking to the Marquis of Exeter, and Gertrude, his wife. Gertrude is talking over supper to the Imperial ambassador, and to the Pole family, who are as papist as they dare to be, who have teetered on the edge of treason these last four years. No one is talking to the French ambassador. But everyone is talking to him, Thomas Cromwell.

In sum, this is the question his new friends are asking: if Henry can retire one wife, and she a daughter of Spain, can he not give a pension to Boleyn's daughter and put her away in some country house, having found defects in the marriage documents? His casting off of Katherine, after twenty years of marriage, offended all Europe. The marriage with Anne is recognised nowhere but in this realm, and has not endured three years; he could annul it, as a folly. After all, he has his own church to do so, his own archbishop.

In his head he rehearses a request. 'Sir Nicholas? Sir William? Will you come to my humble house to dine?'

He does not really mean to ask them. Word would soon reach the queen. A coded glance is enough, a nod and a wink. But once again in his mind he sets the table.

Norfolk at the head. Montague and his sainted mother. Courtenay and his blasted wife. Sliding in behind them, our friend Monsieur Chapuys. 'Oh, dammit,' Norfolk sulks, 'now must we speak French?'

'I will translate,' he offers. But who's this clattering in? It's Duke Dishpan. 'Welcome, my lord Suffolk,' he says. 'Take a seat. Careful not to get crumbs in that great beard of yours.'

'If there were a crumb.' Norfolk is hungry.

Margaret Pole spears him with a glacial stare. 'You have set a table. You have given us all seats. You have given us no napery.'

'My apologies.' He calls for a servant. 'You wouldn't want to get your hands dirty.'

Margaret Pole shakes out her napkin. On it is imprinted the face of the dead Katherine.

A bawling comes from without, the direction of the buttery. Francis Bryan reels in, already a bottle to the good. '*Pastime with good company ...*' He crashes to his place.

Now he, Cromwell, nods to his menials. Extra stools are fetched. 'Squeeze them in,' he says.

Carew and Fitzwilliam enter. They take their places without a smile or a nod. They have come ready to the feast, their knives in their hands.

He looks around at his guests. All are prepared. A Latin grace; English would be his choice, but he will suit his company. Who cross themselves ostentatiously, in papist style. Who look at him, expectant.

He shouts for the waiters. The doors burst open. Sweating men heave the platters to the table. It seems the meat is fresh, in fact not slaughtered yet.

It is just a minor breach of etiquette. The company must sit and salivate.

The Boleyns are laid at his hand to be carved.

Now that Rafe is in the privy chamber, he has closer acquaintance with the musician, Mark Smeaton, who has been promoted among the grooms. When Mark first showed himself at the cardinal's door, he sloped up in patched boots and a canvas doublet that had belonged to a bigger man. The cardinal put him into worsted, but since he joined the royal household he goes in damask, perched on a fine gelding with a saddle of Spanish leather, the reins clutched in gold-fringed gloves. Where is the money coming from? Anne is recklessly generous, Rafe says. The gossip is that she has given Francis Weston a sum to keep his creditors at bay.

You can understand, Rafe says, that because now the king does not admire the queen so much, she is keen to have young men about her who hang on her words. Her rooms are busy thoroughfares, the privy chamber gentlemen constantly calling in on this errand or that, and lingering to play a game or share a song; where there is no message to carry, they invent one.

Those gentlemen who are less in the queen's favour are keen to talk to the newcomer and give him all the gossip. And some things he doesn't need to be told, he can see and hear for himself. Whispering and scuffling behind doors. Covert mockery of the king. Of his clothes, of his music. Hints of his shortcomings in bed. Where would those hints come from, but the queen?

There are some men who talk all the time about their horses. This is a steady mount but I used to have one speedier; that's a fine filly you have there, but you should see this bay I have my eye on. With Henry, it's ladies: he finds something to like in almost any female who crosses his path, and will scratch up a compliment for her, though she be plain and old and sour. With the young ones, he is enraptured twice a day: has she not the finest eyes, is not her throat white, her voice sweet, her hand shapely? Generally it's look and don't touch: the most he will venture, blushing slightly, 'Don't you think she must have pretty little duckies?'

One day Rafe hears Weston's voice in the next room, running on, amused, in imitation of the king: 'Has she not the wettest cunt you ever groped?' Giggles, complicit sniggers. And 'Hush! Cromwell's spy is about.'

Harry Norris has been absent from court lately, spending time on his own estates. When he is on duty, Rafe says, he tries to suppress the talk, sometimes seems angry at it; but sometimes he lets himself smile. They talk about the queen and they speculate …

Go on, Rafe, he says.

Rafe doesn't like telling this. He feels it is below him to be an eavesdropper. He thinks hard before he speaks. 'The queen needs to conceive another child quickly to please the king, but where is it to come from, they ask. Since Henry cannot be trusted to do the business, which of them is to do him a favour?'

'Did they come to any conclusion?'

Rafe rubs the crown of his head and makes his hair stand up. You know, he says, they would not really do it. None of them. The queen is sacred. It is too great a sin even for such lustful men as they be, and they are too much in fear of the king, surely, even though they mock him. Besides, she would not be so foolish.

'I ask you again, did they come to any conclusion?'

'I think it's every man for himself.'

He laughs. '*Sauve qui peut.*'

He hopes none of this will be needed. If he acts against Anne he hopes for a cleaner way. It's all foolish talk. But Rafe cannot unhear it, he cannot unknow it, there it is.

March weather, April weather, icy showers and splinters of sun; he meets Chapuys, indoors, this time.

'You seem pensive, Master Secretary. Come to the fire.'

He shakes away the raindrops from his hat. 'I have a weight on my mind.'

'Do you know, I think you only set up these meetings with me to annoy the French ambassador?'

'Oh yes,' he sighs, 'he is very jealous. In truth I would visit you more often, except that word always gets back to the queen. And she contrives to use it against me in one way or another.'

'I could wish you a more gracious mistress.' The ambassador's implicit question: how is that going, the getting of a new mistress? Chapuys has floated to him, could there not be a new treaty between our sovereigns? Something that would safeguard Mary, her interests, perhaps place her back in the line of succession, after any children Henry might have with a new wife? Assuming, of course, the present queen were gone?

'Ah, Lady Mary.' Lately he has taken to putting his hand to his hat when her name is mentioned. He can see the ambassador is touched by this, he can see him preparing to put it in dispatches. 'The king is willing to hold formal talks. It would please him to be united in friendship to the Emperor. So much he has said.'

'Now you must bring him to the point.'

'I have influence with the king but I cannot answer for him, no subject can. This is my difficulty. To succeed with him, one must anticipate his desires. But one then stands exposed, should he change his mind.'

Wolsey his master had advised, make him say what he wants, do not guess, for by guessing you may destroy yourself. But perhaps, since Wolsey's day, the king's unexpressed commands have become harder to ignore. He fills the room with a seething discontent, stares up into the sky when you ask him to sign a paper: as if he were expecting deliverance.

'You fear he will turn on you,' Chapuys says.

'He will, I suppose. One day.'

Sometimes he wakes in the night and thinks of it. There are courtiers who have honourably retired. He can think of instances. Of course, it is the other kind that loom larger, if you are wakeful around midnight. 'But if that day comes,' the ambassador says, 'what will you do?'

'What can I do? Arm myself with patience and leave the rest to God.' And hope the end is quick.

'Your piety does you credit,' Chapuys says. 'If fortune turns against you, you will need friends. The Emperor –'

'The Emperor would not spare a thought for me, Eustache. Or for any common man. No one raised a finger to help the cardinal.'

'The poor cardinal. I wish I had known him better.'

'Stop buttering me up,' he says sharply. 'Have done.'

Chapuys gives him a searching glance. The fire roars up. Vapours rise from his clothes. The rain patters at the window. He shivers. 'You are ill?' Chapuys enquires.

'No, I am not allowed to be. If I took to my bed the queen would turn me out of it and say I am faking. If you want to cheer me up, get out that Christmas hat of yours. It was a pity you had to put it away for mourning. Easter would be none too soon to see it again.'

'I think you are making jokes, Thomas, at the expense of my hat. I have heard that while it was in your custody it was derided, not only by your clerks but by your stable boys and dog-keepers.'

'The reverse is true. There were many applications to try it on. I wish that we may see it at all major feasts of the church.'

'Once again,' Chapuys says, 'your piety does you credit.'

* * *

He sends Gregory away to his friend Richard Southwell, to learn the art of speaking in public. It is good for him to get out of London, and to get away from the court, where the atmosphere is tense. All around him there are signs of unease, little huddles of courtiers that disperse at his approach. If he is to place all in hazard, and he thinks he is, then Gregory should not have to go through the pain and doubt, hour by hour. Let him hear the conclusion of events; he does not need to live through them. He has no time now to explain the world to the simple and the young. He has to watch the movements of cavalry and ordnance across Europe, and the ships on the seas, merchantmen and men of war: the influx of gold from the Americas to the treasury of the Emperor. Sometimes peace looks like war, you cannot tell them apart; sometimes these islands look very small. The word from Europe is that Mount Etna has erupted, and brought floods throughout Sicily. In Portugal there is a drought; and everywhere, envy and contention, fear of the future, fear of hunger or the fact of it, fear of God and doubt over how to placate him, and in what language. The news, when he gets it, is always a fortnight out of date: the posts are slow, the tides against him. Just as the work of fortifying Dover is coming to an end, the walls of Calais are falling down; frost has cracked the masonry and opened a fissure between Watergate and Lanterngate.

On Passion Sunday a sermon is preached in the king's chapel by Anne's almoner, John Skip. It appears to be an allegory; the force of it appears to be directed against him, Thomas Cromwell. He smiles broadly when those who attended explain it to him, sentence by sentence: his ill-wishers and well-wishers both. He is not a man to be knocked over by a sermon, or to feel himself persecuted by figures of speech.

Once when he was a boy he had been in a rage against his father Walter and he had rushed at him, intent to butt him in the belly with his head. But it was just before the Cornish rebels came swarming up the country, and as Putney reckoned it was in

225

their line of march, Walter had been bashing out body armour for himself and his friends. So when he ran head-first, there was a bang, which he heard before he felt it. Walter was trying on one of his creations. 'That'll teach you,' his father said, phlegmatic.

He often thinks about it, that iron belly. And he thinks he has got one, without the inconvenience and weight of metal. 'Cromwell has plenty stomach,' his friends say; his enemies too. They mean he has appetite, gusto, attack: first thing in the morning or last thing at night, a bloody collop of meat would not disgust him, and if you wake him in the small hours he is hungry then too.

An inventory comes in, from Tilney Abbey: vestments of red turkey satin and white lawn, wrought with beasts in gold. Two altar cloths of white Bruges satin, with drops like spots of blood, made of red velvet. And the contents of the kitchen: weights, tongs and fire forks, flesh hooks.

Winter melts into spring. Parliament is dissolved. Easter Day: lamb with ginger sauce, a blessed absence of fish. He remembers the eggs the children used to paint, giving each speckled shell a cardinal's hat. He remembers his daughter Anne, her hot little hand cupped around the eggshell so the colour ran: 'Look! *Regardez!*' She was learning French that year. Then her amazed face; her curious tongue creeping out to lick the stain from her palm.

The Emperor is in Rome, and the word is that he has had a seven-hour meeting with the Pope; how much of that was devoted to plotting against England? Or did the Emperor speak up for his brother monarch? It is rumoured there will be an accord between the Emperor and the French: bad news for England, if so. Time to push on with negotiations. He sets up a meeting between Chapuys and Henry.

A letter is sent to him from Italy, which begins, 'Molto magnifico signor ...' He remembers Hercules, the labourer.

* * *

Two days after Easter, the Imperial ambassador is welcomed at court by George Boleyn. At the sight of glinting George, teeth and pearl buttons flashing, the ambassador's eye rolls like the eye of a startled horse. He has been received by George before, but he did not expect him today: rather one of his own friends, perhaps Carew. George addresses him at length in his elegant and courtly French. You will please to hear Mass with His Majesty and then, if you will do me the favour, it will be my pleasure to entertain you personally to ten o'clock dinner.

Chapuys is looking around: Cremuel, help!

He stands back, smiling, watching the operations of George. I'll miss him, he thinks, in the days when it is all over for him: when I kick him back to Kent, to count his sheep and take a homely interest in the grain harvest.

The king himself gives Chapuys a smile, a gracious word. He, Henry, sails to his private closet above. Chapuys disposes himself amid George's hangers-on. '*Judica me, Deus,*' intones the priest. 'Judge me, oh God, and separate my cause from the nation that is not holy: deliver me from the unjust and deceitful man.'

Chapuys now turns around and stabs him with a look. He grins. 'Why art thou sad, oh my soul?' asks the priest: in Latin of course.

As the ambassador shuffles towards the altar to receive the sacred host, the gentlemen around him, neat as practised dancers, hesitate half a pace and fall behind him. Chapuys falters; George's friends have surrounded him. He darts a glance over his shoulder. Where am I, what should I do?

At that moment, and exactly in his line of sight, Anne the queen sweeps down from her own private galleried space: head high, velvet and sables, rubies at her throat. Chapuys hesitates. He cannot go forward, for he is afraid to cross her path. He cannot go back, because George and his minions are pressing him. Anne turns her head. A pointed smile: and to the enemy, she makes a reverence, a gracious inclination of her jewelled neck. Chapuys screws up his eyes tight, and bows to the concubine.

After all these years! All these years he has picked his path, so that never, never was he brought face to face with her, never brought to this stark choice, to this damnable politesse. But what else could he do? It will soon be reported. It will get back to the Emperor. Let us hope and pray that Charles will understand.

All this shows on the ambassador's face. He, Cremuel, kneels and takes communion. God turns to paste on his tongue. While this process occurs, it is reverent to close the eyes; but on this singular occasion, God will forgive him for looking about. He sees George Boleyn, pink with pleasure. He sees Chapuys, white with humiliation. He sees Henry dazzle in gold as he descends, ponderous, from the gallery. The king's tread is deliberate, his step is slow; his face is blazing with solemn triumph.

Despite the best efforts of pearly George, as they leave the chapel the ambassador breaks away. He scurries towards him, then his hand fastens with a terrier grip. 'Cremuel! You knew this was planned. How could you so embarrass me?'

'It is for the best, I assure you.' He adds, sombre, thoughtful, 'What use as a diplomat would you be, Eustache, if you did not understand the character of princes? They do not think as other men think. To commoners' minds like ours, Henry seems perverse.'

Light dawns in the ambassador's eye. 'Ahh.' He lets out a long breath. He grasps, in that single moment, why Henry has forced him to make a public reverence to a queen whom he no longer wants. Henry is tenacious of his will, he is stubborn. Now he has carried his point: his second marriage has been acknowledged. Now, if he likes, he can let it go.

Chapuys draws his garments together, as if he feels a draught from the future. He whispers, 'Must I really dine with her brother?'

'Oh yes. You will find him a charming host. After all,' he raises a hand to hide his smile, 'has he not just enjoyed a triumph? He and his whole family?'

Chapuys huddles closer. 'I am shocked to see her. I have not seen her so close. She looks like a thin old woman. Was that Mistress Seymour, in the halcyon sleeves? She is very plain. What does Henry see in her?'

'He thinks she's stupid. He finds it restful.'

'Clearly he is enamoured. There must be something about her not evident to the stranger's eye.' The ambassador sniggers. 'No doubt she has a very fine *enigme*.'

'No one would know,' he says blankly. 'She is a virgin.'

'After so long at your court? Surely Henry is deluded.'

'Ambassador, keep this for later. Your host is here.'

Chapuys folds his hands over his heart. He makes George, Lord Rochford, a sweeping bow. Lord Rochford does the same. Arm in arm, they mince away. It sounds as if Lord Rochford is reciting verses in praise of the spring.

'Hm,' says Lord Audley: 'What a performance.' The weak sunshine glints from the Lord Chancellor's chain of office. 'Come on, my boy, let's go and gnaw a crust.' Audley chuckles. 'The poor ambassador. He looks like someone being carried by slavers to the Barbary coast. He does not know what country he will wake up in tomorrow.'

Nor do I, he thinks. You can rely on Audley to be jovial. He closes his eyes. Some hint, some intimation has reached him, that he has had the best of the day, though it is only ten o'clock. 'Crumb?' the Lord Chancellor says.

It is some time after dinner that it all begins to fall apart, and in the worst possible way. He has left Henry and the ambassador together in a window embrasure, to caress each other with words, to coo about an alliance, to make each other immodest propositions. It is the king's change of colour he notices first. Pink and white to brick red. Then he hears Henry's voice, high-pitched, cutting: 'I think you presume too much, Chapuys. You say I acknowledge your master's right to rule in Milan: but perhaps the

King of France has as good a right, or better. Do not presume to know my policy, ambassador.'

Chapuys jumps back. He thinks of Jane Seymour's question: Master Secretary, have you ever seen a scalded cat?

The ambassador speaks: something low and supplicating. Henry raps back at him, 'You mean to say that what I took as a courtesy, from one Christian prince to the other, is really a bargaining position? You agree to bow to my wife the queen, and then you send me a bill?'

He, Cromwell, sees Chapuys hold up a placating hand. The ambassador is trying to interrupt, to limit the damage, but Henry talks over him, audible to the whole chamber, to the whole gaping assembly, and to those pressing in behind. 'Does your master not remember what I did for him, in his early troubles? When his Spanish subjects rose up against him? I kept the seas open for him. I lent him money. And what do I get back?'

A pause. Chapuys has to send his mind scurrying back, to the years before he was in post. 'The money?' he suggests weakly.

'Nothing but broken promises. Recall, if you will, how I helped him against the French. He promised me territory. Next thing I heard, he was making a treaty with Francis. Why should I trust a word he says?'

Chapuys draws himself up: as far as a little man can. 'Game little cockerel,' Audley says, in his ear.

But he, Cromwell, is not to be distracted. His eyes are fastened on the king. He hears Chapuys say, 'Majesty. That is not a question to be asked, by one prince of another.'

'Is it not?' Henry snarls. 'In times past, I would never have had to ask it. I take every brother prince to be honourable, as I am honourable. But sometimes, Monsieur, I suggest to you, our fond and natural assumptions must give way before bitter experience. I ask you, does your master take me for a fool?' Henry's voice swoops upwards; he bends at the waist, and his fingers make little paddling motions on his knees, as if he were trying to entice a child or a small dog. 'Henry!' he squeaks. 'Come to Charles! Come to your kind master!' He straightens up, almost spitting in his rage. 'The Emperor treats me like an infant. First he whips me, then he pets me, then it is the whip again. Tell him I am not an infant. Tell him I am an emperor in my own realm, and a man, and a father. Tell him to keep out of my family business. I have put up with his interference for too long. First he seeks to tell me who I can marry. Then he wants to show me how to manage my daughter. Tell him, I shall deal with Mary as I see fit, as a father does deal with a disobedient child. No matter who her mother is.'

The king's hand – in fact, dear God, his fist – makes crude contact with the ambassador's shoulder. His path cleared, Henry stamps out. An imperial performance. Except that his leg drags. He shouts over his shoulder, 'I require a profound and public apology.'

He, Cromwell, lets out his breath. The ambassador fizzes across the room, gibbering. Distraught, he seizes his arm. 'Cremuel, I do not know for what I am to apologise. I come here in good faith, I am tricked into coming face to face with that creature, I am forced to exchange compliments with her brother through a whole dinner, and then I am attacked by Henry. He wants my master, he needs my master, he is just playing the old game, trying to sell himself dear, pretending he might send troops to King Francis to fight in Italy – where are these troops? I do not see them, I have eyes, I do not see his army.'

'Peace, peace,' Audley soothes. 'We will do the apologising, Monsieur. Let him cool down. Never fear. Hold back your dispatches to your good master, do not write tonight. We will keep the talks going.'

Over Audley's shoulder, he sees Edward Seymour, gliding through the crowd. 'Ah, ambassador,' he says, with a suave confidence he does not feel. 'Here is an opportunity for you to meet –'

Edward springs forward, '*Mon cher ami ...*'

Black glances from Boleyns. Edward into the breach, armed with confident French. Sweeping Chapuys aside: none too soon. A stir at the door. The king is back, erupting into the midst of the gentlemen.

'Cromwell!' Henry stops before him. He is breathing hard. 'Make him understand. It is not for the Emperor to make conditions to me. It is for the Emperor to apologise, for threatening me with war.' His face congests. 'Cromwell, I know just what you have done. You have gone too far in this matter. What have you promised him? Whatever it is, you have no authority. You have put my honour in hazard. But what do I expect, how can a man like you understand the honour of princes? You have said, "Oh, I am sure of Henry, I have the king in my pocket." Don't deny it, Cromwell, I can hear you saying it. You mean to train me up, don't you? Like one of your boys at Austin Friars? Touch my cap when you come down of a morning and say "How do you, sir?" Walk through Whitehall half a pace behind you. Carry your folios, your inkhorn and your seal. And why not a crown, eh, brought behind you in a leather bag?' Henry is convulsing with rage. 'I really believe, Cromwell, that you think you are king, and I am the blacksmith's boy.'

He will never claim, later, that his heart did not turn over. He is not one to boast of a coolness no reasonable man would possess. Henry could, at any moment, gesture to his guards; he could find himself with cold metal at his ribs, and his day done.

But he steps back; he knows his face shows nothing, neither repentance nor regret nor fear. He thinks, you could never be the blacksmith's boy. Walter would not have had you in his forge. Brawn is not the whole story. In the flames you need a cool head, when sparks are flying to the rafters you must note when they fall on you and knock the fire away with one swat of your hard palm: a man who panics is no use in a shop full of molten metal. And now, his monarch's sweating face thrust into his, he remembers something his father told him: if you burn your hand, Tom, raise your hands and cross your wrists before you, and hold them so till you get to the water or the salve: I don't know how it works, but it confuses the pain, and then if you utter a prayer at the same time, you might get off not too bad.

He raises his palms. He crosses his wrists. Back you go, Henry. As if confused by the gesture – as if almost relieved to be stopped – the king ceases ranting: and he backs off a pace, turning his face away and so relieving him, Cromwell, of that bloodshot stare, of the indecent closeness of the popping blue whites of the king's eyes. He says, softly, 'God preserve you, Majesty. And now, will you excuse me?'

So: whether he will excuse or no, he walks away. He walks into the next room. You have heard the expression, 'My blood was boiling'? His blood is boiling. He crosses his wrists. He sits down on a chest and calls for a drink. When it is fetched he takes into his right hand the cool pewter cup, running the pads of his fingers around its curves: the wine is strong claret, he spills a drop, he blots it with his forefinger and for neatness touches it with his tongue, so it vanishes. He cannot say whether the trick has decreased the pain, as Walter said it would. But he is glad his father is with him. Someone must be.

He looks up. Chapuys's face is hovering over him: smiling, a mask of malice. 'My dear friend. I thought your last hour had come. Do you know, I thought you would forget yourself and hit him?'

He looks up and smiles. 'I never forget myself. What I do, I mean to do.'

'Though you may not mean what you say.'

He thinks, the ambassador has suffered cruelly, just for doing his job. In addition, I have injured his feelings, I have been ironical about his hat. Tomorrow I shall organise him a present, a horse, a horse of some magnificence, a horse for his own riding. I myself, before it departs my stables, will lift a hoof and check the shoe.

* * *

233

The king's council meets next day. Wiltshire, or Monseigneur, is present: the Boleyns are sleek cats, lolling in their seats and preening their whiskers. Their kinsman, the Duke of Norfolk, looks ragged, unnerved; he stops him on the way in – stops him, Cromwell – 'All right, lad?'

Was ever the Master of the Rolls so addressed, by the Earl Marshal of England? In the council chamber Norfolk scuffles the stools about, creaks down on one that suits him. 'That's what he does, you know.' He flashes him a grin, a glimpse of fang. 'You're balanced just so, standing on your feet, then he blows the pavement from under you.'

He nods, smiling patiently. Henry comes in, sits like a great sulky baby on a chair at the head of the table. Meets no one's eye.

Now: he hopes his colleagues know their duties. He has told them often enough. Flatter Henry. Beseech Henry. Implore him to do what you know he must do anyway. So Henry feels he has a choice. So he feels a warm regard for himself, as if he is not consulting his own interests but yours.

Majesty, the councillors say. If it please you. To look favourably, for the sake of the realm and commonweal, on the Emperor's slavish overtures. On his whimpers and pleas.

This occupies fifteen minutes. At last, Henry says, well, if it is for the good of the commonweal, I will receive Chapuys, we will continue negotiations. I must swallow, I suppose, any personal insults I have received.

Norfolk leans forward. 'Think of it like a draught of medicine, Henry. Bitter. But for the sake of England, do not spit.'

The subject of physicians once raised, the marriage of the Lady Mary is discussed. She continues to complain, wherever the king moves her, of bad air, insufficient food, insufficient consideration of her privacy, of dolorous limb pains, headaches and heaviness of spirit. Her doctors have advised that congress with a man would be good for her health. If a young woman's vital spirits are bottled up, she becomes pale and thin, her appetite wanes, she begins to waste; marriage is an occupation for her, she forgets her minor ailments; her womb remains anchored and primed for use, and shows no tendency to go wandering about her body as if it had nothing better to do. In default of a man, the Lady Mary needs strenuous exercise on horseback; difficult, for someone under house arrest.

Henry clears his throat at last, and speaks. 'The Emperor, it is no secret, has discussed Mary with his own councillors. He would like her married out of this realm, to one of his relatives, within his own domains.' His lips tighten. 'In no wise will I suffer her to go out of the country; or indeed to go anywhere at all, while her behaviour to me is not what it ought to be.'

He, Cromwell, says, 'Her mother's death is still raw with her. I have no doubt she will see her duty, over these next weeks.'

'How pleasing to hear from you at last, Cromwell,' says Monseigneur with a smirk. 'You do most usually speak first, and last, and everywhere in the middle, so that we more modest councillors are obliged to speak sotto voce, if at all, and pass notes to each other. May we ask if this new reticence of yours relates, in any way, to yesterday's events? When His Majesty, if I do recall correctly, administered a check to your ambition?'

'Thank you for that,' the Lord Chancellor says, flatly. 'My lord Wiltshire.'

The king says, 'My lords, the subject is my daughter. I am sorry to have to recall you. Though I am far from sure she should be discussed in council.'

'Myself,' Norfolk says, 'I would go up-country to Mary and make her swear the oath, I would plant her hand on the gospel and hold it there flat, and if she would not take her oath to the king and to my niece's child, I would beat her head against the wall till it were as soft as a baked apple.'

'And thank you again,' Audley says. 'My lord Norfolk.'

'Anyway,' the king says sadly. 'We have not so many children that we can well afford to lose one out of the kingdom. I would rather not part with her. One day she will be a good daughter to me.'

The Boleyns sit back, smiling, hearing the king say he seeks no great foreign match for Mary, she is of no importance, a bastard whom one considers only out of charity. They are well content with the triumph afforded them yesterday by the Imperial ambassador; and they are showing their good taste by not boasting about it.

As soon as the meeting ends, he, Cromwell, is mobbed by the councillors: except for the Boleyns, who waft off in the other direction. The meeting has gone well; he has got everything he wants; Henry is back on course for a treaty with the Emperor: why then does he feel so restless, stifled? He elbows his colleagues aside, though in a mannerly fashion. He wants air. Henry passes him, he stops, he turns, he says, 'Master Secretary. Will you walk along with me?'

They walk. In silence. It is for the prince, not the minister, to introduce a topic.

He can wait.

Henry says, 'You know, I wish we would go down to the weald one day, as we have said, to talk to the ironmasters.'

He waits.

'I have had various drawings, mathematical drawings, and advices concerning how our ordnance can be improved, but to be truthful, I cannot make as much of it as you would.'

More humble, he thinks. A little more humble yet.

Henry says, 'You have been in the forest and met charcoal burners. I remember you said to me once, they be very poor men.'

He waits. Henry says, 'One must know the process from the beginning, I think, whether one is making armour or ordnance. It is no use demanding of a metal that it has certain properties, a certain temper, unless you know how it is made, and the difficulties your craftsman may encounter. Now, I have never been too proud to sit down for an hour with the gauntlet maker, who armours my right hand. We must study, I think, every pin, every rivet.'

And? Yes?

He leaves the king to stumble on.

'And, well. And, so. You are my right hand, sir.'

He nods. Sir. How touching.

Henry says, 'So, to Kent, to the weald: will we go? Shall I choose a week? Two, three days should do it.'

He smiles. 'Not this summer, sir. You will be engaged otherwise. Besides, the ironmasters are like all of us. They must have a holiday. They must lie in the sun. They must pick apples.'

Henry looks at him, mild, beseeching, from the tail of his blue eye: give me a happy summer. He says, 'I cannot live as I have lived, Cromwell.'

He is here to take instructions. Get me Jane: Jane, so kind, who sighs across the palate like sweet butter. Deliver me from bitterness, from gall.

'I think I might go home,' he says. 'If you will permit. I have much to do if I am to set this affair in train, and I feel ...' His English deserts him. This sometimes happens. '*Un peu ...*' But his French deserts him too.

'But you are not ill? You will be back soon?'

'I shall seek a consultation with the canon lawyers,' he says. 'It may take some days, you know what they are. It will go no slower than I can help. I shall speak to the archbishop.'

'And perhaps to Harry Percy,' Henry says. 'You know how she ... the betrothal, the whatever, the relationship between them ... well, I think they were as good as married, were they not? And if that won't run ...' He rubs his beard. 'You know that I was, before I was with the queen, I was, on occasion, with her sister, her sister Mary, which –'

'Oh yes, sir. I remember Mary Boleyn.'

'– and it will be seen that, having been linked with kin so near to Anne, I could not make a valid marriage to her ... however, you will only use that if you have to, I do not want unnecessary ...'

He nods. You don't want history to make a liar of you. In public before your courtiers you had me state that you had never had to do with Mary Boleyn, while you sat there and nodded. You removed all impediments: Mary Boleyn, Harry Percy, you swept them aside. But now our requirements have changed, and the facts have changed behind us.

'So fare you well,' Henry says. 'Be very secret. I trust in your discretion, and your skill.'

How necessary, but how sad, to hear Henry apologise. He has developed a perverse respect for Norfolk, with his grunt of 'All right, lad?'

In an antechamber Mr Wriothesley is waiting for him. 'So do you have instructions, sir?'

'Well, I have hints.'

'Do you know when they might take form?'

He smiles. Call-Me says, 'I hear that in council the king declared he will seek to marry Lady Mary to a subject.'

Surely that's not what the meeting concluded? In a moment, he feels like himself again: hears himself laughing and saying, 'Oh for Christ's sake, Call-Me. Who told you that? Sometimes,' he says, 'I think it would save time and work if all the interested parties came to the council, including foreign ambassadors. The proceedings leak out anyway, and to save them mishearing and misconstruing they might as well hear everything at first hand.'

'I've got it wrong, then?' Wriothesley says. 'Because I thought, marrying her to a subject, to some low man, that was a plan thought up by the queen that is now?'

He shrugs. The young man gives him a glassy look. It will be some years before he understands why.

* * *

Edward Seymour seeks an interview with him. There is no doubt in his mind that the Seymours will come to his table, even if they have to sit under it and catch the crumbs.

Edward is tense, hurried, nervous. 'Master Secretary, taking the long view –'

'In this matter, a day would be a long view. Get your girl out of it, let Carew take her to his house down in Surrey.'

'Do not think I wish to know your secrets,' Edward says, picking his words. 'Do not think I wish to pry into matters that are not for me. But for my sister's sake I would like to have some indication –'

'Oh, I see, you want to know if she should order her wedding clothes?' Edward gives him an imploring look. He says soberly, 'We are going to seek an annulment. Just now I do not know on what grounds.'

'But they will fight,' Edward says. 'The Boleyns if they go down will take us with them. I have heard of serpents that, though they are dying, exude poison through their skins.'

'Did you ever pick up a snake?' he asks. 'I did once, in Italy.' He holds out his palms. 'I am unmarked.'

'Then we must be very secret,' Edward says. 'Anne must not know.'

'Well,' he says wryly, 'I do not think we can keep it from her for ever.'

But she will know all the sooner, if his new friends do not stop trapping him in anterooms, blocking his path and bowing to him; if they do not stop this whispering and eyebrow raising and digging each other with their elbows.

He says to Edward, I must go home and shut the door and consult with myself. The queen is plotting something, I know not what, something devious, something dark, perhaps so dark that she herself does not know what it is, and as yet is only dreaming of it: but I must be quick, I must dream it for her, I shall dream it into being.

According to Lady Rochford, Anne complains that since she rose from childbed Henry is always watching her; and not in the way he used to.

For a long time he has noticed Harry Norris watching the queen; and from some eminence, perched like a carved falcon over a doorway, he has seen himself watching Harry Norris.

For now, Anne seems oblivious to the wings that hover over her, to the eye that studies her path as she jinks and swerves. She chatters about her child Elizabeth, holding up on her fingers a tiny cap, a pretty ribboned cap, just come from the embroiderer.

Henry looks at her flatly as if to say, why are you showing me this, what is it to me?

Anne strokes the scrap of silk. He feels a needle point of pity, an instant of compunction. He studies the fine silk braid that edges the queen's sleeve. Some woman with the skills of his dead wife made that braid. He is looking very closely at the queen, he feels he knows her as a mother knows her child, or a child its mother. He knows every stitch in her bodice. He notes the rise and fall of her every breath. What is in your heart, madam? That is the last door to be opened. Now he stands on the threshold and the key is in his hand and he is almost afraid to fit it into the lock. Because what if it doesn't, what if it doesn't fit and he has to fumble there, with Henry's eyes on him, hear the impatient click of the royal tongue, as surely his master Wolsey once heard it?

Well, then. There was an occasion – in Bruges, was it? – when he had broken down a door. He wasn't in the habit of breaking doors, but he had a client who wanted results and wanted them today. Locks can be picked, but that's for the adept with time to spare. You don't need skill and you don't need time if you've got a shoulder and a boot. He thinks, I wasn't thirty then. I was a youth. Absently his right hand rubs his left shoulder, his forearm, as if remembering the bruises. He imagines himself entering Anne, not as a lover but as a lawyer, and rolled in his fist his papers, his writs; he imagines himself entering the heart of the queen. In its chambers he hears the click of his own boot heels.

At home, he takes from his chest the Book of Hours that belonged to his wife. It was given to her by her first husband Tom Williams, who was a good enough fellow, but not a man of substance like himself. Whenever he thinks of Tom Williams now it is as a blank, a faceless waiting man dressed in the Cromwell livery, holding his coat or perhaps his horse. Now that he can handle, at his whim, the finest texts in the king's library, the prayer book seems a poor thing; where is the gold leaf? Yet the essence of Elizabeth is in this book, his poor wife with her white cap, her blunt manner, her sideways smile and busy craftswoman's fingers. Once he had watched Liz making a silk braid. One end was pinned to the wall and on each finger of her raised hands she was spinning loops of thread, her fingers flying so fast he couldn't see how it worked. 'Slow down,' he said, 'so I can see how you do it,' but she'd laughed and said, 'I can't slow down, if I stopped to think how I was doing it I couldn't do it at all.'

II
Master of Phantoms
London, April–May 1536

'Come and sit with me a while.'

'Why?' Lady Worcester is wary.

'Because I have cakes.'

She smiles. 'I am greedy.'

'I even have a waiter to serve them.'

She eyes Christophe. 'This boy is a waiter?'

'Christophe, first Lady Worcester requires a cushion.'

The cushion is plump with down and embroidered with a pattern of hawks and flowers. She takes it in her two hands, strokes it absently, then positions it behind her and leans back. 'Oh, that's better,' she smiles. Pregnant, she rests a composed hand on her belly, like a Madonna in a painting. In this small room, its window open to mild spring air, he is holding a court of inquiry. He does not mind who comes in to see him, who is noticed as they come and go. Who would not pass the time with a man who has cakes? And Master Secretary is always pleasant and useful. 'Christophe, hand my lady a napkin, and go and sit in the sun for ten minutes. Close the door behind you.'

Lady Worcester – Elizabeth – watches the door close; then she leans forward and whispers, 'Master Secretary, I am in such trouble.'

'And this,' he indicates her person, 'cannot be easy. Is the queen jealous of your condition?'

'Well, she keeps me close to her, and she need not. She asks me each day how I do. I could not have a fonder mistress.' But her face shows doubt. 'In some ways it would be better if I were to go home to the country. As it is, kept before the court, I am pointed at by all.'

'Do you think then it is the queen herself who began the murmurs against you?'

'Who else?'

A rumour is going about the court that Lady Worcester's baby is not the earl's child. Perhaps it was spread out of malice; perhaps as someone's idea of a joke: perhaps because someone was bored. Her gentle brother, the courtier Anthony Browne, has stormed into her rooms to take her to task: 'I told him,' she says, 'don't pick on me. Why me?' As if sharing her indignation, the curd tart on her palm quakes in its pastry shell.

He frowns. 'Let me take you back a step. Is your family blaming you because people are talking about you, or because there is truth in what they say?'

Lady Worcester dabs her lips. 'You think I will confess, just for cakes?'

'Let me smooth this over for you. I should like to help you if I can. Has your husband reason to be angry?'

'Oh, men,' she says. 'They are always angry. They are so angry they can't count on their fingers.'

'So it could be the earl's?'

'If it is a strong boy I dare say he will own it.' The cakes are distracting her: 'That white one, is that almond cream?'

Lady Worcester's brother, Anthony Browne, is Fitzwilliam's half-brother. (All these people are related to each other. Luckily, the cardinal left him a chart, which he updates whenever there is a wedding.) Fitzwilliam and Browne and the aggrieved earl have been conferring in corners. And Fitzwilliam has said to him, can you find out, Crumb, for I am sure I cannot, what the devil is going on among the queen's waiting-women?

'And then there's the debts,' he says to her. 'You are in a sad place, my lady. You have borrowed from everyone. What did you buy? I know there are sweet young men about the king, witty young men too, always amorous and ready to write a lady a letter. Do you pay to be flattered?'

'No. To be complimented.'

'You should get that free.'

'I believe that is a gallant speech.' She licks her fingers. 'But you are a man of the world, Master Secretary, and you know that if you yourself wrote a woman a poem you would enclose a bill.'

He laughs. 'True. I know the value of my time. But I did not think your admirers were so miserly.'

'But they have so much to do, these boys!' She selects a candied violet, nibbles it. 'I do not know why we speak of idle youths. They are busy day and night, making their careers. They wouldn't send their account in. But you must buy them a jewel for their cap. Or some gilt buttons for a sleeve. Fee their tailor, perhaps.'

He thinks of Mark Smeaton, in his finery. 'Does the queen pay out in this way?'

'We call it patronage. We don't call it paying out.'

'I accept your correction.' Jesus, he thinks, a man could use a whore, and call it 'patronage'. Lady Worcester has dropped some raisins on the table and he feels the urge to pick them up and feed them to her; probably that would be all right with her. 'So when the queen is a patron, does she ever, does she ever patronise in private?'

'In private? How could I know?'

He nods. It's tennis, he thinks. That shot was too good for me. 'What does she wear, to patronise?'

'I have not myself seen her naked.'

'So you think, these flatterers, you don't think she goes to it with them?'

'Not in my sight or hearing.'

'But behind a closed door?'

'Doors are often closed. It is a common thing.'

'If I were to ask you to bear witness, would you repeat that on oath?'

She flicks a speck of cream away. 'That doors are often closed? I could go so far.'

'And what would be your fee for that?' He is smiling; his eyes rest on her face.

'I am a little afraid of my husband. Because I have borrowed money. He does not know, so please … hush.'

'Point your creditors in my direction. And for the future, if you need a compliment, draw on the bank of Cromwell. We look after our customers and our terms are generous. We are known for it.'

She puts down her napkin; picks a last primrose petal from the last cheese cake. She turns at the door. A thought has struck her. Her hand bunches her skirts. 'The king wants a reason to put her aside, yes? And the closed door will be enough? I would not wish her harm.'

She grasps the situation, at least partly. Caesar's wife must be above reproach. Suspicion would ruin the queen, a crumb or a sliver of truth would ruin her faster; you wouldn't need a bed sheet with a snail-trail left by Francis Weston or some other sonneteer. 'Put her aside,' he says. 'Yes, possibly. Unless these rumours prove to be misunderstandings. As I'm sure they will in your case. I am sure your husband will be contented when the child is born.'

Her face clears. 'So you will speak to him? But not about the debt? And speak to my brother? And William Fitzwilliam? You will persuade them to leave me alone, please? There is nothing I have done, that other ladies have not.'

'Mistress Shelton?' he says.

'That would be no news.'

'Mistress Seymour.'

'That would be news indeed.'

'Lady Rochford?'

She hesitates. 'Jane Rochford does not like the sport.'

'Why, is my lord Rochford inept?'

'Inept.' She seems to taste the word. 'I have not heard her describe it like that.' She smiles. 'But I have heard her describe it.'

Christophe is back. She sails past him, a woman disburdened. 'Oh, look at that,' Christophe says. 'She has picked all the petals off the top, and left the crumb.'

Christophe sits down to stuff his maw with the remnants. He craves honey, sugar. You can never mistake a boy who was brought up hungry. We are coming to the sweet season of the year, when the air is mild and the leaves pale, and lemon cakes are flavoured with lavender: egg custards, barely set, infused with a sprig of basil; elderflowers simmered in a sugar syrup and poured over halved strawberries.

St George's Day. All over England, cloth and paper dragons sway in noisy procession through the streets, and the dragon-slayer after them in his armour of tin, beating an old rusty sword on his shield. Virgins plait wreaths of leaves, and spring flowers are carried into church. In the hall at Austin Friars, Anthony has hung from the ceiling beams a beast with green scales, a rolling eye and a lolling tongue; it looks lascivious, and reminds him of something, but he can't remember what.

This is the day the Garter knights hold their chapter, where they elect a new knight if any member has died. The Garter is the most distinguished order of chivalry in Christendom: the King of France is a member, so is the King of Scots. So is Monseigneur the queen's father, and the king's bastard Harry Fitzroy. This year the meeting is at Greenwich. The foreign members will not attend, it is understood, and yet the chapter serves as a gathering of his new allies: William Fitzwilliam, Henry Courtenay the Marquis of

Exeter, my lord of Norfolk, and Charles Brandon, who seems to have forgiven him, Thomas Cromwell, for shoving him around the presence chamber: who now seeks him out and says, 'Cromwell, we have had our differences. But I always did say to Harry Tudor, now take note of Cromwell, let him not go down with his ingrate master, for Wolsey has taught him his tricks and he may be useful to you accordingly.'

'Did you so, my lord? I am much bound to you for that word.'

'Aye, well, we see the consequence, for now you are a rich man, are you not?' He chuckles. 'And so is Harry rich.'

'And I am always glad to bestow gratitude in the proper quarter. May I ask, who will my lord vote for in the Garter chapter?'

Brandon gives him a strenuous wink. 'Depend on me.'

There is one vacancy, caused by the death of Lord Bergavenny; there are two men who expect to have it. Anne has been pressing the merits of brother George. The other candidate is Nicholas Carew; and when soundings have been taken and the votes have been counted it is Sir Nicholas whose name is read out by the king. George's people are quick to limit the damage, to give out that they didn't expect anything: that Carew was promised the next vacancy, that King Francis himself asked the king three years ago to give it him. If the queen is displeased, she does not show it, and the king and George Boleyn have a project to discuss. The day after May Day, a royal party is to ride down to Dover to inspect the new work on the harbour, and George will accompany it in his capacity as Warden of the Cinque Ports: an office which he fills badly, in his, Cromwell's opinion. He himself plans to ride down with the king. He could even go over to Calais for a day or two, and order matters there; so he gives out, the rumour of his arrival serving to keep the garrison on the *qui vive*.

Harry Percy has come down from his own country for the Garter meeting, and is now at his house at Stoke Newington. That might be useful, he says to his nephew Richard, I might send someone to see him and sound him out, whether he might be prepared to give back word on this pre-contract business. Go myself, if I need to. But we must take this week hour by hour. Richard Sampson is waiting for him, Dean of the Chapel Royal, Doctor of Canon Law (Cambridge, Paris, Perugia, Siena): the king's proctor in his first divorce.

'Here is a pretty pickle,' is all the dean will say, laying down his folios in his precise way. There is a mule cart outside, groaning with further folios, well-wrapped to save them from adverse weather: the documents go all the way back to the king's first expressed dissatisfaction with his first queen. At which time, he says, to the dean, we were all young. Sampson laughs; it is a clerical laugh, like the creak of a vestment chest. 'I barely recall being young, but I suppose we were. And some of us carefree.'

They are going to try for nullity, see if Henry can be released. 'I hear Harry Percy bursts into tears at the sound of your name,' Sampson says.

'They much exaggerate. The earl and I have had many civil interchanges these last months.'

He keeps turning over papers from the first divorce, and finding the cardinal's hand, amending, suggesting, drawing arrows in the margin.

'Unless,' he says, 'Anne the queen would decide to enter religion. Then the marriage would be dissolved of itself.'

'I'm sure she would make an excellent abbess,' Sampson says politely. 'Have you sounded out my lord archbishop yet?'

Cranmer is away. He has been putting it off. 'I have to show him,' he tells the dean, 'that our cause, that is to say, the cause of the English Bible, will get on better without her. We want the living word of God to sound in the king's ears like music, not like Anne's ingrate whining.'

He says 'we', including the dean out of courtesy. He is not at all sure that, in his heart, Sampson is devoted to reform, but it is outward compliance that concerns him, and the dean is always cooperative.

'This little matter of sorcery.' Sampson clears his throat. 'The king does not mean us to pursue it seriously? If it could be proved that some unnatural means were used to draw him into the marriage, then of course his consent could not be free, the contract is of no effect; but surely, when he says he was seduced by charms, by spells, he was speaking, as it were, in figures? As a poet might speak of a lady's fairy charms, her wiles, her seductions ...? Oh, by the Mass,' the dean says mildly. 'Do not look at me in that way, Thomas Cromwell. It is a business I would rather not meddle in. I would rather have Harry Percy again, and between us beat him into sense. I would rather bring out the matter of Mary Boleyn, whose name, I must say, I hoped never to hear again.'

He shrugs. He sometimes thinks about Mary; what it would have been like, if he had taken her up on her offers. That night in Calais, he had been so close he could taste her breath, sweetmeats and spices, wine ... but of course, that night in Calais, any man with functioning tackle would have done for Mary. Gently, the dean breaks into his train of thought: 'May I suggest? Go and talk to the queen's father. Talk to Wiltshire. He's a reasonable man, we were at Bilbao together on embassy a few years back, I always found him to be reasonable. Get him to ask his daughter to go quietly. Save us all twenty years of grief.'

To 'Monseigneur', then: he has Wriothesley to take the record of the meeting. Anne's father brings his own folio, while brother George brings only his delightful self. He is always a sight to see: George likes his clothes braided and tasselled, stippled and striped and slashed. Today he wears white velvet over red silk, scarlet rippling from each gash. He is reminded of a picture he saw once in the Low Countries, of a saint being flayed alive. The skin of the man's calves was folded neatly over his ankles, like soft boots, and his face wore an expression of unblinking serenity.

He puts his papers down on the table. 'I will not waste words. You see the situation. Matters have come to the king's attention that, if he had always known them, would have prevented this pretensed marriage with Lady Anne.'

George says, 'I have spoken to the Earl of Northumberland. He stands by his oath. There was no pre-contract.'

'Then that is unfortunate,' he says. 'I do not see what I am to do. Perhaps you can help me, Lord Rochford, with some suggestions of your own?'

'We will help you to the Tower,' says George.

'Minute that,' he says to Wriothesley. 'My lord Wiltshire, may I recall some circumstances that your son here may be unaware of? In the matter of your daughter and Harry Percy, the late cardinal called you to account, warning you that there could be no match between them, for the lowness of your family and the high estate of the Percy line. And your answer was that you were not responsible for what Anne did, that you could not control your own children.'

Thomas Boleyn arranges his face, as a certain piece of knowledge dawns. 'So it was you, Cromwell. Scribbling in the shadows.'

'I never denied it, my lord. Now on that occasion you did not get much sympathy from the cardinal. Myself, being a father of a family, I understand how these things occur. You would hold to it, at the time, that your daughter and Harry Percy had gone far in the matter. By which you meant – as the cardinal was pleased to put it – a haystack and a warm night. You implied their liaison was consummated, and a true marriage.'

Boleyn smirks. 'But then, the king made known his feelings for my daughter.'

'So you rethought your position. As one does. I am asking you to rethink once more. It would be better for your daughter if she had in fact been married to Harry Percy. Then her marriage to the king could be proclaimed null. And the king would be left free to select another lady.'

251

A decade of self-aggrandisement, since his daughter flashed her cunny at the king, has made Boleyn rich and settled and confident. His era is drawing to a close, and he, Cromwell, sees him decide not to fight it. Women age, men like variety: it's an old story, and even an anointed queen cannot escape it to write her own ending. 'So. What about Anne?' her father says. No particular tenderness attaches to the question.

He says, as Carew did, 'Convent?'

'I should expect a generous settlement,' Boleyn says. 'For the family, I mean.'

'Wait,' George says. 'My lord father, enter into no undertakings with this man. Enter into no discussion.'

Wiltshire speaks coldly to his son. 'Sir. Calmly. Things are as they are. What if, Cromwell, she were to be left in possession of her estate as marchioness? And we, her family, remain in undisturbed possession of ours?'

'I think the king would prefer her to withdraw from the world. I am sure we could find some godly house, well-governed, where her beliefs and views will be comfortable.'

'I am disgusted,' George says. He edges away from his father.

He says, 'Minute Lord Rochford's disgust.'

Wriothesley's pen scratches.

'But our land?' Wiltshire says. 'Our offices of state? I could continue to serve the king as Lord Privy Seal, surely. And my son here, his dignities and titles –'

'Cromwell wants me out,' George shoots to his feet. 'That's the plain truth. He has never ceased to interfere with what I do in defence of the realm, he is writing to Dover, he is writing to Sandwich, his men are swarming everywhere, my letters are redirected to him, my orders are countermanded by him –'

'Oh, sit down,' Wriothesley says. He laughs: as much at his own wearied impertinence, as at George's face. 'Or of course, my lord, stand, if you please.'

Now Rochford does not know which to do. All he can do is reinforce that he is standing, by flouncing on the spot; he can pick up his hat; he can say, 'I pity you, Master Secretary. If you succeed in forcing out my sister, your new friends will make short work of you once she is gone, and if you do not succeed, and she and the king are reconciled, then I shall make short work of you. So whichever way you turn, Cromwell, you have overreached yourself this time.'

He says mildly, 'I only sought this interview, my lord Rochford, because you have influence with your sister, no man more. I am offering you your safety, in return for your kind help.'

The elder Boleyn closes his eyes. 'I'll talk to her. I'll talk to Anne.'

'And talk to your son here, because I will talk to him no more.'

Wiltshire says, 'I marvel, George, that you do not see where this is tending.'

'What?' George says. 'What, what?' He is still whatting as his father tows him away. On the threshold the elder Boleyn bows his head civilly. 'Master Secretary. Master Wriothesley.'

They watch them go out: father and son. 'That was interesting,' Wriothesley says. 'And where is it tending, sir?'

He reshuffles his papers.

'I remember,' Wriothesley says, 'a certain play at court, after the cardinal came down. I remember Sexton, the jester, dressed in scarlet robes, in the character of the cardinal, and how four devils bore him off to Hell, each seizing an extremity. And they were masked. And I wondered, was George –'

'Right forepaw,' he says.

'Ah,' says Call-Me-Risley.

'I went behind the screen at the back of the hall. I saw them pull off their hairy bodies, and Lord Rochford take off his mask. Why did you not follow me? You could have seen for yourself.'

Mr Wriothesley smiles. 'I did not care to go behind that scene. I feared you might confuse me with the players, and for ever after I would be tainted in your mind.'

He remembers it: an evening of feral stench, as the flower of chivalry became hunting dogs, baying for blood, the whole court hissing and jeering as the figure of the cardinal was dragged and bounced across the floor. Then a voice called out from the hall: 'Shame on you!' He asks Wriothesley, 'That was not you who spoke?'

'No.' Call-Me will not lie. 'I think perhaps it was Thomas Wyatt.'

'I believe it was. I have thought about it these many years. Look, Call-Me, I have to go and see the king. Shall we have a glass of wine first?'

Mr Wriothesley on his feet. Searching out a waiting boy. Light shines on the curve of a pewter jug, Gascon wine splashes into a cup. 'I gave Francis Bryan an import licence for this,' he says. 'Would be three months back. No palate, has he? I didn't know he'd be selling it back to the king's buttery.'

He goes to Henry, scattering guards, attendants, gentlemen; he is barely announced, so that Henry looks up, startled, from his music book. 'Thomas Boleyn sees his way. He is only anxious to retain his good name with Your Majesty. But I cannot get any cooperation from his son.'

'Why not?'

Because he's an idiot? 'I think he believes Your Majesty's mind can be changed.'

Henry is piqued. 'He ought to know me. George was a little lad of ten when he first came to court, he ought to know me. I do not change my mind.'

It's true, in the one way. Like a crab the king goes sideways to his destination, but then he sinks his pincers in. It is Jane Seymour who is pinched. 'I tell you what I think about Rochford,' Henry says. 'He is what, thirty-two now, but he is still called Wiltshire's son, he is still called the queen's brother, he does not feel he has come into his own, and he has no heir to follow him, not so much

254

as a daughter. I have done what I can for him. I have sent him abroad many a time to represent me. And that will cease, I suppose, because when he is no longer my brother, no one will take any notice of him. But he will not be a poor man. I may continue to favour him. Though not if he is obstructive. So he should be warned. Must I speak to him myself?'

Henry looks irritated. He should not have to manage this. Cromwell is supposed to manage it for him. Ease out the Boleyns, ease in the Seymours. His business is more kingly: praying for the success of his enterprises, and writing songs for Jane.

'Leave it a day or two, sir, and I will interview him apart from his father. I think in Lord Wiltshire's presence he feels the need to strut and posture.'

'Yes, I am not often wrong,' Henry says. 'Vanity, that's all it is. Now listen.' He sings:

> 'The daisy delectable,
> The violet wan and blue.
> I am not variable ...

'You perceive it is an old song that I am trying to rework. What pairs with blue? Apart from "new"?'

What else do you need, he thinks. He takes his leave. The galleries are lit by torches, from which figures melt away. The atmosphere at court, this Friday evening in April, reminds him of the public bath-houses they have in Rome. The air is thick and the swimming figures of other men glide past you – perhaps men you know, but you don't know them without their clothes. Your skin is hot then cold then hot again. The tiles are slippery beneath your feet. On each side of you are doors left ajar, just a few inches, and outside your line of sight, but very close to you, perversities are occurring, unnatural conjugations of bodies, men and women and men and men. You feel nauseous, from the sticky heat and what you know of human nature, and you wonder why you have

255

come. But you have been told that a man must go to the bath-house at least once in his life, or he won't believe it when other people tell him what goes on.

'The truth is,' Mary Shelton says, 'I would have tried to see you, Master Secretary, even if you had not sent for me.' Her hand shakes; she takes a sip of wine, looks deeply into the bowl as if divining, then raises her eloquent eyes. 'I pray I never pass another day like this one. Nan Cobham wants to see you. Marjorie Horsman. All the women of the bedchamber.'

'Have you something to tell me? Or is it that you just want to cry on my papers and make the ink run?'

She puts down the cup and gives him her hands. He is moved by the gesture, it is like a child showing you her hands are clean. 'Shall we try to disentangle it?' he asks gently.

All day from the queen's rooms, shouting, slamming doors, running feet: hissed conversations in undertones. 'I wish I were gone from the court,' Shelton says. 'I wish myself in another place.' She slides her hands away. 'I should be married. Is that too much, to be married and have some children, while I am still young?'

'Now, do not be sorry for yourself. I thought you were marrying Harry Norris.'

'So did I.'

'I know that there was some falling out between you, but that would be a year ago now?'

'I suppose Lady Rochford told you. You should not listen, you know, she invents things. But yes, it was true, I quarrelled with Harry, or he quarrelled with me, and it was over young Weston coming to the queen's rooms in and out of season, and Harry thought he was casting his fancy to me. And so thought I. But I did not encourage Weston, I swear.'

He laughs. 'But Mary, you do encourage men. It is what you do. You cannot help it.'

'So Harry Norris said, I will give that puppy a kick in the ribs he will not forget. Though Harry is not that sort of man, to go around kicking puppies. And the queen my cousin said, no kicking in my chamber, if you please. Harry said, by your royal favour I will take him out to the courtyard and kick him, and –' she cannot help laugh, though shakily, miserably, '– and Francis standing there all the time, though they were talking about him as if he were absent. So Francis said, well, I should like to see you kick me, for at your great age, Norris, you will wobble over –'

'Mistress,' he says, 'can you make it short?'

'But they go on like this an hour or more, scrapping and digging and scratching around for favour. And my lady the queen is never weary of it, she eggs them on. Then Weston, he said, do not agitate yourself, gentle Norris, for I come not here for Mistress Shelton, I come for the sake of another, and you know who that is. And Anne said, no, tell me, I cannot guess. Is it Lady Worcester? Is it Lady Rochford? Come, tell us, Francis. Tell us who you love. And he said, madam, it is yourself.'

'And what did the queen say?'

'Oh, she defied him. She said, you must not say so, for my brother George will come and kick you too, for the honour of the Queen of England. And she was laughing. But then Harry Norris quarrelled with me, about Weston. And Weston quarrelled with him, about the queen. And both of them quarrelled with William Brereton.'

'Brereton? What had he to do with it?'

'Well, he happened to come in.' She frowns. 'I think it was then. Or it was some other time that he happened to come in. And the queen said, now, here is the man for me, Will is one who shoots his arrow straight. But she was tormenting them all. You cannot understand her. One moment she is reading out Master Tyndale's gospel. Next moment ...' She shrugs. 'She opens her lips and out slides the devil's tail.'

So then, by Shelton's account, a year passes. Harry Norris and Mistress Shelton are speaking again, and soon they have made it up and Harry is creeping to her bed. And all is as before. Until today: 29 April. 'This morning it began with Mark,' Mary Shelton says. 'You know how he hovers? He is always outside the queen's presence chamber. And as she goes by she does not speak to him but laughs and tugs his sleeve or knocks his elbow, and once she snapped off the feather in his cap.'

'I never heard of this as love play,' he says. 'Is it something they do in France?'

'And this morning she said, oh, look at this little doggie, and she tousled him and pulled his ears. And his silly eyes brimming. Then she said to him, why are you so sad, Mark, you have no business to be sad, you are here to entertain us. And he offered to kneel down, saying, "Madam –" and she cut him off. She said to him, oh for Mary's sweet sake, stand on your two feet, I do you favours in noticing you at all, what do you expect, do you think I should talk to you as if you were a gentleman? I cannot, Mark, because you are an inferior person. He said, no, no madam, I do not expect a word, a look suffices for me. So she waited. Because she expected him to praise the power of her glance. That her eyes are lodestones, and so on. But he did not, he just burst into tears, and "Farewell," he said, and walked away. Just turned his back on her. And she laughed. And so we went in to her chamber.'

'Take your time,' he says.

'Anne said, does he think I am some item from Paris Garden? That is, you know –'

'I know what Paris Garden is.'

She blushes. 'Of course you do. And Lady Rochford said, it were well if Mark were dropped from a height, like your dog Purkoy. Then the queen burst into tears. Then she struck Lady Rochford. And Lady Rochford said, do that again and I will buffet you back, you are no queen but a mere knight's daughter,

Master Secretary Cromwell has your measure, your day is over, madam.'

He says, 'Lady Rochford is getting ahead of herself.'

'Then Harry Norris came in.'

'I was wondering where he was.'

'He said, what is this commotion? Anne said, do me a good turn, take away my brother's wife and drown her, then he can have a fresh one who may do him some good. And Harry Norris was amazed. Anne said to him, did you not swear you would do anything I wanted? That you would walk barefoot to China for me? And Harry said, you know he is droll, he said, I think it was barefoot to Walsingham I offered. Yes, she said, and repent your sins there, because you look for dead men's shoes, if aught came to the king but good, you would look to have me.'

He wants to write down what Shelton says, but he dare not move in case she stops saying it.

'Then the queen turned to me, and said, Mistress Shelton, you perceive now why he does not marry you? He is in love with me. So he claims, and has claimed this long while. But he will not prove it, by putting Lady Rochford in a sack and carrying her to the riverbank, which I much desire. Then Lady Rochford ran out.'

'I think I understand why.'

Mary looks up. 'I know you are laughing at us. But it was horrible. For me it was. Because I thought that it was a jest between them that Harry Norris loved her, and then I saw it was not. I swear he had turned pale and he said to Anne, will you spill all your secrets or only some? And he walked away and he did not even bow to her, and she ran after him. And I do not know what she said, because we were all frozen like statues.'

Spill her secrets. All or only some. 'Who heard this?'

She shakes her head. 'Perhaps a dozen people. They could not help but hear it.'

And then, it appears, the queen was frantic. 'She looked at us ranged about her, and she wanted to get Norris back, she said a priest must be fetched, she said Harry must take an oath that he knew her to be chaste, a faithful good wife. She said he must take back everything said, and she would take it back too, and they would put their hands on the Bible in her chamber, and then everybody would know that it was idle talk. She is terrified Lady Rochford will go to the king.'

'I know Jane Rochford likes to carry bad news. But not such bad news as that.' Not to a husband. That his dear friend and his wife have discussed his death, with a view to how they will console themselves after.

It is treason. Possibly. To envisage the death of the king. The law recognises it: how short the step, from dreaming to desiring to encompassing. We call it 'imagining' his death: the thought is father to the deed, and the deed is born raw, ugly, premature. Mary Shelton does not know what she has witnessed. She thinks it is a lovers' quarrel. She thinks it is one incident in her own long career of love and love's misfortunes. 'I doubt,' she says dully, 'that Harry Norris will marry me now, or even trouble himself pretending he is going to marry me. If you had asked me last week has the queen given way to him, I would have told you no, but when I look at them now, it is clear such words have passed between them, such looks, and how can I know what deeds? I think ... I don't know what to think.'

'I'll marry you, Mary,' he says.

She laughs, in spite of herself. 'Master Secretary, you will not, you are always saying you will marry this lady and that, but we know you hold yourself a great prize.'

'Ah well. So it's back to Paris Garden.' He shrugs, he smiles; but he feels the need to be brisk with her, to hurry on. 'Now understand me, you must be discreet and silent. The thing you must do here – you and the other ladies – you must protect yourselves.'

Mary is struggling. 'It could not tend to bad, could it? If the king hears, he will know how to take it, yes? He may suppose it is all light words? No harm? It is all conjecture, perhaps I have spoken in haste, one cannot know that anything has passed between them, I could not swear it.' He thinks, but you will swear it; by and by you will. 'You see, Anne is my cousin.' The girl's voice falters. 'She has done everything for me –'

Even pushed you into the king's bed, he thinks, when she was carrying a child: to keep Henry in the family.

'What will happen to her?' Mary's eyes are solemn. 'Will he leave her? There is talk but Anne does not believe it.'

'She must stretch her credulity a little.'

'She says, I can always get him back, I know how. And you know she always has. But whatever has happened with Harry Norris, I will not continue with her, for I know she would take him from me and no scruple, if she has not already. And gentle-women cannot be on such terms. And Lady Rochford cannot continue. And Jane Seymour is removed, for – well, I will not say why. And Lady Worcester must go home for her lying-in this summer.'

He sees the young woman's eyes move, calculating, counting. To her, a problem is looming: a problem of staffing Anne's privy chamber. 'But I suppose England has enough ladies,' she says. 'It were well she began again. Yes, a new beginning. Lady Lisle in Calais looks to send her daughters over. I mean, her daughters from her first husband. They are pretty girls and I think they will do very well when they are trained.'

It is as if Anne Boleyn has entranced them, men and women both, so that they cannot see what is happening around them and cannot hear the meaning of their own words. They have lived in stupidity such a long season. 'So do you write to Honor Lisle,' Mary says, with perfect confidence. 'She will be for ever your debtor if she gets her girls at court.'

'And you? What will you do?'

'I'll take thought,' she says. She is never put down for long. That's why men like her. There will be other times, other men, other manners. She hops to her feet. She plants a kiss on his cheek.

It is Saturday evening.

Sunday: 'I wish you had been here this morning,' Lady Rochford says with relish. 'It was something to witness. The king and Anne in the great window together, so everybody in the courtyard below could see them. The king has heard about the quarrel she had with Norris yesterday. Well, the whole of England has heard of it. You could see the king was beside himself, his face was purple. She stood with her hands clasped at her breast ...' She shows him, clasping her own hands. 'You know, like Queen Esther, in the king's great tapestry?'

He can picture it easily, that richly textured scene, woven courtiers gathered about their distressed queen. One maid, as if unconcerned, carries a lute, perhaps en route to Esther's apartments; others gossip aside, the women's smooth faces uptilted, the men's heads inclined. Among these courtiers with their jewels and elaborate hats he has looked in vain for his own face. Perhaps he is somewhere else, plotting: a snapped skein, a broken end, an intractable knot of threads. 'Like Esther,' he says. 'Yes.'

'Anne must have sent for the little princess,' Lady Rochford says, 'because then a nurse heaved up with her, and Anne snatched her and held her up, as if to say, "Husband, how can you doubt this is your daughter?"'

'You are supposing that was his question. You could not hear what was said.' His voice is cold; he hears it himself, its coldness surprises him.

'Not from where I stood. But I doubt it bodes any good to her.'

'Did you not go to her, to comfort her? She being your mistress?'

'No. I went looking for you.' She checks herself, her tone suddenly sobered. 'We – her women – we want to speak out and save ourselves. We are afraid she is not honest and that we will be blamed for concealing it.'

'In the summer,' he says, 'not last summer but the one before, you said to me that you believed the queen was desperate to get a child, and was afraid the king could not give her one. You said he could not satisfy the queen. Will you repeat it now?'

'I'm surprised you don't have a note of our talk.'

'It was a long talk, and – with respect to you, my lady – more full of hints than particulars. I want to know what you would stand to, if you were to be put on oath before a court.'

'Who is to be tried?'

'That is what I am hoping to determine. With your kind help.'

He hears these phrases flow out of him. With your kind help. Yourself not offended. Saving his Majesty.

'You know it has come out about Norris and Weston,' she says. 'How they have declared their love for her. They are not the only ones.'

'You do not take it as just a form of courtesy?'

'For courtesy, you do not sneak around in the dark. On and off barges. Slipping through gates by torchlight. Bribes to the porters. It has been happening these two years and more. You cannot know who you have seen, where and when. You would be sharp if you could catch any of them.' She pauses, to be sure she has his attention. 'Let us say the court is at Greenwich. You see a certain gentleman, one who waits on the king. And you suppose his tour of duty is over, and you imagine him to be in the country; but then you are about your own duties with the queen, and you see him whisking around the corner. You think, why are you here? Norris, is that you? Many a time I have thought some one of them is at Westminster, and then I spy him at Richmond. Or he is supposed to be at Greenwich, and there he is at Hampton Court.'

'If they change their duties among themselves, it is no matter.'

'But I do not mean that. It is not the times, Master Secretary. It is the places. It is the queen's gallery, it is her antechamber, it is her threshold, and sometimes the garden stair, or a little gate left unlocked by some inadvertence.' She leans forward, and her fingertips brush his hand as it lies on his papers. 'I mean they come and go by night. And if anyone enquires why they should be there, they say they are on a private message from the king, they cannot say to whom.'

He nods. The privy chamber carry unwritten messages, it is one of their tasks. They come and go between the king and his peers, sometimes between the king and foreign ambassadors, and no doubt between the king and his wife. They do not brook questioning. They cannot be held to account.

Lady Rochford sits back. She says softly, 'Before they were married, she used to practise with Henry in the French fashion. You know what I mean.'

'I have no idea what you mean. Were you ever in France yourself?'

'No. I thought you were.'

'As a soldier. Among the military, the *ars amatoria* is not refined.'

She considers this. A hardness creeps into her voice. 'You wish to shame me out of saying what I must say, but I am no virgin girl, I see no reason not to speak. She induced Henry to put his seed otherwise than he should have. So now he berates her, that she caused him to do so.'

'Opportunities lost. I understand.' Seed gone to waste, slid away in some crevice of her body or down her throat. When he could have been seeing to her in the honest English way.

'He calls it a filthy proceeding. But God love him, Henry does not know where filth begins. My husband George is always with Anne. But I've told you that before.'

'He is her brother, I suppose it is natural.'

'Natural? Is that what you call it?'

'My lady, I know you would like it to be a crime to be a fond brother and a cold husband. But there is no statute that makes it so, and no precedent for your relief.' He hesitates. 'Do not think I am without sympathy for you.'

For what can a woman like Jane Rochford do when circumstances are against her? A widow well-provided can cut a figure in the world. A merchant's wife can with diligence and prudence take business matters into her hands, and squirrel away a store of gold. A labouring woman ill-used by a husband can enlist robust friends, who will stand outside her house all night and bang pans, till the unshaven churl tips out in his shirt to chase them off, and they pull up his shirt and mock his member. But a young married gentlewoman has no way to help herself. She has no more power than a donkey; all she can hope for is a master who spares the whip. 'You know,' he says, 'that your father Lord Morley is a scholar I hold in great esteem. Have you never advised with him?'

'What is the use?' She is scornful. 'When we married he said he was doing his best for me. It is what fathers say. He paid less mind to contracting me to Boleyn than he would to selling a hound puppy. If you think there's a warm kennel and a dish of broken meats, what more do you need to know? You don't ask the animal what it wants.'

'So you have never thought you might be released from your marriage?'

'No, Master Cromwell. My father went into everything thoroughly. Just as thoroughly as you would expect, of a friend of yours. No previous promise, no pre-contract, no shadow of one. Even you and Cranmer between you couldn't get us an annulment. On the wedding day we sat at our supper with our friends, and George told me, I am only doing this because my father says I must. That was good hearing, you will agree, for a girl of twenty who cherished hopes of love. And I defied him, I said the same back to him: I said, if my father did not enforce me, I would be far from you, sir. So then the light faded and we were put to bed.

He put his hand out and flipped my breast and said, I have seen plenty of these, and many better. He said, lie down, open your body, let us do our duty and make my father a grandfather, and then if we have a son we can live apart. I said to him, then do it if you think you can, pray God you may set seed tonight, and then you may take your dibber away and I need not look at it again.' A little laugh. 'But I am barren, you see. Or so I must believe. It may be that my husband's seed is bad or weak. God knows, he spends it in some dubious places. Oh, he is a gospeller, is George, St Matthew be his guide and St Luke protect him. No man as godly as George, the only fault he finds with God is that he made folk with too few orifices. If George could meet a woman with a quinny under her armpit, he would call out "Glory be" and set her up in a house and visit her every day, until the novelty wore off. Nothing is forbidden to George, you see. He'd go to it with a terrier bitch if she wagged her tail at him and said bow-wow.'

For once he is struck silent. He knows he will never get it out of his mind, the picture of George in a hairy grapple with a little ratting dog.

She says, 'I am afraid he has given me a disease and that is why I have never conceived a child. I think there is something destroying me from the inside. I think I might die of it one day.'

She had asked him once, if I die suddenly, have them cut open my corpse to look inside. In those days she thought Rochford might poison her; now she is sure he has done so. He murmurs, my lady, you have borne a great deal. He looks up. 'But this is not to the point. If George knows something about the queen that the king should be told, I can bring him to witness, but I cannot know he will speak out. I can hardly compel the brother against the sister.'

She says, 'I am not talking about his being a witness. I am telling you he spends time in her chamber. Alone with her. And the door closed.'

'In conversation?'

'I have been to the door and heard no voices.'

'Perhaps,' he says, 'they join in silent prayer.'

'I have seen them kiss.'

'A brother may kiss his sister.'

'He may not, not in that way.'

He picks up his pen. 'Lady Rochford, I cannot write down, "He kissed her in that way."'

'His tongue in her mouth. And her tongue in his.'

'You want me to record that?'

'If you fear you won't remember it.'

He thinks, if this comes out in a law court the city will be in an uproar, if it is mentioned in Parliament the bishops will be frigging themselves on their benches. He waits, his pen poised. 'Why would she do this, such a crime against nature?'

'The better to rule. Surely you see it? She is lucky with Elizabeth, the child is like her. But suppose she gets a boy and it has Weston's long face? Or it looks like Will Brereton, what might the king say to that? But they cannot call it a bastard if it looks like a Boleyn.'

Brereton too. He makes a note. He remembers how Brereton once joked with him he could be in two places at once: a chilly joke, a hostile joke, and now, he thinks, now at last, I laugh. Lady Rochford says, 'Why do you smile?'

'I have heard that in the queen's rooms, among her lovers, there was talk of the king's death. Did George ever join in with it?'

'It would kill Henry if he knew how they laugh at him. How his member is discussed.'

'I want you to think hard,' he says. 'Be sure of what you are doing. If you give evidence against your husband, in a court of law or to the council, you may find yourself a lonely woman in the years to come.'

Her face says, am I now so rich in friends? 'I will not bear the blame,' she says. 'You will, Master Secretary. I am thought a woman of no great wit or penetration. And you are what you are, a man of resource who spares no one. It will be thought that you drew the truth out of me, whether I was willing or no.'

It seems to him little more need be said. 'In order to sustain that notion, it will be necessary for you to contain your pleasure and feign distress. Once George is arrested, you must petition for mercy for him.'

'I can do that.' Jane Rochford puts out the tip of her tongue, as if the moment were sugared and she can taste it. 'I am safe, for the king will take no notice, I can guarantee.'

'Be advised by me. Talk to no one.'

'Be advised by me. Talk to Mark Smeaton.'

He tells her, 'I am going to my house at Stepney. I have asked Mark for supper.'

'Why not entertain him here?'

'There has been disturbance enough, don't you think?'

'Disturbance? Oh, I see,' she says.

He watches her out. The door does not close before Rafe and Call-Me-Risley are in the room with him. Pale and set, both of them steady: from which he knows they have not been eavesdropping. 'The king wishes inquiries to begin,' Wriothesley says. 'Utmost discretion, but all possible speed. He can no longer ignore the talk, after the incident. The quarrel. He has not approached Norris.'

'No,' Rafe says. 'They think, the gentlemen in the privy chamber, that it has all blown over. The queen has calmed herself, by all accounts. Tomorrow's jousts are to go ahead as usual.'

'I wonder,' he says, 'would you go to Richard Sampson, Rafe, and tell him that, *entre nous*, matters are out of our hands? It may not be necessary to sue for nullity after all. Or at least, I think the queen will be disposed to give way to anything the king requires of her. She has not much of a negotiating position left. I think we have Henry Norris within bow shot. Weston. Oh, and Brereton too.'

Rafe Sadler raises his eyebrows. 'I would have said the queen hardly knew him.'

'It seems he has the habit of walking in at the wrong moment.'

'You seem very calm, sir,' Call-Me says.

'Yes. Learn from it.'

'What does Lady Rochford say?'

He frowns. 'Rafe, before you go to Sampson, do you sit down there, at the head of the table. Pretend you are the king's council, meeting in privy session.'

'All of them, sir?'

'Norfolk and Fitzwilliam and all. Now, Call-Me. You are a lady of the queen's bedchamber. On your feet. May we have a curtsey? Thank you. Now, I am a page who fetches you a stool. And a cushion on it. Sit down and give the councillors a smile.'

'If you will,' Rafe says uncertainly. But then the spirit of the thing seizes him. He reaches forward and tickles Call-Me under the chin. 'What have you to tell us, delicate madam? Pray, divulge, and part your ruby lips.'

'This beautiful lady alleges,' he says – he, Cromwell, with a wave of his hand – 'that the queen is of light conditions. That her conduct gives rise to suspicion of evil-doing, of flouting of the laws of God, even if no one has witnessed actions contrary to statute.'

Rafe clears his throat. 'Some might say, madam, why did you not speak of this before?'

'Because it was treason to speak against the queen.' Mr Wriothesley is a ready man, and maidenly excuses flow from him. 'We had no choice but to shield her. What could we do, but reason with her, and persuade her to give up her light ways? And yet we could not. She kept us in awe. She is jealous of anyone who has an admirer. She wants to take him from her. She does not scruple to threaten anyone she thinks has erred, whether matron or maid, and she can ruin a woman that way, look at Elizabeth Worcester.'

'So now you can no longer forbear to speak out?' Rafe says.

'Now burst into tears, Wriothesley,' he instructs.

'Consider it done.' Call-Me dabs his cheek.

'What a play it makes.' He sighs. 'I wish now we could all take off our disguises and go home.'

He is thinking, Sion Madoc, a boatman on the river at Windsor: 'She goes to it with her brother.'

Thurston, his cook: 'They are standing in a line frigging their members.'

He remembers what Thomas Wyatt told him: 'That is Anne's tactic, she says yes, yes, yes, then she says no ... the worst of it is her hinting to me, her boasting almost, that she says no to me, but yes to others.'

He had asked Wyatt, how many lovers do you think she has had? And Wyatt had answered, 'A dozen? Or none? Or a hundred?'

He himself thought Anne cold, a woman who took her maidenhead to market and sold it for the best price. But this coldness – that was before she was wed. Before Henry heaved himself on top of her, and off again, and she was left, after he had stumbled back to his own apartments, with the bobbing circles of candlelight on the ceiling, the murmurs of her women, the basin of warm water and the cloth: and Lady Rochford's voice as she scrubs herself, 'Careful, madam, do not wash away a Prince of Wales.' Soon she is alone in the dark, with the scent of masculine sweat on the linen, and perhaps one useless maidservant turning and snuffling on a pallet: she is alone with the small sounds of river and palace. And she speaks, and no one answers, except the girl who mutters in her sleep: she prays, and no one answers; and she rolls on to her side, and smooths her hands over her thighs, and touches her own breasts.

So what if, one day, it's yes, yes, yes, yes, yes? To whoever happens to be standing by when the thread of her virtue snaps? Even if it's her brother?

He says to Rafe, to Call-Me, 'I have heard such matter today as I never thought to hear in a Christian country.'

They wait, the young gentlemen: their eyes on his face. Call-Me says, 'Am I still a lady, or shall I take my seat and pick up my pen?'

He thinks, what we do here in England, we send our children into other households when they are young, and so it is not rare for a brother and sister to meet, when they are grown, as if for the first time. Think how it must be then: this fascinating stranger whom you know, this mirror of you. You fall in love, just a little: for an hour, an afternoon. And then you make a joke of it; the residual drag of tenderness remains. It is a feeling that civilises men, and makes them behave better, to dependent women, than otherwise they might. But to go further, to trespass on forbidden flesh, to leap the great gap from a fleeting thought to action … Priests tell you that temptation slides into sin and you cannot put a hair between. But surely that is not true. You kiss the woman's cheek, very well; then you bite her neck? You say, 'Sweet sister,' and then next minute you flip her back and cant her skirts up? Surely not. There is a room to be crossed and buttons to be undone. You don't sleepwalk into it. You don't fornicate inadvertently. You don't fail to see the other party, who she is. She doesn't hide her face.

But then, it may be that Jane Rochford is lying. She has cause.

'I am not often perplexed,' he says, 'about how to proceed, but I find I have to deal with a matter I hardly dare speak of. I can only partly describe it, so I do not know how to draw up a charge sheet. I feel like one of those men who shows a freak at a fair.'

At a fair the drunken churls throw down their money, and then they disdain what you offer. 'Call that a freak? That's nothing to my wife's mother!'

And all their fellows slap them on the back and chortle.

But then you say to them, well, neighbours, I showed you that only to test your mettle. Part with a penny more, and I shall show you what I have here in the back of the tent. It is a sight to make hardened men quail. And I guarantee that you have never seen devil's work like it.

And then they look. And then they throw up on their boots. And then you count the money. And lock it in your strongbox.

Mark at Stepney. 'He has brought his instrument,' Richard says. 'His lute.'

'Tell him to leave it without.'

If Mark was blithe before, he is suspicious now, tentative. On the threshold, 'I thought, sir, I was to entertain you?'

'Make no doubt of it.'

'I had thought there would be a great company, sir.'

'You know my nephew, Master Richard Cromwell?'

'Still, I am happy to play for you. Perhaps you want me to hear your singing children?'

'Not today. In the circumstances you might be tempted to overpraise them. But will you sit down, and take a cup of wine with us?'

'It would be a charity if you could put us in the way of a rebec player,' Richard says. 'We have but the one, and he is always running off to Farnham to see his family.'

'Poor boy,' he says in Flemish, 'I think he is homesick.'

Mark looks up. 'I did not know you spoke my language.'

'I know you did not. Or you would not have used it to be so disrespectful of me.'

'I am sure, sir, I never meant any harm.' Mark can't remember, what he's said or not said about his host. But his face shows he recalls the general tenor of it.

'You forecast I should be hanged.' He spreads his arms. 'Yet I live and breathe. But I am in a difficulty, and although you do not like me, I have no choice but to come to you. So I ask your charity.'

Mark sits, his lips slightly parted, his back rigid, and one foot pointing to the door, showing he would very much like to be out of it.

'You see.' He puts his palms together: as if Mark were a saint on a plinth. 'My master the king and my mistress the queen are at odds. Everybody knows it. Now, my dearest wish is to reconcile them. For the comfort of the whole realm.'

Give the boy this: he is not without spirit. 'But, Master Secretary, the word about the court is, you are keeping company with the queen's enemies.'

'For the better to find out their practices,' he says.

'If I could believe that.'

He sees Richard shift on his stool, impatient.

'These are bitter days,' he says. 'I do not remember such a time of tension and misery, not since the cardinal came down. In truth I do not blame you, Mark, if you find it hard to trust me, there is such ill-feeling at court that no one trusts anyone else. But I come to you because you are close to the queen, and the other gentlemen will not help me. I have the power to reward you, and will make sure you have everything you deserve, if only you can give me some window into the queen's desires. I need to know why she is so unhappy, and what I can do to remedy it. For it is unlikely she will conceive an heir, while her mind is unquiet. And if she could do that: ah, then all our tears would be dried.'

Mark looks up. 'Why, it is no wonder she is unhappy,' he says. 'She is in love.'

'With whom?'

'With me.'

He, Cromwell, leans forward, elbows on the table: then puts a hand up to cover his face.

'You are amazed,' Mark suggests.

That is only part of what he feels. I thought, he says to himself, that this would be difficult. But it is like picking flowers. He lowers his hand and beams at the boy. 'Not so amazed as you might think. For I have watched you, and I have seen her gestures, her eloquent looks, her many indications of favour. And if these are shown in public, then what in private? And of course it is no surprise any woman would be drawn to you. You are a very handsome young man.'

'Though we thought you were a sodomite,' Richard says.

'Not I, sir!' Mark turns pink. 'I am as good a man as any of them.'

'So the queen would give a good account of you?' he asks, smiling. 'She has tried you and found you to her liking?'

The boy's glance slides away, like a piece of silk over glass. 'I cannot discuss it.'

'Of course not. But we must draw our own conclusions. She is not an inexperienced woman, I think, she would not be interested in a less than masterly performance.'

'We poor men,' Mark says, 'poor men born, are in no wise inferior in that way.'

'True,' he says. 'Though gentlemen keep that fact from ladies, if they can.'

'Otherwise,' Richard says, 'every duchess would be frolicking in a copse with a woodcutter.'

He cannot help laugh. 'Only there are so few duchesses and so many woodcutters. There must be competition between them, you would think.'

Mark looks at him as if he is profaning a sacred mystery. 'If you mean she has other lovers, I have never asked her, I would not ask her, but I know they are jealous of me.'

'Perhaps she has tried them and found them a disappointment,' Richard says. 'And Mark here takes the prize. I congratulate you, Mark.' With what open Cromwellian simplicity he leans forward and asks, 'How often?'

'It cannot be easy to steal the opportunity,' he suggests. 'Even though her ladies are complicit.'

'They are not my friends either,' Mark says. 'They would even deny what I have told you. They are friends of Weston, Norris, those lords. I am nothing to them, they ruffle my hair and call me waiting boy.'

'The queen is your only friend,' he says. 'But such a friend!' He pauses. 'At some point, it will be necessary for you to say who the others are. You have given us two names.' Mark looks up, shocked, at the change of tone. 'Now name them all. And answer Master Richard. How often?'

The boy has frozen under his gaze. But at least he enjoyed his moment in the sun. At least he can say he took Master Secretary by surprise: which few men can say, who are now living.

He waits for Mark. 'Well, perhaps you are right not to speak. Best to get it down in writing, no? I must say, Mark, my clerks will be as astonished as I am. Their fingers will tremble and they will blot the page. So will the council be astonished, when they hear of your successes. There will be many lords who envy you. You cannot expect their sympathy. "Smeaton, what is your secret?" they will demand. You will blush and say, ah, gentlemen, I cannot impart. But you will impart all, Mark, for they will make you. And you will do it freely, or do it enforced.'

He turns away from the boy, as Mark's face falls open in dismay, as his body begins to shake: five rash minutes of boasting, in one ungratified life and, like nervous tradesmen, the gods at once send in their account. Mark has lived in a story of his own devising, where the beautiful princess in her tower hears beyond her casement music of unearthly sweetness. She looks out and sees by moonlight the humble musician with his lute. But unless the musician turns out to be a prince in disguise, this story cannot end well. The doors open and ordinary faces crowd in, the surface of the dream is shattered: you are in Stepney on a warm night at the beginning of spring, the last birdsong is fading into the hush of twilight, somewhere a bolt rattles, a stool is scraped across the floor, a dog barks below the window and Thomas Cromwell says to you, 'We all want our supper, let's get on, here is the paper and the ink. Here is Master Wriothesley, he will write for us.'

'I can give no names,' the boy says.

'You mean, the queen has no lovers but you? So she tells you. But I think, Mark, she has been deceiving you. Which she could easily do, you must admit, if she has been deceiving the king.'

'No.' The poor boy shakes his head. 'I think she is chaste. I do not know how I came to say what I said.'

'Nor do I. No one had hurt you, had they? Or coerced you, or tricked you? You spoke freely. Master Richard is my witness.'

'I take it back.'

'I don't think so.'

There is a pause, while the room repositions itself, figures dispose themselves in the landscape of the evening. Master Secretary says, 'It's chilly, we should have a fire lit.'

Just an ordinary household request, and yet Mark thinks they mean to burn him. He jumps off his stool and makes for the door; perhaps the first bit of sense he's shown, but Christophe is there, broad and amiable, to head him off. 'Seat yourself, pretty boy,' Christophe says.

The wood is laid already. Such a long time it takes, to fan the spark. A little, welcome crackle, and the servant withdraws, wiping his hands on his apron, and Mark watches the door close after him, with a lost expression that may be envy, because he would rather be a kitchen hand now or a boy that scours privy pits. 'Oh, Mark,' Master Secretary says. 'Ambition is a sin. So I am told. Though I have never seen how it is different from using your talents, which the Bible commands we do. So here you are, and here I am, and both of us servants of the cardinal at one time. And if he could see us sitting here tonight, do you know, I don't think he would be the least surprised? Now, to business. Who did you displace in the queen's bed, was it Norris? Or perhaps you have a rota, like the queen's chamber servants?'

'I don't know. I take it back. I can give you no names.'

'It is a shame you should suffer alone, if others are culpable. And of course, they are more culpable than you, as they are gentlemen who the king has personally rewarded and made great, and all of them educated men, and some of them of mature years: whereas you are simple and young, and as much to be pitied as punished, I would say. Tell us now about your adultery with the queen and what you know of her dealings with other men, and then if your confession is prompt and full, clear and unsparing, it is possible that the king will show mercy.'

Mark is hardly hearing him. His limbs are trembling and his breathing is short, he is beginning to cry and to stumble over his words. Simplicity is best now, brisk questions requiring easy answers. Richard asks him, 'You see this person here?' Christophe points to himself, in case Mark is in doubt. 'Do you take him for a pleasant fellow?' Richard asks. 'Would you like to spend ten minutes alone with him?'

'Five would do it,' Christophe predicts.

He says, 'I explained to you, Mark, that Mr Wriothesley will write down what we say. But he will not necessarily write down what we do. You follow me? That will be just between us.'

Mark says, 'Mother Mary, help me.'

Mr Wriothesley says, 'We can take you to the Tower where there is a rack.'

'Wriothesley, may I have a word with you aside?' He waves Call-Me out of the room and on the threshold speaks in an undertone. 'It is better not to specify the nature of the pain. As Juvenal says, the mind is its own best torturer. Besides, you should not make empty threats. I will not rack him. I do not want him carried to his trial in a chair. And if I needed to rack a sad little fellow like this ... what next? Stamping on dormice?'

'I am reproved,' Mr Wriothesley says.

He puts his hand on Wriothesley's arm. 'Never mind. You are doing very well.'

This is a business that tries the most experienced. He remembers that day in the forge when a hot iron had seared his skin. There was no choice of resisting the pain. His mouth dropped open and a scream flew out and hit the wall. His father ran to him and said 'Cross your hands,' and helped him to water and to salve, but afterwards Walter said to him, 'It's happened to us all. It's how you learn. You learn to do things the way your father taught you, and not by some foolish method you hit upon yourself half an hour ago.'

He thinks of this: re-entering the room, he asks Mark, 'Do you know you can learn from pain?'

But, he explains, the circumstances must be right. To learn, you must have a future: what if someone has chosen this pain for you and they are going to inflict it for as long as they like, and only stop once you're dead? You can make sense of your suffering, perhaps. You can offer it up for the struggling souls in Purgatory, if you believe in Purgatory. That might work for saints, whose souls are shining white. But not for Mark Smeaton, who is in mortal sin, a self-confessed adulterer. He says, 'No one wants your pain, Mark. It's no good to anyone, no one's interested in it. Not even God himself, and certainly not me. I have no use for your screams. I want words that make sense. Words I can transcribe. You have already spoken them and it will be easy enough to speak them again. So now what you do is your choice. It is your responsibility. You have done enough, by your own account, to damn you. Do not make sinners of us all.'

It may, even now, be necessary to impress on the boy's imagination the stages on the route ahead: the walk from the room of confinement to the place of suffering: the wait, as the rope is uncoiled or the guiltless iron is set to heat. In that space, every thought that occupies the mind is taken out and replaced by blind terror. Your body is emptied and filled up with dread. The feet stumble, the breath labours. The eyes and ears function but the head can't make sense of what is seen and heard. Time falsifies itself, moments becoming days. The faces of your torturers loom up like giants or they become impossibly distant, small, like dots. Words are spoken: bring him here, seat him, now it is time. They were words attached to other and common meanings, but if you survive this they will only ever have one meaning and the meaning is pain. The iron hisses as it is lifted from the flame. The rope doubles like a serpent, loops itself, and waits. It is too late for you. You will not speak now, because your tongue has swelled and filled your mouth and language has eaten itself. Later you will speak, when you are carried away from the machinery and set down on straw. I have endured it, you will say. I have come through. And pity and self-love will crack open your heart, so that at the first gesture of kindness – let us say, a blanket or a sip of wine – your heart will overflow, your tongue unstop. Out flow the words. You were not brought to this room to think, but to feel. And in the end you have felt too much for yourself.

But Mark will be spared this; for now he looks up: 'Master Secretary, will you tell me again what my confession must be? Clear and … what was it? There were four things but I have already forgot them.' In a thicket of words he is stuck fast, and the more he fights the deeper the thorns rip his flesh. If appropriate, a translation can be made for him, yet his English has always seemed good enough. 'But you understand me, sir, I cannot tell you what I do not know?'

'Can you not? Then you must be my guest tonight. Christophe, you can see to that, I think. In the morning, Mark, your own powers will surprise you. Your head will be clear and your memory perfect. You will see that it is not in your interests to protect the gentlemen who share your sin. Because if the position were reversed, believe me, they would not spare a thought for you.'

* * *

He watches Christophe lead Mark away by the hand, as one might lead a simpleton. He waves away Richard and Call-Me to their suppers. He had intended to join them, but he finds he wants nothing, or only a dish he ate as a boy, a simple salad of purslane, the leaves picked that morning and left wrapped in a damp cloth. He ate it then for want of better and it did not stave off hunger. Now it is enough. When the cardinal fell, he had found posts for many of his poor servants, taking in some himself; if Mark had been less insolent, he might have taken him in too. Then he would not be a ruined being, as now he is ruined. His affectations would have been kindly ridiculed, till he became more manly. His expertise would have been lent out to other households and he would have been shown how to value himself and cost out his time. He would been shown how to make money for himself, and put in the way of a wife: instead of spending his best years snuffling and scraping outside the apartments of a king's wife, and having her jog his elbow and snap the feather in his hat.

At midnight, after the whole household has retired, a message from the king comes, to say that he has called off this week's visit to Dover. The jousts, however, will go ahead. Norris is listed, and George Boleyn. They are drawn on opposite teams, one for the challengers, one for the defenders: perhaps they will damage each other.

He does not sleep. His thoughts race. He thinks, I never lay awake a night for love, though poets tells me that is the procedure. Now I lie awake for its opposite. But then, he does not hate Anne, he is indifferent to her. He does not even hate Francis Weston, any more than you hate a biting midge; you just wonder why it was created. He pities Mark, but then, he thinks, we take him for a boy: when I was as old as Mark is now, I had crossed the sea and the frontiers of Europe. I had lain screaming in a ditch and hauled myself out of it, and got myself on the road: not once but twice, once in flight from my father and once from the Spanish on the battlefield. When I was as old as Mark is now, or

Francis Weston, I had distinguished myself in the houses of the Portinari, the Frescobaldi, and long before I was the age of George Boleyn I had dealt for them in the exchanges of Europe; I had broken down doors in Antwerp; I had come home to England, a changed man. I had made over my language, and to my exultation, and unexpectedly, I spoke my native tongue with more fluency than when I went away; I commended me to the cardinal, and at the same time, I was marrying a wife, I was proving myself in the law courts, I would go into court and smile at the judges and talk, my expertise laggard to my presentation, and the judges were so happy that I smiled at them and didn't smack them round the head, that they saw the case my way, often as not. The things you think are the disasters in your life are not the disasters really. Almost anything can be turned around: out of every ditch, a path, if you can only see it.

He thinks of lawsuits he has never thought of in years. Whether the judgement was good. Whether he would have given it against himself.

He wonders if he will ever sleep, and what he will dream. It is only in his dreams that he is private. Thomas More used to say you should build yourself a retreat, a hermitage, within your own house. But that was More: able to slam the door in everyone's face. In truth you cannot separate them, your public being and your private self. More thought you could, but in the end he had men he called heretics dragged to his house in Chelsea, so he could persecute them conveniently in the bosom of his family. You can insist on separation, if you must: go to your cabinet and say, 'Leave me alone to read.' But outside the room, you can hear breathing and scuffling, as a seething discontent builds up, a rumble of expectation: he is a public man, he belongs to us, when will he come forth? You cannot blank it out, the shuffle of the feet of the body politic.

He turns over in bed and says a prayer. In the depth of the night, he hears screaming. It is more like the wail of a child's nightmare than a man's scream of pain, and he thinks, half-asleep, shouldn't some woman be doing something about that? Then he thinks, it must be Mark. What are they doing to him? I said do nothing yet.

But he does not stir. He does not think his household would go against his orders. He wonders if they are asleep in Greenwich. The armoury is too near the palace itself, and the hours before a joust are often alive with the tap of hammers. The beating, the shaping, the welding, the polishing in the polishing mill, these operations are complete; there is just some last-minute riveting, an oiling and easing, final adjustments to please the anxious combatants.

He wonders, why did I leave Mark that space to boast, to undo himself? I could have condensed the process; I could have told him what I wanted, and threatened him. But I encouraged him; I did it so that he would be complicit. If he told the truth about Anne, he is guilty. If he lied about Anne, he is hardly innocent. I was prepared, if necessary, to put him under duress. In France, torture is usual, as necessary as salt to meat; in Italy, it is a sport for the piazza. In England, the law does not countenance it. But it can be used, at a nod from the king: on a warrant. It is true there is a rack at the Tower. No one withstands it. No one. For most men, since the way it works is so obvious, a glimpse of it is enough.

He thinks, I will tell Mark that. It will make him feel better about himself.

He gathers the sheet about him. Next moment, Christophe comes in to wake him. His eyes seem to flinch from the light. He sits up. 'Oh, Jesus. I have not slept all night. Why was Mark screaming?'

The boy laughs. 'We locked him in with Christmas. I thought of it, myself. You remember when I first saw the star in its sleeves? I said, master, what is that machine that is all over points? I thought it was an engine for torture. Well, it is dark in Christmas.

He fell against the star and it impaled him. Then the peacock wings came out of their shroud and brushed his face with fingers. And he thought a phantom was shut up with him in the dark.'

He says, 'You must do without me for an hour.'

'You are not ill, God forbid?'

'No, just wretched with lack of sleep.'

'Pull the covers over your head, and lie as one dead,' Christophe advises. 'I shall come back in an hour with bread and ale.'

When Mark tumbles out of the room he is grey with shock. Feathers adhere to his clothes, not peacock feathers but fluff from the wings of parish seraphs, and smudged gilding from the Three Kings' robes. Names run out of his mouth so fluently that he has to check him; the boy's legs threaten to give way and Richard has to hold him up. He has never had this problem before, the problem of having frightened someone too much. 'Norris' is somewhere in the babble, 'Weston' is there, so far so likely: and then Mark names courtiers so fast that their names merge and fly, he hears Brereton and says, 'Write that down,' he swears he hears Carew, also Fitzwilliam, and Anne's almoner and the Archbishop of Canterbury; he is in there himself of course, and at one point the child alleges Anne has committed adultery with her own husband. 'Thomas Wyatt ...' Mark pipes ...

'No, not Wyatt.'

Christophe leans forward and flicks his knuckles against the side of the boy's head. Mark stops. He looks around, wonderingly, for the source of the pain. Then once again he is confessing and confessing. He has worked through the privy chamber from gentlemen to grooms and he is naming persons unknown, probably cooks and kitchen boys he knew in his former less exalted life.

'Put him back with the ghost,' he says, and Mark gives one scream, and is silent.

'You have had to do with the queen how many times?' he asks.

Mark says, 'A thousand.'

Christophe gives him a little slap.

'Three times or four.'

'Thank you.'

Mark says, 'What will happen to me?'

'That rests with the court who will try you.'

'What will happen to the queen?'

'That rests with the king.'

'Nothing good,' Wriothesley says: and laughs.

He turns. 'Call-Me. You're early today?'

'I could not sleep. A word, sir?'

So today the positions are reversed, it is Call-Me-Risley who is taking him aside, frowning. 'You will have to bring in Wyatt, sir. You take it too much to heart, this charge his father laid on you. If it comes to it, you cannot protect him. The court has talked for years about what he may have done with Anne. He stands first in suspicion.'

He nods. It is not easy to explain to a young man like Wriothesley why he values Wyatt. He wants to say, because, good fellows though you are, he is not like you or Richard Riche. He does not talk simply to hear his own voice, or pick arguments just to win them. He is not like George Boleyn: he does not write verses to six women in the hope of bundling one of them into a dark corner where he can slip his cock into her. He writes to warn and to chastise, and not to confess his need but to conceal it. He understands honour but does not boast of his own. He is perfectly equipped as a courtier, but he knows the small value of that. He has studied the world without despising it. He understands the world without rejecting it. He has no illusions but he has hopes. He does not sleepwalk through his life. His eyes are open, and his ears for sounds others miss.

But he decides to give Wriothesley an explanation he can follow. 'It is not Wyatt,' he says, 'who stands in my way with the king. It is not Wyatt who turns me out of the privy chamber when I need the king's signature. It is not he who is continually dropping slander against me like poison into Henry's ear.'

Mr Wriothesley looks at him speculatively. 'I see. It is not so much, who is guilty, as whose guilt is of service to you.' He smiles. 'I admire you, sir. You are deft in these matters, and without false compunction.'

He is not sure he wants Wriothesley to admire him. Not on those grounds. He says, 'It may be that any of these gentlemen who are named could disarm suspicion. Or if suspicion remained, they could by some appeal stay the king's hand. Call-Me, we are not priests. We don't want their sort of confession. We are lawyers. We want the truth little by little and only those parts of it we can use.'

Wriothesley nods. 'But still I say, bring in Thomas Wyatt. If you don't arrest him your new friends will. And I have been wondering, sir, forgive me if I am persistent, but what will happen afterwards with your new friends? If the Boleyns go down, and it seems they must, the supporters of the Princess Mary will take the credit. They will not thank you for the part you have played. They may speak you fair now, but they will never forgive you for Fisher and More. They will turn you out of office, and they may destroy you completely. Carew, the Courtenays, those people, they will have all to rule.'

'No. The king will have all to rule.'

'But they will persuade him and entice him. I mean Margaret Pole's children, the old noble houses – they take it as natural they should have sway and they mean to have it. They will undo all the good you have done these last five years. And also they say that Edward Seymour's sister, if he marries her, she will take him back to Rome.'

He grins. 'Well, Call-Me, who will you back in a fight, Thomas Cromwell or Mistress Seymour?'

But of course Call-Me is right. His new allies hold him cheap. They take their triumph as natural, and for a mere promise of forgiveness he is to follow them and work for them and repent everything he has done. He says, 'I do not claim I can tell the future, but I do know one or two things such folk are ignorant of.'

One can never be sure what Wriothesley is reporting to Gardiner. Hopefully, matter that will cause Gardiner to scratch his head in puzzlement, and quiver in alarm. He says, 'What do you hear from France? I understand there is much talk of the book that Winchester wrote, justifying the king's supremacy. The French believe he wrote it under duress. Does he allow people to think that?'

'I am sure –' Wriothesley begins.

He cuts him off. 'No matter. I find I like the picture it puts in my head, Gardiner whining how he is crushed.'

He thinks, let's see if that gets back. It is his contention that Call-Me forgets for weeks at a time that he is the bishop's servant. He is an edgy young man, tense, and Gardiner's bellowing makes him ill; Cromwell is a congenial master, and easy day-to-day. He has said to Rafe, I quite like Call-Me, you know. I am interested in his career. I like watching him. If I ever broke with him, Gardiner would send another spy, who might be worse.

'Now,' he says, turning back to the company, 'we had better get poor Mark to the Tower.' The boy has shrunk to his knees, and is begging not to be put back with Christmas. 'Give him a rest,' he says to Richard, 'in a room clear of phantoms. Offer him food. When he is coherent, take his formal statement, and have it well witnessed before he leaves here. If he proves difficult, leave him to Christophe and Master Wriothesley, it is business more fit for them than for you.' Cromwells do not exhaust themselves on menial work; if they once did, that day has passed. He says, 'If Mark tries to renege once he is out of here, they will know what to do at the Tower. Once you have his confession secure, and all the names you need, go down to the king at Greenwich. He will be expecting you. Trust the message to no one. Drop the word in his ear yourself.'

Richard pulls Mark Smeaton to his feet, handling him as one might handle a puppet: and with no more ill-will than one would spare for a marionette. Through his mind darts, unprompted, the image of old Bishop Fisher tottering to the scaffold, skeletal and obstinate.

It is already nine in the morning. The dews of May Day have burned from the grass. All over England, green boughs are carried in from the woods. He is hungry. He could eat a cut of mutton: with samphire, if any has been sent up from Kent. He needs to sit down for his barber. He has not perfected the art of dictating letters while being shaved. Perhaps I'll grow my beard, he thinks. It would save time. Only then, Hans would insist on committing another portrait against me.

At Greenwich by this time, they will be sanding the arena for the jousts. Christophe says, 'Will the king fight today? Will he fight the Lord Norris and slay him?'

No, he thinks, he will leave that to me. Past the workshops, the store rooms and the jetties, the natural haunt of men such as himself, the pages will be placing silk cushions for the ladies in the towers that overlook the tilt yard. Canvas and rope and tar give way to damask and fine linen. The oil and stench and din, the smell of the river, give way to the perfume of rosewater and the murmurings of the maids as they dress the queen for the day ahead. They sweep away the remnants of her small meal, the crumbs of white bread, the slices of sweet preserves. They bring her petticoats and kirtles and sleeves and she makes choice. She is laced and tied and trussed, she is polished and flounced and studded with gems.

The king – it would be three or four years back and to justify his first divorce – put out a book called *A Glass of the Truth*. Parts of it, they say, he wrote himself.

Now Anne Boleyn calls for her glass. She sees herself: her jaundiced skin, lean throat, collarbones like twin blades.

1 May 1536: this, surely, is the last day of knighthood. What happens after this – and such pageants will continue – will be no

more than a dead parade with banners, a contest of corpses. The king will leave the field. The day will end, broken off, snapped like a shinbone, spat out like smashed teeth. George Boleyn, brother to the queen, will enter the silken pavilion to disarm, laying aside the favours and tokens, the scraps of ribbon the ladies have given him to carry. When he lifts off his helmet he will hand it to his squire, and see the world with misted eyes, falcons emblazoned, leopards couchant, claws, talons, teeth: he will feel his head on his shoulders wobbling as soft as jelly.

Whitehall: that night, knowing Norris is in custody, he goes to the king. A snatched word with Rafe in an outer room: how is he?

'Well,' Rafe says, 'you would expect him to be storming about like Edgar the Peaceable, looking for someone to stick with a javelin.' They exchange a smile, remembering the supper table at Wolf Hall. 'But he is calm. Surprisingly so. As if he knew, long ago. In his heart. And by his express wish he is alone.'

Alone: but who would he be with? Useless to expect Gentle Norris whispering towards him. Norris was keeper of the king's private purse; now one imagines the king's money loose and rolling down the highway. The angels' harps are slashed, and discord is general; purse strings are cut, and the silk ties of garments snapped to spill flesh.

As he stands on his threshold, Henry turns his eyes: 'Crumb,' he says heavily. 'Come and sit.' He waves away the attentions of the groom who hovers by the door. He has wine and pours it himself. 'Your nephew will have told you what passed at the tilting ground.' He says softly, 'He is a good boy, Richard, is he not?' His gaze is distant, as if he would like to wander off the point. 'I was among the spectators today, not an actor at all. She of course was as ever: at ease among her women, her countenance very haughty, but then smiling and stopping to converse with this gentleman or that.' He sniggers, a flat, incredulous sound. 'Oh yes, she has had some conversation.'

Then the bouts began, the heralds calling out each rider. Henry Norris had some ill-luck. His horse, startled by something, jibbed and laid back its ears, danced and tried to shed its rider. (Horse can fail. Boys can fail. Nerve can fail.) The king sent a message down to Norris, advising him to retire; a substitute would be sent to him, one of the king's own string of fighting horses, still kept trimmed and tacked in case it should be his sudden pleasure to take the field.

'It was a usual courtesy,' Henry explains; and shifts in his chair, like one called to justify himself. He nods: of course, sir. Whether Norris did in fact return to the lists, he is unsure. It was mid-afternoon when Richard Cromwell made his way through the crowds to the gallery, and knelt before the king; and at a word, approached to whisper in his ear. 'He explained how the musician Mark was taken,' the king says. 'He had confessed all, your nephew said. What, confessed freely? I asked him. Your nephew said, nothing was done against Mark. Not a hair of his head harmed.'

He thinks, but I shall have to burn the peacock wings.

'And then ...' the king says. For a moment he baulks, as Norris's horse did: and falls silent.

He will not continue. But he, Cromwell, already knows what occurred. Upon hearing the word from Richard, the king rose from his place. His servants eddied about him. He signed to a page, 'Find out Henry Norris, and tell him I ride to Whitehall, now. I want his company.'

He gave no explanation. He did not tarry. He did not speak to the queen. But covered the miles back, Norris beside him: Norris puzzled, Norris astonished, Norris almost slipping from the saddle with fright. 'I taxed him with the matter,' Henry says. 'With the boy Mark's confession. He would say nothing, but of his innocence.' Again that flat, scornful little laugh. 'But since then, Master Treasurer has questioned him. Norris admits it, he says he loved her. But when Fitz put it to him that he is an adulterer, that he desired my death so he could marry her, he said no, no and no. You will put questions to him, Cromwell, but when you do, tell him again what I told him as we rode. There can be mercy. There may be mercy, if he confesses and names the others.'

'We have names from Mark Smeaton.'

'I would not trust him,' Henry says contemptuously. 'I would not trust some little fiddle-player with the lives of men I have called my friends. I await some corroboration of his story. We will see what the lady says when she is taken.'

'Their confessions will be enough, sir, surely. You know who is suspected. Let me take them all in ward.'

But Henry's mind has strayed. 'Cromwell, what does it mean, when a woman turns herself about and about in the bed? Offering herself, this way and that? What would put it into her head to do such a thing?'

There is only one answer. Experience, sir. Of men's desires and her own. He does not need to say it.

'One way is apt for the procreation of children,' Henry says. 'The man lies on her. Holy church sanctions it, on the permitted days. Some churchmen say that though it is a grievous thing for a brother to copulate with a sister, it is still more grievous should a woman sit astride a man, or should a man approach a woman as if she were a bitch. For these practices, and others I will not name, Sodom was destroyed. I fear that any Christian man or woman who is in thrall to such vices will incur a judgement: what do you say? Where would a woman, not bred in a whorehouse, get knowledge of such things?'

'Women talk among themselves,' he says. 'As men do.'

'But a sober, a godly matron, whose only duty is to get a child?'

'I suppose she might want to pique her good man's interest, sir. So he does not venture to Paris Garden or some other ill-reputed place. If, let's say, they were long married.'

'But three years? Is that long?'

'No, sir.'

'It is not even three.' For a moment the king has forgotten that we are not talking about himself, but about some notional, God-fearing Englishman, some forester or ploughman. 'Where would she get the idea?' he persists. 'How would she know the man would like it?'

He bites back the obvious answer: perhaps she talked to her sister, who was in your bed first. Because now the king has wandered away from Whitehall and back to the country, to the blunt-fingered cottar and his wife in apron and cap: the man who crosses himself and asks leave of the Pope before he pinches out the light and sombrely tups his spouse, her knees to the roof beams and his backside bobbing. Afterwards, this godly couple, they kneel by their bed: they join in prayer.

But one day when the cottar is about his employment, the woodsman's little apprentice sneaks in and takes out his tool: now Joan, he says, now Jenny, bend over the table and let me teach you a lesson your mother never taught you. And so she trembles; and so he teaches her; and when the honest cottar comes home and mounts her that night, she thinks with every thrust and grunt of a newer way of doing things, a sweeter way, a dirtier way, a way that makes her eyes widen with surprise and another man's name jerk out of her mouth. Sweet Robin, she says. Sweet Adam. And when her husband recalls that his own name is Henry, does that not cause him to scratch his pate?

It is dusk now, outside the king's windows; his kingdom is growing chilly, his councillor too. They need lights and a fire. He opens the door and at once the room is full of folk: around the king's person, the grooms dart and swerve like early swallows in the twilight. Henry barely notices their presence. He says, 'Cromwell, do you suppose the rumours did not come to me? When every ale wife knew them? I am a simple man, you see. Anne told me she was untouched and I chose to believe her. She lied to me for seven years that she was a maid pure and chaste. If she could carry on such a deceit, what else might she be capable of? You can arrest her tomorrow. And her brother. Some of these acts alleged against her are not fit for discussion among decent people, lest they are moved by examples to sins they would not otherwise have dreamed to exist. I ask you and all my councillors to be close and discreet.'

'It is easy,' he says, 'to be deceived about a woman's history.'

For suppose Joan, suppose Jenny, had another life before her cottage life? You thought she grew up in a clearing at the other side of the wood. Now you hear, from reliable sources, that she came to womanhood in a harbour town, and danced naked on a table for sailors.

Did Anne, he will wonder later, understand what was coming? You would have thought that at Greenwich she would have been praying, or writing letters to her friends. Instead, if reports are true, she has walked blindly through her last morning, doing what she always used to do: she has been to the tennis courts, where she placed bets on the outcome of the matches. Late morning, a messenger came to ask her to appear before the king's council, sitting in His Majesty's absence: in the absence, too, of Master Secretary, who is busy elsewhere. The councillors told her that she would be charged with adultery with Henry Norris and Mark Smeaton: and with one other gentleman, for the moment unnamed. She must go to the Tower, pending proceedings against her. Her manner, Fitzwilliam tells him later, was incredulous and haughty. You cannot put a queen on trial, she said. Who is competent to try her? But then, when she was told that Mark and Henry Norris had confessed, she burst into tears.

From the council chamber, she is escorted to her own rooms, to dine. At two o'clock, he is heading there, with Audley the Lord Chancellor, and Fitzwilliam by his side. Mr Treasurer's affable face is creased with strain. 'I was not happy this morning in council, to hear her told so bluntly that Harry Norris has confessed. He confessed to me he loved her. He didn't confess to any act.'

'So what did you do, Fitz?' he asks him. 'Did you speak up?'

'No,' Audley says. 'He fidgeted and stared into the middle distance. Didn't you, Master Treasurer?'

'Cromwell!' It is Norfolk who is roaring, swatting his way through the throng of courtiers towards him. 'Now, Cromwell! I hear the singer has sung to your tune. What did you do to him? I wish I had been there. This will furnish a pretty ballad from the printer's shop. Henry fingering the lute, while the lutenist fingers his wife's quim.'

'If you hear of any such printer,' he says, 'tell me and I will close him down.'

Norfolk says, 'But listen to me, Cromwell. I do not intend this bag of bones to be the ruin of my noble house. If she has misconducted herself, it must not bear on the Howards, only the Boleyns. And I don't need Wiltshire finished off. I just want his foolish title taken off him. *Monseigneur*, if you please.' The duke bares his teeth in glee. 'I want to see him diminished, after his pride these past years. You will recall that I never promoted this marriage. No, Cromwell, that was you. I always warned Henry Tudor of her character. Perhaps this will teach him that in the future he should listen to me.'

'My lord,' he says, 'do you have the warrant?'

Norfolk flourishes a parchment. When they enter Anne's rooms, her gentlemen servants are just rolling away the great tablecloth, and she is still seated under her canopy of estate. She is wearing crimson velvet and she turns – the bag of bones – the perfect ivory oval of her face. Hard to think she has eaten anything; there is a fretful silence in the room, strain visible on every face. They must wait, the councillors, until the rolling is performed, till the folding of the napery is accomplished, and the correct reverences made.

293

'So you are here, uncle,' she says. Her voice is small. One by one she acknowledges them. 'Lord Chancellor. Master Treasurer.' Other councillors are pushing in behind them. Many people, it seems, have dreamed of this moment; they have dreamed that Anne would plead with them on her knees. 'My lord Oxford,' she says. 'And William Sandys. How are you, Sir William?' It is as if she finds it soothing, to name them all. 'And you, Cremuel.' She leans forward. 'You know, I created you.'

'And he created you, madam,' Norfolk snaps. 'And be sure he repents him of it.'

'But I was sorry first,' Anne says. She laughs. 'And I am sorry more.'

'Ready to go?' Norfolk says.

'I do not know how to be ready,' she says simply.

'Just come with us,' he says: he, Cromwell. He holds out a hand.

'I would rather not go to the Tower.' The same small voice, empty of everything except politeness. 'I would rather go to see the king. Can I not be taken up to Whitehall?'

She knows the answer. Henry never says goodbye. Once, on a summer's day of still heat, he rode away from Windsor and left Katherine behind; he never saw her again.

She says, 'Surely, masters, you will not take me like this, as I stand? I have no necessities, not a change of shift, and I should have my women with me.'

'Your clothes will be brought to you,' he says. 'And women to serve you.'

'I had rather have my own ladies of my privy chamber.'

Glances are exchanged. She seems not to know it is these women who have given evidence against her, these women who crowd around Master Secretary everywhere he moves, keen to tell him anything he wants, desperate to protect themselves. 'Well, if I cannot have my choice ... some persons at least from my household. So I can keep my proper state.'

Fitz clears his throat. 'Madam, your household is to be dissolved.'

She flinches. 'Cremuel will find them places,' she says lightly. 'He is good about servants.'

Norfolk nudges the Lord Chancellor. 'Because he grew up with them, eh?' Audley turns his face away: he is always Cromwell's man.

'I do not think I shall come with any of you,' she says. 'I will go with William Paulet, if he is pleased to escort me, because in the council this morning you all abused me, but Paulet was a very gentleman.'

'By God,' Norfolk chuckles. 'Go with Paulet, is it? I'll lock you under my arm and drag you to the boat with your arse in the air. Is that what you want?'

With one accord, the councillors turn on him, and glare. 'Madam,' Audley says, 'be assured, you will be handled as befits your status.'

She stands. Gathers her crimson skirts, raising them, fastidious, as if she will not now touch the common ground. 'Where is my lord brother?'

Last seen at Whitehall, she is told: which is true, though by now the guards may have come for him. 'And my father Monseigneur? This is what I do not understand,' she says. 'Why is Monseigneur not here with me? Why does he not sit down with you gentlemen and resolve this?'

'No doubt there will be resolution hereafter.' The Lord Chancellor is almost purring. 'Everything will be provided to keep you in comfort. It is arranged.'

'But arranged for how long?'

No one answers her. Outside the chamber, William Kingston waits for her, the Constable of the Tower. Kingston is a huge man, the king's own build; he conducts himself nobly, but his office, and his appearance, have struck terror into the hearts of the strongest men. He remembers Wolsey, when Kingston went

295

up-country to arrest him: the cardinal's legs went from under him, and he had to sit down on a chest to recover. We should have left Kingston at home, he whispers to Audley, and taken her ourselves. Audley murmurs, 'We could have, certainly; but don't you think, Master Secretary, that you're frightening enough on your own account?'

It amazes him, the Lord Chancellor's levity, as they pass into the open air. At the king's landing stage, the heads of stone beasts swim in the water, and so do their own shapes, the shapes of gentlemen, their forms broken by ripples, and the everted queen, flickering like a flame in a glass: around them, the dance of mild afternoon sunshine, and a flood of birdsong. He hands Anne into the barge, as Audley seems reluctant to touch her, and she shies away from Norfolk; and as if fishing his thoughts out of his mind, she whispers, 'Cremuel, you have never forgiven me for Wolsey.' Fitzwilliam gives him a glance, murmurs something he does not catch. Fitz was a favourite of the cardinal's in his day, and perhaps they are sharing a thought: now Anne Boleyn knows what it is like to be turned out of your house and put upon the river, your whole life receding with every stroke of the oars.

Norfolk takes a place opposite his niece, twitching and tutting. 'You see? You see now, madam! You see what happens, when you spurn your own family?'

'I do not think "spurn" is the word,' Audley says. 'She hardly did that.'

He gives Audley a black look. He has asked for discretion on the charges against brother George. He does not want Anne to start flailing about and knock someone out of the boat. He withdraws into himself. Watches the water. A company of halberdiers are their escort, and he admires each fine axe edge, the sharp gleam on their blades. From an armoury's point of view, they are surprisingly cheap to produce, halberds. But probably, as a weapon of war, they've had their day. He thinks of Italy, the battlefield, the forward push of pike. There is a powder house at the Tower and he likes to go in and talk to the firemasters. But perhaps that is a task for another day.

Anne says, 'Where is Charles Brandon? I am sure he is sorry not to have seen this.'

'He is with the king, I suppose,' Audley says. He turns to him and whispers, 'Poisoning his mind against your friend Wyatt. You have your work cut out there, Master Secretary.'

His eyes are on the far bank. 'Wyatt is too good a man to lose.'

The Lord Chancellor sniffs. 'Verses will not save him. Damn him, rather. We know he writes in riddles. But I think perhaps the king will feel they have been solved.'

He thinks not. There are codes so subtle that they change their whole meaning in half a line, or in a syllable, or in a pause, a caesura. He has prided himself, will pride himself, on asking Wyatt no questions that will force him to lie, though he may dissimulate. Anne should have dissimulated, Lady Rochford has explained to him: on her first night with the king she should have acted the virgin's part, lain rigid and weeping. 'But, Lady Rochford,' he had objected, 'faced with such fear, any man might falter. The king is not a rapist.'

Oh, well then, Lady Rochford had said. She should at least have flattered him. She should have acted like a woman who was getting a happy surprise.

He did not relish the topic; he sensed in Jane Rochford's tone the peculiar cruelty of women. They fight with the poor weapons God has bestowed – spite, guile, skill in deceit – and it is likely that in conversations between themselves they trespass in places where a man would never trust his footing. The king's body is borderless, fluent, like his realm: it is an island building itself or eroding itself, its substance washed out into the waters salt and fresh; it has its shores of polder, its marshy tracts, its reclaimed margins; it has tidal waters, emissions and effusions, quags that slough in and out of the conversation of Englishwomen, and dark mires where only priests should wade, rush lights in their hands.

On the river the breeze is cold; summer still weeks away. Anne is watching the water. She looks up and says, 'Where is the archbishop? Cranmer will defend me and so will all my bishops, they owe their promotion to me. Fetch Cranmer and he will swear I am a good woman.'

Norfolk leans forward and speaks into her face: 'A bishop would spit on you, niece.'

'I am the queen and if you do me harm, then a curse will come on you. No rain will fall till I am released.'

A soft groan from Fitzwilliam. The Lord Chancellor says, 'Madam, it is such foolish talk of curses and spells that has brought you here.'

'Oh? I thought you said I was a false wife, are you now saying I am a sorcerer too?'

Fitzwilliam says, 'It was none of us raised the subject of curses.'

'You cannot do anything against me. I will swear on oath I am true, and the king will listen. You can bring no witnesses. You do not even know how to charge me.'

'Charge you?' Norfolk says. 'Why charge you, I ask myself. It would save us trouble if we pitched you out and drowned you.'

Anne shrinks into herself. Huddled as far as she can get from her uncle, she looks the size of a child.

As the barge moors at the Court Gate he sees Kingston's deputy, Edmund Walsingham, scanning the river; in conversation with him, Richard Riche. 'Purse, what are you doing here?'

'I thought you might want me, sir.'

The queen steps on to dry land, steadies herself on Kingston's arm. Walsingham bows to her. He seems agitated; he looks around, wondering to which councillor he should address himself. 'Are we to fire the cannon?'

'That's usual,' Norfolk says, 'is it not? When a person of note comes in, at the king's pleasure. And she is of note, I suppose?'

'Yes, but a queen ...' the man says.

'Fire the cannon,' Norfolk demands. 'The Londoners ought to know.'

'I think they know already,' he says. 'Didn't my lord see them running along the banks?'

Anne looks up, scans the stonework above her head, the narrow loupe windows and the gratings. There are no human faces, just the flap of a raven's wing, and its voice above her, startling in its human quality. 'Is Harry Norris here?' she asks. 'Has he not cleared my name?'

'I fear not,' Kingston says. 'Nor his own.'

Something happens to Anne then, which later he will not quite understand. She seems to dissolve and slip from their grasp, from Kingston's hands and his, she seems to liquefy and elude them, and when she resolves herself once more into woman's form she is on hands and knees on the cobbles, her head thrown back, wailing.

Fitzwilliam, the Lord Chancellor, even her uncle, step back; Kingston frowns, his deputy shakes his head, Richard Riche looks stricken. He, Cromwell, takes hold of her – since no one else will do it – and sets her back on her feet. She weighs nothing, and as he lifts her, her wail breaks off, as if her breath had been stopped. Silent, she steadies herself against his shoulder, leans into him: intent, complicit, ready for the next thing they will do together, which is kill her.

As they turn back to the royal barge, Norfolk barks, 'Master Secretary? I need to see the king.'

'Alas,' he says, as if the regret were genuine: alas, that will not be possible. 'His Majesty has asked for peace and seclusion. Surely, my lord, in the circumstances you would do the same.'

'In the circumstances?' Norfolk echoes. The duke is dumb, at least for a minute, as they inch out into the central channel of the Thames: and he frowns, no doubt thinking of his own ill-used wife and the chances of her straying. A snort of derision is best, the duke decides: 'I tell you what, Master Secretary, I know you're friendly with my duchess, so what do you say? Cranmer can have us annulled, and she's yours for the asking. What, you won't have her? She comes with her own bedding and a riding mule, and she doesn't eat much. I'll make over forty shillings a year and we'll shake hands on it.'

'My lord, curb yourself,' Audley says fiercely. He is driven to the reproach of last resort: 'Remember your ancestry.'

'It's more than Cromwell can,' the duke sniggers. 'Now listen to me, Crumb. If I say I need to see the Tudor, no blacksmith's boy will say me nay.'

'He may weld you, my lord,' Richard Riche says. They had not noticed him slip aboard. 'He may take upon him to beat and reshape your head. Master Secretary has skills you have never imagined.'

A sort of giddiness has seized them, a reaction to the horrible sight they have left behind on the quay. 'He may pound you into a different shape entirely,' Audley says. 'You may wake up a duke and by noon you may be curved into a horseboy.'

'He may melt you,' Fitzwilliam says. 'You begin as a duke and end as a leaden drip.'

'You may live out your days as a trivet,' Riche says. 'Or a hinge.'

He thinks, you must laugh, Thomas Howard, you must laugh or burst into flames: which will it be? If you combust we can at least throw water on you. With a spasm, a shudder, the duke turns his back on them to master himself: 'Tell Henry,' he says. 'Tell him I renounce the wench. Tell him I no longer call her niece.'

He, Cromwell, says, 'You will have the chance to show loyalty. If it comes to a trial, you will preside over the court.'

'At least, we think that is the procedure,' Riche chips in. 'A queen has never come to trial before. What does the Lord Chancellor say?'

'I say nothing.' Audley holds up his palms. 'You and Wriothesley and Master Secretary have worked it all between you, as you usually do. Only – Cromwell, you will not put the Earl of Wiltshire among the judges?'

He smiles. 'Her father? No. I would not do that.'

'How will we charge Lord Rochford?' Fitzwilliam asks. 'If he is indeed to be charged?'

Norfolk says, 'It is the three for trial? Norris, Rochford, and the fiddle player?'

'Oh no, my lord,' he says calmly.

'There's more? By the Mass!'

'How many lovers has she had?' Audley says, with a keenness barely suppressed.

Riche says, 'Lord Chancellor, you have seen the king? I have seen him. He is pale and ill from the strain. That, in fact, is treason in itself, if any harm should happen to his royal body. Indeed, I think we may say harm has already occurred.'

If dogs could smell out treason, Riche would be a bloodhound, that prince among trufflers.

He says, 'I keep an open mind as to how these gentlemen are to be charged, whether with concealing a treason or with the offence itself. If they claim to be only a witness to the misdeeds of others they must say who those others are, they must earnestly and openly tell us what they know; but if they withhold names, we must suspect they are themselves among the guilty.'

The boom of the cannon catches them unawares, shuddering across the water; you feel the jolt inside, in your bones.

That evening a message comes to him from Kingston at the Tower. Write down everything she says and everything she does, he had told the constable, and Kingston – a dutiful, civil and prudent man, though sometimes obtuse – can be relied on for that. As the councillors walked away to the barge, Anne asked him, 'Master Kingston, shall I go into a dungeon?' No, madam, he had assured her, you shall have the chambers where you lay before your coronation.

At that, he reports, she fell into a storm of weeping, 'It is too good for me. Jesus have mercy on me.' Then she knelt down on the stones and prayed and wept, said the constable: then, most strangely, or so it seemed to him, she began to laugh.

Without a word, he passes the letter to Wriothesley. Who looks up from it, and when he speaks his tone is hushed. 'What has she done, Master Secretary? Perhaps something we have not yet imagined.'

He looks at him, exasperated. 'You are not going to begin on that witchcraft business?'

'No. But. If she says she is not worthy, she is saying she is guilty. Or so it seems to me. But I do not know guilty of what.'

'Remind me what I said. What kind of truth do we want? Did I say, the whole truth?'

'You said, only the truth we can use.'

'I reiterate the point. But you know, Call-Me, I shouldn't have to. You're quick on the uptake. Once should be enough.'

It is a warm evening, and he sits by an open window, his nephew Richard for company. Richard knows when to keep silence and when to talk; it is a family trait, he supposes. Rafe Sadler is the only other company he would have liked, and Rafe is with the king.

Richard looks up. 'I had a letter from Gregory.'

'Oh yes?'

'You know Gregory's letters.'

'"The sun is shining. We have had good hunting and great cheer. I am well, how are you? And now no more for lack of time."'

Richard nods. 'He doesn't change, Gregory. Though he does, I suppose. He wants to come here to you. He should be with you, he thinks.'

'I was trying to spare him.'

'I know. But perhaps you should let him. You cannot keep him a child.'

He broods. If his son is to become accustomed to the king's service, perhaps he should know what it involves. 'You can leave me,' he says to Richard. 'I might write to him.'

Richard pauses to shut out the night air. Outside the door his voice runs on, giving kindly commands: bring down my uncle's furred gown, he may want it, and take in to him more lights. He is sometimes surprised if he knows someone cares for him, cares enough to think of his bodily comfort: except for his servants, who are paid to do it. He wonders how the queen finds herself, amid her new Tower household: Lady Kingston has been set among her attendants, and though he has placed women of the Boleyn family around her, they might not be those she would have chosen for herself. They are women of experience, who will know how the tide is running. They will listen keenly to weeping and laughter, and any words like, 'It is too good for me.'

He believes he understands Anne, as Wriothesley does not. When she said the queen's lodgings were too good for her, she did not mean to admit her guilt, but to say this truth: I am not worthy, and I am not worthy because I have failed. One thing she set out to do, this side of salvation: get Henry and keep him. She has lost him to Jane Seymour, and no court of law will judge her more harshly than she judges herself. Since Henry rode away from her yesterday, she has been an impostor, like a child or a court fool, dressed in the costumes of a queen and now ordered to live in the queen's rooms. She knows adultery is a sin and treason a crime, but to be on the losing side is a greater fault than these.

Richard puts his head back in and says, 'Your letter, shall I write it for you? Save your eyes?'

He says, 'Anne is dead to herself. We shall have no trouble with her now.'

* * *

He has asked the king to keep to his privy chamber, admit as few people as possible. He has strictly instructed the guards to turn away petitioners, whether men or women. He does not want the king's judgement contaminated, as it can be, by the last person he talked to; he does not want Henry persuaded or cajoled or pushed off course. Henry seems inclined to obey him. These last years, the king has tended to retire from public view: at first because he wanted to be with his concubine Anne, and then because he wanted to be without her. Behind his privy chamber, he has his secret lodgings; and sometimes, after he has been put into his great bed and the bed has been blessed, after the candles have been snuffed, he pushes away the damask counterpane and slides from the mattress and pads into a secret chamber, where he creeps into another, unofficial bed, and sleeps like a natural man, naked and alone.

So it is in the muffled silence of these secret rooms, hung with tapestries of the Fall of Man, that the king says to him, 'Cranmer has sent a letter from Lambeth. Read it to me, Cromwell. I have had it read once, but do you read it again.'

He takes the paper. You can feel Cranmer shrinking as he writes, hoping the ink will run and the words blur. Anne the queen has favoured him, Anne has listened to him and promoted the cause of the gospel; Anne has made use of him, too, but Cranmer can never see that. '"*I am in such perplexity,*" he writes, "*that my mind is clean amazed; for I never had better opinion in woman, than I had in her.*"'

Henry interrupts him. 'See how we were all deceived.'

'"*... which maketh me to think,*"' he reads, '"*that she should not be culpable. And again, I think your Highness would not have gone so far, except she had surely been culpable.*"'

'Wait till he hears it all,' Henry says. 'He will not have heard the like. At least, I hope he has not. I do not think there has ever been an instance in the world like this.'

'"*Now I think that your Grace best knoweth, that next unto your Grace I was most bound unto her of all creatures living ...*"'

Henry breaks in again. 'But you will see he goes on to say, if she is culpable she should be punished without mercy, and held for an example. Seeing how I raised her from nothing. And further he says, that no one who loves the gospel will favour her, rather hate her.'

Cranmer adds, '*Wherefore I trust that your Grace will bear no less entire favour unto the truth of the gospel, than you did before forsomuch as your grace's favour to the gospel was not led by affection unto her, but by zeal unto the truth.*'

He, Cromwell, puts the letter down. That seems to cover everything. She cannot be guilty. But yet she must be guilty. We, her brethren, repudiate her.

He says, 'Sir, if you want Cranmer, send for him. You could comfort each other, and perhaps between you try to understand all this. I will tell your people to let him in. You look as if you need fresh air. Go down the stair into the privy garden. You will not be disturbed.'

'But I have not seen Jane,' Henry says. 'I want to look at her. We can bring her here?'

'Not yet, sir. Wait till the business is more forward. There are rumours on the streets, and crowds who want to see her, and ballads made, deriding her.'

'Ballads?' Henry is shocked. 'Find out the authors. They must be straitly punished. No, you are right, we must not bring Jane here until the air is pure. So you go to her, Cromwell. I want you to carry a certain token.' He produces from among his papers a tiny, jewelled book: the kind a woman keeps at her girdle, looped on a gold chain. 'It was my wife's,' he says. Then he checks himself and looks away in shame. 'I mean to say, it was Katherine's.'

He does not want to take the time to go down to Surrey to Carew's house, but it seems he must. It is a well-proportioned house put up some thirty years ago, its great hall especially splendid and much copied by gentlemen building their own houses.

He has been there before, with the cardinal in his time. It looks as though since then Carew has brought Italians in to replan the gardens. The gardeners doff their straw hats to him. The walks are coming into their early summer glory. Birds twitter from an aviary. The grass is shorn as close as velvet pile. Nymphs watch him with stone eyes.

Now that the business is tending one way and one way only, the Seymours have begun teaching Jane how to be a queen. 'This business you get up to with doors,' Edward Seymour says. Jane blinks at him. 'The way you hold the door still and slide yourself around it.'

'You told me to be discreet.' Jane lowers her eyes, to show him what discretion means.

'Now. Go out of the room,' Edward says. 'Come back in. Like a queen, Jane.'

Jane sneaks out. The door creaks behind her. In the hiatus, they look at each other. The door swings open. There is a long pause – as it might be, a regal pause. The doorway stands empty. Then Jane appears, inching around the corner. 'Is that better?'

'Do you know what I think?' he says. 'I think that from now on Jane won't be opening her own doors, so it doesn't matter.'

'My belief is,' Edward says, 'this modesty could pall. Look up at me, Jane. I want to see your expression.'

'But what makes you think,' Jane murmurs, 'that I want to see yours?'

In the gallery the whole family is assembled. The two brothers, prudent Edward and hasty Tom. Worthy Sir John, the old goat. Lady Margery, the noted beauty of her day, about whom John Skelton once penned a line: 'benign, courteous and meek', he called her. The meekness is not evident today: she looks grimly triumphant, like a woman who has squeezed success from life, though it's taken her nearly sixty years to do it.

Bess Seymour, the widowed sister, sails in. She has a parcel wrapped in linen in her hands. 'Master Secretary,' she says, with a reverence. She says to her brother, 'Here, Tom, hold this. Sit down, sister.'

Jane sits on a stool. You expect someone to hand her a slate and begin her on A.B.C. 'Now,' Bess says. 'Off with this.' For a moment, she looks as if she is attacking her sister: with a vigorous double-handed tug, she rips off her half-moon headdress, flips up its veil and bundles the whole into the waiting hands of her mother.

Jane in her white cap looks naked and pained, her face as small and wan as a face on a sickbed. 'Cap off too, and start again,' Bess orders. She drags at the knotted string under her sister's chin. 'What have you done with this, Jane? It looks as if you've been sucking it.' Lady Margery produces a pair of embroidery scissors. With a snip, Jane is freed. Her sister whisks the cap off and Jane's pale hair, a thin ribbon of light, streaks over her shoulder. Sir John ahems and looks away, the old hypocrite: as if he'd seen something beyond the male remit. The hair has a moment's freedom before Lady Margery plucks it up and wraps it around her hand, as unfeeling as if it were a hank of wool; Jane frowns as it is whipped up from her nape, coiled, and crammed under a newer, stiffer cap. 'We're going to pin this,' Bess says. She works, absorbed. 'More elegant, if you can stand it.'

'Never liked strings myself,' Lady Margery says.

'Thank you, Tom,' Bess says, and takes her parcel. She casts aside the wrappings. 'Cap tighter,' she decrees. Her mother pinches as directed, repins. The next moment a fabric box is crammed on Jane's head. Her eyes turn up, as if for help, and she utters one little bleat, as the wire frame bites into her scalp. 'Well, I am surprised,' Lady Margery says. 'You've got a bigger head than I thought, Jane.' Bess applies herself to bending the wire. Jane sits mute. 'That'll do,' Lady Margery says. 'It's got a bit of give in it. Push it down. Turn up the lappets. About chin level, Bess. That's how the old queen used to like it.' She stands back to assess her daughter, now imprisoned in an old-fashioned gable hood, the kind that hasn't been seen since Anne came up. Lady Margery sucks in her lips and studies her daughter. 'Tilting,' she pronounces.

'That's Jane, I think,' Tom Seymour says. 'Sit up straight, sister.'

Jane puts her hands to her head, gingerly, as if the construction might be hot. 'Leave it alone,' her mother snaps. 'You wore it before. You'll get used to it.'

From somewhere Bess produces a length of fine black veiling. 'Sit still.' She begins to pin it to the back of the box, her face absorbed. Ouch, that was my neck, Jane says, and Tom Seymour gives a heartless laugh; some private joke of his, too unseemly to share, but one can guess. 'I'm sorry to keep you, Master Secretary,' Bess says, 'but she has to get this right. We cannot have her reminding the king of, you know.'

Just take care, he thinks, uneasy: it is only four months since Katherine died, perhaps the king does not want to be reminded of her either.

'We have several more frames at our command,' Bess tells her sister, 'so if you really can't balance it, we can take the whole thing down and try again.'

Jane closed her eyes. 'I'm sure it will do.'

'How did you get them so quickly?' he asks.

'They have been put away,' Lady Margery says. 'In chests. By women like myself who knew they would be needed again. We shall not see the French fashions now, not for many a year, please God.'

Old Sir John says, 'The king has sent her jewels.'

'Things La Ana had no use for,' Tom Seymour says. 'But they will all come to her soon.'

Bess says, 'I suppose Anne will not want them, in her convent.'

Jane glances up: and now she does it, now she meets the eyes of her brothers, and pulls her gaze away again. It is always a surprise to hear her voice, so soft and so unpractised, its tone so at odds with what she has to say. 'I do not see how that can work, the convent. First Anne would claim that she was carrying the king's child. Then he would be forced to wait on her, without result, for there is never a result. After that she would think of new delays. And meanwhile none of us would be safe.'

Tom says, 'She knows Henry's secrets, I dare say. And would sell them to her friends the French.'

'Not that they are her friends,' Edward says. 'Not any more.'

'But she would try,' Jane says.

He sees them, closing ranks: a fine old English family. He asks Jane, 'Would you do anything you can, to ruin Anne Boleyn?' His tone implies no reproach; he's just interested.

Jane considers: but only for a moment. 'No one need contrive at her ruin. No one is guilty of it. She ruined herself. You cannot do what Anne Boleyn did, and live to be old.'

He must study Jane, now, the expression on her downturned face. When Henry courted Anne she looked squarely at the world, her chin tilted upwards, her shallow-set eyes like pools of darkness against the glow of her skin. But one searching glance is enough for Jane, and then she casts her eyes down. Her expression is withdrawn, brooding. He has seen it before. He has been looking at pictures these forty years. When he was a boy, before he ran away from England, a picture was a splayed cunt chalked on a wall, or a flat-eyed saint you studied while you yawned through Sunday Mass. But in Florence the masters had painted silver-faced virgins, demure, reluctant, whose fate moved within them, a slow reckoning in the blood; their eyes were turned inwards, to images of pain and glory. Has Jane seen such pictures? Is it possible that the masters drew from life, that they studied the face of some woman betrothed, some woman being walked by her kin to the church door? French hood, gable hood, it is not enough. If Jane could veil her face completely, she would do it, and hide her calculations from the world.

'Well now,' he says. He feels awkward, attracting attention back to himself. 'The reason I have come, the king has sent me with a gift.'

It is wrapped in silk. Jane looks up as she turns it over in her hands. 'You once gave me a gift, Master Cromwell. And in those days no one else did so. You may be sure I shall remember that, when it is in my power to do you good.'

Just in time to frown at this, Sir Nicholas Carew has made an entrance. He does not come into a room like lesser men, but rolls in, like a siege engine or some formidable hurling device: and now, halting before Cromwell, he looks as if he wishes to bombard him. 'I have heard about these ballads,' he says. 'Cannot you suppress them?'

'They're nothing personal,' he says. 'Just warmed-over libels from when Katherine was queen and Anne was the pretender.'

'The two cases are in no way alike. This virtuous lady, and that ...' Words fail Carew; and indeed, her judicial status uncertain, the charges not yet framed, it is hard to describe Anne. If she is a traitor she is, pending the verdict of the court, technically dead; though at the Tower, Kingston reports, she eats heartily enough, and giggles, like Tom Seymour, over private jokes.

'The king is rewriting old songs,' he says. 'Reworking their references. A dark lady is taken out and a fair lady brought in. Jane knows how these things are managed. She was with the old queen. If Jane has no illusions, a little maid such as she, then you should get rid of yours, Sir Nicholas. You are too old for them.'

Jane sits unmoving with her present in her hands, still wrapped. 'It's all right to undo it, Jane,' her sister says kindly. 'Whatever it is, it's yours to keep.'

'I was listening to Master Secretary,' Jane says. 'One can learn a great deal from him.'

'Hardly apt lessons for you,' Edward Seymour says.

'I don't know. Ten years in the train of Master Secretary, and I might learn to stand up for myself.'

'Your happy destiny,' says Edward, 'is to be a queen, not a clerk.'

'So do you,' Jane says, 'give thanks to God I was born a woman?'

'We thank God on our knees daily,' Tom Seymour says, with leaden gallantry. It is new to him, to have this meek sister require compliments, and he is not swift to respond. He gives brother Edward a glance and a shrug: sorry, best I can do.

Jane unwraps her prize. She runs the chain through her fingers; it is as fine as one of her own hairs. She holds the tiny book in the palm of her hand and turns it over. In the gold and black enamel of its cover, initials are studded in rubies, and entwined: 'H' and 'A'.

'Think nothing of it, the stones can be replaced,' he says quickly. Jane hands him the object. Her face has fallen; she does not yet know how thrifty the king can be, this most magnificent prince. Henry should have warned me, he thinks. Beneath Anne's initial you can still distinguish the 'K'. He passes it to Nicholas Carew. 'You take note?'

The knight opens it, fumbling with the tiny clasp. 'Ah,' he says. 'A Latin prayer. Or a Bible verse?'

'If I may?' He takes it back. 'Here is the Book of Proverbs. "Who can find a good, a virtuous woman? Her price is beyond rubies."' Evidently it's not, he thinks: three presents, three wives, and only one jeweller's bill. He says to Jane, smiling, 'Do you know this woman who is mentioned here? Her clothing is silk and purple, says the author. I could tell you much more about her, from verses this page cannot contain.'

Edward Seymour says, 'You should have been a bishop, Cromwell.'

'Edward,' he says, 'I should have been Pope.'

He is taking his leave, when Carew crooks a peremptory finger. Oh, Lord Jesus, he breathes to himself, I am in trouble now, for not being humble enough. Carew motions him aside. But it is not to reproach him. 'The Princess Mary,' Carew murmurs, 'is very hopeful of a call to her father's side. What better remedy and comfort at such a time, for the king, than to have the child of his true marriage in his house?'

'Mary is better where she is. The subjects discussed here, in the council and on the street, are not fit for the ears of a young girl.'

Carew frowns. 'There may be something in that. But she looks to have messages from the king. Tokens.'

Tokens, he thinks; that can be arranged.

'There are ladies and gentlemen from the court,' Carew says, 'who wish to ride up-country to pay their respects, and if the princess is not to be conducted here, surely the terms of her confinement should be relaxed? It is hardly suitable, now, to have Boleyn women around her. Perhaps her old governor, the Countess of Salisbury ...'

Margaret Pole? That haggard papist battleaxe? But now is not the time to deliver hard truths to Sir Nicholas; that can wait. 'The king will dispose,' he says comfortably. 'It is a close family matter. He will know what is best for his daughter.'

By night, when the candles are lit, Henry leaks easy tears over Mary. But by daylight he sees her for what she is: disobedient, self-willed, still unbroken. When all this is tidied away, the king says, I shall turn my attention to my duties as father. I am sad that the Lady Mary and I have become estranged. After Anne, reconciliation will become possible. But, he adds, there will be certain conditions. To which, mark my words, my daughter Mary will adhere.

'One more thing,' Carew says. 'You must pull Wyatt in.'

Instead, he has Francis Bryan fetched. Francis comes in grinning: he thinks himself the untouchable man. His eye patch is decorated with a small winking emerald, which gives a sinister effect: one green eye, and the other ...

He examines it: says, 'Sir Francis, what colour are your eyes? I mean, your eye?'

'Red, generally,' Bryan says. 'But I try not to drink during Lent. Or Advent. Or on Fridays.' He sounds lugubrious. 'Why am I here? You know I'm on your side, don't you?'

'I only asked you to supper.'

'You asked Mark Smeaton to supper. And look where he is now.'

'It is not I who doubts you,' he says with a heavy, actor's sigh. (How he enjoys Sir Francis.) 'It is not I, but the world at large, who asks where your loyalties lie. You are, of course, the queen's kinsman.'

'I am Jane's kinsman too.' Bryan is still at ease, and he shows it by leaning back in his chair, his feet thrust out under the table. 'I hardly thought I should be interrogated.'

'I am talking to everyone who is close to the queen's family. And you are certainly close, you have been with them since the early days; did you not go to Rome, chasing the king's divorce, pressing the Boleyns' case with the best of them? But what should you fear? You are an old courtier, you know everything. Used wisely, wisely shared, knowledge may protect you.'

He waits. Bryan has sat up straight.

'And you want to please the king,' he says. 'All I ask is to be sure that, if you are put to it, you will give evidence on any point I require.'

He could swear that Francis sweats Gascon wine, his pores leaking that mouldy, ropey stuff he's been buying cheap and selling dear to the king's own cellars.

'Look, Crumb,' Bryan says. 'What I know is, Norris always imagined rutting with her.'

'And her brother, what did he imagine?'

Bryan shrugs. 'She was sent to France and they never knew each other till they were grown. I have known such things happen, have not you?'

'No, I cannot say I have. We never went in for incest where I grew up, God knows we had crimes enough and sins, but there were places our fantasy did not stretch.'

'You saw it in Italy, I wager. Only sometimes people see it and they don't dare name it.'

'I dare name anything,' he says calmly. 'As you will see. My imagination may lag behind each day's revelations, but I am working hard to catch up with them.'

'Now she is not queen,' Bryan says, 'because she is not, is she ... I can call her what she is, a hot minx, and where has she better opportunity, than with her family?'

He says, 'By that reasoning, do you think she goes to it with Uncle Norfolk? It could even be you, Sir Francis. If she has a mind to her relatives. You are a great gallant.'

'Oh, Christ,' Bryan says. 'Cromwell, you would not.'

'I only mention it. But as we are at one in this matter, or we appear to be, will you do me a service? You could ride over to Great Hallingbury, and prepare my friend Lord Morley for what is coming. It is not the sort of news you can break in a letter, not when the friend is elderly.'

'You think it's better face to face?' An incredulous laugh. 'My lord, I shall say, I come myself to spare you a shock – your daughter Jane will soon be a widow, because her husband is to be decapitated for incest.'

'No, the matter of incest we leave to the priests. It is for treason he will die. And we do not know the king will choose decapitation.'

'I do not believe I can do it.'

'But I do. I have great faith in you. Think of it as a diplomatic mission. You have performed those. Though I wonder how.'

'Sober,' Francis Bryan says. 'I shall need a drink for this one. And you know, I have a dread of Lord Morley. He is always pulling out some ancient manuscript, and saying, "Look here,

Francis!" and laughing heartily at the jokes in it. And you know my Latin, any schoolboy would be ashamed of it.'

'Don't wheedle,' he says. 'Saddle your horse. But before you ride to Essex, do me a further service. Go see your friend Nicholas Carew. Tell him I agree to his demands and I will talk to Wyatt. But warn him, tell him not to push me because I will not be pushed. Remind Carew that there may be more arrests, I am not yet able to say who. Or rather, if I am able, I am not willing. Understand, and make your friends understand, that I must have a free hand to deal. I am not their waiting boy.'

'Am I free to go?'

'Free as air,' he says, blandly. 'But what about supper?'

'You can eat mine,' Francis says.

Though the king's chamber is dark, the king says, 'We must look into a glass of truth. I think I am to blame, as what I suspected I did not own.'

Henry looks at Cranmer as if to say, it's your turn now: I admit my fault, so give me absolution. The archbishop looks harrowed; he does not know what Henry will say next, or if he can trust himself to respond. This is not a night for which Cambridge ever trained him. 'You were not remiss,' he tells the king. He darts a questioning look, like a long needle, at him, Cromwell. 'In these matters, surely the accusation should not come before the evidence.'

'You must bear in mind,' he says to Cranmer – for he is bland and easy and full of phrases – 'you must bear in mind that not I but the whole council examined the gentlemen who now stand accused. And the council called you in, laid the matter before you, and you did not demur. As you have said yourself, my lord archbishop, we would not have gone so far in the matter without grave consideration.'

'When I look back,' Henry says, 'so much falls into place. I was misled and betrayed. So many friends lost, friends and good servants, lost, alienated, exiled from court. And worse ... I think of Wolsey. The woman I called my wife practised against him with all her ingenuity, with every weapon of slyness and rancour.'

Which wife would that be? Both Katherine and Anne worked against the cardinal. 'I do not know why I have been so crossed,' Henry says. 'But does not Augustine call marriage "a mortal and slavish garment"?'

'Chrysostom,' Cranmer murmurs.

'But let that pass,' he, Cromwell, says hastily. 'If this marriage is dissolved, Majesty, Parliament will petition you to marry again.'

'I dare say it will. How may a man do his duty, to both his realm and to God? We sin even in the very act of generation. We must have offspring, and kings especially must, and yet we are warned against lust even in marriage, and some authorities say, do they not, that to love your wife immoderately is a kind of adultery?'

'Jerome,' Cranmer whispers: as if he would just as soon disown the saint. 'But there are many other teachings that are more comfortable, and that praise the married state.'

'Roses snatched from the thorns,' he says. 'The church does not offer much comfort to the married man, though Paul says we should love our wives. It is hard, Majesty, not to think marriage is sinful inherently, since the celibates have spent many centuries saying that they are better than we are. But they are not better. Repetition of false teachings does not make them true. You agree, Cranmer?'

Just kill me now, the archbishop's face says. Against all the laws of king and church, he is a married man; he married in Germany when he was among the reformers, he keeps Frau Grete secretly, he hides her in his country houses. Does Henry know? He must know. Will Henry say? No, because he is intent on his own plight. 'Now I cannot see why I ever wanted her,' the king says. 'That is why I think she has practised on me with charms and enchantments. She claims she loves me. Katherine claimed she loved me. They say love, and mean the opposite. I believe Anne has tried to undermine me at every turn. She was always unnatural. Think how she would taunt her uncle, my lord of Norfolk. Think how she would scorn her father. She would presume to censure my own conduct, and press on me advice in matters well beyond her understanding, and give me such words as no poor man would willingly hear from his wife.'

Cranmer says, 'She was bold, it is true. She knew it for a fault and would try to bridle herself.'

'Now she shall be bridled, by God.' Henry's tone is ferocious; but the next moment he has modulated it, to the plaintive accents of the victim. He opens his walnut writing box. 'Do you see this little book?' It is not really a book, or not yet, just a collection of loose leaves, tied together; there is no title page, but a sheet black with Henry's own laboured hand. 'It is a book in the making. I have written it. It is a play. It is a tragedy. It is my own case.' He offers it.

He says, 'Keep it sir, till we have more leisure to do justice to it.'

'But you ought to know,' the king insists. 'Her nature. How ill she has behaved to me, when I gave her everything. All men should know and be warned about what women are. Their appetites are unbounded. I believe she has committed adultery with a hundred men.'

Henry looks, for a moment, like a hunted creature: hounded by women's desire, dragged down and shredded. 'But her brother?' Cranmer says. He turns away. He will not look at the king. 'Is it likely?'

'I doubt she could resist him,' Henry says. 'Why spare? Why not drink the cup to the filthy dregs? And while she was indulging her own desires, she was killing mine. When I would approach her, only to do my duty, she would give me such a look

317

as would daunt any man. I know now why she did so. She wanted to be fresh for her lovers.'

The king sits. He begins to talk, to ramble. Anne took him by the hand, these ten years ago and more. She led him into the forest, and at the sylvan edge, where the broad light of day splinters and filters into green, he left his good judgement, his innocence. She drew him on all day, till he was trembling and exhausted, but he could not stop even to catch his breath, he could not go back, he had lost the path. All day he chased her, until the light faded, and he followed her by the light of torches: and then she turned on him, and stifled the torches, and left him alone in the dark.

The door opens softly: he looks up, and it is Rafe, where once it would have been Weston, perhaps. 'Majesty, my lord of Richmond is here to say good night. May he come in?'

Henry breaks off. 'Fitzroy. Of course.'

Henry's bastard is now a princeling of sixteen, though his fine skin, his open gaze, make him seem younger than his age. He has the red-gold hair of King Edward IV's line; he has a look of Prince Arthur too, Henry's elder brother who died. He is hesitant as he confronts his bull of a father, hovering in case he is unwanted. But Henry rises and embraces the boy, his face wet with tears. 'My little son,' he says, to the child who will soon make six foot. 'My only son.' The king is crying so hard now that he has to blot his face on his sleeve. 'She would have poisoned you,' he moans. 'Thank God that by the cunning of Master Secretary the plot was found out in time.'

'Thank you, Master Secretary,' the boy says formally. 'For finding out the plot.'

'She would have poisoned you and your sister Mary, both of you, and made that little blotch she spawned the heir to England. Or my throne would have passed to whatever she whelped next, God save me, if it lived. I doubt a child of hers could live. She was too wicked. God abandoned her. Pray for your father, pray God does not abandon me. I have sinned, I must have. The marriage was illicit.'

'What, this one was?' the boy says. 'This one as well?'

'Illicit and accursed.' Henry rocks the boy back and forth, gripping him ferociously, fists clenched behind his back: so, perhaps, does a bear crush her cubs. 'The marriage was outside God's law. Nothing could make it lawful. Neither of them was my wife, not this one and not the other, thank God she is in her grave now, and I do not have to listen to her snuffling and praying and entreating and meddling in my business. Do not tell me there were dispensations, I do not want to hear it, no Pope can dispense from the law of Heaven. How did she ever come near me, Anne Boleyn? Why did I ever look at her? Why did she blind my eyes? There are so many women in the world, so many fresh and young and virtuous women, so many good and kind women. Why have I been cursed with women who destroy the children in their own wombs?'

He lets the boy go, so abruptly that he staggers.

Henry sniffs. 'Go now, child. To your own guiltless bed. And you, Master Secretary, to your ... back to your own people.' The king blots his face with his handkerchief. 'I am too tired to confess tonight, my lord archbishop. You may go home too. But you will come again, and absolve me.'

It seems a comfortable idea. Cranmer hesitates: but he is not one to press for secrets. As they leave the chamber, Henry takes up his little book; absorbed, he turns the pages, and settles down to read his own story.

Outside the king's chamber he gives the signal to the hovering gentlemen. 'Go in and see if he wants anything.' Slow, reluctant, his body servants creep towards Henry in his lair: unsure of their welcome, unsure of everything. Pastime with good company: but where's the company now? It's cringing against the wall.

319

He takes his leave of Cranmer, embracing him, whispering: 'All will work for good.' Young Richmond touches his arm: 'Master Secretary, there is something I must tell you.'

He is tired. He was up at dawn writing letters into Europe. 'Is it urgent, my lord?'

'No. But it is important.'

Imagine having a master who knows the difference. 'Go ahead, my lord, I am all attention.'

'I want to tell you, I have had a woman now.'

'I hope that she was all you desired.'

The boy laughs uncertainly. 'Not really. She was a whore. My brother Surrey arranged it for me.' Norfolk's son, he means. By the light of a sconce, the boy's face flickers, gold to black to cross-hatched gold again, as if he were dipped in shadows. 'But this being so, I am a man, and I think Norfolk should let me live with my wife.'

Richmond has already been married off, to Norfolk's daughter, little Mary Howard. For reasons of his own, Norfolk has kept the children apart; if Anne had given Henry a son in wedlock, the bastard boy would be worthless to the king, and it has entered Norfolk's calculations that in that case, if his daughter was a virgin, he could perhaps marry her more usefully elsewhere.

But all those calculations are needless now. 'I'll speak to the duke for you,' he says. 'I think he will now be keen to fall in with your wishes.'

Richmond flushes: pleasure, embarrassment? The boy is no fool and knows his situation, which in a few days has improved beyond all measure. He, Cromwell, can hear the voice of Norfolk, as clear as if he were reasoning in the king's council: Katherine's daughter has been made a bastard already, Anne's daughter will follow, so all three of Henry's children are illegitimate. If that is so, why not prefer the male to the female?

'Master Secretary,' the boy says, 'the servants in my household are saying Elizabeth is not even the queen's child. They say she

320

was smuggled into the bedchamber in a basket, and the queen's dead child carried out.'

'Why would she do that?' He is always curious to hear the reasoning of household servants.

'It is because, to be queen, she struck a bargain with the devil. But the devil always cheats you. He let her be queen, but he would not let her bear a live child.'

'You would think the devil would have sharpened her wit, though. If she was bringing in a baby in a basket, surely she would have brought in a boy?'

Richmond manages a miserable smile. 'Perhaps she laid hold of the only baby she could get. After all, people do not leave them in the street.'

They do, though. He is bringing in a bill to the new Parliament, to provide for the orphan boys of London. His idea is, look after the orphan boys, and they will look after the girls.

'Sometimes,' the boy says, 'I think about the cardinal. Do you ever think of him?' He sinks down to sit on a chest; and he, Cromwell, sits down with him. 'When I was a very little child, and very foolish as children are, I used to think the cardinal was my father.'

'The cardinal was your godfather.'

'Yes, but I thought … Because he was so tender to me. He would visit me and carry me, and though he gave me great gifts of gold plate, he brought me a silk ball and also a doll, which you know, boys do like …' he drops his head, 'when they are little children, and I am speaking of when I was still in a gown. I knew there was some secret about me, and I thought that was it, that I was a priest's son. When the king came he was a stranger to me. He brought me a sword.'

'And did you guess then that he was your father?'

'No,' says the boy. He opens his hands, to show his helpless nature, the nature he had as a little child. 'No. It had to be explained to me. Do not tell him, please. He would not understand.'

Of all the shocks the king has received, it could be the greatest, to know that his son did not recognise him. 'Has he many other children?' Richmond asks. He speaks, now, with the authority of a man of the world. 'I suppose he must have.'

'To my knowledge, he has no child who could hurt your claim. They said Mary Boleyn's son was his, but she was married at the time and the boy took her husband's name.'

'But I suppose he will marry Mistress Seymour now, when this marriage,' the boy stumbles over his words, 'when whatever is to happen, when it happens. And she will have a son, perhaps, because the Seymours are fertile stock.'

'If that occurs,' he says gently, 'you must stand ready, the first to congratulate the king. And you must be prepared all your life to place yourself at the service of this little prince. But on a more immediate matter, if I may advise ... if your living with your wife should be further delayed, it is best to find a kind and clean young woman and make an arrangement with her. Then when you part from her, pay her some small retainer so she does not talk about you.'

'Is that what you do, Master Secretary?' The question is ingenuous, but for a moment he wonders if the boy is spying for someone.

'It is better not discussed between gentlemen,' he says. 'And emulate your father the king, who in speaking of women is never coarse.' Violent, perhaps, he thinks: but never coarse. 'Be prudent and do not deal with whores. You must not catch a disease, like the French king. Then also, if your young woman gives you a child, you have its keeping and bringing up, and you know it is not another man's.'

'But you cannot be sure ...' Richmond breaks off. The realities of the world are tumbling in fast on this young man. 'If the king can be deceived, surely any man can be deceived. If married ladies are false, any gentleman could be bringing up another man's child.'

He smiles. 'But another gentleman would be bringing up his.'

He means to begin, when he has time to plan it, some form of registration, documentation to record baptisms so he can count the king's subjects and know who they are, or at least, who their mothers say they are: family name and paternity are two different things, but one must start somewhere. He scans the faces of the Londoners as he rides through the city, and he thinks of streets in other cities where he has lived or passed through, and he wonders. I could do with more children, he thinks. He has been continent in his living as far as it is reasonable for a man to be, but the cardinal used to invent scandals about him and his many concubines. Whenever some stout young felon was dragged to the gallows, the cardinal would say, 'There, Thomas, that will be one of yours.'

The boy yawns. 'I am so tired,' he says. 'Yet I have not been hunting today. So I don't know why.'

Richmond's servants are hovering: their badge a demi-lion rampant, their livery of blue and yellow faded in the failing light. Like nursemaids snatching up a child from muddy puddles, they want to sweep the young duke away from whatever Cromwell is plotting. There is a climate of fear and he has created it. Nobody knows how long the arrests will go on and who else will be taken. He feels even he does not know, and he is in charge of it. George Boleyn is lodged in the Tower. Weston and Brereton have been allowed a last night to sleep in the world, a few hours' grace to arrange their affairs; this time tomorrow the key will have turned on them: they could run, but where to? None of the men except Mark have been properly interrogated: that is to say, interrogated by him. But the scrapping for the spoils has begun. Norris had not been in ward for a day before the first letter came in, seeking a share of his offices and privileges, from a man who pleaded he had fourteen children. Fourteen hungry mouths: not to mention the man's own needs, and the snapping teeth of his lady wife.

* * *

Next day, early, he says to William Fitzwilliam, 'Come with me to the Tower to talk to Norris.'

Fitz says, 'No, you go. I cannot do it a second time. I have known him all my years. The first time nearly killed me.'

Gentle Norris: chief bottom-wiper to the king, spinner of silk threads, spider of spiders, black centre of the vast dripping web of court patronage: what a spry and amiable man he is, past forty but wearing it lightly. Norris is a man always in equipoise, a living illustration of the art of *sprezzatura*. No one has ever seen him ruffled. He has the air of a man who has not so much achieved success, as become resigned to it. He is as courteous to a dairy maid as to a duke; at least, for as long he has an audience. A master of the tournament ground, he breaks a lance with an air of apology, and when he counts the coin of the realm he washes his hands afterwards, in spring water scented with rose petals.

Nevertheless, Harry has grown rich, as those about the king cannot help but grow rich, however modestly they strive; when Harry snaps up some perquisite, it is as if he, your obedient servant, were sweeping away from your sight something distasteful. And when he volunteers for some lucrative office, it is as if he is doing it out of a sense of duty, and to save lesser men the trouble.

But look at Gentle Norris now! It is a sad thing to see a strong man weep. He says so, as he sits down, and enquires after his keeping, whether he is being served with the food he likes and how he has slept. His manner is benign and easy. 'During the days of Christmas last, Master Norris, you impersonated a Moor, and William Brereton showed himself half-naked in the guise of a hunter or wild man of the woods, going towards the queen's chamber.'

'For God's sake, Cromwell,' Norris sniffs. 'Are you in earnest? You are asking me in all seriousness about what we did when we were costumed for a masque?'

'I counselled him, William Brereton, against exposing his person. Your retort was that the queen had seen it many a time.'

Norris reddens: as he did on the date in question. 'You mistake me on purpose. You know I meant that she is a married woman and so a man's … a man's gear is no strange sight to her.'

'You know what you meant. I only know what you said. You must admit that such a remark would not strike the king's ear as innocent. On the same occasion as we were standing in conversation we saw Francis Weston, disguised. And you remarked he was going to the queen.'

'At least he wasn't naked,' Norris says. 'In a dragon suit, wasn't he?'

'He was not naked when we saw him, I agree. But what did you say next? You spoke to me of the queen's attraction to him. You were jealous, Harry. And you didn't deny it. Tell me what you know against Weston. It will be easier for you thereafter.'

Norris has pulled himself together and blown his nose. 'All you are alleging is some loose words capable of many interpretations. If you are seeking proofs of adultery, Cromwell, you will have to do better than this.'

'Oh, I don't know. By the nature of the thing, there is seldom a witness to the act. But we consider circumstances and opportunities and expressed desires, we consider weighty probabilities, and we consider confessions.'

'You will have no confession from me or Brereton either.'

'I wonder.'

'You will not put gentlemen to the torture, the king would not permit it.'

'There don't have to be formal arrangements.' He is on his feet, he slams his hand down on the table. 'I could put my thumbs in your eyes, and then you would sing "Green Grows the Holly" if I asked you to.' He sits down, resumes his former easy tone. 'Put yourself in my place. People will say I have tortured you anyway. They will say I have tortured Mark, they are already putting the word about. Though not a gossamer thread of him is snapped, I swear. I have Mark's free confession. He has given me names. Some of them surprised me. But I have mastered myself.'

'You are lying.' Norris looks away. 'You are trying to trick us into betraying, each man the other.'

'The king knows what to think. He does not ask for eyewitnesses. He knows your treason and the queen's.'

'Ask yourself,' Norris says, 'how likely is it, that I should so forget my honour, as to betray the king who has been so good to me and to place in such terrible danger a lady I revere? My family has served the King of England time out of mind. My great-grandfather served King Henry VI, that saintly man, God rest his soul. My grandfather served King Edward, and would have served his son if he had lived to reign, and after he was driven out of the realm by the scorpion Richard Plantagenet, he served Henry Tudor in exile, and served him still when he was crowned king. I have been at the side of Henry since I was a boy. I love him like a brother. Do you have a brother, Cromwell?'

'None living.' He looks at Norris, exasperated. He seems to think that with eloquence, with sincerity, with frankness, he can change what is happening. The whole court has seen him slobbering over the queen. How could he expect to go shopping with his eyes, and finger the goods no doubt, and not have an account to settle at the end of it?

He gets up, he walks away, he turns, he shakes his head: he sighs. 'Ah, for God's sake, Harry Norris. Have I to write it on the wall for you? The king must be rid of her. She cannot give him a son and he is out of love with her. He loves another lady and he cannot come at her unless Anne is removed. Now, is that simple enough for your simple tastes? Anne will not go quietly, she warned me of it once; she said, if ever Henry puts me aside, it will be war. So if she will not go, she must be pushed, and I must push her, who else? Do you recognise the situation? Will you take your mind back? In a like case, my old master Wolsey could not gratify the king, and then what? He was disgraced and driven to his death. Now I mean to learn from him, and I mean the king to be gratified in every respect. He is now a miserable cuckold, but he will forget it when he is a bridegroom again, and it will not be long.'

'I suppose the Seymours have the wedding feast ready.'

He grins. 'And Tom Seymour is having his hair curled. And on that wedding day, the king will be happy, I will be happy, all England will be happy, except Norris, for I fear he will be dead. I see no help for it, unless you confess and throw yourself on the king's mercy. He has promised mercy. And he keeps his promises. Mostly.'

'I rode with him from Greenwich,' Norris says, 'away from the tournament, all that long ride. Every stride he badgered me, what have you done, confess. I will tell you what I told him, that I am an innocent man. And what is worse,' and now he is losing his composure, he is irate, 'what is worse is that you and he both know it. Tell me this, why is it me? Why not Wyatt? Everyone suspects him with Anne, and has he ever directly denied it? Wyatt knew her before. He knew her in Kent. He knew her from her girlhood.'

'And so what of it? He knew her when she was a simple maid. What if he did meddle with her? It may be shameful but it is no treason. It is not like meddling with the king's wife, the Queen of England.'

'I am not ashamed of any dealings I have had with Anne.'

'Are you ashamed of your thoughts about her, perhaps? You told Fitzwilliam as much.'

'Did I?' Norris says bleakly. 'Is that what he took away, from what I said to him? That I am ashamed? And if I am, Cromwell, even if I am … you cannot make my thoughts a crime.'

He holds out his palms. 'If thoughts are intentions, if intentions are malign … if you did not have her unlawfully, and you say you did not, did you intend to have her lawfully, after the king's death? It is getting on six years since your wife died, why have you not married again?'

'Why haven't you?'

He nods. 'A good question. I ask myself. But I have not promised myself to a young woman, and then broken my promise, as you have. Mary Shelton has lost her honour to you –'

Norris laughs. 'To me? To the king, rather.'

'But the king was not in a position to marry her, and you were, and she had your pledge, and yet you dallied. Did you think the king would die, so you could marry Anne? Or did you expect her to dishonour her marriage vows during the king's life, and become your concubine? It is one or the other.'

'If I say either, you will damn me. You will damn me if I say nothing at all, taking my silence for agreement.'

'Francis Weston thinks you are guilty.'

'That Francis thinks anything, is news to me. Why would he …?' Norris breaks off. 'What, is he here? In the Tower?'

'He is in ward.'

Norris shakes his head. 'He is a boy. How can you do this to his people? I admit he is a careless, headstrong boy, he is known to be no favourite of mine, it is known we have cut across each other –'

'Ah, rivals in love.' He puts his hand to his heart.

'By no means.' Ah, Harry is ruffled now: he has flushed darkly, he is trembling with rage and fear.

'And what do you think to brother George?' he asks him. 'You may have been surprised to encounter rivalry from that quarter. I hope you were surprised. Though the morals of you gentlemen astonish me.'

'You do not trap me that way. Any man you name, I will say nothing against him and nothing for him. I have no opinion on George Boleyn.'

'What, no opinion on incest? If you take it so quietly and without objection, I am forced to conjecture there may be truth in it.'

'And if I were to say, I think there might be guilt in that case, you would say to me, "Why, Norris! Incest! How can you believe such an abomination? Is it a ploy to lead me away from your own guilt?"'

He looks at Norris with admiration. 'Not for nothing have you known me twenty years, Harry.'

'Oh, I have studied you,' Norris says. 'As I studied your master Wolsey before you.'

'That was politic in you. Such a great servant of the state.'

'And such a great traitor at the end.'

'I must take your mind back. I do not ask you to remember the manifold favours you received at the cardinal's hands. I only ask you to recall an entertainment, a certain interlude played at court. It was a play in which the late cardinal was set upon by demons and carried down to Hell.'

He sees Norris's eyes move, as the scene rises before him: the firelight, the heat, the baying spectators. Himself and Boleyn grasping the victim's hands, Brereton and Weston laying hold of him by his feet. The four of them tossing the scarlet figure, tumbling him and kicking him. Four men, who for a joke turned the cardinal into a beast; who took away his wit, his kindness and his grace, and made him a howling animal, grovelling on the boards and scrabbling with his paws.

It was not truly the cardinal, of course. It was the jester Sexton in a scarlet robe. But the audience catcalled as if it had been real, they yelled and shook their fists, they swore and mocked. Behind a screen the four devils pulled off their masks and their hairy jerkins, cursing and laughing. They saw Thomas Cromwell leaning against the panelling, silent, wrapped in a robe of mourning black.

Now, Norris gapes at him: 'And that is why? It was a play. It was an entertainment, as you said yourself. The cardinal was dead, he could not know. And while he was alive, was I not good to him in his trouble? Did I not, when he was exiled from court, ride after him, and come to him on Putney Heath with a token from the king's own hand?'

He nods. 'I concede that others behaved worse. But you see, none of you behaved like Christians. You behaved like savages instead, falling on his estates and possessions.'

He sees he need not continue. The indignation on Norris's face is replaced by a look of blank terror. At least, he thinks, the fellow has the wit to see what this is about: not one year's grudge or two, but a fat extract from the book of grief, kept since the cardinal came down. He says, 'Life pays you out, Norris. Don't you find? And,' he adds gently, 'it is not all about the cardinal, either. I would not want you to think I am without motives of my own.'

Norris raises his face. 'What has Mark Smeaton done to you?'

'Mark?' He laughs. 'I don't like the way he looks at me.'

Would Norris understand if he spelled it out? He needs guilty men. So he has found men who are guilty. Though perhaps not guilty as charged.

A silence falls. He sits, he waits, his eyes on the dying man. He is already thinking what he will do with Norris's offices, his Crown grants. He will try to oblige the humble applicants, like the man with fourteen children, who wants the keeping of a park at Windsor and a post in the administration of the castle. Norris's offices in Wales can be parcelled out to young Richmond, and that will bring the posts in effect back to the king and under his own supervision. And Rafe could have the Norris estate at Greenwich, he could house Helen and the children there when he has to be at court. And Edward Seymour has mentioned he would like Norris's house in Kew.

Harry Norris says, 'I assume you will not just lead us out to execution. There will be a process, a trial? Yes? I hope it will be quick. I suppose it will. The cardinal used to say, Cromwell will do in a week what will take another man a year, it is not worth your while to block him or oppose him. If you reach out to grip him he will not be there, he will have ridden twenty miles while you are pulling your boots on.' He looks up. 'If you intend to kill me in public, and mount a show, be quick. Or I may die of grief alone in this room.'

He shakes his head. 'You'll live.' He once thought it himself, that he might die of grief: for his wife, his daughters, his sisters, his father and master the cardinal. But the pulse, obdurate, keeps its rhythm. You think you cannot keep breathing, but your ribcage has other ideas, rising and falling, emitting sighs. You must thrive in spite of yourself; and so that you may do it, God takes out your heart of flesh, and gives you a heart of stone.

Norris touches his ribs. 'The pain is here. I felt it last night. I sat up, breathless. I durst not lie down again.'

'When he was brought down, the cardinal said the same. The pain was like a whetstone, he said. A whetstone, and the knife was drawn across it. And it ground away, till he was dead.'

He rises, picks up his papers: inclining his head, takes his leave. Henry Norris: left forepaw.

William Brereton. Gentleman of Cheshire. Servant in Wales to the young Duke of Richmond, and a bad servant too. A turbulent, arrogant, hard-as-nails man, from a turbulent line.

'Let's go back,' he says, 'let's go back to the cardinal's time, because I do remember someone of your household killed a man during a bowls match.'

'The game can get very heated,' Brereton says. 'You know yourself. You play, I hear.'

'And the cardinal thought, it is time for a reckoning; and your family were fined because they impeded the investigation. I ask myself, has anything changed since then? You think you can do anything because you are the Duke of Richmond's servant, and because Norfolk favours you –'

'The king himself favours me.'

He raises his eyebrows. 'Does he? Then you should complain to him. Because you are ill-lodged, are you not? Sadly for you, the king is not here, so you must make do with me and my long memory. But let us not cast back for instances. Look, for instance, at the case of the Flintshire gentleman, John ap Eyton. That is so recent you have not forgot it.'

'So that is why I am here,' Brereton says.

'Not entirely, but leave aside now your adultery with the queen and concentrate on Eyton. The facts of the case are known to you. There is a quarrel, blows exchanged, one of your household ends up dead, but the man Eyton is tried in due form before a London jury, and is acquitted. Now, having no respect for either law or justice, you swear revenge. You have the Welshman abducted. Your servants hang him out of hand, all this – do not interrupt me, man – all this with your permission and contrivance. I give this as one instance. You think this is only one man and he doesn't matter, but you see he does. You think a year or more has passed and no one remembers, but I remember. You believe the law should be what you would like it to be, and it is on that principle that you conduct yourself in your holdings on the marches of Wales, where the king's justice and the king's name are brought into contempt every day. The place is a stronghold of thieves.'

'You say I am a thief?'

'I say you consort with them. But your schemes end here.'

'You are judge and jury and hangman, is that it?'

'It is better justice than Eyton had.'

And Brereton says, 'I concede that.'

What a fall this is. Only days ago, he was petitioning Master Secretary for spoils, when the abbey lands in Cheshire should be given out. Now no doubt the words run through his head, the words he used to Master Secretary when he complained of his high-handed ways: I must tutor you in realities, he had said coldly. We are not creatures of some lawyers' conclave at Gray's Inn. In my own country, my family upholds the law, and the law is what we care to uphold.

Now he, Master Secretary, asks, 'Do you think Weston has had to do with the queen?'

'Perhaps,' Brereton looks as if he hardly cares, one way or the other. 'I barely know him. He is young and foolish and good-looking, isn't he, and women regard these things? And she may be a queen but she is only a woman, who knows what she might be persuaded to?'

'You think women more foolish than men?'

'In general, yes. And weaker. In matters of love.'

'I note your opinion.'

'What about Wyatt, Cromwell? Where is he in this?'

'You are in no place,' he says, 'to put questions to me.' William Brereton; left hindpaw.

George Boleyn is well past thirty, but he still has the sheen we admire in the young, the sparkle and the clear gaze. It is hard to associate his pleasant person with the kind of bestial appetite of which his wife accuses him, and for a moment he looks at George and wonders if he can be guilty of any offences, except a certain pride and elation. With the graces of his person and mind, he could have floated and hovered above the court and its sordid machinations, a man of refinement moving in his own sphere: commissioning translations of the ancient poets, and causing them to be published in exquisite editions. He could have ridden pretty white horses that curvet and bow in front of ladies. Unfortunately, he liked to quarrel and brag, intrigue and snub. As we find him now, in his light circular room in the Martin Tower, we find him pacing, hungry for conflict, we ask ourselves, does he know why he is here? Or is that surprise still to come?

'You are perhaps not much to blame,' he says, as he takes his seat: he, Thomas Cromwell. 'Join me at this table,' he directs. 'One hears of prisoners wearing a path through stone, but I do not believe it can really happen. It would take three hundred years perhaps.'

333

Boleyn says, 'You are accusing me of some sort of collusion, concealment, concealing misconduct on my sister's part, but this charge will not stand, because there was no misconduct.'

'No, my lord, that is not the charge.'

'Then what?'

'That is not what you are accused of. Sir Francis Bryan, who is a man of great imaginative capacities –'

'Bryan!' Boleyn looks horrified. 'But you know he is an enemy of mine.' His words tumble over each other. 'What has he said, how can you credit anything he says?'

'Sir Francis has explained it all to me. And I begin to see it. How a man may hardly know his sister, and meet her as a grown woman. She is like himself, yet not. She is familiar, yet piques his interest. One day his brotherly embrace is a little longer than usual. The business progresses from there. Perhaps neither party feels they are doing anything wrong, till some frontier is crossed. But I myself am far too lacking in imagination to imagine what that frontier could be.' He pauses. 'Did it begin before her marriage, or after?'

Boleyn begins to tremble. It is shock; he can hardly speak. 'I refuse to answer this.'

'My lord, I am accustomed to dealing with those who refuse to answer.'

'Are you threatening me with the rack?'

'Well, now, I didn't rack Thomas More, did I? I sat in a room with him. A room here at the Tower, such as the one you occupy. I listened to the murmurs within his silence. Construction can be put on silence. It will be.'

George says: 'Henry killed his father's councillors. He killed the Duke of Buckingham. He destroyed the cardinal and harried him to his death, and struck the head off one of Europe's great scholars. Now he plans to kill his wife and her family and Norris who has been his closest friend. What makes you think it will be different with you, that are not the equal of any of these men?'

He says, 'It ill becomes anyone of your family to evoke the cardinal's name. Or Thomas More's, for that matter. Your lady sister burned for vengeance. She would say to me, what, Thomas More, is he not dead yet?'

'Who began this slander against me? It is not Francis Bryan, surely. Is it my wife? Yes. I should have known.'

'You make the assumption. I do not confirm it. You must have a guilty conscience towards her, if you think she has such cause to hate you.'

'And will you believe something so monstrous?' George begs. 'On the word of one woman?'

'There are other women who have been recipients of your gallantry. I will not bring them before a court if I can help it, I can do that much to protect them. You have always regarded women as disposable, my lord, and you cannot complain if in the end they think the same of you.'

'So am I to be put on trial for gallantry? Yes, they are jealous of me, you are all jealous, I have had some success with women.'

'You still call it success? You must think again.'

'I never heard it was a crime. To spend time with a willing lover.'

'You had better not say that in your defence. If one of your lovers is your sister ... the court will find it, what shall we say ... pert and bold. Lacking in gravity. What would save you now – I mean, what might preserve your life – would be a full statement of all you know about your sister's dealings with other men. Some suggest there are liaisons which would put yours in the shade, unnatural though it may be.'

'You are a Christian man, and you ask me this? To give evidence to kill my sister?'

He opens his hands. 'I ask nothing. I only point out what some would see as the way forward. I do not know whether the king would incline to mercy. He might let you live abroad, or he might grant you mercy as to the manner of your death. Or not. The traitor's penalty, as you know, is fearful and public; he dies in great pain and humiliation. I see you do know, you have witnessed it.'

Boleyn folds into himself: narrowing himself, arms across his body, as if to protect his guts from the butcher's knife, and he slumps to a stool; he thinks, you should have done that before, I told you to sit, you see how without touching you I have made you sit? He tells him softly, 'You profess the gospel, my lord, and that you are saved. But your actions do not suggest you are saved.'

'You may take your thumbprints off my soul,' George says. 'I discuss these matters with my chaplains.'

'Yes, so they tell me. I think you have become too assured of forgiveness, believing you have years ahead of you to sin and yet though God sees all he must be patient, like a waiting man: and you will notice him at last, and answer his suit, if only he will wait till you are old. Is that your case?'

'I will speak to my confessor about that.'

'I am your confessor now. Did you say, in the hearing of others, that the king was impotent?'

George sneers at him. 'He can do it when the weather is set fair.'

'In doing so, you called into question the parentage of the Princess Elizabeth. You will readily see this is treason, as she is the heir to England.'

'*Faute de mieux*, as far as you're concerned.'

'The king now believes he could not have a son from this marriage, as it was not lawful. He believes there were hidden impediments and that your sister was not frank about her past. He means to make a new marriage, which will be clean.'

'I marvel you explain yourself,' George says. 'You never did so before.'

'I do so for one reason – so that you can realise your situation and entertain no false hope. These chaplains you speak of, I will send them to you. They are fit company for you now.'

'God grants sons to every beggar,' George says. 'He grants them to the illicit union, as well as the blessed, to the whore as well as the queen. I wonder that the king can be so simple.'

'It is a holy simplicity,' he says. 'He is an anointed sovereign, and so very close to God.'

Boleyn scrutinises his expression, for levity or scorn: but he knows his face says nothing, he can rely on his face for that. You could look back through Boleyn's career, and say, 'There he went wrong, and there.' He was too proud, too singular, unwilling to bridle his whims or turn himself to use. He needs to learn to bend with the breeze, like his father; but the time he has to learn anything is running out fast. There is a time to stand on your dignity, but there is a time to abandon it in the interests of your safety. There is a time to smirk behind the hand of cards you have drawn, and there is a time to throw down your purse on the table and say, 'Thomas Cromwell, you win.'

George Boleyn, right forepaw.

By the time he gets to Francis Weston (right hindpaw) he has been approached by the young man's family and offered a great deal of money. Politely, he has refused them; in their circumstances he would do just the same, except that it is hard to imagine Gregory or any member of his household to be such a fool as this young man has been.

The Weston family go further: they approach the king himself. They will make an offering, they will make a benevolence, they will make a large and unconditional donation to the king's treasury. He discusses it with Fitzwilliam: 'I cannot advise His Majesty. It is possible that lesser charges can be brought. It depends how much His Majesty thinks his honour is touched.'

But the king is not disposed to be lenient. Fitzwilliam says grimly, 'If I were Weston's people, I would pay the money anyway. To ensure favour. Afterwards.'

That is the very approach he has settled on himself, thinking of the Boleyn family (those who survive) and the Howards. He will shake the ancestral oaks and gold coins will drop each season.

Even before he comes to the room where Weston is held, the young man knows what to expect; he knows who is gaoled with him; he knows or has a good idea of the charges; his gaolers must have babbled, because he, Cromwell, has cut off communication between the four men. A talkative gaoler can be useful; he can nudge a prisoner towards cooperation, towards acceptance, towards despair. Weston must guess his family's initiative has failed. You look at Cromwell and you think, if bribery won't do it, nothing else will. It's useless to protest or disclaim or contradict. Abasement might just do it, it's worth a try. 'I taunted you, sir,' Francis says. 'I belittled you. I am sorry I ever did so. You are the king's servant and it was proper for me to respect that.'

'Well, that is a handsome apology,' he says. 'Though you should beg forgiveness of the king and of Jesus Christ.'

Francis says, 'You know I am not long married.'

'And your wife left at home in the country. For obvious reasons.'

'Can I write to her? I have a son. He is not yet a year.' A silence. 'I wish my soul to be prayed for after I am dead.'

He would have thought God could make his own decisions, but Weston believes the creator may be pushed and coaxed and maybe bribed a little. As if following his thought, Weston says, 'I am in debt, Master Secretary. To the tune of a thousand pounds. I am sorry for it now.'

'No one expects a gallant young gentleman like yourself to be thrifty.' His tone is kindly, and Weston looks up. 'Of course, these debts are more than you could reasonably pay, and even set against the assets you will have when your father dies, they are a heavy burden. So your extravagance gives people to think, what expectations had young Weston?'

For a moment, the young man looks at him with a dumb, rebellious expression, as if he does not see why this should be brought against him: what have his debts to do with anything? He does not see where it is leading. Then he does. He, Cromwell, puts out a hand to grab his clothes, to stop him slumping forward in shock. 'A jury will easily grasp the point. We know the queen gave you money. How could you live as you did? It is easy to see. A thousand pounds is nothing to you, if you hoped to marry her once you had contrived the king's death.'

When he is sure that Weston can sit upright, he opens his fist and eases his grip. Mechanically, the boy reaches up and straightens his clothes, straightens the little ruff of his shirt collar.

'Your wife will be taken care of,' he tells him. 'Have no unease on that score. The king never extends animosity to widows. She will be cared for better, I dare say, than you ever cared for her.'

Weston looks up. 'I cannot fault your reasoning. I see how it will weigh when it is given in evidence. I have been a fool and you have stood by and seen it all. I know how I have undone myself. I cannot fault your conduct either, because I would have injured you if I could. And I know I have not lived a good … I have not lived … you see, I thought I should have another twenty years or more to live as I have, and then when I am old, forty-five or fifty, I should give to hospitals and endow a chantry, and God would see I was sorry.'

He nods. 'Well, Francis,' he says. 'We know not the hour, do we?'

'But Master Secretary, you know that whatever wrong I have done, I am not guilty in this matter of the queen. I see by your face you know it, and all the people will know it too when I am brought out to die, and the king will know it and think about it in his private hours. I shall be remembered, therefore. As the innocent are remembered.'

It would be cruel to disturb that belief; he looks to his death to give him greater fame than his life has done. All the years that stretched before him, and no reason to believe that he meant to make any better use of them than he made of the first twenty-five; he himself says not. Brought up under the wing of his sovereign, a courtier since he was a child, from a family of courtiers: never a moment's doubt about his place in the world, never a moment's anxiety, never a moment's thankfulness for the great privilege of having been born Francis Weston, born in the eye of fortune, born to serve a great king and a great nation: he will leave nothing but his debt, and a tarnished name, and a son: and anyone can father a son, he says to himself: until he remembers why we are here and what all this is about. He says, 'Your wife has written for you to the king. Asking for mercy. You have a great many friends.'

'Much good they will do me.'

'I do not think you realise that at this juncture, many men would find themselves alone. It should cheer you. You should not be bitter, Francis. Fortune is fickle, every young adventurer knows that. Resign yourself. Regard Norris. No bitterness there.'

'Perhaps,' the young man blurts, 'perhaps Norris thinks he has no reason for bitterness. Perhaps his regrets are honest ones, and necessary. Perhaps he deserves to die, as I do not.'

'He is well paid out, you think, for meddling with the queen.'

'He is always in her company. It is not to discuss the gospel.'

He is, perhaps, on the verge of a denunciation. Norris had begun on some admission to William Fitzwilliam, but he bit it back. Perhaps the facts will come out now? He waits: sees the boy's head sink into his hands; then, impelled by something, he does not know what, he stands up, says, 'Francis, excuse me,' and walks out of the room.

Outside Wriothesley is waiting, with gentlemen of his house-hold. They are leaning against the wall, sharing some joke. They stir at the sight of him, look expectant. 'Are we finished?' Wriothesley says. 'He has confessed?'

He shakes his head. 'Each man will give a good account of himself, but he will not absolve his fellows. Also, they will all say

340

"I am innocent," but they do not say, "She is innocent." They are not able. It may be she is, but none of them will give his word on it.'

It is just as Wyatt once told him: 'The worst of it is,' he had said, 'her hinting to me, her boasting almost, that she says no to me, but yes to others.'

'Well, you have no confessions,' Wriothesley says. 'Do you want us to get them?'

He gives Call-Me a look that knocks him back, so he steps on the foot of Richard Riche. 'What, Wriothesley, do you think I am too soft to the young?'

Riche rubs his foot. 'Shall we draw up specimen charges?'

'The more the merrier. Forgive me, I need a moment …'

Riche assumes he has gone out to piss. He does not know what caused him to break off from Weston and walk out. Perhaps it was when the boy said 'forty-five or fifty'. As if, past mid-life, there is a second childhood, a new phase of innocence. It touched him, perhaps, the simplicity of it. Or perhaps he just needed air. Let us say you are in a chamber, the windows sealed, you are conscious of the proximity of other bodies, of the declining light. In the room you put cases, you play games, you move your personnel around each other: notional bodies, hard as ivory, black as ebony, pushed on their paths across the squares. Then you say, I can't endure this any more, I must breathe: you burst out of the room and into a wild garden where the guilty are hanging from trees, no longer ivory, no longer ebony, but flesh; and their wild lamenting tongues proclaim their guilt as they die. In this matter, cause has been preceded by effect. What you dreamed has enacted itself. You reach for a blade but the blood is already shed. The lambs have butchered and eaten themselves. They have brought knives to the table, carved themselves, and picked their own bones clean.

* * *

May is blossoming even in the city streets. He takes flowers in to the ladies in the Tower. Christophe has to carry the bouquets. The boy is filling out and looks like a bull garlanded for sacrifice. He wonders what they did with their sacrifices, the pagans and the Jews of the Old Testament; surely they would not waste fresh meat, but give it to the poor?

Anne is housed in the suite of rooms that were redecorated for her coronation. He himself had overseen the work, and watched as goddesses, with their soft and brilliant dark eyes, blossomed on the walls. They bask in sunlit groves, under cypress trees; a white doe peeps through foliage, while the hunters head off in another direction, and hounds lollop ahead of them, making their hound music.

Lady Kingston rises to greet him, and he says, 'Sit down, dear madam ...' Where is Anne? Not here in her presence chamber.

'She is praying,' one of the Boleyn aunts says. 'So we left her to it.'

'She has been a while,' the other aunt says. 'Are we sure she hasn't got a man in there?'

The aunts giggle; he does not join them; Lady Kingston gives them a hard look.

The queen emerges from the little oratory; she has heard his voice. Sunlight strikes her face. It is true what Lady Rochford says, she has begun to line. If you did not know she was a woman who had held a king's heart in her hand, you would take her for a very ordinary person. He supposes there will always be a strained levity in her, a practised coyness. She will be one of those women who at fifty thinks she is still in the game: one of those tired old experts in innuendo, women who simper like maids and put their hand on your arm, who exchange glances with other women when a prospect like Tom Seymour heaves into view.

But of course, she will never be fifty. He wonders if this is the last time he will see her, before the courtroom. She sits down, in shadow, in the midst of the women. The Tower always feels damp from the river and even these new, bright rooms feel clammy. He asks if she would like furs brought in, and she says, 'Yes. Ermine. Also, I do not want these women. I should like women of my own choosing, not yours.'

'Lady Kingston attends you because –'

'Because she is your spy.'

'– because she is your hostess.'

'Am I then her guest? A guest is free to leave.'

'I thought you would like to have Mistress Orchard,' he says, 'as she is your old nurse. And I didn't think you would object to your aunts.'

'They have grudges against me, both of them. All I see and hear is sniggering and tutting.'

'Jesus! Do you expect applause?'

This is the trouble with the Boleyns: they hate their own kin. 'You will not speak in that way to me,' Anne says, 'when I am released.'

'I apologise. I spoke without thinking.'

'I do not know what the king means by holding me here. I suppose he does it to test me. It is some stratagem he has devised, yes?'

She does not really think that, so he does not answer.

'I should like to see my brother,' Anne says.

One aunt, Lady Shelton, looks up from her needlework. 'That is a foolish demand, in the circumstances.'

'Where is my father?' Anne says. 'I do not understand why he does not come to my aid.'

'He is lucky to be at liberty,' Lady Shelton says. 'Expect no help there. Thomas Boleyn always looked after himself first, and I know it, for I am his sister.'

Anne ignores her. 'And my bishops, where are they? I have nourished them, I have protected them, I have furthered the cause of religion, so why do they not go to the king for me?'

The other Boleyn aunt laughs. 'You expect bishops to intervene, to make excuses for your adultery?'

It is evident that, in this court, Anne has already been tried. He says to her, 'Help the king. Unless he is merciful your cause is lost, you can do nothing for yourself. But you may do something for your daughter Elizabeth. The more humbly you hold yourself, the more penitent you show yourself, the more patiently you bear with the process, the less bitterness will His Majesty feel when your name is raised hereafter.'

'Ah, the process,' Anne says, with a flash of her old sharpness. 'And what is this process to be?'

'The confessions of the gentlemen are now being compiled.'

'The what?' Anne says.

'You heard,' Lady Shelton says. 'They will not lie for you.'

'There may be other arrests, other charges, though by speaking out now, by being open with us, you could shorten the pain for all concerned. The gentlemen will come to trial together. For yourself and my lord your brother, since you are ennobled, you will be judged by your peers.'

'They have no witnesses. They can make any accusation, and I can say no to it.'

'That is true,' he concedes. 'Though it is not true about the witnesses. When you were at liberty, madam, your ladies were intimidated by you, forced to lie for you, but now they are emboldened.'

'I am sure they are.' She holds his gaze; her tone is scornful. 'In the way Seymour is emboldened. Tell her from me, God sees her tricks.'

He stands to take his leave. She unnerves him, the wild distress she is keeping in check, holding back but only just. There seems no point in prolonging the business, but he says, 'If the king begins a process to nullify your marriage, I may return, to take statements from you.'

'What?' she says. 'That too? Is it necessary? Murder will not be enough?'

He bows and turns away. 'No!' She fetches him back. She is on her feet, detaining him, timidly touching his arm; as if it is not her release she wants, so much as his good opinion. 'You do not believe these stories against me? I know in your heart you do not. Cremuel?'

It is a long moment. He feels himself on the edge of something unwelcome: superfluous knowledge, useless information. He turns, hesitates, and reaches out, tentative …

But then she raises her hands and clasps them at her breast, in the gesture Lady Rochford had showed him. Ah, Queen Esther, he thinks. She is not innocent; she can only mimic innocence. His hand drops to his side. He turns away. He knows her for a woman without remorse. He believes she would commit any sin or crime. He believes she is her father's daughter, that never since child-hood has she taken any action, coaxed or coerced, that might damage her own interests. But in one gesture, she has damaged them now.

She has seen his face change. She steps back, puts her hands around her throat: like a strangler she closes them around her own flesh. 'I have only a little neck,' she says. 'It will be the work of a moment.'

Kingston hurries out to meet him; he wants to talk. 'She keeps doing that. Her hands around her neck. And laughing.' His honest gaoler's face is dismayed. 'I cannot see that it is any occasion for laughter. And there are other foolish sayings, which my wife has reported. She says, it will not stop raining till I am released. Or start raining. Or something.'

He casts a glance at the window and he sees only a summer shower. In a moment the sun will scorch the moisture from the stones. 'My wife tells her,' Kingston says, 'to leave off such fool-ish talk. She said to me, Master Kingston, shall I have justice? I said to her, madam, the poorest subject of the king has justice. But she just laughs,' Kingston says. 'And she orders her dinner. And she eats it with a good appetite. And she says verses. My wife cannot follow them. The queen says they are verses of Wyatt's. And she says, Oh, Wyatt, Thomas Wyatt, when shall I see you here with me?'

At Whitehall he hears Wyatt's voice and walks towards it, attendants wheeling after him; he has more attendants than ever he did, some of them people he has never seen before. Charles Brandon, Duke of Suffolk, Charles Brandon big as a house: he is blocking Wyatt's path, and they are yelling at one another. 'What are you doing?' he shouts, and Wyatt breaks off and says over his shoulder, 'Making peace.'

He laughs. Brandon stumps away, grinning behind his vast beard. Wyatt says, 'I have begged him, set aside your old enmity for me, or it will kill me, do you want that?' He looks after the duke with disgust. 'I suspect he does. This is his chance. He went to Henry long ago, blustering that he had suspicions of me with Anne.'

'Yes, but if you recall, Henry kicked him back to the east country.'

'Henry will listen now. He will find him easy to believe.'

He takes Wyatt by the arm. If he can move Charles Brandon, he can move anybody. 'I am not going to dispute in a public place. I sent for you to come to my house, you fool, not to go raging about in public view and making people say, What, Wyatt, is he still at large?'

Wyatt puts a hand over his. He takes in a deep breath, trying to calm himself. 'My father told me, get to the king, and stay with him day and night.'

'That is not possible. The king is seeing no one. You must come to me at the Rolls House, but then –'

'If I go to your house people will say I am arrested.'

He drops his voice. 'No friend of mine will suffer.'

'They are strange and sudden friends you have this month. Papist friends, Lady Mary's people, Chapuys. You make common cause with them now, but what about afterwards? What will happen if they abandon you before you abandon them?'

'Ah,' he says equably, 'so you think the whole house of Cromwell will come down? Trust me, will you? Well, you have no choice, really, have you?'

From Cromwell's house, to the Tower: Richard Cromwell as escort, and the whole thing done so lightly, in such a spirit of friendliness, that you would think they were going out for a day's hunting. 'Beg the constable to do all honour to Master Wyatt,' he tells Richard. And to Wyatt, 'It is the only place you are safe. Once you are in the Tower no one can question you without my permission.'

Wyatt says, 'If I go in I shall not come out. They want me sacrificed, your new friends.'

'They will not want to pay the price,' he says easily. 'You know me, Wyatt. I know how much everyone has, I know what they can afford. And not only in cash. I have your enemies weighed and assessed. I know what they will pay and what they will baulk at, and believe me, the grief they will expend if they cross me in this matter, it will bankrupt them of tears.'

When Wyatt and Richard have gone on their way, he says to Call-Me-Risley, frowning: 'Wyatt once said I was the cleverest man in England.'

'He didn't flatter,' Call-Me says. 'I learn much daily, from mere proximity.'

'No, it is him. Wyatt. He leaves us all behind. He writes himself and then he disclaims himself. He jots a verse on some scrap of paper, and slips it to you, when you are at supper or praying in the chapel. Then he slides a paper to some other person, and it is the same verse, but a word is different. Then that person says to you, did you see what Wyatt wrote? You say yes, but you are talking of different things. Another time you trap him and say, Wyatt, did you really do what you describe in this verse? He smiles and tells you, it is the story of some imaginary gentleman, no one we know; or he will say, this is not my story I write, it is yours, though you do not know it. He will say, this woman I describe here, the brunette, she is really a woman with fair hair, in disguise. He will declare, you must believe everything and nothing of what you read. You point to the page, you tax him: what about this line, is this true? He says, it is poet's truth. Besides, he claims, I am not free to write as I like. It is not the king, but metre that constrains me. And I would be plainer, he says, if I could: but I must keep to the rhyme.'

'Someone should take his verses to the printer,' Wriothesley says. 'That would fix them.'

'He would not consent to that. They are private communications.'

'If I were Wyatt,' Call-Me says, 'I would have made sure no one misconstrued me. I would have stayed away from Caesar's wife.'

'That is the wise course.' He smiles. 'But it is not for him. It is for people like you and me.'

When Wyatt writes, his lines fledge feathers, and unfolding this plumage they dive below their meaning and skim above it. They tell us that the rules of power and the rules of war are the same, the art is to deceive; and you will deceive, and be deceived in your turn, whether you are an ambassador or a suitor. Now, if a man's subject is deception, you are deceived if you think you grasp his meaning. You close your hand as it flies away. A statute is written to entrap meaning, a poem to escape it. A quill, sharpened, can stir and rustle like the pinions of angels. Angels are messengers. They are creatures with a mind and a will. We do not know for a fact that their plumage is like the plumage of falcons, crows, peacocks. They hardly visit men nowadays. Though in Rome he knew a man, a turnspit in the papal kitchens, who had come face to face with an angel in a passage dripping with chill, in a sunken store room of the Vatican where cardinals never tread; and people bought him drinks to make him talk about it. He said the angel's substance was heavy and smooth as marble, its expression distant and pitiless; its wings were carved from glass.

When the indictments come to his hand, he sees at once that, though the script is a clerk's, the king has been at work. He can hear the king's voice in every line: his outrage, jealousy, fear. It is not enough to say that she incited Norris to adultery with her in October 1533, nor Brereton in November the same year; Henry must imagine the 'base conversations and kisses, touchings, gifts'. It is not enough to cite her conduct with Francis Weston, in May 1534, or to allege that she lay down for Mark Smeaton, a man of low degree, in April last year; it is necessary to speak of the lovers' burning resentment of each other, of the queen's furious jealousy of any other woman they look at. It is not enough to say that she sinned with her own brother: one must imagine the kisses, presents, jewels that passed between them, and how they looked when she was 'alluring him with her tongue in the said George's mouth, and the said George's tongue in hers'. It is more like a conversation with Lady Rochford, or any other scandal-loving woman, than it is like a document one carries into court; but all the same, it has its merits, it makes a story, and it puts into the heads of those who will hear it certain pictures that will not easily be got out again. He says, 'You must add at every point, and to every offence, "and several days before and after". Or a similar phrase, that makes it clear the offences are numerous, perhaps more numerous than even the parties themselves recollect. For in that way,' he says, 'if there is specific denial of one date, one place, it will not be enough to injure the whole.'

And look what Anne has said! According to this paper, she has confessed, 'she would never love the king in her heart'.

349

Never has. Does not now. And never could.

He frowns over the documents and then gives them out to be picked over. Objections are raised. Is Wyatt to be added? No, by no means. If he must be tried, he thinks, if the king goes so far, then he will be pulled away from this contaminated crew, and we will start again with a blank sheet; with this trial, with these defendants, there is no way but one, no exit, no direction except the scaffold.

And if there are discrepancies, visible to those who keep accounts of where the court resides on this day or that? He says, Brereton once told me he could be in two places at once. Come to think of it, so did Weston. Anne's lovers are phantom gentlemen, flitting by night with adulterous intent. They come and go by night, unchallenged. They skim over the river like midges, flicker against the dark, their doublets sewn with diamonds. The moon sees them, peering from her hood of bone, and Thames water reflects them, glimmering like fish, like pearls.

His new allies, the Courtenays and the Pole family, profess themselves unsurprised by the charges against Anne. The woman is a heretic and so is her brother. Heretics, it is well known, have no natural limits, no constraints, fear neither the law of the land nor the law of God. They see what they want and they take it. And those who (foolishly) have tolerated heretics, out of laziness or pity, then discover at last what their true nature is.

Henry Tudor will learn harsh lessons from this, the old families say. Perhaps Rome will stretch out a hand to him in his trouble? Perhaps, if he creeps on his knees, then after Anne is dead the Pope will forgive him, and take him back?

And I? he asks. Oh, well, you, Cromwell ... his new masters look at him with various expressions of bemusement or disgust. 'I shall be your prodigal son,' he says, smiling. 'I shall be the sheep that was lost.'

At Whitehall, little huddles of men, muttering, drawn into tight circles, their elbows pointing backwards as hands caress the daggers at their waist. And among lawyers a subfusc agitation, conferences in corners.

Rafe asks him, could the king's freedom be obtained, sir, with more economy of means? Less bloodshed?

Look, he says: once you have exhausted the process of negotiation and compromise, once you have fixed on the destruction of an enemy, that destruction must be swift and it must be perfect. Before you even glance in his direction, you should have his name on a warrant, the ports blocked, his wife and friends bought, his heir under your protection, his money in your strong room and his dog running to your whistle. Before he wakes in the morning, you should have the axe in your hand.

When he, Cromwell, arrives to see Thomas Wyatt in prison, the constable Kingston is anxious to assure him that his word has been obeyed, that Wyatt has been treated with all honour.

'And the queen, how is she?'

'Restless,' Kingston says. He looks uneasy. 'I am used to all sorts of prisoners, but I have never had one like this. One moment she says, I know I must die. Next moment, much contrary to that. She thinks the king will come in his barge and take her away. She thinks a mistake has been made, that there is a misapprehension. She thinks the King of France will intervene for her.' The gaoler shakes his head.

He finds Thomas Wyatt playing dice against himself: the kind of time-wasting pursuit old Sir Henry Wyatt reprehends. 'Who's winning?' he asks.

Wyatt looks up. 'That trolling idiot, my worst self, plays that canting fool, my best self. You can guess who wins. Still, there is always the possibility it will come up different.'

'Are you comfortable?'

'In body or spirit?'

'I only answer for bodies.'

351

'Nothing makes you falter,' Wyatt says. He says it with a reluctant admiration that is close to dread. But he, Cromwell, thinks, I did falter but no one knows it, reports have not gone abroad. Wyatt did not see me walk away from Weston's interrogation. Wyatt did not see me when Anne laid her hand on my arm and asked me what I believed in my heart.

He rests his eyes on the prisoner, he takes his seat. He says softly, 'I think I have been training all my years for this. I have served an apprenticeship to myself.' His whole career has been an education in hypocrisy. Eyes that once skewered him now kindle with simulated regard. Hands that would like to knock his hat off now reach out to take his hand, sometimes in a crushing grip. He has spun his enemies to face him, to join him: as in a dance. He means to spin them away again, so they look down the long cold vista of their years: so they feel the wind, the wind of exposed places, that cuts to the bone: so they bed down in ruins, and wake up cold. He says to Wyatt, 'Any information you give me I will note, but I give you my word that I will destroy it once this thing is accomplished.'

'Accomplished?' Wyatt is querying his choice of word.

'The king is informed his wife has betrayed him with various men, one her brother, one his closest friend, another a servant she says she hardly knows. The glass of truth has shattered, he says. So, yes, it would be an accomplishment to pick up the pieces.'

'But you say he is informed, how is he informed? No one admits anything, except Mark. What if he is lying?'

'When a man admits guilt we have to believe him. We cannot set ourselves to proving to him that he is wrong. Otherwise the law courts would never function.'

'But what is the evidence?' Wyatt persists.

He smiles. 'The truth comes to Henry's door, wearing a cloak and hood. He lets it in because he has a shrewd idea of what lies beneath, it is not a stranger who comes calling. Thomas, I think he has always known. He knows if she was not false to him in body she was so in words, and if not in deeds then in dreams. He thinks she never esteemed or loved him, when he laid the world at her feet. He thinks he never pleased or satisfied her and that when he lay next to her she imagined someone else.'

'That is common,' Wyatt said. 'Is it not usual? That is how marriage works. I never knew it was an offence in the eyes of the law. God help us. Half England will be in gaol.'

'You understand that there are the charges that are written down in an indictment. And then there are the other charges, those we don't commit to paper.'

'If feeling is a crime, then I admit …'

'Admit nothing. Norris admitted. He admitted he loved her. If what someone wants from you is an admission, it is never in your interest to give it.'

'What does Henry want? I am honestly perplexed. I cannot see my way through it.'

'He changes his mind, day to day. He would like to rework the past. He would like never to have seen Anne. He would like to have seen her, but to have seen through her. Mostly he wishes her dead.'

'Wishing is not doing it.'

'It is, if you are Henry.'

'As I understand the law, a queen's adultery is no treason.'

'No, but the man who violates her, he commits treason.'

'You think they used force?' Wyatt says drily.

'No, it is just the legal term. It is a pretence, that allows us to think well of any disgraced queen. But as for her, she is a traitor too, she has said so out of her own mouth. To intend the king's death, that is treason.'

'But again,' Wyatt says, 'forgive my poor understanding, I thought Anne had said, "If he dies," or some such words. So let me put a case to you. If I say "All men must die," is that a forecast of the king's death?'

353

'It would be well not to put cases,' he says pleasantly. 'Thomas More was putting cases when he tipped into treason. Now let me come to the point with you. I may need your evidence against the queen. I will accept it in writing, I do not need it aired in open court. You once told me, when you visited my house, how Anne conducts herself with men: she says, "Yes, yes, yes, yes, no."' Wyatt nods; he recognises those words; he looks sorry he spoke them. 'Now you may have to transpose one word of that testimony. Yes, yes, yes, no, yes.'

Wyatt does not answer. The silence extends, settles around them: a drowsy silence, as elsewhere leaves unfurl, may blossoms on the trees, water tinkles into fountains, young people laugh in gardens. At last Wyatt speaks, his voice strained: 'It was not testimony.'

'What was it then?' He leans forward. 'You know I am not a man with whom you can have inconsequential conversations. I cannot split myself into two, one your friend and the other the king's servant. So you must tell me: will you write down your thoughts, and if you are requested, will you say one word?' He sits back. 'And if you can reassure me on this point, I will write to your father, to reassure him in turn. To tell him you will come out of this alive.' He pauses. 'May I do so?'

Wyatt nods. The smallest possible gesture, a nod to the future.

'Good. Afterwards, for your trouble, to compensate you for this detention, I will arrange for you to have a sum of money.'

'I don't want it.' Wyatt turns his face away, deliberately: like a child.

'Believe me, you do. You are still trailing debts from your time in Italy. Your creditors come to me.'

'I'm not your brother. You're not my keeper.'

He looks about him. 'I am, if you think about it.'

Wyatt says, 'I hear Henry wants an annulment too. To kill her and be divorced from her, all in one day. That is how she is, you see. Everything is ruled by extremes. She would not be his mistress, she must be queen of England; so there is breaking of faith and making of laws, so the country is set in an uproar. If he had such trouble to get her, what must it cost him to be rid? Even after she is dead, he had better make sure to nail her down.'

He says curiously, 'Have you no tenderness left for her?'

'She has exhausted it,' Wyatt says shortly. 'Or perhaps I never had any, I do not know my own mind, you know it. I dare say men have felt many things for Anne, but no one except Henry has felt tenderness. Now he thinks he's been taken for a fool.'

He stands up. 'I shall write some comfortable words to your father. I will explain you must stay here a little space, it is safest. But first I must ... we thought Henry had dropped the annulment, but now, as you say, he revives it, so I must ...'

Wyatt says, as if relishing his discomfort, 'You'll have to go and see Harry Percy, won't you?'

It is now almost four years since, with Call-Me-Risley at his heels, he had confronted Harry Percy at a low inn called Mark and the Lion, and made him understand certain truths about life: the paramount truth being, that he was not, whatever he thought, married to Anne Boleyn. On that day he had slammed his hand on the table and told the young man that if he did not get himself out of the way of the king, he would be destroyed: that he, Thomas Cromwell, would let his creditors loose to destroy him, and rip away his earldom and his lands. He had slammed his hand on the table and told him that, further, if he did not forget Anne Boleyn and any claim he made on her, her uncle the Duke of Norfolk would find out where he hid and bite his bollocks off.

Since then, he has done much business with the earl, who is now a sick and broken young man, heavily in debt, his hold on his affairs slipping away from him day by day. In fact, the judgement is almost accomplished, the judgement he had invoked: except that the earl still has his bollocks, as far as anybody knows. After their talk at Mark and the Lion the earl, who had been drinking for some days, had caused his servants to sponge his clothes, wiping away trails of vomit: sour-smelling, rawly shaven, trembling and green with nausea, he had presented himself before the king's council, and obliged him, Thomas Cromwell, by rewriting the history of his infatuation: by forswearing any claim on Anne Boleyn; by affirming that no contract of marriage had ever existed between them; that on his honour as a nobleman he had never tupped her, and that she was completely free for the king's hands, heart and marriage bed. On which, he had taken his Bible oath, the book held by old Warham, who was archbishop before Thomas Cranmer: on which, he had received the Holy Sacrament, with Henry's eyes boring into his back.

Now he, Cromwell, rides over to meet the earl at his country house in Stoke Newington, which lies north and east of the city on the Cambridge road. Percy's servants take their horses, but rather than entering at once he stands back from the house to take a view of the roof and chimneys. 'Fifty pounds spent before next winter would be a good investment,' he says to Thomas Wriothesley. 'Not counting the labour.' If he had a ladder he could go up and look at the state of the leads. But that would perhaps not be consonant with his dignity. Master Secretary can do anything he likes, but the Master of the Rolls has to think of his ancient office and what is due to it. Whether, as the king's Vicegerent in Spirituals, he is allowed to climb about on roofs … who knows? The office is too new and untried. He grins. Certainly, it would be an affront to the dignity of Master Wriothesley, if he were asked to foot the ladder. 'I'm thinking about my investment,' he tells Wriothesley. 'Mine and the king's.'

The earl owes him considerable sums, but he owes the king ten thousand pounds. After Harry Percy is dead, his earldom will be swallowed by the Crown: so he examines the earl too, to judge how sound he is. He is jaundiced, hollow-cheeked, looks older than his age, which is some thirty-four, thirty-five; and that sour smell that hangs in the air, it takes him back to Kimbolton, to the old queen shut up in her apartments: the fusty, unaired room like a gaol, and the bowl of vomit that passed him, in the hands of one of her girls. He says without much hope, 'You haven't been sick because of my visit?'

The earl looks at him from a sunken eye. 'No. They say it is my liver. No, on the whole, Cromwell, you have dealt very reasonably with me, I must say. Considering –'

'Considering what I threatened you with.' He shakes his head, rueful. 'Oh, my lord. Today I stand before you a poor suitor. You will never guess my errand.'

'I think I would.'

'I put it to you, my lord, that you are married to Anne Boleyn.'

'No.'

'I put it to you that in or about the year 1523, you made a secret contract of marriage with her, and that therefore her so-called marriage with the king is null.'

'No.' From somewhere, the earl finds a spark of his ancestral spirit, that border fire which burns in the north parts of the kingdom, and roasts any Scot in its path. 'You made me swear, Cromwell. You came to me where I was drinking at Mark and the Lion, and you threatened me. I was dragged before the council and I was made to swear on the Bible that I had no contract with Anne. I was made to go with the king and take communion. You saw me, you heard me. How can I take it back now? Are you saying I committed perjury?'

The earl is on his feet. He remains seated. He does not mean any discourtesy; rather he thinks that, if he stands up, he might fetch the earl a slap, and he has never to his knowledge assaulted a sick man. 'Not perjury,' he says amicably. 'I put it to you that on that occasion, your memory failed.'

'I was married to Anne, but had forgotten?'

He sits back and considers his adversary. 'You have always been a drinker, my lord, which is how, I believe, you are reduced to your present condition. On the day in question I found you, as you say, at a tavern. Is it possible that when you came before the council, you were still drunk? And therefore you were confused about what you were swearing?'

'I was sober.'

'Your head ached. You were nauseous. You were afraid you might be sick on the reverend shoes of Archbishop Warham. The possibility so perturbed you that you could think of nothing else. You were not attentive to the questions put to you. That was hardly your fault.'

'But,' the earl says, 'I was attentive.'

'Any councillor would understand your plight. We have all been in drink, one time or another.'

'Upon my soul, I was attentive.'

'Then consider another possibility. Perhaps there was some slackness in the taking of the oath. Some irregularity. The old archbishop, he was ill himself that day. I remember how his hands trembled as he held the holy book.'

'He was palsied. It is common in age. But he was competent.'

'If there was some defect in the procedure, your conscience should not trouble you, if you were now to repudiate your oath. Perhaps, you know, it was not even a Bible?'

'It was bound like a Bible,' the earl says.

'I have a book on accountancy that is often mistaken for a Bible.'

'Especially by you.'

He grins. The earl is not entirely addle-witted, not yet.

'And what about the sacred host?' Percy says. 'I took the sacrament to seal my oath, and was that not the very body of God?'

He is silent. I could give you an argument about that, he thinks, but I will not give you an opening to call me a heretic.

'I will not do it,' Percy says. 'And I cannot see why I should. All I hear is, that Henry means to kill her. Isn't it enough for her to be dead? After she is dead what does it matter who she was contracted to?'

'It does, in the one way. He is suspicious about the child Anne had. But he does not want to press inquiries into who is her father.'

'Elizabeth? I have seen the thing,' Percy says. 'She's his. I can tell you that much.'

'But if she were … even if she were, he now thinks to put her out of the succession, so if he was never married to her mother – well, at a stroke the matter is clear. The way is open for the children of his next wife.'

The earl nods. 'I see that.'

'So if you want to help Anne, this is your last chance.'

'How will it help her, to have her marriage annulled and her child bastardised?'

'It might save her life. If Henry's temper cools.'

'You will make sure to keep it hot. You will heap on the fuel and apply the bellows, will you not?'

He shrugs. 'It is nothing to me. I do not hate the queen, I leave that to others. So, if you had ever any regard for her –'

'I cannot help her any more. I can only help myself. God knows the truth. You made me a liar as I stood before God. Now you want to make me a fool as I stand before men. You must find another way, Master Secretary.'

'I will do that,' he says easily. He stands up. 'I am sorry you lose a chance to please the king.' At the door, he turns back. 'You are stubborn,' he says, 'because you are weak.'

Harry Percy looks up at him. 'I am worse than weak, Cromwell. I am dying.'

'You'll last until the trial, won't you? I shall put you on the panel of peers. If you are not Anne's husband, you are clear to be her judge. The court has need of wise and experienced men like yourself.'

Harry Percy cries out after him, but he leaves the hall with long strides, and gives the gentlemen outside the door a shake of the head. 'Well,' Master Wriothesley says, 'I made sure you would bounce him into sense.'

'Sense has fled.'

'You look gloomy, sir.'

'Do I, Call-Me? I can't think why.'

'We can still free the king. My lord archbishop will see a way. Even if we have to bring Mary Boleyn into it, and say the marriage was unlawful through affinity.'

'Our difficulty is, in the case of Mary Boleyn, the king was apprised of the facts. He may not have known if Anne was secretly married. But he always knew she was Mary's sister.'

'Have you ever done anything like that?' Master Wriothesley asks thoughtfully. 'Two sisters?'

'Is that the kind of question that absorbs you at this time?'

'Only one wonders. How it would be. They say Mary Boleyn was a great whore when she was at the French court. Do you think King Francis had them both?'

He looks at Wriothesley with new respect. 'There is an angle I might explore. Now ... because you have been a good boy and not struck out at Harry Percy or called him names, but waited patiently outside the door as you were bade, I'll tell you something you will like to know. Once, when she found herself between patrons, Mary Boleyn asked me to marry her.'

Master Wriothesley gapes at him. He follows, uttering broken syllables. What? When? Why? Only when they are on horseback does he speak to the purpose. 'God strike me. You would have been the king's brother-in-law.'

'But not for much longer,' he says.

The day is breezy and fine. They make good speed back to London. In other days, in other company, he would have enjoyed the journey.

But what company would that be, he wonders, dismounting at Whitehall. Bess Seymour's? 'Master Wriothesley,' he asks, 'can you read my mind?'

'No,' says Call-Me. He looks baffled, and somehow affronted.

'Do you think a bishop could read my mind?'

'No, sir.'

He nods. 'Just as well.'

The Imperial ambassador comes to see him, wearing his Christmas hat. 'Especially for you, Thomas,' he says, 'because I know it makes you happy.' He sits down, signals to the servant for wine. The servant is Christophe. 'Do you use this ruffian for every purpose?' Chapuys asks. 'Is it not he who tortured the boy Mark?'

'Firstly, Mark is not a boy, he is only immature. Secondly, no one tortured him.' At least, he says, 'not in my sight or hearing, not at my command nor suggestion, nor with my permission, expressed or implied'.

'I feel you preparing yourself for the courtroom,' Chapuys says. 'A knotted rope, was it not? Tightened around the brow? So you threatened to pop out his eyes?'

He is angry. 'This may be what they do where you were brought up. I have never heard of such a practice.'

'So it was the rack instead?'

'You can see him at his trial. You can judge for yourself whether he is damaged. I have seen men who have been racked. Not here. Abroad, I have seen it. They have to be carried in a chair. Mark is as nimble as in his dancing days.'

'If you say so.' Chapuys seems pleased to have provoked him. 'And how is your heretic queen now?'

'Brave as a lion. You will be sorry to learn.'

'And proud, but she will be humbled. She is no lion, and no more than one of your London cats that sing on rooftops.'

He thinks of a black cat he used to have. Marlinspike. After some years of fighting and scavenging he ran off, as cats do, to make his career elsewhere. Chapuys says, 'As you know, a number of ladies and gentlemen of the court have ridden up to the Princess Mary, to assure her of their services in the time which is at hand. I thought you might go yourself.'

361

God damn it, he thinks, I am already fully employed, and more than fully; it is no small enterprise, to bring down a queen of England. He says, 'I trust the princess will forgive my absence at this time. It is to do her good.'

'You have no trouble calling her "the princess" now,' Chapuys observes. 'She will be reinstated, of course, as Henry's heir.' He waits. 'She expects, all her loyal supporters expect, the Emperor himself expects …'

'Hope is a great virtue. But,' he adds, 'I hope you will warn her not to receive any persons without permission from the king. Or from me.'

'She cannot stop them resorting to her. All her old household. They flock. It will be a new world, Thomas.'

'The king will be eager, is eager, for a reconciliation with her. He is a good father.'

'A pity he has not had more opportunity to show it.'

'Eustache …' He pauses, waves Christophe away. 'I know you have never married, but have you no children? Do not look so startled. I am curious about your life. We must come to know each other better.'

The ambassador bristles at the change of topic. 'I do not meddle with women. Not like you.'

'I would not turn away a child. No one ever makes a claim on me. If they did, I would meet it.'

'The ladies do not wish to prolong the encounter,' Chapuys suggests.

That makes him laugh. 'You may be right. Come, my good friend, let us have our supper.'

'I look forward to many more such convivial evenings,' the ambassador says, beaming. 'Once the concubine is dead, and England is at ease.'

* * *

The men in the Tower, though they lament their likely fate, do not complain as sorely as the king does. By day he walks around like an illustration from the Book of Job. By night he glides down the river, accompanied by musicians, to visit Jane.

For all the beauties of Nicholas Carew's house, it is eight miles from the Thames and so not convenient for evening journeys, even in these light nights of early summer; the king wants to stay with Jane till darkness falls. So the queen-in-waiting has come up to London, to be housed by her supporters and friends. Crowds surge about from one rumoured spot to another, trying to catch a glimpse of her, necks craning, eyes popping, the curious blocking gateways and hoisting each other up on walls.

Her brothers throw out largesse to the Londoners, in the hope of winning their voices for her. The word is put about that she is an English gentlewoman, one of our own; unlike Anne Boleyn, whom many believe to be French. But the crowds are puzzled, even rancorous: ought not the king to marry a great princess, like Katherine, from a faraway land?

Bess Seymour tells him, 'Jane is squirrelling away money in a locked chest, in case the king changes his mind.'

'So should we all. A locked chest is a good thing to have.'

'She keeps the key in her bosom,' Bess says.

'No one is likely to come at it there.'

Bess gives him a merry look, out of the tail of her eye.

By now, the news of Anne's arrest is beginning to ripple through Europe, and though Bess does not know it, offers for Henry are coming in hour by hour. The Emperor suggests that the king might like his niece the Infanta of Portugal, who would come with 400,000 ducats; and the Portuguese Prince Dom Luis could marry the Princess Mary. Or if the king does not want the Infanta, what would he say to the dowager Duchess of Milan, a very pretty young widow, who would bring him a good sum also?

These are days of omens and portents for those who value such things and can read them. The malign stories have come out of the books and are enacting themselves. A queen is locked in a tower, accused of incest. The commonwealth, nature herself, is perturbed. Ghosts are glimpsed in doorways, standing by windows, against walls, hoping to overhear the secrets of the living. A bell rings of itself, touched by no human hand. There is a burst of speech where no one is present, a hissing in the air like the sound of a hot iron plunged into water. Sober citizens are moved to shout in church. A woman pushes through the crowd at his gate, grabbing at the bridle of his horse. Before the guards force her away, she shouts at him, 'God help us, Cromwell, what a man the king is! How many wives does he mean to have?'

For once, Jane Seymour has a blush of colour in her cheeks; or perhaps it is reflected from her gown, the soft clear rose of quince jelly.

Statements, indictments, bills are circulated, shuffled between judges, prosecutors, the Attorney General, the Lord Chancellor's office; each step in the process clear, logical, and designed to create corpses by due process of law. George Rochford will be tried apart, as a peer; the commoners will be tried first. The order goes to the Tower, 'Bring up the bodies.' Deliver, that is, the accused men, by name Weston, Brereton, Smeaton and Norris, to Westminster Hall for trial. Kingston fetches them by barge; it is 12 May, a Friday. They are brought in by armed guards through a fulminating crowd, shouting the odds. The gamblers believe that Weston will get off; this is his family's campaign at work. But for the others, the odds are even that they live or die. For Mark Smeaton, who has admitted everything, no wagers are being taken; but a book is open on whether he will be hanged, beheaded, boiled or burned, or subject to some novel penalty of the king's invention.

They do not understand the law, he says to Riche, looking down from a window at the scenes below. There is only one penalty for high treason: for a man, to be hanged, cut down alive

and eviscerated, or for a woman, to be burned. The king may vary
the sentence to decapitation; only poisoners are boiled alive. The
court can give just the one sentence in this case, and it will be
transmitted from the court to the crowds, and misunderstood, so
that those who have won will be gnashing their teeth, and those
who have lost will be demanding their money, and there will be
fights and torn clothes and smashed heads, and blood on the
ground while the accused are still safe in the courtroom, and days
away from death.

They will not hear the charges till they hear them in court and,
as is usual in treason trials, they will have no legal representation.
But they will have a chance to speak, and represent themselves,
and they can call witnesses: if anybody will stand up for them.
Men have been tried for treason, these last few years, and walked
free, but these men know they will not escape. They have to think
of their families left behind; they want the king to be good to
them and that alone should still any protest, prevent any strident
pleas of innocence. The court must be allowed to work unim-
peded. In return for their cooperation it is understood, more or
less understood, that the king will grant them the mercy of death
by the axe, which will not add to their shame; though there are
murmurs among the jurors that Smeaton will hang because, being
a man of low birth, he has no honour to protect.

Norfolk presides. When the prisoners are brought in, the three
gentlemen draw away from Mark; they want to show him their
scorn, and how they are better than he. But this brings them into
proximity with each other, more than they will allow; they will
not look at each other, he notices, they shuffle to create as much
space as they can, so they seem to be shrinking from each other,
twitching at coats and sleeves. Only Mark will declare his guilt.
He has been kept in irons in case he tries to destroy himself:
surely a charity, as he would bungle it. So he arrives before the
court intact, as promised, no marks of injury, but unable to keep
himself from tears. He pleads for mercy. The other defendants are

succinct but respectful to the court: three heroes of the tilting ground who see, bearing down on them, the indefeasible opponent, the King of England himself. There are challenges they could make, but the charges, their dates and their details, go by them so fast. They can win a point, if they insist; but it only slows the inevitable, and they know it. When they go in, the guards stand with halberds reversed; but when they come out, convicted, the axe edge is turned to them. They push through the uproar, dead men: hustled through the lines of halberdiers to the river, and back to their temporary home, their anteroom, to write their last letters and make spiritual preparations. All have expressed contrition, though none but Mark has said for what.

A cool afternoon: and once the crowds have drifted off, and the court broken up, he finds himself sitting by an open window with the clerks bundling the records, and he watches it done, and then says, I will go home now. I am going to my city house, to Austin Friars, send the papers to Chancery Lane. He is the overlord of the spaces and the silences, the gaps and the erasures, what is missed or misconstrued or simply mistranslated, as the news slips from English to French and perhaps via Latin to Castilian and the Italian tongues, and through Flanders to the Emperor's eastern territories, over the borders of the German principalities and out to Bohemia and Hungary and the snowy realms beyond, by merchantmen under sail to Greece and the Levant; to India, where they have never heard of Anne Boleyn, let alone her lovers and her brother; along the silk routes to China where they have never heard of Henry the eighth of that name, or any other Henry, and even the existence of England is to them a dark myth, a place where men have their mouths in their bellies and women can fly, or cats rule the commonwealth and men crouch at mouse holes to catch their dinner. In the hall at Austin Friars he stands for a moment before the great image of Solomon and Sheba; the tapestry belonged to the cardinal once, but the king took it, and then, after

Wolsey was dead, and he, Cromwell, had risen in favour, the king had made him a gift of it, as if embarrassed, as if slipping back to its true owner something that should never have been away. The king had seen him look with longing, and more than once, at Sheba's face, not because he covets a queen but because she takes him back to his past, to a woman whom by accident she resembles: Anselma, an Antwerp widow, whom he might have married, he often thinks, if he had not made up his mind suddenly to take himself off back to England and pick up with his own people. In those days he did things suddenly: not without calculation, not without care, but once his mind was made up he was swift to move. And he is still the same man. As his opponents will find.

'Gregory?' His son is still in his riding coat, dusty from the road. He hugs him. 'Let me look at you. Why are you here?'

'You did not say I must not come,' Gregory explains. 'You did not absolutely forbid it. Besides, I have learned the art of public speaking now. Do you want to hear me make a speech?'

'Yes. But not now. You ought not to ride about the country with just one attendant or two. There are people who would hurt you, because you are known to be my son.'

'How am I known?' Gregory says. 'How would they know that?' Doors open, there are feet on the stairs, there are questioning faces crowding the hall; the news from the courtroom has preceded him. Yes, he confirms, they are all guilty, all condemned, whether they will go to Tyburn I do not know, but I will move the king to grant them the swifter end; yes, Mark too, because when he was under my roof I offered him mercy, and this is all the mercy I can deliver.

'We heard they are all in debt, sir,' says his clerk Thomas Avery, who does the accounts.

'We heard there were perilous crowds, sir,' says one of his watchmen.

Thurston the cook comes out, looking floury: 'Thurston has heard there were pies on sale,' says the jester Anthony. 'And I, sir? I hear that your new comedy was very well-received. And everybody laughed except the dying.'

Gregory says, 'But there could still be reprieves?'

'Undoubtedly.' He does not feel like adding anything. Someone has given him a drink of ale; he wipes his mouth.

'I remember when we were at Wolf Hall,' Gregory says, 'and Weston spoke so boldly to you, and so me and Rafe, we caught him in our magic net and dropped him from a height. But we would not really have killed him.'

'The king is wreaking his pleasure, and so many fine gentlemen will be spoiled.' He speaks for the household to hear. 'When your acquaintances tell you, as they will, that it is I who have condemned these men, tell them that it is the king, and a court of law, and that all proper formalities have been observed, and no one has been hurt bodily in pursuit of the truth, whatever the word is in the city. And you will not believe it, please, if ill-informed persons tell you these men are dying because I have a grudge against them. It is beyond grudge. And I could not save them if I tried.'

'But Master Wyatt will not die?' Thomas Avery asks. There is a murmur; Wyatt is a favourite in his household, for his open-handed ways and his courtesy.

'I must go in now. I must read the letters from abroad. Thomas Wyatt ... well, let us say I have advised him. I think we shall soon see him here among us, but bear in mind that nothing is certain, the will of the king ... No. Enough.'

He breaks off, Gregory trails him. 'Are they really guilty?' he asks, the moment they are alone. 'Why so many men? Would it not have stood better with the king's honour if he named only one?'

He says wryly, 'That would distinguish him too much, the gentleman in question.'

'Oh, you mean that people would say, Harry Norris has a bigger cock than the king, and he knows what to do with it?'

'What a way with words you have indeed. The king is inclined to take it patiently, and where another man would strive to be secret, he knows he cannot be, because he is not a private man. He believes, or at least he wishes to show, that the queen has been indiscriminate, that she is impulsive, that her nature is bad and she cannot control it. And now that so many men are found to have erred with her, any possible defence is stripped away, do you see? That is why they have been tried first. As they are guilty, she must be.'

Gregory nods. He seems to understand, but perhaps seeming is as far as it goes. When Gregory says, 'Are they guilty?' he means, 'Did they do it?' But when he says, 'Are they guilty?' he means, 'Did the court find them so?' The lawyer's world is entire unto itself, the human pared away. It was a triumph, in a small way, to unknot the entanglement of thighs and tongues, to take that mass of heaving flesh and smooth it on to white paper: as the body, after the climax, lies back on white linen. He has seen beautiful indictments, not a word wasted. This was not one: the phrases jostled and frotted, nudged and spilled, ugly in content and ugly in form. The design against Anne is unhallowed in its gestation, untimely in its delivery, a mass of tissue born shapeless; it waited to be licked into shape as a bear cub is licked by its mother. You nourished it, but you did not know what you fed: who would have thought of Mark confessing, or of Anne acting in every respect like an oppressed and guilty woman with a weight of sin upon her? It is as the men said today in court: we are guilty of all sorts of charges, we have all sinned, we all are riddled and rotten with offences and, even by the light of church and gospel, we may not know what they are. Word has come from the Vatican, where they are specialists in sin, that any offers of friendship, any gesture of reconciliation from King Henry, would be viewed kindly at this difficult time; because, whoever else is surprised, they are not surprised in Rome about the turn events have taken. In Rome, of course, it would be unremarkable:

adultery, incest, one merely shrugs. When he was at the Vatican, in Cardinal Bainbridge's day, he quickly saw that no one in the papal court grasped what was happening, ever; and least of all the Pope. Intrigue feeds on itself; conspiracies have neither mother nor father, and yet they thrive: the only thing to know is that no one knows anything.

Though in Rome, he thinks, there is little pretence at process of law. In the prisons, when an offender is forgotten and starves, or when he is beaten to death by his gaolers, they just stuff the body into a sack then roll and kick it into the river, where it joins the Tiber's general effluent.

He looks up. Gregory has been sitting quietly, respectful of his thoughts. But now he says, 'When will they die?'

'It cannot be tomorrow, they need time to settle their business. And the queen will be tried in the Tower on Monday, so it must be after that, Kingston cannot ... the court will sit in public, you see, the Tower will be awash with people ...' He pictures an unseemly scramble, the condemned men having to fight to the scaffold through the incoming hordes who want to see a queen on trial.

'But will you be there to watch?' Gregory insists. 'When it does occur? I could attend them at the last to offer them my prayers, but I could not do it unless you were there. I might fall down on the ground.'

He nods. It is good to be realistic in these matters. He has heard street brawlers in his youth boast of their stomach, then blench at a cut finger, and anyway being at an execution is not like being in a fight: there is fear, and fear is contagious, whereas in a scrap there is no time for fear, and not until it's over do your legs begin to shake. 'If I am not there, Richard will be. It is a kindly thought and though it would give you pain I feel it shows respect.' He cannot guess the shape of the next week. 'It depends ... the annulment must go through, so it rests with the queen, on how she helps us, will she give her assent.' He is thinking aloud: 'It may be I am at Lambeth with Cranmer. And please, my dear son, don't ask me why there has to be an annulment. Just know it's what the king wants.'

He finds he cannot think of the dying men at all. Into his mind instead strays the picture of More on the scaffold, seen through the veil of rain: his body, already dead, folding back neatly from the impact of the axe. The cardinal when he fell had no persecutor more relentless than Thomas More. Yet, he thinks, I did not hate him. I exercised my skills to the utmost to persuade him to reconcile with the king. And I thought I would win him, I really thought I would, for he was tenacious of the world, tenacious of his person, and had a good deal to live for. In the end he was his own murderer. He wrote and wrote and he talked and talked, then suddenly at a stroke he cancelled himself. If ever a man came close to beheading himself, Thomas More was that man.

The queen wears scarlet and black, and instead of a hood a jaunty cap, with feathers of black and white sweeping across its brim. Remember those plumes, he tells himself; this will be the last time, or almost so. How did she look, the women will ask. He will be able to say she looked pale, but unafraid. How can it be for her, to enter that great chamber and to stand before the peers of England, all men and none of them desiring her? She is tainted now, she is dead meat, and instead of coveting her – bosom, hair, eyes – their gaze slides away. Only Uncle Norfolk glares at her fiercely: as if her head were not Medusa's head.

In the centre of the great hall at the Tower they have built a platform with benches for the judges and peers, and there are some benches too in the side arcades, but the most part of the spectators will be standing, pushing in behind each other till the guards say 'No more,' and block the doorways with staves. Even then they push, and the noise rises as those who have been let through jostle in the well of the court, till Norfolk, his white baton of office in his hand, calls for silence, and from the ferocious expression on his face, the most ignorant person in that throng knows he means it.

Here is the Lord Chancellor seated by the duke, to supply him with the best legal advice in the kingdom. Here is the Earl of Worcester, whose wife, you might say, started all this; and the earl gives him a filthy look, he does not know why. Here is Charles Brandon, Duke of Suffolk, who has hated Anne since he set eyes on her and has made it plain to the king's face. Here is the Earl of Arundel, the Earl of Oxford, the Earl of Rutland, the Earl of Westmorland: among them he moves softly, plain Thomas Cromwell, a greeting here and a word there, spreading reassurance: the Crown's case is in order, no upsets are expected or will be tolerated, we shall all be home for supper and sleep safely in our own beds tonight. Lord Sandys, Lord Audley, Lord Clinton and many lords more, each pricked off on a list as they take their seats: Lord Morley, George Boleyn's father-in-law, who reaches for his hand and says, please, Thomas Cromwell, as you love me, let not this sordid business rebound on my poor little daughter Jane.

She was not so much your poor little daughter, he thinks, when you married her off without asking her; but it is common, you cannot blame him as a father, for as the king once said to him ruefully, it is only very poor men and women who are free to choose who they love. He clasps Lord Morley's hand in return, and wishes him courage, and bids him take his seat, for the prisoner is among us and the court prepared.

He bows to the foreign ambassadors; but where is Chapuys? Word is passed forward, he is suffering from a quartan fever: word is passed back, I am sorry to hear that, let him send to my house for anything that might make him more comfortable. Say his fever is up today, day one: its tide ebbing tomorrow, by Wednesday he is on his feet but shaky, but by Thursday night he will be down again, as it shakes him in its grip.

The Attorney General reads the indictment, and it takes some time: crimes under statute, crimes under God. As he gets to his feet to prosecute he is thinking, the king expects a verdict by mid-afternoon; and glancing across the court he sees Francis Bryan, still in his outdoor coat, ready to get on the river with word to the Seymours. Steady, Francis, he thinks, this may take some time, it may get hot in here.

The substance of the case is the work of an hour or two, but when there are ninety-five names to be verified, of the justices and the peers, then the mere shuffling and the throat-clearing, the nose-blowing, the adjustment of robes and the settling of belt sashes – all those distracting rituals that some men need before they speak in public – with all that, it is clear the day will wear on; the queen herself is a still presence, listening intently from her chair as the list of her crimes is read out, the dizzying catalogue of times, dates, places, of men, their members, their tongues: into the mouth, out of the mouth, into divers crannies of the body, at Hampton Court and Richmond Palace, at Greenwich and Westminster, in Middlesex and in Kent; and then the loose words and taunts, the jealous quarrels and twisted intentions, the declaration, by the queen, that when her husband is dead, she will choose some one of them to be her husband, but she cannot yet say which. 'Did you say that?' She shakes her head. 'You must answer aloud.'

Icy little voice: 'No.'

It is all she will say, no, no and no: and once she answers 'Yes,' when she is asked if she has given money to Weston, and she hesitates and admits it; and there is a whoop from the crowd, and Norfolk stops proceedings and threatens he will have them all arrested if they do not keep silence. In any well-ordered country, Suffolk said yesterday, the trial of a noblewoman would be conducted in seemly privacy; he had rolled his eyes and said, but my lord, this is England.

Norfolk has obtained quiet, a rustling calm punctuated by coughs and whispers; he is ready for the prosecution to resume, and says, 'Very well, go on, er – you.' Not for the first time, he is baffled by having to speak to a common man, who is not an ostler or a carter, but a minister of the king: the Lord Chancellor leans forward and whispers, reminding him perhaps that the prosecutor is Master of the Rolls. 'Carry on, Your Mastership,' he says, more politely. 'Please do proceed.'

She denies treason, there is the point: she never raises her voice, but she disdains to enlarge, to excuse, extenuate: to mitigate. And there is no one to do it for her. He remembers what Wyatt's old father had once told him, how a dying lioness can maul you, flash out with her claw and scar you for life. But he feels no threat, no tension, nothing at all. He is a good speaker, known for eloquence, style and audibility, but today he has no interest in whether he is heard, not beyond the judges, the accused, as whatever the populace hear they will misconstrue: and so his voice seems to fade to a drowsy murmur in the room, the voice of a country priest droning through his prayers, no louder than a fly buzzing in a corner, knocking against glass; out of the corner of his eye he sees the Attorney General stifle a yawn, and he thinks, I have done what I thought I could never achieve, I have taken adultery, incest, conspiracy and treason, and I have made them routine. We do not need any false excitement. After all, it is a law court, not the Roman circus.

The verdicts drag in: it is a lengthy business; the court implores brevity, no speeches please, one word will suffice: ninety-five vote guilty, and not one nay-sayer. When Norfolk begins to read the sentence, the roar rises again, and one can feel the pressure of the people outside trying to get in, so it seems the hall gently rocks, like a boat at its mooring. 'Her own uncle!' someone wails, and the duke bangs his fist on his table and says he will do slaughter. That produces some quiet; the hush allows him to conclude, '... thy judgement is this: Thou shalt be burned here, within the Tower, or else to have thy head smitten off, as the king's pleasure shall be further known –'

374

There is a yelp from one of the justices. The man is leaning forward, whispering furiously; Norfolk looks irate; the lawyers are going into a huddle, the peers crane forward to find out what is the delay. He strolls over. Norfolk says, 'These fellows tell me I have not done it right, I cannot say burning or beheading, I have to say one, and they say it must be burning, that is how a woman suffers when she is a traitor.'

'My lord Norfolk has his instructions from the king.' He means to crush objection and he does. 'The phrasing is the king's pleasure and moreover, do not tell me what can be done and what cannot, we have never tried a queen before.'

'We're just making it up as we go,' says the Lord Chancellor amiably.

'Finish what you were saying,' he tells Norfolk. He steps back.

'I think I have done,' Norfolk says, scratching his nose. '... head smitten off, as the king's pleasure shall be further known of the same.'

The duke drops his voice and concludes at conversational pitch; so the queen never hears the end of her sentence. She has the gist, though. He watches her rise from her chair, still composed, and he thinks, she doesn't believe it; why doesn't she believe it? He looks across to where Francis Bryan was hovering, but the messenger has already gone.

Rochford's trial has now to go forward; they must get Anne out, before her brother comes in. The solemnity of the occasion has dissipated. The more elderly members of the court have to totter out to piss, and the younger to stretch their legs and have a gossip, and collect the latest odds on an acquittal for George. The betting runs in his favour, though his face, as he is brought in, shows he is not deceived. To those who insist he will be acquitted, he, Cromwell has said, 'If Lord Rochford can satisfy the court, he will be let go. Let us see what defence he will make.'

He has only one real fear: that Rochford is not vulnerable to the same pressure as the other men, because he is not leaving behind anyone he cares for. His wife has betrayed him, his father deserted him, and his uncle will preside over the court that tries him. He thinks George will speak with eloquence and spirit, and he is correct. When the charges are read to him, he asks that they be put one by one, clause by clause: 'For what is your worldly time, gentlemen, against God's assurance of eternity?' There are smiles: admiration for his suavity. Boleyn addresses him, Cromwell, directly. 'Put them to me one by one. The times, the places. I will confound you.'

But the contest is not even. He has his papers, and if it comes to it, he can lay them on the table and make his case without them; he has his trained memory, he has his accustomed self-possession, his courtroom voice that places no strain on his throat, his urbanity of manner that places no strain on his emotions; and if George thinks he will falter, reading out the details of caresses administered and received, then George does not know the place he comes from: the times, the manners, that have formed Master Secretary. Soon enough, Lord Rochford will begin to sound like a raw, tearful boy; he is fighting for his life, and thus unequal to a man who seems so indifferent to the outcome; let the court acquit if it will, there will be another court, or a process, more informal, that will end with George a broken corpse. He thinks, too, that soon young Boleyn will lose his temper, that he will show his contempt for Henry, and then it will all be up with him. He hands Rochford a paper: 'Certain words are written here, which the queen is said to have spoken to you, and you in your turn passed them on. You need not read them aloud. Just tell the court, do you recognise those words?'

George smiles in disdain. Relishing the moment, he smirks: he takes a breath; he reads the words aloud. 'The king cannot copulate with a woman, he has neither skill nor vigour.'

He has read it because he thinks the crowd will like it. And so they do, though the laughter is shocked, incredulous. But from his judges – and it is they who matter – there is an audible hiss of deprecation. George looks up. He throws out his hands. 'These are not my words. I do not own them.'

But he owns them now. In one moment of bravado, to get the applause of the crowd, he has impugned the succession, derogated the king's heirs: even though he was cautioned not to do it. He, Cromwell, nods. 'We have heard that you spread rumours that the Princess Elizabeth is not the king's child. It seems you do. You have spread them even in this court.'

George is silent.

He shrugs and turns away. It is hard on George that he cannot even mention the charges against him without becoming guilty of them. As prosecutor, he would rather it had gone unmentioned, the king's difficulty; yet it is no more of a shame to Henry to have it declared in court than have it said in the street, and in taverns where they are singing the ballad of King Littleprick and his wife the witch. In such circumstances, the man blames the woman, as often as not. Something she has done, something she has said, the black look she gave him when he faltered, the derisive expression on her face. Henry is afraid of Anne, he thinks. But he will be potent with his new wife.

He gathers himself, gathers his papers; the judges wish to confer. The case against George is flimsy enough in all truth, but if the charges are thrown out, Henry will arraign him on some other matter, and it will go hard with his family, not just the Boleyns but the Howards too: for this reason, he thinks, Uncle Norfolk will not let him escape. And no one has denounced the charges as incredible, at this trial or the trials that preceded it. It has become a thing one can believe, that these men would plot against the king and copulate with the queen: Weston because he is reckless, Brereton because he is old in sin, Mark because he is ambitious, Henry Norris because he is familiar, he is close, he has confused his own person with the person of the king; and George Boleyn, not despite being her brother, but because he is her brother. Boleyns, it is known to all, will do what they need to do to rule; if Anne Boleyn put herself on the throne, walking on the bodies of the fallen, can she not put a Boleyn bastard there too?

He looks up at Norfolk, who gives him a nod. The verdict is in no doubt then, nor the sentence. The only surprise is Harry Percy. The earl rises from his place. He stands, his mouth open slightly, and a silence falls, not the rustling, whispering apology for a silence which the court has endured till now, but a still, expectant hush. He thinks of Gregory: do you want to hear me make a speech? Then the earl pitches forward, unleashes a groan, he crumples, and with a clatter and a thud he hits the floor. At once his prone body is swamped by guardsmen, and a great roar arises, 'Harry Percy is dead.'

Unlikely, he thinks. They'll bring him round. It is now mid-afternoon, warm and airless, and the evidence placed before the judges, the written statements alone, would fell a healthy man. There is a length of blue cloth laid over the new boards of the platform on which the judges sit, and he watches the guardsmen rip it up from the floor and improvise a blanket in which to carry the earl; and a memory stabs him, Italy, heat, blood, heaving and rolling and flopping a dying man on to knotted saddlecloths, cloths themselves scavenged from the dead, hauling him into the shade of the wall of – what, a church, a farmhouse? – only so that he could die, cursing, a few minutes later, trying to pack his guts back into the wound from which they were spilling, as if he wanted to leave the world tidy.

He feels sick, and he sits down by the Attorney General. The guardsmen carry the earl out, head lolling, eyes closed, feet dangling. His neighbour says, 'There is another man the queen has ruined. I suppose we will not know them all for years.'

It is true. The trial is a provisional arrangement, a fix for getting Anne out, Jane in. The effects of it have not been tested yet, the resonances have not been felt; but he expects a quaking at the heart of the body politic, a heaving in the stomach of the common-wealth. He gets up and goes over to urge Norfolk to get the trial under way again. George Boleyn – suspended as he is between trial and conviction – looks as though he might collapse himself, and has begun to weep. 'Help Lord Rochford to a chair,' he says. 'Give him something to drink.' He is a traitor, but still an earl; he can hear his death sentence sitting down.

Next day, 16 May, he is at the Tower, with Kingston in the constable's own lodgings. Kingston is fretting because he does not know what sort of scaffold to prepare for the queen: she lies under a dubious sentence, waiting for the king to speak. Cranmer is with her in her lodgings, come to hear her confession, and he will be able to hint to her, delicately, that her cooperation now will spare her pain. That the king still has mercy in him.

A guardsman at the door, addressing the constable: 'There is a visitor. Not for yourself, sir. For Master Cromwell. It is a foreign gentleman.'

It is Jean de Dinteville, who was here on embassy round about the time Anne was crowned. Jean stands poised in the doorway: 'They said I should find you here, and as time is short –'

'My dear friend.' They embrace. 'I did not even know you were in London.'

'I am straight off the boat.'

'Yes, you look it.'

'I am no sailor.' The ambassador shrugs; or at least, his vast padding moves, and subsides again; on this balmy morning, he is wrapped up in bewildering layers, much as a man dresses to face November. 'Anyway, it seemed best to come here and catch you before you are back playing bowls, which I believe you generally do when you should be receiving our representatives. I am sent to speak to you about young Weston.'

Good God, he thinks, has Sir Richard Weston managed to bribe the King of France?

'Not a moment too soon. He is sentenced to die tomorrow. What about him?'

'One is uneasy,' the ambassador says, 'if gallantry should be punished. Surely the young man is guilty of nothing more than a poem or two? Paying compliments and making jests? Perhaps the king might spare his life. One understands that for a year or two he would be advised to keep away from the court – travelling, perhaps?'

'He has a wife and young son, Monsieur. Not that the thought of them has ever constrained his behaviour.'

'So much the worse, if the king puts him to death. Does Henry not regard his reputation as a merciful prince?'

'Oh yes. He talks about it a lot. Monsieur, my advice is to forget Weston. Much as my master reveres and respects yours, he will not take it kindly if King Francis were to interfere in something which is, after all, a family matter, something he feels very near his own person.'

Dinteville is amused. 'One might well call it a family matter.'

'I notice you do not ask mercy for Lord Rochford. He has been an ambassador, one thought the King of France would be more interested in him.'

'Ah well,' the ambassador says. 'George Boleyn. One understands there is a change of regime, and what that entails. The whole French court hopes, of course, that Monseigneur will not be destroyed.'

'Wiltshire? He has been a good servant to the French, I see you would miss him. He is in no danger at present. Of course, you cannot look for his influence to be what it was. A change of regime, as you say.'

'May I say …' the ambassador stops to sip wine, to nibble a wafer that Kingston's servants have provided, 'that we in France find this whole business incomprehensible? Surely if Henry wishes to be rid of his concubine he can do it quietly?'

The French do not understand law courts or parliaments. For them, the best actions are covert actions. 'And if he must parade his shame to the world, surely one or two adulteries are enough? However, Cremuel,' the ambassador runs his eye over him, 'we can speak man to man, can we not? The great question is, can Henry do it? Because what we hear is, he prepares himself, and then his lady gives him a certain look. And his hopes collapse. That seems to us like witchcraft, as witches do commonly render men impotent. But,' he adds, with a look of sceptical contempt, 'I cannot imagine that any Frenchman would be so afflicted.'

'You must understand,' he says, 'though Henry is at all points a man, he is a gentleman, and not a cur grunting in the gutter with ... well, I say nothing of your own king's choice of women. These last months,' he takes a breath, 'these last weeks particularly, have been a time of great trial and grief for my master. He now seeks happiness. Have no doubt that his new marriage will secure his realm and promote the welfare of England.'

He is talking as if he is writing; already he is casting his version into dispatches.

'Oh, yes,' the ambassador says, 'the little person. One hears no great praise either of her beauty or her wit. He will not really marry her, another woman of no importance? When the Emperor offers him such lucrative matches ... or so we hear. We understand everything, Cremuel. As a man and a woman, the king and the concubine may have their disputes, but there are more than the two of them in the world, this is not the Garden of Eden. When all's said, it is the new politics she doesn't suit. The old queen was, in some sort, the concubine's protector, and ever since she died Henry has been plotting how he may become a respectable man again. So he must wed the first honest woman he sees, and in all truth it really does not matter whether she is the Emperor's relative or no, because with the Boleyns gone, Cremuel is riding high, and he will be sure to pack the council with good imperialists.' His lip curls; it might be a smile. 'Cremuel, I wish you would say how much the Emperor Charles pays you. I have no doubt we could match it.'

381

He laughs. 'Your master is seated on thorns. He knows my king has money flowing in. He is afraid that he might pay France a visit, and in arms.'

'You know what you owe King Francis.' The ambassador is annoyed. 'Only our negotiations, most astute and subtle negotiations, prevent the Pope from striking your country from the list of Christian nations. We have, I think, been loyal friends to you, representing your cause better than you can yourselves.'

He nods. 'I always enjoy hearing the French praise themselves. Will you dine with me later this week? Once this is over? And your queasiness has settled down?'

The ambassador inclines his head. His cap badge glitters and winks; it is a silver skull. 'I shall report to my master that sadly I have tried and failed in the matter of Weston.'

'Say you came too late. The tide was against you.'

'No, I shall say Cremuel was against me. By the way, you know what Henry has done, don't you?' He seems amused. 'He sent last week for a French executioner. Not from one of our own cities, but the man who chops heads in Calais. It seems there is no Englishman whom he trusts to behead his wife. I wonder he does not take her out himself and strangle her in the street.'

He turns to Kingston. The constable is an elderly man now, and though he was in France on the king's business fifteen years ago he has not had much use for the language since; the cardinal's advice was, speak English and shout loud. 'Did you get that?' he asks. 'Henry has sent to Calais for the headsman.'

'By the Mass,' Kingston says. 'Did he do it before the trial?'

'So monsieur the ambassador tells me.'

'I am glad of the news,' Kingston says, loudly and slowly. 'My mind. Much relieved.' He taps his head. 'I understand he employs a …' He makes a swishing motion.

'Yes, a sword,' Dinteville says in English. 'You may expect a graceful performance.' He touches his hat, '*Au revoir*, Master Secretary.'

They watch him go out. It is a performance in itself; his servants need to truss him in further wrappings. When he was here on his last mission, he spent the time sweltering under quilts, trying to sweat out a fever picked up from the influence of the English air, the moisture and the gnawing cold.

'Little Jeannot,' he says, looking after the ambassador. 'He still fears the English summer. And the king – when he had his first audience with Henry, he could not stop shaking from terror. We had to hold him up, Norfolk and myself.'

'Did I misunderstand,' the constable says, 'or did he say Weston was guilty of poems?'

'Something like that.' Anne, it appears, was a book left open on a desk for anyone to write on the pages, where only her husband should inscribe.

'Anyway, there's a matter off my mind,' the constable says. 'Did you ever see a woman burned? It is something I wish never to see, as I trust in God.'

When Cranmer comes to see him on the evening of 16 May, the archbishop looks ill, shadowed grooves running from nose to chin. Were they there a month ago? 'I want all this to be over,' he says, 'and to get back to Kent.'

'Did you leave Grete there?' he says gently.

Cranmer nods. He seems hardly able to say his wife's name. He is terrified every time the king mentions marriage, and of course these days the king mentions little else. 'She is afraid that, with his next queen, the king will revert to Rome, and we shall be forced to part. I tell her, no, I know the king's resolve. But whether he will change his thinking, so a priest can live openly with his wife ... if I thought there was no hope of that, then I think I should have to let her go home, before there is nothing there for her. You know how it is, in a few years people die, they forget you, you forget your own language, or so I suppose.'

'There is every hope,' he says firmly. 'And tell her, within a few months, in the new Parliament, I shall have wiped out all remnants of Rome from the statute books. And then, you know,' he smiles, 'once the assets are given out ... well, once they have been directed to the pockets of Englishmen, they will not revert to the pockets of the Pope.' He says, 'How did you find the queen, did she make her confession to you?'

'No. It is not yet the time. She will confess. At the last. If it comes to it.'

He is glad for Cranmer's sake. What would be worse at this point? To hear a guilty woman admit everything, or to hear an innocent woman beg? And to be bound to silence, either way? Perhaps Anne will wait until there is no hope of a reprieve, preserving her secrets till then. He understands this. He would do the same.

'I told her the arrangements made,' Cranmer says, 'for the annulment hearing. I told her it will be at Lambeth, it will be tomorrow. She said, will the king be there? I said no, madam, he sends his proctors. She said, he is busy with Seymour, and then she reproached herself, saying, I should not speak against Henry, should I? I said, it would be unwise. She said to me, may I come there to Lambeth, to speak for myself? I said no, there is no need, proctors have been appointed for you too. She seemed downcast. But then she said, tell me what the king wants me to sign. Whatever the king wants, I will agree. He may allow me to go to France, to a convent. Does he want me to say I was wed to Harry Percy? I said to her, madam, the earl denies it. And she laughed.'

He looks doubtful. Even the fullest disclosure, even a complete and detailed admission of guilt, it would not help her, not now, though it might have helped before the trial. The king doesn't want to think about her lovers, past or present. He has wiped them out of his mind. And her too. She would not credit the extent to which Henry has erased her. He said yesterday, 'I hope these arms of mine will soon receive Jane.'

Cranmer says, 'She cannot imagine that the king has abandoned her. It is not yet a month since he made the Emperor's ambassador bow to her.'

'I think he did that for his own sake. Not for hers.'

'I don't know,' Cranmer says. 'I thought he loved her. I thought there was no estrangement between them, up until the last. I am forced to think I don't know anything. Not about men. Not about women. Not about my faith, nor the faith of others. She said to me, "Shall I go to Heaven? Because I have done many good deeds in my time."'

She has made the same enquiry of Kingston. Perhaps she is asking everybody.

'She talks of works.' Cranmer shakes his head. 'She says nothing of faith. And I hoped she understood, as I now understand, that we are saved, not by our works, but only through Christ's sacrifice, and through his merits, not our own.'

'Well, I do not think you should conclude that she was a papist all this time. What would it have availed her?'

'I am sorry for you,' Cranmer says. 'That you should have the responsibility of uncovering it all.'

'I did not know what I would find, when I began. That is the only reason I could do it, because I was surprised at every turn.' He thinks of Mark's boasting, of the gentlemen before the court twitching away from each other, and evading each other's eyes; he has learned things about human nature that even he never knew. 'Gardiner in France is clamouring to know the details, but I find I do not want to write the particulars, they are so abominable.'

'Draw a veil over it,' Cranmer agrees. Though the king himself, he does not shrink from the details, it seems. Cranmer says, 'He is taking it around with him, the book he has written. He showed it the other evening, at the Bishop of Carlisle's house, you know Francis Bryan has the lease there? In the midst of Bryan's entertainments, the king took out this text, and began to read it aloud, and press it on all the party. Grief has unhinged him.'

'No doubt,' he says. 'Anyway, Gardiner will be content. I have told him he will be the gainer, when the spoils are given out. The offices, I mean, and the pensions and payments that now revert to the king.'

But Cranmer is not listening. 'She said to me, when I die, shall I not be the king's wife? I said, no, madam, for the king would have the marriage annulled, and I have come to seek your consent to that. She said, I consent. She said to me, but will I still be queen? And I think, under statute, she will be. I did not know what to say to her. But she looked satisfied. But it seemed so long. The time I was with her. One moment she was laughing, and then praying, and then fretting … She asked me about Lady Worcester, the child she is carrying. She said she thought the child was not stirring as it should, the lady being now in her fifth month or so, and she thinks it is because Lady Worcester has taken fright, or is sorrowing for her. I did not like to tell her that this lady had given a deposition against her.'

'I will enquire,' he says. 'About my lady's health. Though not of the earl. He glared at me. I do not know for what cause.'

A number of expressions, all of them unfathomable, chase themselves across the archbishop's face. 'Do you not know why? Then I see the rumour is not true. I am glad of it.' He hesitates. 'You really do not know? The word at court is that Lady Worcester's child is yours.'

He is dumbfounded. 'Mine?'

'They say you have spent hours with her, behind closed doors.'

'And that is proof of adultery? Well, I see that it would be. I am paid out. Lord Worcester will run me through.'

'You do not look afraid.'

'I am afraid, but not of Lord Worcester.'

More of the times that are coming. Anne climbing the marble steps to Heaven, her good deeds like jewels weighting wrists and neck.

Cranmer says, 'I do not know why, but she thinks there is still hope.'

All these days he is not alone. His allies are watching him. Fitzwilliam is at his side, disturbed still by what Norris half-told him and then took back: always talking about it, taxing his brain, trying to make complete sentences from broken phrases. Nicholas Carew is mostly with Jane, but Edward Seymour flits between his sister and the privy chamber, where the atmosphere is subdued, vigilant, and the king, like the minotaur, breathes unseen in a labyrinth of rooms. He understands his new friends are protecting their investment. They watch him for any sign of wavering. They want him as deep in the matter as they can contrive, and their own hands hidden, so that if later the king expresses any regret, or questions the haste with which things were done, it is Thomas Cromwell and not they who will suffer.

Riche and Master Wriothesley keep turning up too. They say, 'We want to give attendance on you, we want to learn, we want to see what you do.' But they can't see. When he was a boy, fleeing to put the Narrow Sea between himself and his father, he rolled penniless into Dover, and set himself up in the street with the three-card trick. 'See the queen. Look well at her. Now … where is she?'

The queen was in his sleeve. The money was in his pocket. The gamblers were crying, 'You will be whipped!'

He takes the warrants to Henry to be signed. Kingston has still received no word of how the men are to die. He promises, I will make the king concentrate his mind. He says, 'Majesty, there is no gallows at Tower Hill, and I do not think it would be a good idea to take them to Tyburn, the crowds might be unruly.'

'Why would they?' Henry says. 'The people of London do not love these men. Indeed they do not know them.'

'No, but any excuse for disorder, and if the weather stays fine ...'

The king grunts. Very well. The headsman.

Mark too? 'After some sort, I promised him mercy if he confessed, and you know he did confess freely.'

The king says, 'Has the Frenchman come?'

'Yes, Jean de Dinteville. He has made representations.'

'No,' Henry says.

Not that Frenchman. He means the Calais executioner. He says to the king, 'Do you think that it was in France, when the queen was at court there in her youth, do you think it was there she was first compromised?'

Henry is silent. He thinks, then speaks. 'She was always pressing me, do you mark what I say ... always pressing on me the advantage of France. I think you are right. I have been thinking about it and I do not believe it was Harry Percy took her maidenhead. He would not lie, would he? Not on his honour as a peer of England. No, I believe it was in the court of France she was first debauched.'

So he cannot tell if the Calais headsman, so expert in his art, is a mercy at all; or if this form of death, dealt to the queen, simply meets Henry's severe sense of the fitness of things.

But he thinks, if Henry blames some Frenchman for ruining her, some foreigner unknown and perhaps dead, so much the better. 'So it was not Wyatt?' he says.

'No,' Henry says sombrely. 'It was not Wyatt.'

He had better stay where he is, he thinks, for now. Safer so. But a message can go to him, to say he is not to be tried. He says, 'Majesty, the queen complains of her attendants. She would like to have women from her own privy chamber.'

'Her household is broken up. Fitzwilliam has seen to it.'

'I doubt the ladies have all gone home.' They are hovering, he knows, in the houses of their friends, in expectation of a new mistress.

Henry says, 'Lady Kingston must stay, but you can change the rest. If she can find any willing to serve her.'

It is possible Anne still does not know how she has been abandoned. If Cranmer is right, she imagines her former friends are lamenting her, but really they are in a sweat of fear until her head is off. 'Someone will do her the charity,' he says.

Henry now looks down at the papers before him, as if he does not know what they are. 'The death sentences. To endorse,' he reminds him. He stands by the king while he dips his pen and sets his signature to each of the warrants: square, complex letters, lying heavy on the paper; a man's hand, when all is said.

He is at Lambeth, in the court convened to hear the divorce proceedings, when Anne's lovers die: this is the last day of the proceedings, it must be. His nephew Richard is there to represent him on Tower Hill and bring him the word of how it was accomplished. Rochford made an eloquent speech, appearing in command of himself. He was killed first and needed three blows of the axe; after which, the others said not much. All proclaimed themselves sinners, all said they deserved to die, but once again they did not say for what; Mark, left till last and slipping in the blood, called for God's mercy and the prayers of the people. The executioner must have steadied himself, since after his first blunder all died cleanly.

On paper it is done. The records of the trials are his, to carry to the Rolls House, to keep or destroy or mislay, but the bodies of the dead men are a dirty, urgent problem. The corpses must be put in a cart and brought within the Tower walls: he can see them, a heap of entangled bodies without heads, heaped promiscuously as if on a bed, or as if, like corpses in war, they have already been buried and dug up. Within the fortress they are stripped of their clothes, which are the perquisite of the headsman and his assistants, and left in their shirts. There is a graveyard huddled to the walls of St Peter ad Vincula, and the commoners will be buried there, with Rochford to go alone beneath the floor of the chapel. But now the dead are without the badges of their ranks there is some confusion. One of the burial party said, fetch the queen, she knows their body parts; but others, Richard says, cried shame on him. He says, gaolers see too much, they soon lose their sense of what is fitting. 'I saw Wyatt looking down from a grate in the Bell Tower,' Richard says. 'He signed to me and I wanted to give him hope, but I did not know how to signal that.'

He will be released, he says. But perhaps not until Anne is dead.

The hours to that event seem long. Richard hugs him; says, 'If she had reigned longer she would have given us to the dogs to eat.'

'If we had let her reign longer, we would have deserved it.'

At Lambeth, the two proctors for the queen had been present: as the king's substitutes, Dr Bedyll and Dr Tregonwell, and Richard Sampson as his counsel. And himself, Thomas Cromwell: and the Lord Chancellor, and other councillors, including the Duke of Suffolk, whose own marital affairs have been so entangled that he has learned a certain amount of canon law, swallowing it like a child taking medicine; today Brandon had sat making faces and shifting in his chair, while the priests and lawyers sifted the circumstances. They had talked over Harry Percy, and agreed he was no use to them. 'I cannot think why you did not get his cooperation, Cromwell,' the duke says. Reluctantly they had talked over Mary Boleyn, and agreed she would have to furnish the impediment; though the king was as culpable as anyone, for he knew, surely, he could not be contracted to Anne if he had slept with her sister? I suppose the point was not entirely obvious, Cranmer says gently. There was affinity, that is clear, but he had a dispensation from the Pope, which he thought held good at the time. He did not know that, in so grave a matter, the Pope cannot dispense; that point was settled later.

It is all most unsatisfactory. The duke says suddenly, 'Well, you all know she is a witch. And if she witched him into marriage ...'

'I don't think the king means that,' he says: he, Cromwell.

'Oh, he does,' says the duke. 'I thought that was what we had come here to discuss. If she witched him into marriage it was null, is my understanding.' The duke sits back, his arms folded.

The proctors look at each other. Sampson looks at Cranmer. No one looks at the duke. Eventually Cranmer says, 'We don't have to make it public. We can issue the decree but keep the grounds secret.'

A release of breath. He says, 'I suppose it is some consolation, that we need not be laughed at in public.'

The Lord Chancellor says, 'The truth is so rare and precious that sometimes it must be kept under lock and key.'

The Duke of Suffolk speeds to his barge, crying out that at last he is free of the Boleyns.

The end of the king's first marriage was protracted, public and discussed throughout Europe, not only in the councils of princes but in the market square. The end of his second, if decency prevailed, would be swift, private, unspoken and obscure. Yet it is necessary to have it witnessed by the city and by men of rank. The Tower is a town. It is an armoury, a palace, a mint. Workmen of all sorts, officials come and go. But it can be policed, and foreigners evacuated. He sets Kingston to do this. Anne, he is sorry to learn, has mistaken the day of her death, rising at 2 a.m. to pray on the morning of 18 May, sending for her almoner and for Cranmer to come to her at dawn so she can purge herself of her sins. No one seems to have told her that Kingston comes without fail at dawn on the morning of an execution, to warn the dying person to be ready. She is not familiar with the protocol, and why would she be? Kingston says, see it from my point of view: five deaths in one day, and to be ready for a queen of England the next? How can she die, when the appropriate officials from the city are not here? The carpenters are still making her scaffold on Tower Green, though thankfully she cannot hear the knocking from the royal lodging.

Still, the constable is sorry for her misapprehension; especially since her mistake ran on, late into the morning. The situation is a great strain on both himself and his wife. Instead of being glad of another dawn, he reports, Anne had cried, and said she was sorry not to die that day: she wished she were past her pain. She knew about the French executioner and, 'I told her,' Kingston says, 'it shall be no pain, it is so subtle.' But once again, Kingston says, she closed her fingers around her throat. She had taken the Eucharist, declaring on the body of God her innocence.

Which surely she would not do, Kingston says, if she were guilty?

She laments the men who are gone.

She makes jokes, saying that she will be known hereafter as Anne the Headless, Anne sans Tête.

He says to his son, 'If you come with me to witness this, it will be almost the hardest thing you ever do. If you can go through it with a steady countenance, it will be remarked on and it will be much in your favour.'

Gregory just looks at him. He says, 'A woman, I cannot.'

'I will be beside you to show you that you can. You need not look. When the soul passes, we kneel, and we drop our eyes, and pray.'

The scaffold has been set up in an open place, where once they used to hold tournaments. A guard of two hundred yeomen is assembling, drawing up to lead the procession. Yesterday's bungling, the confusion over the date, the delays, the misinformation: none of that must be repeated. He is there early, when they are putting the sawdust down, leaving his son back in Kingston's lodgings, with the others who are collecting: the sheriffs, aldermen, London's officers and dignitaries. He stands himself on the steps of the scaffold, testing them to see if they take his weight; one of the sawdust men says to him, it's sound, sir, we have all run up and down, but I suppose you want to check it yourself. When he looks up the executioner is already there, talking to Christophe. The young man is well-dressed, an allowance having been made him for a gentleman's apparel, so that he will not be easy to pick out from the other officials; this is done to save alarm to the queen, and if the clothes are spoiled, at least he is not out of pocket himself. He walks up to the executioner. 'How will you do this?'

'I shall surprise her, sir.' Switching into English, the young man indicates his feet. He is wearing soft shoes, such as one might wear indoors. 'She never sees the sword. I have put it there, in the straw. I shall distract her. She will not see from where I come.'

'But you will show me.'

The man shrugs. 'If you like. Are you Cremuel? They told me you are in charge of everything. In fact they joke to me, saying, if you faint because she is so ugly, there is one who will pick up the sword, his name is Cremuel and he is such a man, he can chop the head off the Hydra, which I do not understand what it is. But they say it is a lizard or serpent, and for each head that is chopped two more will grow.'

'Not in this case,' he says. Once the Boleyns are done, they are done.

The weapon is heavy, needing a two-handed grip. It is almost four foot in length: two inches broad, round at the tip, a double edge. 'One practises, like this,' the man says. He whirls like a dancer on the spot, his arms held high, his fists together as if he were gripping the sword. 'Every day one must handle the weapon, if only to go through the motions. One may be called at any time. We do not kill so many in Calais, but one goes to other towns.'

'It is a good trade,' Christophe says. He wants to handle the sword, but he, Cromwell, does not want to let go of it yet.

The man says, 'They tell me I may speak French to her and she will understand me.'

'Yes, do so.'

'But she will kneel, she must be informed of this. There is no block, as you see. She must kneel upright and not move. If she is steady, it will be done in a moment. If not, she will be cut to pieces.'

He hands back the weapon. 'I can answer for her.'

The man says, 'Between one beat of the heart and the next it is done. She knows nothing. She is in eternity.'

They walk away. Christophe says, 'Master, he has said to me, tell the women that she should wrap her skirts about her feet when she kneels, in case she falls bad and shows off to the world what so many fine gentlemen have already seen.'

He does not reprove the boy for his coarseness. He is crude but correct. And when the moment comes, it will prove, the women do it anyway. They must have discussed it among themselves.

Francis Bryan has appeared beside him, steaming inside a leather jerkin. 'Well, Francis?'

'I am charged that as soon as her head is off I ride with the news to the king and Mistress Jane.'

'Why?' he says coldly. 'Do they think the headsman might in some way fail?'

It is almost nine o'clock. 'Did you eat any breakfast?' Francis says.

'I always eat my breakfast.' But he wonders if the king did. 'Henry has hardly spoken of her,' Francis Bryan says. 'Only to say he cannot see how the whole thing occurred. When he looks back on the last ten years, he cannot understand himself.'

They are silent. Francis says, 'Look, they are coming.'

The solemn procession, through Coldharbour Gate: the city first, aldermen and officials, then the guard. In the midst of them the queen with her women. She wears a gown of dark damask and a short cape of ermine, a gable hood; it is the occasion, one supposes, to hide the face as much as possible, to guard the expression. That ermine cape, does he not know it? It was wrapped around Katherine, he thinks, when I saw it last. These furs, then, are Anne's final spoils. Three years ago when she went to be crowned, she walked on a blue cloth that stretched the length of the abbey – so heavy with child that the onlookers held their breath for her; and now she must make shift over the rough ground, picking her way in her little lady's shoes, with her body hollow and light and just as many hands around her, ready to retrieve her from any stumble and deliver her safely to death. Once or twice the queen falters, and the whole procession must slow; but she has not stumbled, she is turning and looking behind her. Cranmer had said, 'I do not know why, but she thinks there is still hope.' The ladies have veiled themselves, even Lady Kingston; they do not want their future lives to be associated with this morning's work, they do not want their husbands or their suitors to look at them and think of death.

Gregory has slipped into place beside him. His son is trembling and he can feel it. He puts out a gloved hand and rests it on his arm. The Duke of Richmond acknowledges him; he stands in prominent view, with his father-in-law Norfolk. Surrey, the duke's son, is whispering to his father, but Norfolk gazes straight ahead. How has the house of Howard come to this?

When the women strip the queen of her cape she is a tiny figure, a bundle of bones. She does not look like a powerful enemy of England, but looks can deceive. If she could have brought Katherine to this same place, she would have. If her sway had continued, the child Mary might have stood here; and he himself of course, pulling off his coat and waiting for the coarse English axe. He says to his son, 'It will be but a moment now.' Anne has given alms out as she walks, and the velvet bag is empty now; she slips her hand inside it and turns it inside out, a prudent housewife's gesture, checking to see that nothing is thrown away.

One of the women stretches out a hand for the purse. Anne passes it without looking at her, then moves to the edge of the scaffold. She hesitates, looks over the heads of the crowd, then begins to speak. The crowd as one sways forward, but can only shuffle by inches towards her, every man with his head lifted, staring. The queen's voice is very low, her words barely heard, her sentiments the usual ones on the occasion: '... pray for the king, for he is a good, gentle, amiable and virtuous prince ...' One must say these things, as even now the king's messenger might come ...

She pauses ... But no, she has finished. There is nothing more to say and not more than a few moments left of this world. She takes in a breath. Her face expresses bewilderment. *Amen*, she says, *amen*. Her head goes down. Then she seems to draw herself together, to control the tremor that has seized her entire body from head to foot.

One of the veiled women moves to her side and speaks to her. Anne's arm shakes as she raises it to lift off her hood. It comes easily, no fumbling; he thinks, it cannot have been pinned. Her hair is gathered in a silk net at the nape of her neck and she shakes it out, gathers up the strands, raising her hands above her head, coiling it; she holds it with one hand, and one of the women gives her a linen cap. She pulls it on. You would not think it would hold her hair, but it does; she must have rehearsed with it. But now she looks about as if for direction. She lifts the cap half off her head, puts it back. She does not know what to do, he sees she does not know if she should tie the cap's string beneath her chin – whether it will hold without fastening or whether she has time to make a knot and how many heartbeats she has left in the world. The executioner steps out and he can see – he is very close – Anne's eyes focus on him. The Frenchman bobs to his knees to ask pardon. It is a formality and his knees barely graze the straw. He has motioned Anne to kneel, and as she does so he steps away, as if he does not want contact even with her clothes. At arm's length, he holds out a folded cloth to one of the women, and raises a hand to his eyes to show her what he means. He hopes it is Lady Kingston who takes the blindfold; whoever it is, she is adept, but a small sound comes from Anne as her world darkens. Her lips move in prayer. The Frenchman waves the women back. They retreat; they kneel, one of them almost sinks to the ground and is propped up by the others; despite the veils one can see their hands, their helpless bare hands, as they draw their own skirts about them, as if they were making themselves small, making themselves safe. The queen is alone now, as alone as she has ever been in her life. She says, Christ have mercy, Jesus have mercy, Christ receive my soul. She raises one arm, again her fingers go to the coif, and he thinks, put your arm down, for God's sake put your arm down, and he could not will it more if – the executioner calls out sharply, 'Get me the sword.' The blinded head whips around. The man is behind Anne, she is misdirected, she does not sense him. There is a groan, one single sound from the whole crowd. Then a silence, and into that silence, a sharp sigh or a sound like a whistle through a keyhole: the body exsanguinates, and its flat little presence becomes a puddle of gore.

The Duke of Suffolk is still standing. Richmond too. All others, who have knelt, now get to their feet. The executioner has turned away, modestly, and already handed over his sword. His assistant is approaching the corpse but the four women are there first, blocking him with their bodies. One of them says fiercely, 'We do not want men to handle her.'

He hears young Surrey say, 'No, they have handled her enough.' He says to Norfolk, my lord, take your son in charge, and take him away from this place. Richmond, he sees, looks ill, and he sees with approval how Gregory goes to him and bows, friendly as one young boy can be to another, saying, my lord, leave it now, come away. He does not know why Richmond did not kneel. Perhaps he believes the rumours that the queen tried to poison him, and will not offer her even that last respect. With Suffolk, it is more understandable. Brandon is a hard man and owes Anne no forgiveness. He has seen battle. Though never a bloodletting like this.

It seems Kingston did not think further than the death, to the burial. 'I hope to God,' he, Cromwell says to no one in particular, 'that the constable has remembered to have the flags taken up in the chapel,' and someone answers him, I think so, sir, for they were levered up two days ago, so her brother could go under.

The constable has not helped his reputation these last few days, though he has been kept in uncertainty by the king and, as he will admit later, he had thought all morning that a messenger might suddenly arrive from Whitehall, to stop it: even when the queen was helped up the steps, even to the moment she took off her hood. He has not thought of a coffin, but an elm chest for arrows has been hastily emptied and carried to the scene of the carnage. Yesterday it was bound for Ireland with its freight, each shaft ready to deal separate, lonely damage. Now it is an object of public gaze, a death casket, wide enough for the queen's little body. The executioner has crossed the scaffold and lifted the severed head; in a yard of linen he swaddles it, like a newborn. He waits for someone to take the burden. The women, unassisted, lift the queen's sodden remains into the chest. One of them steps forward, receives the head, and lays it – no other space – by the queen's feet. Then they straighten up, each of them awash in her blood, and stiffly walk away, closing their ranks like soldiers.

That evening he is at home at Austin Friars. He has written letters into France, to Gardiner. Gardiner abroad: a crouching brute nibbling his claws, waiting for his moment to strike. It has been a triumph, to keep him away. He wonders how much longer he can do it.

He wishes Rafe were here, but either he is with the king or he has gone back to Helen in Stepney. He is used to seeing Rafe most days and he cannot get used to the new order of things. He keeps expecting to hear his voice, and to hear him and Richard, and Gregory when he is at home, scuffling in corners and trying to push each other downstairs, hiding behind doors to jump on each other, doing all those tricks that even men of twenty-five or thirty do when they think their grave elders are not nearby. Instead of Rafe, Mr Wriothesley is with him, pacing. Call-Me seems to think someone should give an account of the day, as if for a chronicler; or if not that, that he should give an account of his own feelings. 'I stand, sir, as if upon a headland, my back to the sea, and below me a burning plain.'

'Do you, Call-Me? Then come in from the wind,' he says, 'and have a cup of this wine Lord Lisle sends me from France. I do usually keep it for my own drinking.'

Call-Me takes the glass. 'I smell burning buildings,' he says. 'Fallen towers. Indeed there is nothing but ash. Wreckage.'

'But it's useful wreckage, isn't it?' Wreckage can be fashioned into all sorts of things: ask any dweller on the sea shore.

'You have not properly answered on one point,' Wriothesley says. 'Why did you let Wyatt go untried? Other than because he is your friend?'

'I see you do not rate friendship highly.' He watches Wriothesley take that in.

'Even so,' Call-Me says. 'Wyatt I see poses you no threat, nor has he slighted or offended you. William Brereton, he was high-handed and offended many, he was in your way. Harry Norris, young Weston, well, there are gaps where they stood, and you can put your own friends in the privy chamber alongside Rafe. And Mark, that squib of a boy with his lute; I grant you, the place looks tidier without him. And George Rochford struck down, that sends the rest of the Boleyns scurrying away, Monseigneur will have to scuttle back to the country and sing small. The

399

Emperor will be gratified by all that has passed. It is a pity the ambassador's fever kept him away today. He would like to have seen it.'

No he would not, he thinks. Chapuys is squeamish. But you ought to get up from your sickbed if you need to, and see the results you have willed.

'Now we shall have peace in England,' Wriothesley says.

A phrase runs through his head – was it Thomas More's? – 'the peace of the hen coop when the fox has run home'. He sees the scattered carcasses, some killed with one snap of the jaw, the rest bitten and shredded as the fox whirls and snaps in panic as the hens flap about him, as he spins around and deals death: the remnants then to be sluiced away, the mulch of scarlet feathers plastered over the floor and walls.

'All the players gone,' Wriothesley says. 'All four who carried the cardinal to Hell; and also the poor fool Mark who made a ballad of their exploits.'

'All four,' he says. 'All five.'

'A gentleman asked me, if this is what Cromwell does to the cardinal's lesser enemies, what will he do by and by to the king himself?'

He stands looking down into the darkening garden: transfixed, the question like a knife between his shoulderblades. There is only one man among all the king's subjects to whom that question would occur, only one who would dare pose it. There is only one man who would dare question the loyalty he shows to his king, the loyalty he demonstrates daily. 'So ...' he says at last. 'Stephen Gardiner calls himself a gentleman.'

Perhaps, caught in the little panes which distort and cloud, Wriothesley sees a dubious image: confusion, fear, emotions that do not often mark Master Secretary's face. Because if Gardiner thinks this, who else? Who else will think it in the months and years ahead? He says, 'Wriothesley, surely you don't expect me to justify my actions to you? Once you have chosen a course, you should not apologise for it. God knows, I mean nothing but good to our master the king. I am bound to obey and serve. And if you watch me closely you will see me do it.'

He turns, when he thinks it is fit for Wriothesley to see his face. His smile is implacable. He says, 'Drink my health.'

III
Spoils
London, Summer 1536

The king says, 'What happened to her clothes? Her headdress?'

He says, 'The people at the Tower have them. It is their perquisite.'

'Buy them back,' the king says. 'I want to know they are destroyed.'

The king says, 'Call in all the keys that admit to my privy chamber. Here and elsewhere. All the keys to all the rooms. I want the locks changed.'

There are new servants everywhere, or old servants in new offices. In place of Henry Norris, Sir Francis Bryan is appointed chief of the privy chamber, and is to receive a pension of a hundred pounds. The young Duke of Richmond is appointed Chamberlain of Chester and North Wales, and (replacing George Boleyn) Warden of the Cinque Ports and Constable of Dover Castle. Thomas Wyatt is released from the Tower and granted a hundred pounds also. Edward Seymour is promoted Viscount Beauchamp. Richard Sampson is appointed Bishop of Chichester. The wife of Francis Weston announces her remarriage.

He has conferred with the Seymour brothers on the motto Jane should adopt as queen. They settle on, 'Bound to Obey and Serve'.

403

cry it out on Henry. A smile, a nod: perfect contentment.
...ing's blue eyes are serene. Through the autumn of this year,
...6, in glass windows, in carvings of stone or wood, the badge
of the phoenix will replace the white falcon with its imperial
crown; for the heraldic lions of the dead woman, the panthers of
Jane Seymour are substituted, and it is done economically, as the
beasts only need new heads and tails.

The marriage is swift and private, in the queen's closet at
Whitehall. Jane is found to be the king's distant cousin, but all
dispensations are granted in proper form.

He, Cromwell, is with the king before the ceremony. Henry is
quiet, and more melancholy that day than any bridegroom ought to
be. He is not thinking about his last queen; she is ten days dead and
he never speaks of her. But he says, 'Crumb, I don't know if I will
have any children now. Plato says that a man's best offspring are
born when he is between thirty years and thirty-nine. I am past that.
I have wasted my best years. I don't know where they have gone.'

The king feels he has been cheated of his fate. 'When my
brother Arthur died, my father's astrologer predicted that I
should enjoy a prosperous reign and father many sons.'

You're prosperous at least, he thinks: and if you stick with me,
richer than you can ever have imagined. Somewhere, Thomas
Cromwell was in your chart.

The debts of the dead woman now fall to be paid. She owes
some thousand pounds, which her confiscated estate is able to
meet: to her furrier and her hosier, her silkwomen, her apothecary,
her linen draper, her saddler, her dyer, her farrier and her pinmaker.
The status of her daughter is uncertain, but for now the child is
well provided with gold fringing for her bed, and with caps of
white and purple satin with gilt trim. The queen's embroiderer is
owed fifty-five pounds, and one can see where the money went.

The fee to the French executioner is over twenty-three pounds,
but it is an expense unlikely to be repeated.

* * *

At Austin Friars, he takes the keys and lets himself into the little room where they store Christmas: where Mark was held, and where he cried out in fear in the night. The peacock wings will have to be destroyed. Rafe's little girl will probably not ask for them again; children do not remember from one Christmas to the next.

When the wings are shaken out of their linen bag he stretches the fabric, holds it up to the light and sees that the bag is slit. He understands how the feathers crept out and stroked the dead man's face. He sees that the wings are shabby, as if nibbled, and the glowing eyes dulled. They are tawdry things after all, not worth setting store by.

He thinks about his daughter Grace. He thinks, was my wife ever false to me? When I was away on the cardinal's business as I so often was, did she take up with some silk merchant she knew through her business, or did she, as many women do, sleep with a priest? He can hardly believe it of her. Yet she was a plain woman, and Grace was so beautiful, her features so fine. They blur in his mind these days; this is what death does to you, it takes and takes, so that all that is left of your memories is a faint tracing of spilled ash.

He says to Johane, his wife's sister, 'Do you think Lizzie ever had to do with another man? I mean, while we were married?'

Johane is shocked. 'Whatever put that into your head? Put it right out again.'

He tries to do that. But he cannot escape the feeling that Grace has slipped further from him. She was dead before she could be painted or drawn. She lived and left no trace. Her clothes and her cloth ball and her wooden baby in a smock are long ago passed to other children. But his elder daughter, Anne, he has her copy book. Sometimes he takes it out and looks at it, her name inked in her bold hand, Anne Cromwell, Anne Cromwell her book; the fish and birds she drew in the margin, mermaids and griffins. He keeps it in a wooden box faced and lined with red leather. On the

.olour has faded to a pale rose. Only when you open it up
ɔu see the original, shocking scarlet.

These light nights find him at his desk. Paper is precious. Its offcuts and remnants are not discarded, but turned over, reused. Often he takes up an old letter-book and finds the jottings of chancellors long dust, of bishop-ministers now cold under inscriptions of their merits. When he first, in this fashion, turned up Wolsey's hand after his death – a hasty computation, a discarded draft – his heart had clenched small and he had to put down his pen till the spasm of grief passed. He has grown used to these encounters, but tonight, as he flicks over the leaf and sees the cardinal's writing, it is strange to him, as if some trick, perhaps a trick of the light, has altered the letter forms. The hand could be that of a stranger, of a creditor or a debtor you have dealt with just this quarter and don't know well; it could be that of some humble clerk, taking dictation from his master.

A moment passes: a soft flicker of the beeswax flame, a nudge of the book towards the light, and the words take on their familiar contours, so he can see the dead hand that inscribed them. During daylight hours he thinks only of the future, but sometimes late at night memory comes to nag him. However. His next task is somehow to reconcile the king and the Lady Mary, to save Henry from killing his own daughter; and before that, to stop Mary's friends from killing him. He has helped them to their new world, the world without Anne Boleyn, and now they will think they can do without Cromwell too. They have eaten his banquet and now they will want to sweep him out with the rushes and the bones. But this was his table: he runs on the top of it, among the broken meats. Let them try to pull him down. They will find him armoured, they will find him entrenched, they will find him stuck like a limpet to the future. He has laws to write, measures to take, the good of the commonwealth to serve, and his king: he has titles and honours still to attain, houses to build, books to read, and who knows, perhaps children to father, and Gregory to dispose in marriage. It would be some compensation for the children lost, to have a grandchild. He imagines standing in a daze of light, holding up a small child so the dead can see it.

He thinks, strive as I might, one day I will be gone and as this world goes it may not be long: what though I am a man of firmness and vigour, fortune is mutable and either my enemies will do for me or my friends. When the time comes I may vanish before the ink is dry. I will leave behind me a great mountain of paper, and those who come after me – let us say it is Rafe, let us say it is Wriothesley, let us say it is Riche – they will sift through what remains and remark, here is an old deed, an old draft, an old letter from Thomas Cromwell's time: they will turn the page over, and write on me.

Summer, 1536: he is promoted Baron Cromwell. He cannot call himself Lord Cromwell of Putney. He might laugh. However. He can call himself Baron Cromwell of Wimbledon. He ranged all over those fields, when he was a boy.

The word 'however' is like an imp coiled beneath your chair. It induces ink to form words you have not yet seen, and lines to march across the page and overshoot the margin. There are no endings. If you think so you are deceived as to their nature. They are all beginnings. Here is one.

AUTHOR'S NOTE

The circumstances surrounding the fall of Anne Boleyn have been controversial for centuries. The evidence is complex and sometimes contradictory; the sources are often dubious, tainted and after-the-fact. There is no official transcript of her trial, and we can reconstruct her last days only in fragments, with the help of contemporaries who may be inaccurate, biased, forgetful, elsewhere at the time, or hiding under a pseudonym. Eloquent and lengthy speeches, put into Anne's mouth at her trial and on the scaffold, should be read with scepticism, and so should the document often called her 'last letter', which is almost certainly a forgery or (to put it more kindly) a fiction. A mercurial woman, elusive in her lifetime, Anne is still changing centuries after her death, carrying the projections of those who read and write about her.

In this book I try to show how a few crucial weeks might have looked from Thomas Cromwell's point of view. I am not claiming authority for my version; I am making the reader a proposal, an offer. Some familiar aspects of the story are not to be found in this novel. To limit the multiplication of characters, it omits mention of a deceased lady called Bridget Wingfield, who may (from beyond the grave) have had something to do with the rumours that began to circulate against Anne before her fall. The

ᴜmitting any source of rumour may be to throw more
on Jane, Lady Rochford, than perhaps she deserves; we
ᴜ to read Lady Rochford backwards, as we know the destruc-
ᴜve role she played in the affairs of Katherine Howard, Henry's
fifth wife. Julia Fox has given a more positive reading of Jane's
character in her book *Jane Boleyn* (2007).

Connoisseurs of Anne's last days will notice other omissions,
including that of Richard Page, a courtier who was arrested at
about the same time as Thomas Wyatt, and who was never
charged or tried. As he plays no part in this story otherwise, and
as no one has an idea why he was arrested, it seemed best not to
burden the reader with one more name.

I am indebted to the work of Eric Ives, David Loades, Alison
Weir, G.W. Bernard, Retha M. Warnicke and many other historians of the Boleyns and their downfall.

This book is of course not about Anne Boleyn or about Henry
VIII, but about the career of Thomas Cromwell, who is still in
need of attention from biographers. Meanwhile, Mr Secretary
remains sleek, plump and densely inaccessible, like a choice plum
in a Christmas pie; but I hope to continue my efforts to dig him
out.

ACKNOWLEDGEMENTS

I am truly grateful to the open-minded historians who took the time to read *Wolf Hall*, to comment on it and encourage this project, and to the many readers who have contacted me with family trees and snippets of family legend, with piquant information about lost places and almost forgotten names. Thank you to Sir Bob Worcester for showing me Allington Castle, once owned by the Wyatt family, and to Rupert Thistlethwayte, descendant of William Paulet, for inviting me to Cadhay, his beautiful house in Devon. And thank you to all those people who have issued kind invitations I hope to take up in the course of writing my next novel.

I owe special gratitude to my husband Gerald McEwen, who has to share a house with so many invisible people, and who never fails in his support and practical kindness.